Now, *that* was a move he hadn't seen coming

In fact, Harry still couldn't quite believe Pippa had shoved the envelope of money —payment he hadn't asked for and *wasn't* going to keep—down the waistband of his shorts.

Briefly he toyed with  her, letting her know he wasn't interested himself chasing her corner until she was take the envelope back. She'd protest, no doubt, but he'd simply look into those rich chocolate-brown eyes of hers and—

He put the cash in his pocket and turned away from the thought that had been about to insinuate itself into his head. Pippa was off-limits. She was trying to raise Alice on her own. Pippa was all about responsibility and commitment. Nothing that Harry had to offer.

Walk away, mate.

Too bad his libido wasn't getting the message.

Dear Reader,

I've written two sequels in my career so far—this one and *One Good Reason*—and both were completely unplanned. It wasn't until I started writing about a character who I assumed would be a supporting player that I realized that I wanted to tell that story, too.

Harry came to life in *All They Need*, which tells the story of his sister, Mel, and Flynn, the man who teaches her that love is not about pain and shame. I loved Harry from the moment he opened his mouth. His tattoos, his attitude, his blue-collar decency. I talked about him with my editor, and she—wise, wise woman—said, "For some reason I see him with a woman who has a child." My brain lit up like a slot machine hitting jackpot. Of course Harry had to fall in love with a woman with a child! What better way to rock the world of a committed party boy?

When I started thinking about who this woman might be, it occurred to me that the lives of men like Harry revolve around their mates. They party together, they hang together, they have each other's backs. But what if one of those mates turns out to have done the wrong thing by an ex-lover who wound up pregnant? And what if Harry had always really liked this woman because she was smart and funny and sassy? Beneath his tough exterior, Harry is a huge pussycat. I figured he'd be powerless to resist the urge to step in and step up on his friend's behalf.

Those basic ideas sent my imagination off. I loved writing this book! Pippa and Harry were so much fun. I hope you enjoy reading their journey. I love hearing from readers, so please feel free to drop me a line at sarah@sarahmayberry.com.

Oh, and in case you're wondering, I've never fallen through the ceiling. But I have come very, very close!

Happy reading,

Sarah Mayberry

SUDDENLY YOU

BY
SARAH MAYBERRY

MILLS & BOON

First published in Great Britain 2013
by Mills & Boon, an imprint of Harlequin (UK) Limited,
Eton House, 18-24 Paradise Road, Richmond, Surrey TW9 1SR

© Small Cow Productions Pty Ltd. 2012

ISBN: 978 0 263 90075 0
ebook ISBN: 978 1 472 00427 7

23-0113

Harlequin (UK) policy is to use papers that are natural, renewable and recyclable products and made from wood grown in sustainable forests. The logging and manufacturing processes conform to the legal environmental regulations of the country of origin.

Printed and bound in Spain
by Blackprint CPI, Barcelona

Sarah Mayberry lives in Melbourne in a house by the bay, happily sharing her days with her partner (now husband!) of twenty years and a small black, tan and white cavoodle called Max. She adores them both. When she isn't writing, she is feeling guilty about not being out in the garden more and indulging in shoe shopping and re-imagining her soon-to-be renovated home. She also loves to read, cook, go to the movies and sleep, and is fully aware that the word *exercise* should be in that list somewhere, too.

This book was written with the undeniable distraction of a new puppy in the house. So it would be remiss of me not to thank Max for the many hours he stole from my work while simultaneously making me laugh and gnash my teeth. Bless your little furry everything. As usual, Wanda held my hand and gave sage counsel and helped me see the wood for the trees. There would be no me without you, my dear.

And Chris. What can I say? You really are the best. The funniest. The smartest. The sweetest. (There are more -ests, but I don't want to embarrass you. You know where I'm going with this, though.)

Lastly, a big thanks to the readers who take the time to put fingers to keyboard to write to me. Your letters really do make my day.

CHAPTER ONE

BEER. ICY COLD, preferably accompanied by a big, greasy burger. Oh, yeah.

Harry Porter rolled down the window of his 1972 HQ Monaro GTS and grinned into the resulting wind as he sped toward the pub. A vintage Midnight Oil song played on the radio and he tapped out the rhythm on the steering wheel, the burble of the V8 engine providing a bass beat.

It was Friday afternoon, it was summer, he'd just been paid, and half a dozen of his best mates were waiting at the Pier Hotel ten minutes up the road to kick off the weekend's adventures.

Life didn't get much better.

Whoever was in charge at the radio station seemed to agree because Midnight Oil's "Power and the Passion" was followed by Nirvana's "Smells Like Teen Spirit." He was reaching for the volume to crank it higher when he spotted the bright yellow car in the emergency stopping lane to the left of the highway, its hood pushed up in the universal signal that someone was shit out of luck.

The mechanic in him automatically diagnosed the problem—in this weather, most likely the car's cooling system—before returning his gaze to the road. Fortunately, being a mechanic wasn't like being a doctor—Harry wasn't obliged to stop for emergencies. Which was just as well, because he'd spend half his life riding to the rescue if that was the case.

Something tickled at the back of his brain as he approached the car. He realized what it was as he sped past. He knew this car—at least, he knew its owner. He hadn't seen her for nearly six months, but that was definitely her bright yellow hatchback, a fact he confirmed when he looked in his rear vision mirror and saw Pippa White standing with her hands on her hips staring into the engine bay.

He swerved into the unsealed emergency lane and glanced in the rearview mirror as Pippa turned to watch his big black car reverse toward her. She was frowning, clearly trying to work out who was coming to her rescue.

The worried expression vanished from her face when he exited his car. It was replaced with the wry, appreciative smile he'd come to associate with her during the six months she'd dated his best mate, Steve.

Pippa pushed her heavy black-framed glasses up her nose and scanned him head to toe as he approached.

"You're definitely not what I was expecting when I sent up a prayer for a guardian angel."

"Long time no see," he said easily.

Pippa's smile slipped a fraction and he knew that—like him—she was remembering the last time they'd seen each other. Driven by god-knows-what stupid impulse, he had visited her at the hospital after the birth of her daughter, Alice. The most uncomfortable fifteen minutes of his life so far, hands down. She recovered quickly, pushing her glasses up her nose again.

"How have you been, Harry? How's Hogwarts going? Cast any good spells lately?"

The Harry Potter/Porter jokes had gotten old around

the time Ms. Rowling had made her second billion, but Pippa was one of the few people he allowed to get away with them. They'd always got on well and, unlike most of Steve's girlfriends, he'd regretted it when things had gone pear-shaped and she'd disappeared off the scene. She'd always had something interesting to say, and she'd always laughed at his jokes, even when they sucked.

"Made some underwear disappear the other night, if that's what you mean."

She laughed appreciatively. "Dirty dog."

"How about you? How are things?"

"I've had better days, you know." She shrugged, her dark, wavy hair brushing her shoulders. A sparkly clip was pinned at one temple. Combined with her heavy glasses, it gave her an arty, slightly eccentric look that was reinforced by her old-fashioned floral dress and timeworn tan oxfords.

Not for the first time he wondered how she and Steve had ever hooked up. She was a million miles from the tight-T-shirted, tight-jeaned women his mate usually went for, and Harry had always figured Steve wasn't exactly Pippa's normal dating material, either. Which only made it more problematic that they'd created a little girl between them.

"How's Alice?" he asked, glancing at the backseat.

The baby seat was empty, however.

"Mum's visiting, so she's got her for the day. I was supposed to be getting a few chores sorted, but Old Yeller had other ideas." Her tone was heavy with irony as she gave her car a rueful glance.

"Let me guess—it overheated?"

"To be honest, I have no idea. One minute I was driving along, the next minute there was this bang and then steam and smoke was pouring out from under the hood…"

Harry frowned. Steam sounded right for overheating, but not smoke. He moved closer to lean over the engine bay. It took him only a moment to spot the oil dripping down the engine block and sprayed across the other engine components.

"Looks like you've blown a head gasket."

Pippa joined him, peering at the engine. "That's bad, right?"

"It's not great. It basically means the engine is no longer sealed properly, so the oil that's supposed to stop things from seizing up when they get hot leaks out."

"Does that mean the engine is seized now?" She looked alarmed.

"Not if you pulled over immediately."

"I did. Straight away."

"Then it's probably okay. But the only way to know for sure is to crack the engine block open and take a look."

"That sounds expensive. Am I right?" A worried expression filled her brown eyes.

"It can be. Depends on parts, what they find when they get in there…"

She nodded. "Right. Well, I guess me standing here swearing at it won't change any of that."

Harry pulled out his phone. Since he couldn't help her, the least he could do was organize a tow truck.

"Who normally services the car?" He knew most of the workshops in this part of the Mornington Peninsula, as well as a number of the tow truck operators.

"Oh, um, I don't know the name off the top of my head. A place down in Mornington." She waved a hand vaguely.

"Sweet Motors? Beachside Workshop?" he suggested.

Pippa shook her head, her gaze sliding from his face to the car. "I think I've got their card at home."

"Do you want to get it towed to your place, then?"

"No, then I'd have to pay twice. I'll just go home and sort it from there. But thanks for the thought."

Her words were light but the frown creasing her forehead remained. Harry hesitated, but there was something about the way she was trying to be so casual about what was clearly a major hassle that made him want to help out. Even though it wasn't his place, and they weren't really friends anymore.

"My dad owns the workshop in Mount Eliza Village. I could give him a ring. I'm sure he wouldn't mind helping out with a tow." Technically, this was true, since Mike Porter had always been a soft touch for someone in distress, but it didn't mean Harry wouldn't cop some grief for his impulsive offer. He could almost hear his dad now: *It'd be different if you actually worked for Village Motors, mate. Then you'd be within your rights to make offers on my behalf.*

The fact that Harry had chosen to work for someone else once he'd finished his apprenticeship had always been a minor bone of contention between him and his father, although lately it seemed there was more weight behind his father's comments and jokey asides.

Still, Harry was willing to wear the inevitable heat if it meant helping Pippa.

"That's really nice of you, but I don't want to put anyone out. Besides, my car club offers free roadside assistance. I can call them from home and get everything sorted."

"You won't be putting anyone out. The workshop is up the road. It's no big deal."

Pippa's expression became determined. "Thanks, but I've got it covered." She softened her rejection by touching his forearm briefly. "I appreciate you stopping, Harry. A lot of other guys would have kept going."

He frowned. The reality was, if she'd been one of Steve's other exes, he would have simply blown past without a second thought. He wasn't sure why it was different with Pippa, except he'd always liked her. And—maybe—because he felt a little sorry for her, given her situation and the way things had turned out.

"Can I give you a lift home, then?" he heard himself offer. Even though every minute that ticked past chewed up his weekend and delayed the moment when he had an ice-cold glass of beer in his hand.

"Thanks, but Mum can come get me."

Pippa tried to pull the hood stand from its notch on the side of the engine bay. Harry watched her struggle for a few seconds before leaning across her and pulling it loose. He got a whiff of hot engine oil and a rich vanilla scent—Pippa's perfume most likely—as the hood shut with a dull thud.

"Where are you living these days?" he asked.

"Frankston South. Off Karrs Road."

"Perfect. I'm driving past on the way to the pub."

She started to protest again but he walked to the driver's side of the hatchback and leaned in to grab her handbag.

"You need anything else before we lock it up?" he asked as he passed her the bag.

Her expression became rueful. "You're not going to let this drop, are you?"

"Can't be a knight in shining armor if the princess won't get up on my horse."

She scanned his face, almost as though she was looking for evidence of something. His sincerity, perhaps? Or maybe she was thinking more of his association with Steve.

"It's just a lift, Pippa."

"True. And I wouldn't want to deprive you of the chance to play Sir Galahad."

"Especially since the urge only hits once every five years or so."

She laughed, the sound loud and honest. "I bet. I've got some shopping in the back that should come home with me."

He followed her to the trunk and grabbed the bags.

"Thanks."

"All part of the service."

"There's a service? And here I was thinking I was getting special treatment."

She was so dry he couldn't help turning on the charm a little. "That's part of the service, too." He winked, deepened his voice a notch.

Pippa laughed again as they headed for his car. "My God, Harry. No wonder half the women in Frankston love to hate you."

They were on familiar ground now—Pippa giving him a hard time about the "revolving door" to his bedroom.

"You've been talking to the wrong women."

"Sure I have." She gave him a look over her shoulder before opening the passenger door.

Harry smiled. He hadn't been so sure earlier, but now he was glad he'd stopped. It was good to see her again, and even better to help her out of a jam, even in a very minor way.

Digging his keys from his pocket, he prepared himself for a challenging, entertaining five minutes.

PIPPA PRESSED A hand against her belly as Harry stowed her shopping. For some unknown reason, seeing and talking to him again had made her nervous.

A different kind of nervous, obviously, than the way she'd felt when his black car had swerved into the emergency lane so abruptly. The Nepean Highway was a public enough road that she hadn't been afraid for her personal safety, but she'd be lying if she said she hadn't been a little concerned. Then her rescuer had unfolded himself from his car and she'd known she was in good hands.

The car dipped as Harry slid into the driver's seat. Pippa eyed his worn jeans, faded black T-shirt and tattooed arms, acknowledging the irony that someone who looked so fierce could make her feel so safe.

At first glance, Harry looked exactly like the sort of man that should make a woman worry—the military-short hair, the honed power of his arms and shoulders, the sheer height and breadth of him. And, of course, there were those tribal tattoos snaking around his arms. Inky-black and impossible to miss, they marked him as an outlaw, someone who didn't color between the lines.

Not exactly your usual white-knight material, yet she knew Harry well enough to know he was a big softie underneath his fierce exterior.

"Got a big weekend planned?" she asked as he started the car.

"Always." The smile he flashed her was confident, bordering on cocky.

"Fathers of Melbourne, lock up your daughters."

"Fat lot of good that'll do."

It was true. She'd seen Harry in action enough times to know he didn't have to go hunting for women. They came to him, flicking their teased blond hair and sashaying their miniskirted hips. Watching him charm them out of their underwear had fascinated her—but then she'd long recognized that she had a self-destructive penchant for bad boys. Witness her six months with Steve, who was the blond, blue-eyed version of Harry—a teenage boy's mind in a grown man's body, all about fun and good times and no responsibility.

As always, thoughts of Steve Lawson tightened her stomach, so she pushed them away. There was no point getting herself all bunged up over a situation she could do nothing to change.

"Let me guess—you're kicking off at the Pier. Then you'll move on to the Grand or the Twenty-First Century, and you'll wind up at Macca's place playing pool in the garage till three in the morning," she said.

"Sounds pretty good, except Macca's moved in with Sherry and the pool table went west."

It wasn't hard to interpret the disapproving note in Harry's voice. He and Steve had never been shy about their disgust with their mates who'd met the right woman, married and bowed out of their boys' club.

"Oh, dear. Another one bites the dust. Next thing you know you'll be taking on a mortgage and buying golf clubs, too, Harry."

"When hell freezes over."

He sounded so grimly determined she had to laugh. "How old are you?"

"Thirty."

"Getting up there."

He shot her a look before taking a right turn off the highway. "You sound like my sister."

"Relax. I'm only yanking your chain. I honestly can't imagine you settling down. You and Steve like your lives too much the way they are to change them."

She bit her tongue, but it was too late. She'd drawn attention to the elephant in the room. A short silence followed. Harry glanced at her but she kept her gaze front and center.

"For what it's worth, for a while there I thought you had him on the ropes."

"The question is, would I have wanted him once I got him?" Again, the words were out of her mouth before she could stop them. She held up a hand immediately, signaling she knew she'd stepped over the line. "Pretend I didn't say that, okay? Strike it from the record."

Harry was the last person she wanted to vent to about Steve. The absolute last.

"So is Alice walking and talking and stuff yet?" Harry asked after a small silence.

"She's six months old, Harry." Was he really so clueless?

He raised his eyebrows, clearly wondering what he'd gotten wrong. Apparently he *was* that clueless.

"Babies don't generally start doing any of that until twelve months," she explained.

"Right. So what does she do?"

"At the moment? Eat. Sleep. Cry. Poo. She's starting to crawl, too."

"And that's all going well, then?"

She laughed. He was trying. She had to give him points for that.

"She poos like a champion. And no one can reach the high notes like Alice when she's really cranky." Her street was coming up and she gestured with her chin. "This is me."

He made a left turn.

"The one with the broken letterbox," she said, indicating the fifties brick veneer that she'd been renting since she found out she was pregnant.

Harry pulled into the driveway, eyeing the unkempt, overgrown garden and the house's faded sun awnings. Pippa felt an uncomfortable tug of shame over the shabbiness of it all. Between work and university and caring for Alice, she could barely stay on top of the inside of the house, let alone the outside. And no way could she spare any money from her already tight weekly budget to pay someone to worry about it for her.

She opened her mouth to explain, then shut it without saying a word. She didn't owe Harry an explanation. He was breezing through her life. In all likelihood, she wouldn't run into him again for another six months, probably even longer. Which was the way it should be.

"Thanks for the lift and the help with my car," she said.

"Like I did anything to help with your car."

"You destroyed my last vestiges of hope. Sometimes that's very necessary."

"Great. I'll add that to my repertoire. 'Crusher of hope.' Has a real ring to it."

"Actually, it sounds like a heavy metal band."

He laughed. She smiled and slid out of the car.

"Have a good weekend, Harry, and a great Christmas." It was only seven weeks away, after all, and it was unlikely she'd see him again before then.

"You, too, Pippa."

She turned away, then spun back. "Nearly forgot my stuff."

"Right."

Before she could protest, Harry jumped out of the car.

"Don't even think about carrying my shopping to the door for me, Harry. You've done more than enough." Plus she wasn't used to being fussed over like this.

Harry brandished the key at her. "This is an old-school car. No auto trunk release."

"Oh." She felt heat climb into her cheeks and attempted to cover her blush by pushing her glasses up the bridge of her nose.

A small smile played around Harry's mouth as he lifted out the bags and set them on the lawn.

"I'm leaving it here because I don't want you having conniptions again."

"Trust me, neither of us wants that."

"Look after yourself, okay?" His gray eyes were direct and honest.

"I will. You, too. And keep dodging those bullets. The world wouldn't be the same if you were domesticated."

"I'll do my best, don't worry."

Once inside the car, he backed onto the street. Pippa raised her hand in farewell. He waved in return, then was gone, the sound of the engine fading into the distance.

She headed for the house. Running into Harry had been the highlight of her day, which was probably a sad indictment of how pitiful her life was, but what the hell.

"Mum, I'm home," she called as she let herself into the house.

"We're in the sunroom."

Pippa dumped her things in the kitchen before following her mother's voice to the room that overlooked the rear garden. The carpet was a faded floral—probably original—the walls a grubby cream. Huge windows let in the afternoon sun. Her mother was sitting on the Art Deco couch Pippa had rescued from the side of the road and reupholstered a few years ago, a crossword puzzle book open on her knees, while Alice lay on a quilt at her feet, fascinated with one of her own small, pink toes.

"I was starting to get a little worried," her mother said as Pippa dropped a kiss onto her cheek.

"Sorry. I had car trouble."

The vague concern in her mother's eyes became real worry. "Nothing too bad, I hope?"

"Nothing I can't sort," Pippa lied, because she knew if she didn't the next words out of her mother's mouth would be an offer to help pay for the repairs.

Julie White had retired from teaching three years ago and was on a limited, fixed income. Despite her financial limitations, she'd bent over backward to help Pippa once she'd learned of her daughter's pregnancy. Pippa had been doing her damnedest to stem the tide of her mother's generosity in recent months—she point-blank refused to be the reason her mother had to cut corners in her retirement—and little white lies like this were becoming more and more commonplace in their conversations.

Still, Pippa figured it was better to tell a few porky pies now, than have her mother sell her small condo or car later on.

As she'd hoped, the fib worked. "Oh, good. Because the last thing you need right now is car trouble."

"I know. How has little miss been while I was out?"

Pippa sank to her knees to rest a hand on her daughter's warm belly. Alice gazed at her with big blue eyes, her mouth working.

"Did you miss Mummy?"

Alice beamed, both hands gripping Pippa's wrist.

"She's been a little sweetie," her mother said.

"That's because she's a shameless little con artist. Aren't you, Ali bear? Have you been charming your grandma?" Pippa kissed her daughter's cheek before rising to her feet. "Are you staying for dinner?"

"I can't. Not if I want to make it home before midnight. I promised Mrs. Young that I'd drive her to bingo tomorrow and I don't want to let her down."

Her mother lived in Bendigo, a three-hour drive north. Single since Pippa's father died when Pippa was sixteen years old, she was heavily involved in her local community, volunteering at the local retirement village and a number of charity shops.

Pippa did her best not to act relieved as she said her goodbyes. At least she didn't have to put on a brave face for the rest of the evening—the only upside she could find to her situation right now.

She waited until her mother's car had turned the corner before walking slowly into the house, Alice a heavy weight on her hip. She fed Alice, then made dinner for herself. With her daughter settled in her bassinet, happily gurgling away, Pippa fired up her laptop and logged on to her bank account to work out how on earth she would get together enough money to fix her car.

It was a depressing exercise. Despite months of scrimping and saving, she had just enough in the account to cover rent, utilities and food for the next month, but precious little contingency. Certainly nothing near the amount that Harry had implied she might need.

She stared at the figures on the screen, elbows

propped on the table, fingers digging into her temples as she racked her brain. There had to be some way to find the money.

She could ask for more shifts at the local art gallery where she worked, but that would mean bailing on classes at university and she had exams coming up... Plus she was already sailing close to the wind in the attendance department. The last thing she needed was to fail because she hadn't attended the requisite number of hours in class. The whole point of getting her Diploma of Education was to escape this cycle of hand-to-mouth, one-day-at-a-time living by landing a decent-paying job. She was halfway through her diploma, but all her hard work would be a complete write-off if she failed because of skipping class.

Of course, if she had completed her teaching degree ten years ago when she'd graduated with a Bachelor of Arts degree, none of this would be an issue. She would have a decent job, a good income, and Alice would have a stable home. But Pippa had turned her nose up at teaching then, even though her mother had encouraged her to have "something to fall back on." Pippa had been convinced that something else was out there for her, something amazing and creative and exciting. She'd spent a decade searching and had nothing to show for it except a woefully empty bank account and her beautiful, painfully precious daughter.

A headache started behind her left eye and she willed away the panic fluttering in her chest. She might not be able to see it right now, but there was a solution to her problem. She simply had to wait for it to reveal itself.

If Steve was even close to being a responsible adult, you wouldn't have to think twice about calling a mechanic.

Pippa hated the impotent, acidic burn she got in her stomach every time she thought about her ex. Hated how helpless it made her feel. How stupid.

For six incredibly foolhardy months, she'd been infatuated with a real-life version of Peter Pan. She'd laughed at his antics, been beguiled by his laid-back, take-things-as-they-come lifestyle and ignored the little voice in her head telling her nobody could live like that forever. Then she'd discovered she was pregnant, and Steve had turned from a funny, irreverent larrikin to an angry, resentful asshole. Six months of laughs, good times and fun had gone up in smoke and Pippa had been left holding the baby. Literally.

I don't want this. I didn't ask for it. I'll give you the money to make it go away. But if you decide to keep it, it's all on you. I don't want anything to do with it.

His words on that fateful day still lived large in her memory. She'd hoped his attitude would change once he'd gotten over the shock of her announcement, but he hadn't budged on his stance. She'd been forced to contact Child Support Services to pursue him for support payments. She hadn't wanted to, had tried everything in her power to work it out with him, not wishing it to become official and complicated, but Steve had point-blank refused to even come to the table. Pippa had been left with no choice but to take steps to ensure Alice had what she needed.

In theory, the law had supported her cause, but Steve had arrived with the books for his house-painting business and told the caseworker he was barely staying afloat. Alice had been awarded a paltry fifteen dollars per week based on Steve's hugely under-reported annual income. She'd listened with disbelief when her caseworker explained the outcome. She knew how Steve lived. He never denied himself anything, from holidays to Bali to a new truck to three-hundred-dollar sunglasses. But because he was self-employed, he was able to manipulate the figures to make it look as though he barely made ends meet. She'd walked away with nothing but disillusionment and the advice that she needed to file a change of assessment request to empower the agency to go after Steve through tax and bank records. She'd done so two months ago, and was still waiting to hear the result.

No surprises there. She had no doubt that Steve was doing everything to avoid, delay and prevaricate. Meanwhile, she and Alice teetered on the brink of insolvency.

Pippa rubbed her eyes. No matter how much she willed it, the figure on the screen hadn't suddenly grown an extra decimal point. She abandoned the computer and picked up Alice out of her bassinet and then lay on the floor with her baby resting on her belly. Alice pushed up on her arms and stared, eyes bright with curiosity. As usual Pippa felt the bulk of her worries slip away as she looked into her daughter's trusting face.

This is what's important. Only this.

Everything else would take care of itself. University, the car, the bills… Things would work out. She'd make them work out. She might not be loaded, but she was thirty-one years old and she was resourceful and resilient. If she had to sic yet another government agency on Steve, she would. If she had to somehow squeeze in more work shifts around her classes, she'd do that, too. Whatever it took.

She cupped her hand around her daughter's silken head and pressed a kiss to her cheek.

Whatever it took.

CHAPTER TWO

HARRY WOKE THE next morning feeling thirsty and thick in the head. No doubt the result of the many beers he'd sunk last night, along with the fact he'd crawled into bed in the early hours.

He lay in the morning sun trying to muster the energy to get out of bed and take care of both his thirst and complaining bladder.

Details from the night returned: Steve crowing as he won yet another game of pool at the pub, completely ungracious in victory. Nugga making a fool of himself chatting up a girl way too young for him. The hot brunette with the tight tank top—no bra—who had punched her number into Harry's phone and told him to call her.

Yeah, it had been a good one. Not quite up to the glory days of five years ago, when there had been more of them and fewer girlfriends and wives at home, but still a good night.

After a few minutes of drowsing, Harry threw off the covers and shuffled into the bathroom to take care of business. He hit the kitchen afterward, pouring himself a huge glass of OJ and took it to bed, which was when he noticed the sand in the sheets. He grinned, remembering the last part of the evening, when he, Steve and Bluey had played an unholy game of tag on the beach, whooping and hollering as they ran in and out of the surf and up and down the sand. They'd finally been sent home by one of the boys in blue, with a heavy-handed suggestion that they all grow up.

Harry finished the juice in one long pull. He checked his phone for the time and saw he had a text from Nugga asking if he wanted to catch a wave or two at Gunnamatta. He thought about it for a second. He didn't have any other major plans for the day beyond a vague idea that he might drop in on his sister, Mel, and her husband, Flynn. A surf was a safer bet—the moment his sister saw him she'd be sure to invent some gardening job that required muscle strain, sweat and four-letter words. Not that she wouldn't be in there right alongside him and Flynn, pulling her weight, but still.

He texted Nugga to say he was on the way, then rolled out of bed and stretched until his shoulders popped. Ten minutes later he was out the door in a pair of board shorts, a towel under his arm, a pair of thongs on his feet.

He threw his wetsuit and board into the back of his old truck and wended his way through quiet residential streets until he hit the highway.

Harry saw Pippa's car from a mile off, a bright yellow beacon on the opposite side of the road. He frowned as he sped past. He'd thought she would call her mechanic yesterday to take care of it. But maybe she'd had trouble contacting him at the end of the working week. She'd need to deal with it in short order, however, because the local council had strong feelings about abandoned cars. If Pippa wasn't careful, her car would be towed and she'd have to pay a release fee on top of everything else.

Seeing Pippa's car reminded him of something else that had happened last night. Maybe it had been stupid of him given the circumstances and how close-mouthed Steve had always been about Pippa and Alice, but when he'd hit the pub he'd taken Steve aside to let him know what had happened with Pippa. Harry had figured that if it was his ex, the mother of his child, he'd want to know. But Steve had simply nodded as though Harry was talking about someone he barely knew and changed the subject. No interest whatsoever.

Big deal. They're not together. And she sicced some government agency on to him to squeeze more money out of him. He's got every right to feel the way he does.

It wasn't as though Steve had gone looking to be a father, after all, and no one knew better than Harry how messed up and angry Steve had been when Pippa broke the news. And yet…his mate's indifference didn't sit well with Harry.

But he wasn't in the habit of sticking his nose where it didn't belong. So Pippa would have to sort her car out on her own.

Except she didn't.

When he drove to work on Monday morning the car was still there, and when he drove home at the end of the day. Tuesday, same deal. Wednesday morning he kept his eyes peeled and the moment he saw her hatchback, he pulled over. After three minutes of searching an online phone directory, he realized she must have an unlisted number. He drummed his fingers on the steering wheel for a few seconds, then waited for a break in traffic before doing a U-turn.

Five minutes later he climbed the steps to Pippa's front porch. It was only after he'd knocked that he questioned what he was doing. She was an adult, after all. She didn't need him ordering her life or breathing down her neck.

Too late. Footsteps sounded within the house, then the front door opened and a bemused Pippa stared at him.

"Harry. Hi."

Her hair was tousled, her eyes heavy. A fluffy dressing gown swamped her body, her bare feet peeking out beneath the hem.

She should have looked a mess—mumsy and suburban—but she looked good. Soft and warm and gently pretty.

"What's going on with your car?"

She blinked and it occurred to him that he may have actually dragged her out of bed.

"Sorry if I woke you, but you should know that the Peninsula council is all over abandoned cars like white on rice. If someone reports you, your car will be towed and impounded."

"Oh. Right."

Somewhere inside the house, a baby cried. Pippa glanced distractedly over her shoulder.

"I'm a bit slow this morning. I've been up since five with Alice. I only got her down again half an hour ago."

She backed up a step and gestured for him to follow her.

"Come in."

She was gone before he could explain he'd already said what he'd come to say, neatly sidestepping her way around a detached door leaning against the hall wall before disappearing from sight. He hesitated on the threshold, uneasy.

"Do you want a coffee?"

Pippa's question echoed up the hallway. He shook his head, then realized she couldn't see him.

"I'm fine, thanks."

Harry entered the house, navigating his way past the detached door. He found Pippa cradling a blond-haired, blue-eyed baby in the bright kitchen, rocking from foot to foot as she attempted to soothe her.

"Shh, sweetheart, you're all right. It's all good." Pippa's voice was soft and achingly tender. She glanced at him. "There's juice, too, if you'd prefer something cold."

He was too busy staring at Alice to respond immediately. He hadn't seen her since the day she was born. She'd been red and squashed-looking then, her eyes squeezed tightly shut, her hands clenched into tight little fists. Now, she was pink and plump, with pale, wispy hair. She looked like Steve. Almost disconcertingly so. It was weird seeing his friend's features replicated on a tiny baby girl.

"She looks like Steve," he said.

"Yes."

The way she said the single word made him remember he had no business being here. Steve was his mate, after all. Harry owed his first loyalty to him.

He cleared his throat. "Anyway. The car. You should chase up your mechanic because the council are real sticklers about towing anything that looks like it's been abandoned."

"I didn't realize. I thought I'd have a few weeks…"

A few weeks? To do what?

Then it hit him—her worry at the roadside, the slightly shabby house, the fact that she was a single mother.

She couldn't afford to get her car fixed.

Hence her delaying tactics when he'd mentioned having her car towed, and hence her need to wait *a few weeks* before she had the funds to repair it.

He glanced around the room, racking his brain for

a way to offer help without stepping on her toes—because he might not know Pippa that well, but he knew she had way too much pride to ask for help.

"Listen, Pippa, why don't I get my dad to tow the car to your place? At least you won't have to worry about it being impounded."

She was shaking her head before he'd even finished speaking. "It's great of you to offer again, Harry, but I'll sort it. Thanks, though. And thanks for the heads up. I appreciate it." She glanced at the wall clock. "I don't want to hold you up."

She was fobbing him off. Getting ready to send him on his way.

"How are you going to sort it?" he asked bluntly.

"Sorry?"

"How are you going to sort the car when you can't afford to get it fixed?"

Her chin jerked with surprise. "That's not what this is about."

She was a terrible liar, her eyes blinking rapidly behind her glasses.

"So I should call Al Towing and get them to take the car to my work and ask my boss to quote on it for you, then?"

She stared at him, her expression half frustrated, half chagrined. After a second she shook her head. "You don't beat around the bush, do you?"

"I'm hoping I might have a chance of getting to work on time if we cut some of the back and forth out of the way."

She gave a short, sharp laugh. "You always were honest to a fault. Okay, you're right, Harry. I can't afford to fix the car right now. I'm scraping some money together but the gas bill came in and I figure we need hot water more than we need a car. So maybe the council will impound my car and I'll have to live with that until I can figure something out."

Pippa shrugged as though she didn't give a damn but her cheeks were pink and her shoulders tense.

He ran a hand over the top of his head, unsure where to go now that he'd gotten her to admit the truth. If it was one of his mates, he'd simply open his wallet and offer a loan on the spot. But as much as he liked her, Pippa wasn't really his friend and he had no idea how she'd react if he offered her money.

"What about Steve?" Because it seemed to him that was the next natural step, no matter the tensions between them.

"No."

One word, very firm.

"I know you guys have some issues, but he'd help out if he knew you needed it."

"I appreciate that you're trying to help. You're very sweet. But I can handle this."

"I'll ask him. If it'd make it easier for you to swallow."

He didn't know why he was making a federal case out of it. It was her car, her life. She was free to do whatever she liked. Certainly none of it was his responsibility. So why was he offering to be her mouthpiece with his best mate?

Pippa sighed. "It's incredibly generous of you to offer, but you don't want to do that."

"I wouldn't offer if I didn't mean it."

"I know. But it won't make any difference. Steve won't want to help me."

"Look, even if Steve's pissed with you, he'll step up."

"It's nice you believe that, but since he's gone to the

trouble of falsifying the books for his business to avoid paying child support, you'll understand if I don't hold my breath on that one."

He was ready to jump to his mate's defense. No way would Steve turn his back on his responsibilities. Alice was his kid, after all. His daughter.

Something stopped him before the denial left his mouth, however.

Maybe it was the world-weary note to Pippa's voice and the steadiness of her gaze.

Or maybe it was the memory of the utterly blank, disinterested expression on Steve's face Friday night.

"Like I said, I appreciate the heads up, Harry."

A phone rang in the next room.

"I need to get that. It's probably my boss...."

She slipped into the adjacent room. A few seconds later he heard her take the call. Harry glanced around the kitchen again, his gaze landing on a stack of textbooks on the table. He read the title of the top book— *Teaching Studies of Society & Environment in the Primary School*—before his attention was drawn to the large bowl in the center of the table. Filled with odds and ends, it clearly functioned as a tabletop junk drawer— and right on top was a key ring with two car keys.

In the next room, Pippa told someone she was ready and willing to do any and all extra shifts that were on offer. He could hear the strain in her voice. The fear.

He didn't stop to consider it, simply pocketed the keys. When Pippa returned, he said goodbye and bowed out. Once he got to his car, he tossed her keys onto the passenger seat then drove to work.

He'd taken them on impulse, because the idea of walking away from her when she was clearly in need stuck in his craw, and because he couldn't see any other way of convincing her to accept his help. Maybe it had been a mistake. Maybe he'd overstepped the mark, big time. After all, he had no vested interest in her or Alice or any of it.

But he couldn't stop thinking about what she'd said about Steve, about him having engineered his finances to minimize his child support commitments. Harry couldn't conceive of a circumstance where the mate he knew would do that. Steve was always first to buy a round of drinks or help out a friend moving furniture or some other favor. No way could all that generosity dry up when it came to his own flesh and blood.

Pippa must be exaggerating. It wasn't as though things had ended well between her and Steve. She was probably bitter and angry with him. Disappointed, too.

Except she hadn't exactly volunteered the information. Harry had had to push a few times before she'd spelled it out for him.

Deeply uneasy, he grabbed his phone and dialed his father at the workshop.

"It's me. I need a favor. There's an acid-yellow hatchback on the Nepean near the turnoff for the winery. Can you tow it to the workshop and I'll come by to take care of it after work?"

"You think I've got nothing better to do than run around doing favors for your mates?" His father's words were tough, but there was no rancor behind them.

"No. Can you do it?"

Harry half expected his father to have another go at him, but he didn't.

"What's the problem?"

"Head gasket, I think. I'll do the work if you don't mind me using the garage tonight."

"I'll make sure you've got the parts on hand. Who am I doing this for, by the way? Steve? That red-headed idiot?"

"Her name's Pippa. She's a single mum. I'm helping her out."

A profound silence ensued on the other end of the line and Harry could practically hear his father's brain grinding away.

"She's Steve's ex," Harry added.

Just in case his father started getting crazy ideas.

"Fair enough. I guess I'll see you tonight, then."

"Thanks, Dad."

"Don't thank me yet. You haven't seen my bill."

There would be no bill. Mike Porter might look like a hard-ass, but he was the softest touch in town.

As Harry turned in to the parking lot at work, it occurred to him that instead of pulling out all the stops for Pippa himself, he could have simply called Steve and filled him in and let him take care of things. Proving to himself—and Pippa—that she was wrong.

If it hadn't been for the blank look on Steve's face the other night, Harry might have, too. But that look… that look combined with Pippa's comments had sprouted some ugly ideas in his head, and the fact was, he wasn't ready to have them confirmed.

He and Steve had grown up together. Played footy together. Had their first beers, their first fights, their first girlfriends together. He didn't want to think that his mate was capable of letting down people he should care about so profoundly.

So Harry would help Pippa. And he would hold off talking to Steve until he'd had a day or two to digest. And he'd hope that someone, somewhere, had got it wrong.

Two days later, Pippa eased back onto the couch and propped her aching feet on a cushion. Alice lay on her play mat, batting at the Fisher Price mobile Pippa had bought from the local charity shop. It was Friday night and she was exhausted.

It wasn't ordinary, run-of-the-mill exhaustion, either. Having no car meant everything had to be started early and finished late, which meant she was waking earlier, going to bed later. Alice's day care might be around the corner and the gallery only a little farther than that, but when she threw in grocery shopping and other errands, plus getting to the university and back, Pippa figured she was walking more than ten kilometers a day. Great for her thighs and ass, not so great for her feet or her schedule.

In short, it sucked, hard. And she still had no idea how she would get her car repaired. She'd managed to scrape together nearly five hundred dollars, but the two mechanics she'd called had quoted a minimum of one thousand to fix a head gasket.

Pippa pressed her lips together, staring at her much-abused feet. There was no getting around it—she'd have to ask her mum for the money. She would pay her back, of course—but it would take time. And it was humiliating.

Thirty-one and running to Mummy. Well done, Phillipa. Way to be an adult.

To think that not so long ago she'd prided herself on being unconventional and marching to the beat of her own drum. Whenever one of her more conservative friends had asked if she ever worried about the future, about owning a house or being able to afford to retire or having a career, Pippa had laughed and assured them she didn't lose sleep over that stuff because she was too busy enjoying the journey.

What a load of old bullocks.

She'd been off with the fairies, tripping around in a fantasy world. Alice had been a cosmic wake-up call that it was time to stop playing around and grow up—there was nothing like being responsible for a tiny, helpless human being to sort a person's priorities out, quick smart.

Pippa propped an ankle on the opposite knee and massaged the arch of her foot, digging in her thumbs until it hurt. Her thoughts drifted to Harry's visit the other morning. He'd been the last person she'd expected to find on her doorstep at 7:30 a.m. Definitely he was one of the last people she would have chosen to catch her in her fluffy robe, complete with tangled bed hair and smudgy glasses. There was something very unsettling about being caught unprepared for the day by someone as dynamic and charismatic as Harry.

Still, it had been nice of him to drop in and warn her about the council's policy on towing abandoned cars. The bit where he'd forced her to confess that she couldn't afford to have her car fixed hadn't been so great, but since he'd followed it with yet another offer of help, she figured his heart was in the right place. Fortunately, she wasn't that desperate a case yet—stress on the *yet*.

That's right. You're only at the mooching-off-your-retired-mother stage. Mooching-off-strangers is a highlight for coming months, yet to be enjoyed.

A knock echoed through the house. She almost welcomed the interruption, even though it meant she had to get to her feet. Anything was better than lying around brooding.

"Ow," she said as she started up the hallway. "Ow. Ow. Ow. Ow."

Funny how shoes that she'd thought were perfectly comfortable had turned on her after a few days of hard labor. Once she'd dealt with whoever was at the door, she would run herself a bath and soak her feet.

She pushed Alice's stroller out of the way so she could reach the door. Because it was clearly her lucky day, the lock stuck and she swore under her breath.

Like the broken bedroom door, the dodgy lock had been reported to the landlord, but Pippa figured both would be repaired around the same time that Dairy Queen opened a concession in hell. The pitfalls of paying low rent in a working-class suburb.

She shouldered the door, pushing the lock up before twisting it. It gave grudgingly and she—finally—opened it to find Harry filling the frame for the second time in as many days.

"Harry," she said, blinking up at six foot two of solid male dressed in an old gray surf T-shirt, faded jeans and steel-toed boots.

Why did she keep forgetting how *big* he was? And why did he keep turning up on her doorstep?

"These are yours." He caught her hand and dropped a set of keys into it. "Before you say anything, it was my pleasure. Consider it an early birthday present for Alice."

It took her brain a full ten seconds to process his words and understand their meaning.

"You fixed my car," she said stupidly.

Sure enough, Old Yeller was in the driveway, brighter and larger than life.

"It was no big deal. Like I said the other day, it was the gasket. A few hours and the problem was solved."

"But...how did you get my keys?"

Then she remembered she'd left him alone in the kitchen while she took the phone call from her boss.

The first emotion to hit her was shame. She'd thought she'd been doing a decent job of covering how damned desperate she was, but clearly Harry had seen straight through her. That he understood exactly how powerless she'd been to change her situation and had been moved to act was galling and humiliating in the extreme.

Hard on the heels of shame came anger, a knee-jerk, defensive, irrational response to feeling so vulnerable and exposed. Who was he to take so much upon himself? To force his charity on her—stealing her car keys, no less—without asking if she wanted his help?

Finally, relief hit, so profound, so all-encompassing there was no room for anything else and she clenched her jaw to stop an instinctive, deeply pathetic sob from escaping. She curled her fingers around the keys, squeezing them tight, trying very, very hard not to cry with gratitude and relief. She blinked repeatedly but wasn't entirely successful in vanquishing the tears.

"I don't know what to say. You shouldn't have. It's too much. It's amazing.... But it's too much, Harry."

"It was a couple of hours' work, and Dad let me use his shop. Like I said, not a big deal."

Pippa took in his tired eyes, five-o'clock shadow and fingernails still dark with grease. She knew from her inquiries that replacing a head gasket in a standard, four-cylinder car was an eight-hour job, minimum. He must have worked around the clock after hours to do this for her.

A thousand thoughts battled for supremacy, but there was only one thing she could say.

"Thank you. This means so much to me and Alice. You've literally saved my bacon."

She held Harry's gaze as she said it, wanting him to see how sincere she was, how grateful. It might embarrass her to have to be the recipient of his charity, but no way was she rewarding his generosity with anything other than sincere appreciation. The shame was her problem, not his.

He stuck his hands into his back pockets, stretching his T-shirt across his broad chest. "It wasn't anywhere near as bad as it could have been. A clean replacement, no complications."

He was clearly uncomfortable, which, oddly, made it easier to swallow her own discomfort. She felt a rush of fondness for her ex's best friend. Harry had always been her favorite of Steve's mates. No competition.

"You're a good man, Harry."

He frowned.

"If I can be a gracious receiver, the least you can do is accept my thanks," she said.

"Thanks are fine. But we both know I'm no saint."

"Did I call you a saint? I said you were a good man." She stepped to one side. "Come in so I can make you even more uncomfortable with my gratitude."

He glanced over his shoulder as though looking for an escape route.

"Come on. A little slavish gratitude won't hurt you," she teased.

His gray eyes creased at the corners as his mouth curled into a reluctant smile. He stepped over the threshold, brushing past her, and she caught the scent of clean sweat and spicy deodorant. Her gaze scanned his broad back before dropping to his butt.

She stopped the moment she realized what she was

doing. Harry was Steve's best friend. In every way that counted, he was completely and utterly off-limits. She didn't need or want to register him as a man. She definitely didn't want to notice he had a nice ass.

Even if he did.

Pippa shut the door, being careful to shoulder it so the lock slipped into place. She was aware of Harry watching her and she shrugged philosophically.

"This place is a bit of a work in progress," she said and headed down the hall.

She heard Harry follow, his tread steady and sure. When they entered the kitchen she threw him a quick smile.

"One sec while I check on Alice."

She ducked her head into the sunroom. Her daughter was chewing on the sleeve of her Onesie, a sure sign she was hungry. Pippa scooped her into her arms.

"We've got a visitor. You want to come and say hello?"

Harry stood in front of the photographic montage she'd made of the first few months of Alice's life, his expression unreadable.

"Sorry about that," she said. "Now, can I offer you a coffee or a tea? I think I may even have a stray beer in the fridge. And have you had dinner?"

"Coffee's great, thanks." He turned from the photographs, and his expression softened when he saw who she was holding. "Hello, little lady."

Alice blew a bubble and gurgled in the back of her throat.

"That's hello in baby-speak, in case you were wondering."

Pippa settled Alice on her hip and crossed to the kettle to set it boiling. Acting on a hunch, she pulled out the leftover roast potatoes and chicken schnitzel from dinner and ferried them toward the microwave.

"If that's for me, please don't bother," he said.

She slid the plate into the microwave before facing him.

"Tell me what you had for dinner and I'll put it in the fridge." She was aware of Alice latching on to one of the buttons on her bodice and she ran a finger distractedly over her daughter's head.

He eyed her for a beat before responding. "Okay. I haven't eaten yet, but I've got food at home."

"If I can accept you repairing my car for me, you can accept a meal." She hit the button to start the microwave and waved him toward one of the two stools tucked beneath the kitchen counter. "Especially when the reason you went hungry is because you were doing me a favor. Grab a seat."

"I don't remember you being this bossy."

"Maybe you don't know me as well as you think you do."

"Maybe."

He sat as she collected coffee-making paraphernalia from the cupboard.

She laid out a knife and fork for him, grabbed a glass of juice, too, then folded a paper napkin and placed it beside the cutlery.

"Don't go to any trouble." He seemed awkward as hell sitting there, waiting for her to feed him.

"Relax. It's a paper napkin." She went very still when his gaze dropped to her breasts.

In all the time she'd dated Steve, she'd never—not once—gotten the vibe that Harry was interested in her as a woman. His attitude toward her had always been strictly friendly—no eye drops, no ass checks, no speculative looks. If she'd been asked by someone to describe the way he treated her, she'd have said his attitude was fraternal. Big brotherly.

Yet right now, right this second, he was staring at her chest with a single-minded intensity that made her belly tighten with nervous self-consciousness.

The moment seemed to stretch. Then Harry lifted his gaze to hers and realized he'd been busted. Dull color stained his cheeks.

"Sorry. It's just…your dress…" He gestured toward her chest, his gaze trained resolutely over her shoulder now.

She glanced down and discovered that the top two buttons of her bodice were undone, offering him an untrammeled view of her deep red bra and a whole lot of cleavage.

CHAPTER THREE

SHE GATHERED THE sides of her dress together in her free hand, heat burning its way into her face. "Sorry. Alice must have— She's never done that before...."

It was true. Alice was always fiddling—with Pippa's necklace, her earring, the collar of her shirt or the buttons on her coat—but she'd never unbuttoned anything before.

Pippa tucked her chin and tried to rebutton her bodice one-handed, very aware of the warmth in her cheeks. Unlike many of the women in her mothers' group, she had been unsuccessful at breast-feeding. A series of infections and an inadequate milk supply led her pediatrician to recommend bottle-feeding Alice when her daughter was barely a month old. Consequently, Pippa wasn't nearly as casual about flinging her breasts around as some of her friends. To her, they were about sex and intimacy, not sustenance.

And Harry had copped a very decent eyeful.

"Here, I'll take her." Harry held out his hands, ready to accept the baby so she could secure her dress.

"You're sure?" she asked, surprised. He didn't exactly seem the baby type.

"She hasn't just eaten, right?"

"She won't throw up on you, if that's what you're worried about."

"Then we're cool."

She had to release her dress to pass Alice to him, and Harry kept his eyes averted during the exchange. She quickly refastened her dress, fingers racing to push the buttons home.

"Sorry about that," she said once she was decent. "Bit more than you bargained for."

She couldn't quite make herself meet his eye.

"Should I slip the kid a tip or would that be overkill?"

He surprised a laugh out of her. "I don't think she needs the encouragement."

"Guess it depends on where you're sitting."

She risked a glance at his face. He was smiling, a devilish glint in his eyes. She grinned.

"You're hopeless."

"Because I've got eyes in my head?"

"Something like that." She glanced at Alice, who was happily balanced on his knee, her back supported by one of Harry's big hands.

"Are you okay with holding her for a few more minutes or are you going to break out in hives from all the responsibility?"

"I can handle it."

"Brave man."

"Weren't you making me dinner?"

She rolled her eyes comically before checking on the microwave. The timer was almost done and she opened the door to test the temperature of the potatoes. She was aware of Harry watching her as she worked and an odd little frisson ran up her spine. A couple of minutes later, she slid the plate in front of him, complete with gravy and a slice of fresh bread.

"Looks good," he said.

"Well, it's food, anyway," she said modestly.

She enjoyed cooking, but she wasn't about to volunteer for *Masterchef* or anything. Definitely her efforts veered more toward the everyday and practical than haute cuisine.

She reached for Alice, sliding her daughter off his thigh so he could eat his meal unhindered. At the last minute, Alice caught a fistful of Harry's T-shirt in her small hand, clinging to it as though her life depended on it.

"Alice. Sorry, Harry. She's not used to men, so you're a bit of a novelty item."

"It's all part of being a babe magnet."

She winced to let him know his joke was really bad before prying Alice's fingers loose. Her daughter had a fierce grip, however, and it took Pippa a few seconds to convince her to let Harry go. She was very aware of the firm warmth of his chest beneath the fabric and how close she stood to him. It hit her that this was the most intimate she'd been with a member of the opposite sex since she'd gotten pregnant. A less than impressive reflection of her social life, but also a solid explanation for the way her heart suddenly pounded in her chest.

"You live to fight another day," she said as Alice finally relinquished her prize.

"Phew," Harry said. "Thought it was all over for a moment there."

Pippa moved to a safe distance and gestured for him to eat. "Dig in. Don't let it get cold."

He dutifully picked up his cutlery and started eating. She took a deep breath and let it out slowly, trying to regain her equilibrium. From the moment he'd dropped her car keys into her hand she'd been off balance. Exposing herself and then prying her daughter off him hadn't helped matters.

Funny, but she'd never thought of Harry as someone she could ever be nervous around. But then she'd never been alone with him at nine o'clock on a Friday night before, either.

Right, because so much is going to happen. He's probably just waiting for his moment to pounce, single mothers being a huge turn-on for him and all. Add to that the fact you're his best mate's ex and you're practically irresistible. It's a wonder he's still got his pants on.

The thought calmed her. The very idea of Harry being interested in her or her being interested in Harry was absurd. Beyond absurd, really, moving into insane territory.

Common sense restored, Pippa crossed to the sideboard to find her handbag. She grabbed her checkbook from the side pocket and found a pen.

Behind her, Harry made an appreciative noise. "This is really good. I love schnitzel."

"It's my Aunt Bev's recipe. She married an Austrian."

"Go Aunty Bev."

She opened the checkbook to a fresh page.

Harry's eyebrows rose as he registered what she was doing. "That had better not be what I think it is."

"You have to at least let me pay for parts. I've gotten some money together, so I'm not a total charity case."

"It was a gasket and some oil. A few bucks. Like I said, consider it Alice's birthday present."

"Except it's going to be another seventeen-odd years before she actually needs her own car." She fixed Harry with a level look. "I appreciate your generosity, and I know I can't fully repay you for your time, but please let me make sure you're not out of pocket."

He gestured toward his plate. "You cooked me dinner. We're square."

She made a frustrated noise. Harry cut another slice of schnitzel and popped it into his mouth. He chewed slowly, purposefully, a steady, confident expression in his eyes that as good as said, "I just had the final word and you can't do anything about it."

He really was a cheeky bastard. Too cocky and smug and charming for his own good.

"I'll find a way to pay you back, Porter."

"You can try. But I don't like your chances."

She harrumphed to let him know she didn't agree, then crossed to the fridge and refilled his juice glass. Alice started fiddling with her buttons again and Pippa switched her to the opposite hip in the hope that it might distract her.

"I have to ask—what's with all the books on teaching?" Harry asked.

"I'm studying to get my Dip. Ed."

"You're going to be a teacher?"

"No need to sound so surprised. It's not *that* shocking."

"You've never mentioned it before, that's all."

She pulled a strand of her hair free from Alice's grasping fingers. "I need a job. A real job, not a joke job that I can pick up and put down whenever I feel like it."

Harry's gaze went to Alice and she knew he understood.

"Do you like it?"

"Sometimes. I've had two class placements so far and they both went pretty well. No one died on my watch, at least."

"Setting the bar pretty low there."

"These days I find it's best to have low expectations."

They talked about her studies as he finished his meal, leaving nothing but a thin trail of gravy. Testament, she hoped, to how much he'd enjoyed it. Afterward, he set his knife and fork neatly side by side on the plate and carried it to the sink. She watched as he glanced around for the dishwasher—there wasn't one—then proceeded to wash his plate.

"Wow. You're actually house-trained. Who knew?"

There was a reluctant grin on his lips as he glanced over his shoulder at her. "Jesus, you're a smart-ass. To think I used to miss you hanging around."

If the look on his face was anything to go by, he'd surprised himself as well as her with his inadvertent admission. She smiled, oddly touched, as he focused on rinsing his plate. She'd missed him, too, when things had gone south with Steve. Harry's irreverence and easygoing charm had always appealed to her. In another time and place, perhaps, they might have been friends. In this lifetime, however, it was never going to happen. Too many old loyalties on his side and too many bad associations on hers.

"I should get going," Harry said as he set the plate on the drainer.

"Okay."

She led him to the hallway, edging past the broken door. "Sorry about the obstacle course. The landlord assures me he's going to fix this thing before the turn of the next century."

This time, thankfully, the lock opened easily and she watched Harry step onto the porch.

"Thanks for dinner. And the show," he said.

Trust him to bring up the moment with her bra again. "And I'm the smart-ass?"

"Maybe it takes one to know one."

"Maybe." The smile faded from her lips as she held his eyes. "Harry, what you did tonight… I will never be able to tell you how much your generosity means. I feel as though I've had a visit from my fairy godmother or something."

He shrugged modestly. "Honestly, I could do it in my sleep. It's really not a big deal."

"It is to me and Alice. A very big deal."

On impulse, she stepped forward, stood on tiptoes and flung her free arm around his shoulders.

"Thank you for being so damn kind," she said fiercely, pressing a kiss to the angle of his jaw. His shoulders were warm and firm beneath her arm and his five-o'clock shadow tickled her cheek. She inhaled the good, honest smell of him, touched all over again by what he'd done.

Before she could withdraw, his arms came around her, returning her embrace, and for a split second she and Alice were pressed firmly against his chest and side. Then he let go and she sank onto her heels. When she went to step away, however, she discovered Alice had once again grabbed Harry's T-shirt and was not about to let go.

"Maybe you really are a babe magnet."

Harry eyed Alice indulgently. "Nah. She's just got good taste."

He brushed his forefinger across the back of Alice's knuckles. Alice lifted her face to his, eyes wide, her mouth open in an almost-smile. Full of curiosity and wonder.

"Come on, cutie," he said gently, smiling in return.

He brushed her hand again and Alice let go, transferring her grip to his finger. Pippa stepped back, and after a long second Alice let Harry's finger slip from her grasp.

"Should have known you'd be an expert at the cut and run," she said.

"Lots of practice."

For a moment they simply smiled at each other.

"I'll see you around."

"Yeah. Look after yourself, okay?" she said, a little alarmed to feel her throat closing over with unexpected emotion.

Although maybe it wasn't that unexpected—he'd saved her ass tonight, after all.

"Sure thing."

He raised his hand in farewell and headed for his car. She watched him, only belatedly realizing it must have been quite an operation to get both her car and his here. She wondered how many favors he'd called in and knew she'd never know. Just as she'd never know how much she really owed him for parts and labor.

Grateful tears stung the back of her eyes as she waved him off. Pippa wasn't one of those people who had random good things fall in her lap every day, and she'd never considered herself particularly lucky, but there was no doubt the universe had been smiling on her when Harry drove past on the highway last week.

Suddenly she wished she'd said more to him, even if it would almost certainly have made him deeply uncomfortable. They'd been so busy giving each other a hard time, playing up their old dynamic, that she didn't feel as though she'd properly expressed her feelings.

Right now, Harry was her hero. Pure and simple.

She felt a tug, and when she looked down she discovered Alice was once again undressing her. Clearly, she needed to either invest in some safety pins or a pair of mittens for her daughter. Or, alternatively, some truly excellent underwear if she was destined to be flashing all and sundry on a regular basis.

For a split second—the most fleeting of moments—she allowed herself to wonder what Harry had thought of the "show" she'd put on tonight. Then she as quickly pushed the thought from her mind.

After all, it was absurd to even think—

Shaking her head, Pippa went to put her daughter to bed.

HARRY DIDN'T CONSIDER himself a saint. Not by a long shot. He had his faults and flaws, and some of them were worse than others, but one thing he'd never done was look twice at a mate's girlfriend or wife.

It simply wasn't in his makeup. As far as he was concerned, there were more than enough single, ready and willing women in the world without him even considering a woman who was taken.

So why in the name of all that was good couldn't he get the memory of Pippa's creamy, curvy breasts out of his head?

It wasn't just that she'd been wearing a cherry-red bra—not what he would have guessed was under her old-fashioned dress, that was for sure—although the way the bright lace had cupped her pale skin had been pretty damn memorable.

It was everything. The sway of her body as she'd moved around the kitchen, the way she'd tilted her head when she sent smart-mouthed zingers his way, the way she'd turned pink when she'd realized what her enterprising daughter had done.

Pippa White, it turned out, was sexy. In a quiet, subversive, get-under-a-man's-skin kind of way. She might not put it all out there like the brunette who'd punched her number into his phone last week, but there was something about Pippa that made a man think about things he shouldn't be thinking about when she was his best friend's ex-girlfriend—or, better yet, the mother of his best friend's child.

The worst thing was, Harry suspected he'd always been aware of her in that way on some level. When she'd been going out with Steve, Harry had always been able to pick her voice out in a crowd. Same with her laugh. And he'd whiled away more than one night lounging around a pool table with her, shooting the shit, laughing at her jokes and enjoying her sharp take on the world. Enjoying her.

Not gonna happen. Ever. So get that dirty little thought out of your head right now.

Harry pulled into his driveway and braked with more force than necessary, slamming the car door hard as he exited and headed for the house.

It was just as well he wouldn't be running into Pippa again in the near future, because he wasn't interested in being either the nobly-tortured, self-restrained chump or the dick-driven moron who threw away years of friendship for a roll in the hay. He liked things nice and easy. No complications. Lots of fun. Pippa didn't fall under any of those headings.

He strode into the living room, automatically reaching for the remote to flick on the TV. He wasn't really hungry, but he went into the kitchen and made himself a big bowl of ice cream. He sat on the couch and dug in, kidding himself that he was watching the cricket report when really he was thinking about the way Pippa had hugged and kissed him on her doorstep.

She'd called him kind, which was a pretty big joke given all he'd been able to think about was her breast pressed against his biceps. And when he'd returned her embrace—an impulse he hadn't been able to control—he'd sucked in a lungful of her perfume and the warm, milky smell of her daughter.

Who—yeah—had totally been in Pippa's arms while he was thinking about how soft her breast felt against his arm.

He was *so* kind. Practically a saint.

Disgusted with himself, he pushed his half-full bowl onto the coffee table and dropped his head against the cushion, trying to find some clarity. Or at the very least a little peace of mind.

He'd left as soon as he'd registered his own interest—he figured that counted in his favor. And he'd held her for only a second. And even though he wouldn't swear on it, he was pretty sure he'd helped out with the car with absolutely no expectations. Just as, even now, a part of him itched to grab his toolbox and go over to her place to fix that ridiculous abandoned door leaning against the wall, as well as that stupid, half-assed lock she had to wrestle with.

So what? She's Steve's ex. Doesn't matter what good deeds you want to perform, Boy Scout. She's out-of-bounds.

She was. Even if she and Steve had ended things amicably, the same would be true.

Which meant it really was time to stop thinking about her.

Harry reached for the remote, cranked up the volume and pretended that that was what he was doing.

PIPPA PRACTICALLY LEAPED down the steps the next morning, eager to get into the day. She had a car again! She

felt as though she was rejoining the modern world after
a week in the Stone Age.

Alice talked to herself in the backseat as Pippa drove
to the village, her head full of plans. Once she had re-
stocked the pantry, she might make a run to the library
to check if the textbooks she'd ordered for her classes
had arrived. Then she should probably get a head start
on the five-thousand-word assignment that was due before the end of the month.

But first there was something she wanted to do. She
parked in front of the liquor store and strapped Alice
into her stroller, then went inside and bought some beer.
The salesman helped her stow it on the rack at the back
of the stroller before she exited and crossed the road.
A bell rang as she entered the cement-floored reception area of Village Motors and a young girl looked up
from behind the counter.

"Hi. How can I help you?"

Pippa offered up her best smile. "Would it be possible to speak to Mr. Porter?"

The girl's gaze flicked between Pippa, Alice and the
beer. Lord only knew what she was thinking.

"I'll see if he's busy," she said primly.

Pippa pushed the stroller back and forth while she
waited, hoping to keep Alice distracted. When Alice
started vocalizing, she squatted to play peek-a-boo,
making her daughter smile.

"I'm Mike Porter. How can I help you?" a deep voice
asked.

She glanced up to find a powerfully built older man
with a graying horseshoe mustache and Harry's eyes
and nose towering over her. Like Harry, he was tall
and broad. She would have recognized him as Harry's
father anywhere.

She stood. "My name is Pippa White. I own a bright yellow hatchback. Your son Harry repaired it for me...."

"Right. The head gasket."

"That's me. I wanted to drop by and say thank you for your help, and to offer you a small token of my appreciation."

She collected the carton of beer from the luggage rack, offering it to him. His forehead pleated into a perplexed frown.

"You didn't have to do that," he said gruffly.

"I wanted to. I really appreciate what you and Harry did for us. I can't tell you what a relief it is to have a car again." Her arms were starting to get tired and she adjusted her grip a fraction. "Unless you like your beer frothy, you might want to grab this. I'm afraid my upper-body strength isn't what it should be."

"Sorry." Mike took the carton, placing it on the counter. He looked uncomfortable and a little uncertain as he faced her. Pippa stifled a smile. Like Harry, he didn't know what to do with her gratitude.

"Please take it. It's a tiny fraction of what the repairs would have cost, and I really want to acknowledge your generosity."

"Harry won't like this. He was pretty keen to help you out."

For some reason, his words sent a wash of warmth up her chest and into her face.

"I know. But he needs to accept that I'm pretty keen to thank you for that help, too."

Mike's gaze moved to Alice, his mustache twitching around his smile as he studied her round face. "This your daughter?"

"Yes. Alice."

"How old is she?"

"A little over six months."

His gaze returned to her and she could tell he'd made a decision. "Thanks for the beer, Pippa. It won't go to waste. And I'll be sure to direct Harry's comments your way when he hears about it."

She smiled. "You do that. I can handle it." She slid her hand into her handbag and grasped her checkbook. "Now, I don't suppose you could tell me what I owe for parts?"

Mike's eyebrows shot toward his hairline. "You don't need to worry about all that. Harry covered everything."

"I know. That's why I want to make sure he isn't out of pocket. It's one thing to give up his time, but I can't let him pay for parts, as well."

Mike shook his head. "Sorry, but that's something you'll have to take up with Harry."

"Mr. Porter—"

"Mike."

"Mike. Harry is a great guy, but I don't feel comfortable having him pay out money on my behalf. I know I didn't ask and he offered, but I can afford to cover the parts, and I really want to. It's important to me. I've got Alice to look after now and standing on my own two feet means a lot." She could hear the emotion vibrating in her voice and she swallowed. For a woman who had spent much of her adult life merely getting by, being responsible for another person was a profound shift. More than anything, she wanted to be up to the challenge, to be worthy of Alice. That meant not relying on her mother or anyone else. Definitely it meant not taking handouts if she didn't have to.

"I understand where you're coming from," Mike said after a short silence. "Things were tough when we first had Justine, our eldest, but I still had my fair share of pride. I get it."

"So you'll let me reimburse you?" she asked hopefully.

He allowed himself a small smile at her persistence, but he shook his head. "I'll tell you what the parts are worth. You can take repayment up with Harry."

Which meant she had yet another battle on her hands, but so be it.

Mike pulled open the top drawer of a beaten-up filing cabinet. After a few seconds he extracted a folder and opened it.

"Okay. The gasket itself was fifty, but you've got an aluminum head, which had to be resurfaced before the gasket was replaced, so that was three hundred. Then there was five liters of oil at thirty, a new oil filter at twenty-five for a grand total of four-oh-five." He glanced at her. "Which Harry can well afford, by the way."

Pippa pulled out her phone and made a note of the figure on the notepad app. "So can I. Thanks for this, Mike. I appreciate it."

"My pleasure. I appreciate you taking the time to drop in. Not sure I'll feel the same once Harry hears what went down, but I'm still bigger than he is so he can suck it up."

Pippa wasn't too sure about him being bigger than Harry—it looked like a pretty close call to her—but she offered Mike her hand, said thanks once again, then pushed a dozing Alice outside. She paused, thinking about how Harry had shouldered four hundred and five dollars on her behalf without so much as batting an eyelid, yet his best friend wouldn't even pick up the phone to discuss his daughter's welfare.

Someone sure picked the wrong hell-raiser to fall into bed with.

It was a dumb thought and she pushed it away the moment it occurred to her. It wasn't as though she'd ever had a choice between Steve and Harry—Harry hadn't even been around when she'd started going out with Steve. He'd been on holiday, touring the U.S., and she and Steve had been seeing each other for nearly a month by the time he returned home.

She could still remember the day she'd first set eyes on him. He'd walked in the door of Steve's place, two small silver rings shining in his right earlobe, tattoos black against tanned arms, and more than a little intimidating in a plain black T-shirt, worn jeans and steel-toed boots. *Here comes trouble* had been her first thought. Then he'd smiled and she'd seen the mischief, curiosity and intelligence in his eyes and she'd realized he *was* trouble—just not the kind she'd first anticipated.

Alice shifted, making the stroller rock, and Pippa snapped to. She had things to do. She didn't have time to stand around lollygagging. Especially not over Harry.

Her step brisk, she headed for the supermarket.

CHAPTER FOUR

THE REST OF the day sped by. She left Alice with a fellow student she traded babysitting duties with while she went to the university to get a head start on her assignment, a dry-as-dust examination of "the effect of government policy on the new national curriculum." She collected Alice midafternoon and swung by the gallery to check her roster for the next week. She'd requested extra shifts when she'd still been flailing around, trying to work out how to pay for car repairs, and she saw that her boss, Gaylene, had come to the party. The two extra shifts would mean some juggling of Pippa's schedule, but the extra money would give her the opportunity to build a little nest egg so that the next time life threw her a curve ball, she wouldn't feel quite so desperate.

In theory.

She thanked Gaylene, then checked the time. It was a little after five. She chewed her lip, then decided that this was as good a time as any to swing by Harry's place to see if he was around. It was tempting to simply leave the money in an envelope under his door when she knew he'd be at work, but leaving it without talking to him smacked of cowardice, and she wasn't afraid of him or the argument they were bound to have over her insistence on repayment. Far from it.

Pippa had only been to his place once when Steve had parked in the drive and honked the horn to let Harry know they were there to pick him up. Consequently, she knew the street but not the house number, but the big black muscle car in the driveway put paid to any doubts she might have had that she had the right place. The house itself was nondescript, a seventies brown brick with a neatly manicured lawn and a garage to the rear.

She pulled into the driveway, aware that her pulse had sped up and butterflies were doing a lap of her stomach in anticipation of the battle to come. She checked on Alice and discovered she was fast asleep. Well, Pippa was only going to be a minute, so there was no point disturbing her. She cracked the window to ensure there was a breeze and got out of the car.

The Red Hot Chili Peppers' "Under the Bridge" filtered through the warm afternoon air as she made her way to the front door. She knocked and waited. Seconds ticked past and she grew more and more tense. Which was ridiculous. This was Harry, and she'd already established she wasn't even remotely scared of locking horns with him.

When he didn't appear, she knocked again and tapped her foot impatiently. When he still didn't answer, she stepped back and regarded the house. The music told her that someone was home, and it belatedly occurred to her that he might not be able to hear her over the racket. She walked to the side of the house and peered up the driveway. The side door of the garage was open, and the music seemed to be emanating from there. Maybe he was working on a car or something.

She checked on Alice, then made her way past the house. The music switched to Pearl Jam as she neared the garage and she took a deep breath.

"Knock knock," she said as she stepped into the doorway.

And promptly lost the power of speech.

Harry was lying on his back on an incline bench, part of what was clearly an elaborate home gym. His chest was bare, sweat glistening on the muscles, his legs bent at the knee, his feet planted wide. A pair of faded tracksuit pants cut off raggedly at the knee rode low on his hips, and his stomach muscles rippled with effort as he pumped a loaded barbell above his head.

He looked…amazing. Huge. Sweaty. Ridiculously masculine. For the first time she saw that the tribal tattoos that snaked around his arms also flowed onto the left side of his chest, licking up his side like sinuous black flames. His pecs were powerfully defined, his nipples flat brown circles. A dark trail of hair bisected his belly, traveling down from his navel and disappearing beneath his low waistband.

She swallowed and became aware that she was clutching the envelope in her fist and staring like a nun at a strip show. She blinked, cleared her throat.

She'd seen near-naked men before, after all. So what if none of them had looked like Conan the Barbarian? It was no big deal. She wasn't even that into muscle-bound men anyway.

She cleared her throat a second time and knocked on the open door.

"Hey. Harry, you got a minute?" she called over the music.

The barbell crashed onto the uprights on either side of the bench as Harry registered her presence.

"Pippa." He looked surprised—and, unless she was wildly mistaken, pleased. As though he was happy to see her.

He sat up, an action which caused his abdominal

muscles to do amazing things, then leaned over to turn down the volume on the stereo. "What's up?"

"I came by to drop this off." She waved the envelope.

His gaze went from it to her, then he snagged a hand towel from the adjacent bench and wiped first his face then his chest.

"If that's money, I don't want it."

"It's four hundred and five dollars. Fifty for the gasket. Three hundred for resurfacing the head. Twenty-five for the oil filter and thirty for the oil."

"You spoke to Dad."

"I did. I took him some beer to say thank you."

"You didn't have to do that."

"Yeah, I did. Just like I have to do this."

She took a few steps into the room and slid the envelope onto the workbench that ran along the rear wall.

"Pippa…"

She held up a hand. "Harry, you need to let me do this. I am incredibly grateful for what you did, but it's enough that you gave me eight-plus hours of your time. I can't let you cover the parts, as well."

He scowled and pushed himself to his feet, setting off another chain reaction of rippling muscles. She fought the need to take a step backward as he advanced on her, reaching to grab the envelope.

"I'm not taking this," he said, thrusting it into her hand.

"Well, that makes two of us," she said, pulling her hand away before he could release the money.

His scowl deepened. This close she could see that his skin was still damp. She could smell his deodorant, too, and see the veins in his arms where his muscles were pumped from his workout.

"I can't take money from you. Put it toward something else," he said.

"*You* put it toward something else."

Like maybe a pair of workout pants that didn't seem as though they were in imminent danger of falling off his narrow hips.

"You mentioned being a graceful receiver the other night. Here's a newsflash for you—you could do with some lessons," he said.

"I *am* grateful. But I'm not a charity case. I don't need you paying my way."

"Who said anything about you being a charity case?"

An inch of what looked like black boxer-briefs showed at his waist. She felt a little dizzy, a little overwhelmed by all the raw masculinity on display.

"If you don't think I'm a charity case, let me pay for the parts," she said, trying to stop her gaze from sliding down his body.

"No. I wanted to help you and Alice. I did. End of story. I'm not taking your money." He grabbed her hand, slapping the envelope into it. "Save it for when the car breaks down next time, which it will, because it's a piece of yellow crap."

He was probably right, but her back went up anyway.

"Just because it's not some big macho muscle car from the days when dinosaurs roamed the planet doesn't mean it's a piece of crap."

"For the record, there weren't many dinosaurs roaming Australia in the seventies. And that hatchback is a piece of crap, and we both know it."

"Fine. Whatever. The point is, it's my piece of crap, and it's my responsibility. What you did was fantastically generous, but you need to let me cover the parts, Harry."

"Not gonna happen."

"Harry."

He shook his head slowly, his jaw set. She glared at him.

"I'm not letting this drop," she warned.

"Then I guess you've got a problem, because I'm not taking your money."

For a split second Pippa almost caved. Almost. But then she thought about how desperate she'd felt this week, and how relieved and pathetic she'd felt when Harry had shown up last night. She didn't want to be a damsel in distress. She needed to be strong, for both her and Alice's sake. That was what getting her Diploma of Education was all about. That was why it was so important that Harry let her pay her way.

"You know what Mick Jagger says. You can't always get what you want," she said.

Then she stuffed the envelope down the front of his shorts and swiveled on her heel, but not before she saw the shock on his face. She raced out the door. She figured she had the shortest of leads before he came after her. Sure enough, she was nearing the car when she heard him calling her name.

She scrambled into the driver's seat, jammed the keys into the ignition and hit the locks. Harry strode toward her, looking for all the world like an escapee from *Gladiator*.

"Sorry," she mouthed as she reversed out of the driveway.

HARRY STOPPED IN his tracks, hands on his hips, a pissed/resigned expression on his face. She hoped the resigned part signaled he would accept her money.

She glanced in the rearview mirror to find that Alice

was awake again, her blue eyes taking in the world. A smile crept onto Pippa's face, quickly turning into a grin.

She'd stuck a wad of cash down Harry's pants. She probably needed to get out more, but it was the most outrageous thing she'd done in months. Possibly even years. And it felt good.

You do *need to get out more.*

She was still buzzing with triumph when she turned onto her own street. Then she realized that the butterflies-doing-a-lap feeling was still there and in a flash of insight understood it wasn't nervousness. Not by a long shot.

It was excitement—because she'd seen Harry.

That quickly her goofy smile was gone, as was the feeling of triumph.

Harry was Steve's best friend. Furthermore, he was as feckless, as childish, as immature as her ex. Another overgrown teenager who viewed life as a big amusement park.

She didn't want to be excited about seeing him. God, no.

She parked and got Alice out of the car. As it had the other night, holding her daughter's warm, soft body grounded her. Alice was the ultimate invitation to live in the now, to experience only this present moment. Rubbing her cheek against her daughter's, Pippa let whatever silliness had gripped her this afternoon slide away.

Harry was not someone to get excited about. Lovely and funny and generous as he was.

It's hardly going to be a problem. There's no reason on earth for you to see him again now your car is fixed and the money sorted.

She should have felt relieved, but she didn't. She felt disappointed, which went to show that she really was an idiot.

HARRY RETURNED TO the garage. The envelope with Pippa's money lay on the floor where he'd dropped it—after he'd pulled it out of his pants.

Now, *that* was a move he hadn't seen coming. In fact, he still couldn't quite believe she'd done it.

Briefly he toyed with the idea of going after her, letting her know in no uncertain terms that he wasn't interested in her money. He imagined himself chasing her down, backing her into a corner until she was forced to take the envelope back. She'd protest, no doubt, but he'd look into those rich chocolate-brown eyes of hers and—

He bent and collected the money, pushing it into his pocket and turning away from the thought that had been about to insinuate itself into his head.

It wasn't quite so easy to ignore he had the beginnings of a hard-on, however. All because of a schoolboy fantasy that involved Pippa and a hard wall.

What is going on with you?

It was a good question. He wasn't sure what the answer was. Pippa wasn't the sort of woman he usually went for. She was older, for starters. Smarter, too. Then there was the not-insignificant fact she was a mother.

He gave himself a mental shake. It didn't matter why he liked Pippa or how different she was from his usual type. The important thing was that she was Steve's ex, and therefore officially off-limits.

As if his thoughts had conjured him, he heard the distinctive, low rumble of Steve's new truck pull into the drive. Guilt stabbed at him, but he rejected it instinctively. He hadn't done anything wrong.

Yet.

And it was going to stay that way, because Steve was one of his oldest friends.

He reached for his T-shirt and pulled it on as he exited the garage. Steve was sliding from the cab of his shiny red truck, a six-pack under his arm.

"Yo. What's up?" he called out. He was dressed in board shorts and a loose tank, his hair held back by a pair of sunglasses pushed high on his forehead.

"You been out today?"

"Hell, yeah. Suicide was going off," Steve said, naming a brutal surf beach farther south on the peninsula. "You should have come, man."

Harry shrugged. He'd been through this with Steve during that morning's phone call. "Mel needed my help with installing the rose arbors."

Steve tugged a can free from the plastic ring holding it to the six-pack, passing it to Harry. "Don't know why Mr. Richy-Rich doesn't hire a bunch of muscle to do it all for him. Not like he can't afford it."

"Flynn likes getting his hands dirty," Harry said, shrugging to let Steve know that he didn't want to get into yet another conversation about what Steve would do if he had the Randall millions at his disposal. The truth was, Harry's brother-in-law never flaunted his wealth and Harry had long ago stopped thinking of him as anything other than a good friend and the man who'd made his sister smile again.

"Yeah, yeah, whatever. So, what are we up to tonight? The Pier? Or do you want to hit the Portsea pub for a change, crash at Nugga's place?"

Harry led the way inside. "Not fussed. Whatever tickles your fancy."

Steve sat on the couch and propped his legs on the table, crossing them at the ankles. "You think that little blonde chick will be working at the Pier tonight? The new girl?"

"Who knows?"

"If I had to give her ass a score out of ten, it'd be eleven." Steve laughed and took a pull from his beer.

Harry drank a mouthful of his own can, his head full of everything that had happened with Pippa. He wasn't used to feeling guilty, and he didn't like it.

"So, did you call that girl from last week yet?" Steve asked.

It took Harry a beat to drag his head out of his own thoughts. "Didn't get around to it."

Steve made a disgusted sound. "Dude. What's wrong with you?"

"You want her number, it's yours."

Steve paused with his beer halfway to his mouth. "Seriously? You're not going to call her?"

Harry shook his head.

"Bloody hell. Never thought I'd live to see the day. You losing it in your old age, mate? Having trouble getting it up?"

"Thanks for the touching concern, asshole, but everything is in perfect working order."

Steve laughed and reached for the remote, flicking on the TV. "Did you catch any of the cricket today?"

Harry paused before answering, unable to shake the sense of unease dogging him. He felt like he was holding back. And it was because of Pippa. Because of how she made him feel, and—more importantly—because of what she'd said about Steve.

He grabbed the remote from Steve's hand and killed the TV.

"Hey. I was watching that."

"We need to talk. About Pippa."

The look of comic outrage on Steve's face disappeared as he put on his poker face. "What about her?"

"I told you about her car breaking down last week.

Well, I wound up helping her out. Had her car towed to Dad's and fixed the gasket head for her after hours."

Steve's eyes narrowed. "Why'd you do that?"

"Because she couldn't afford to have her car fixed, and she needed to get around."

"Pity you're not in the Scouts still. That'd earn you a merit badge for sure." Steve lifted his beer in a mock-toast. "Here's to Mr. Good Deeds."

"I told Pippa that if she wanted, I'd let you know what had happened on her behalf. See if you couldn't help her out, since she's struggling at the moment."

Steve leaned back in the chair and rested his right ankle across his left knee. "I bet she loved that."

There was no mistaking the resentment in his tone.

"She told me not to. And when I kept pushing she told me you'd dodged paying child support for Alice, so she doubted you'd be helping with the car." Harry didn't say anything more, simply waited for Steve to set him straight.

His friend gave him a derisive look. "What? Is this the bit where I'm supposed to step in and defend my-self? Sorry, mate, but I'm not playing that game."

"That's all you have to say?"

"Yeah, it is. I don't even know why we're having this conversation, to be honest." Steve's gaze was hard with anger and suspicion.

Harry could only think of one reason why his friend would come out swinging so hard: because it was true. Because he really was ignoring his obligation to help support his daughter.

"She's your kid, man," he said quietly, hoping to cut through the bull. "Pippa's doing it tough and Alice is your kid. You should be helping them out."

"Should I?" Steve's tone was deceptively mild.

"You know you should."

"I'll tell you what I know. I told Pippa at the time that I wasn't up for a kid. Even gave her the money to get rid of it. She knew that, and she decided to keep it anyway. Her decision, right? That's what all the women's libbers tell us. So she made her decision, and I made mine. And I'm not changing it."

Harry blinked at the unvarnished fury in his friend's voice.

"Mate, it wasn't like she got pregnant on purpose."

"Yeah? How do you know that? How do you know she didn't see me as the perfect meal ticket?"

"Pippa wouldn't do that. She's not like that." He knew that in his gut. Pippa had far too much integrity to trap a man like that.

"So you're an expert on her now, are you?" There was an ugly suggestion behind Steve's words.

Harry gave his friend a look. "Pull your head in. As if."

"So why am I getting the public service message, then?"

"Because she needs help. And whether you like it or not, Alice is your kid."

"Like I said, Pippa wanted to keep the baby. I'm not wearing the consequences."

"*The consequences* is six months old, man. She looks like you. She's your kid."

Steve stood. "This is getting old, fast."

"So, what? You're going to pretend she doesn't exist? That your kid isn't walking around out there in the world without your protection?"

"Man, she really did a number on you, didn't she? What'd she do? Turn on the waterworks?" Steve's posture was tense, his expression ugly.

Harry pushed to his feet, not liking feeling at a disadvantage. "She didn't say a word about you that I didn't push out of her. She knows we're mates. She respects that."

"So why are we even having this conversation?"

Steve seemed genuinely puzzled, as though it was beyond him why Harry would take up the cudgels on behalf of Pippa and Alice without someone holding a gun to his head.

"Because she needs your help," Harry repeated.

"Not gonna happen." Steve headed for the door. "And you might want to think about whose side you're on in this, *mate*."

The door slammed as Steve exited the house. Harry stared after his oldest friend, trying to reconcile the man he knew—the guy who could make him laugh till his sides ached, who he trusted to have his back through thick and thin—with what he'd just heard.

And couldn't.

Not a single excuse sprang to mind for Steve's refusal to step up and take responsibility for his own child. Being angry wasn't enough. Feeling trapped also didn't cut it. No doubt Pippa must have felt all those things when she first found out she was pregnant, yet she had taken on motherhood with an open heart and mind.

Harry walked to the kitchen and dumped what was left of his beer down the sink. He watched the amber fluid circle the drain, going over Steve's words, wondering if there was anything he could have said that might have made a difference. It was so obvious to him that Steve was in the wrong, however, that he simply couldn't conceive of the mind-set that allowed Steve to carry on with his life as though things hadn't changed six months ago when Alice was born. Harry might prefer to live his life a certain way—no strings, no heavy responsibilities or burdens to get in the way of having a good time—but if he'd found himself in Steve's shoes he would do the right thing, no questions asked.

And not only because it was the right thing, either. If he'd helped make a new life, he'd want to get to know him or her, to pass on what skills or knowledge or advice he might have. He'd want to be a part of his child's life.

Steve clearly didn't feel the same compulsion or curiosity, however. Again, a mind-set that was so far beyond Harry's comprehension it baffled him.

He tossed the empty can in the trash and walked to the bathroom. He left his sweaty workout gear on the floor and stepped beneath the shower spray. Steve's angry departure had left him with an evening to fill. Which was just as well. He didn't particularly want to spend time with Steve right now.

An uncomfortable thought. When they were younger, he and Steve had fought over stupid stuff all the time. Once, Steve had even broken Harry's nose with a badly aimed punch. As adults, however, they pretty much saw eye to eye on everything.

Until now.

Harry scrubbed his face with his hands and dropped his head forward, letting the water pour down his back and shoulders.

He wasn't a grudge keeper, and he didn't consider himself any more or less stubborn than the next guy, but there was a heavy feeling in his gut that told him he would have a hard time forgetting what had gone down with Steve today. Which would be a problem, because he knew that Steve sure as hell wasn't going to be changing his position anytime soon. Harry knew his friend too well to even pretend that that would happen.

Now he was in the unenviable position of having a bone-deep moral objection to his best mate's actions.

The thought was so foreign to him he made a spluttering sound, half appalled, half bemused by the workings of his own mind. As his sisters were only too keen to point out, he wasn't exactly a choirboy. He'd never set himself up to judge anyone in his life. And yet here he was.

He dressed in jeans and a fresh T-shirt before returning to the living room. Habit told him to call Bluey or Macca, but the thought of spending the night at the pub had lost its appeal. Plus the odds were good Steve had called them as his backup plan once he'd blown Harry off.

Sitting on the edge of the couch, Harry stared down the barrel of a Saturday night home alone. Not something he'd done for a long time.

He turned on the TV and flipped through the stations, searching for something—anything—to grab his attention. If he found something decent to watch, he could grab a pizza and chill for the evening. Might even be good for a change.

He scrolled through all the likely channels without finding anything that hooked him and started all over again. When the second trawl still didn't produce fruit, he went in search of his car keys. Maybe he'd go over to Mel and Flynn's place, see what they were up to.

He found his keys in the pocket of his workout shorts—along with Pippa's wad of cash.

He stared at the creased and battered envelope, key scenes from this afternoon playing in his head. Pippa standing tall and proud, telling him she wasn't a charity case, that she could pay her own way. Steve, denying he had a duty to support his own flesh and blood.

The memory alone was enough to make Harry burn with shame for his friend. He felt an absurd, ridiculous urge to pick up the phone and apologize to Pippa on Steve's behalf.

He wanted to tell her that Steve was a good guy, even if he was acting like an asshole right now. He wanted to somehow impart to her all the positive things he knew about Steve, all the memories and goodwill they'd built between them over the years.

Not a call she'd be likely to take well. And not one he would ever make, either. He wasn't stupid. He wasn't about to get involved in Steve and Pippa's very private business.

He opened the envelope, eyeing the crisp fifties inside. Money that Pippa had had to scramble to find. Because Steve had his head up his own ass.

His jaw set, Harry tossed the money onto the couch and headed for the door.

He couldn't fix Steve, but there were other things he could do. And it wasn't like he had anything better to do tonight.

CHAPTER FIVE

PIPPA CLOSED HER eyes and breathed deeply, willing her body to relax into the warm water. Alice was asleep— bless her little cotton socks—the world was quiet, and the bathwater was scented with jasmine. Not a bad combination.

And yet her mind still refused to let go of the usual fistful of worries that were on high rotation in her mind. Money—naturally—study, Alice, the situation with Steve and Child Support Services...

Stop thinking. Breathe and relax and enjoy this little slice of paradise.

She made a conscious effort to relax the muscles of her neck and shoulders. She was floating with her eyes closed, contemplating running the hot tap to heat the water a little when a loud knock echoed through the house. Her eyes popped open and she scowled at the ceiling.

Who on earth would come calling unannounced on a Saturday night? And why had they come when she was finally giving herself over to the whole sinking-into-relaxation thing?

Muttering beneath her breath, she stood and grabbed a towel. Water splashed onto the floor as she climbed from the tub. She blotted the towel against her heat-flushed skin as she made her way to her bedroom. She put on her robe and headed for the front door. Whoever was there knocked for a second time as she paused to cinch her belt. She checked the spyhole.

A muscular male back filled the lens, along with a strong neck and a well-shaped skull covered with close-cropped dark hair.

What on earth was Harry doing on her doorstep again? This was seriously becoming a habit.

If he was here to make her take her money back, he was wasting his time. Something she was more than happy to tell him to his face.

She did the usual shoulder-against-the-door routine to unstick the lock, then pulled the door open. Harry had been contemplating her overgrown lawn but he turned to face her.

A jolt of awareness zinged through her as she met his gaze. Man-woman awareness—the kind she had no business feeling around Steve's best friend.

She was so thrown she launched straight into speech, sidestepping niceties like saying hello and asking after his health. "Before you start, there is no way in the world I'm taking that money back. So forget about trying to browbeat me into accepting. It's not going to happen."

"I'm not here about the money."

"Oh." She blinked, nonplussed.

"I came to fix your bedroom door. And the lock." For the first time she noticed the honking great toolbox at his feet.

"Why on earth would you want to do that?"

"Because it needs doing. The hall's a fire hazard the way it is. And that lock is a disaster waiting to happen. I figure it will take me an hour, two at the most, then I'll be out of your hair."

He stooped to pick up his toolbox and stepped forward. She held up a hand to halt his advance.

"Whoa, whoa, whoa. Hold your horses a second." She shook her head, trying to get her brain working. "I still don't understand."

It was Saturday night, after all. Prime partying time. What on earth was he doing on her doorstep, preparing to DIY?

"What's to understand?" He shifted impatiently, clearly ready to jump in.

She stared at him, perplexed, even as a little voice in her head told her to simply thank him profusely and take him up on his offer. After all, she'd been sidestepping that stupid door for months now, and the lock had never worked properly. If she waited around for the landlord to take action, she'd be pushing daisies before it was done. And having both issues fixed would make her life infinitely more pleasant.

But there was no reason for Harry to be volunteering to help her out like this. No reason that she could think of, anyway. Harry wasn't her friend, he was Steve's friend. But clearly *something* was motivating him.

"At the risk of sounding like an ungrateful cow, I really don't get why you would want to do this for me. Don't get me wrong, it's awesome, but until you saw me on the side of the road last week we hadn't seen each other for months."

Harry's dark brows creased into a frown. After a long beat he set his toolbox down and met her eyes. "I talked to Steve today. Told him what had happened with your car."

She crossed her arms over her chest. She could imagine exactly how that conversation had gone, how completely disinterested Steve would have been. "Right."

"I'll be honest, when you said that stuff about him not paying any child support, I didn't believe you. Not that I thought you were lying, but I thought there must have been more to it."

She didn't like the idea that Harry—or anyone, for that matter—might see her as a bitter, resentful ex, ready to tarnish her former lover at the drop of a hat. This was why she didn't talk about Steve to anyone other than her mother, as a general rule.

"And what did Steve say?" she asked carefully.

"He told me that you'd made your decision, and he'd made his."

She gave a tight nod. "That's about it, yes."

If she ignored the part where he'd lied to the government to avoid paying for his daughter.

"I didn't know any of this stuff. He never talks about you or Alice. I figured things were just ticking over...."

Harry looked acutely uncomfortable. She felt a stab of sympathy for him. She knew how much history he and Steve shared. Discovering that someone you respected and admired had feet of clay was never a pleasant experience.

"He thinks I tricked him into becoming a father because I didn't have a termination."

Harry winced. She tilted her head, trying to work him out. "So you talked to Steve, and your first thought was to grab your toolbox and come over to fix my door?"

"I figured that if he wasn't going to step up, the least I could do was make sure things are okay for you. It's not much, but it's something."

She stared at him as the meaning behind his words hit her.

He felt sorry for her.

He pitied her because her no-good ex wouldn't cough up child support and she'd been left to manage on her own. He thought she was barely keeping her head above water, that she needed all the help she could get, and he'd come rushing to her rescue.

It felt like a slap in the face, like a huge, unequivocal vote of no confidence. It felt as though he'd judged her and found her wanting and was now stepping in to sweep up the broken pieces and glue them back together for poor, struggling Pippa.

Suddenly she felt acutely, inordinately foolish for that small zing of pleasure she'd gotten when she'd opened the door. For a few silly, pointless seconds, she'd allowed herself to believe that he had come calling again *for her*. Because of the way he'd looked at her breasts the other night and teased her and returned her impulsive hug. She'd been flattered, excited and energized by the notion that sexy, bad-boy Harry might find her attractive. She hadn't planned to do anything about it—dear God, there were so many reasons *that* was a bad idea she couldn't even begin listing them—but there was no denying that her feminine ego had stretched and purred a little at the notion that he might be interested.

And he'd come calling because he felt sorry for her.

Yeah.

She took a deep breath, conscious of the embarrassed heat that was rising in a slow wave from her chest, up her neck and into her face. "I appreciate the thought, Harry," she said tightly, "but I'm not quite at the begging bowl, prostrate on the sidewalk stage just yet."

His scowl deepened. "What's that supposed to mean?"

"What it sounds like. I don't need you playing knight

errant for me. The car was one thing, but this… No. Alice and I are getting by just fine."

"Did I say anything about how you and Alice are getting by?" Harry sounded aggrieved and baffled in equal measure.

"Yeah, you did, when you came thundering over here full of good intentions. It would be different if we were friends, Harry, because then I would know that I could return the favor for you some time in the future. We'd have a history of give and take. But we're not friends, are we? And you're doing this because you think I've gotten a raw deal and you feel sorry for me. Right? I'm the human equivalent of one of those plastic seeing-eye dogs that you slip a coin into at the supermarket."

"Does it matter? Isn't the important thing that the door is fixed and the lock works properly?"

It was such a rational, calm, measured response that a red haze came over her vision.

"What, just because I'm a single mother, I don't get to have any dignity, is that it? Just because I've hit a temporary rough patch, I get to be painted as a victim who needs to be rescued? Well, guess what, Harry, I don't need your help. I can get my own damn door fixed. And I definitely don't need you feeling sorry for me."

He held up his hands, palms out, as though he was warding off a madwoman. "Okay. Calm down. I was only trying to help."

"Well, *don't*. I'm not your responsibility. I'm *my* responsibility, and so is Alice, and everything here is fine, thank you."

"Fine. Whatever. *Jesus*."

She grabbed the door. "Boy, am I glad I got out of a nice warm bath for *this*."

She swung the door shut, remembering the temperamental lock at the last second. Before she could catch it, the door hit the striking plate and bounced open. The door was open for only a split second, but it was more than long enough for her to see the I-told-you-so expression on Harry's face. She pushed the door shut again and woman-handled it into position, swearing under her breath. Finally the latch clicked closed and she exhaled in an angry, impatient rush.

She heard Harry's heavy tread on the steps, then, a few seconds later, the sound of an engine starting. She swiveled on her heel and made her way up the hall to the bathroom.

How dare he come over here to shove his good intentions down her throat like that? How dare he take her up as his own personal charity?

She wrenched the tie on her robe free and tossed it into the corner. Every muscle tense, she stepped into the bath and sat in the water.

The whole thing was made even worse by the fact that for a few crazy seconds she'd thought he was here because he'd been thinking about her as much as she'd been thinking about him. So much worse. While she'd been battling an unwanted attraction, he'd been giving his pity gland a good workout.

She rested against the end of the tub, flinching at its coldness. The water was tepid, too, and instead of being a comforting haven, the bath suddenly felt wrong and awful and irritating.

Another thing to thank Harry for: ruining her first moment of decent alone time in months.

Oh, yeah, what an evil despot he is. The way he came over wanting to help you out because he'd learned that his friend is a jerk. Lock the man up and throw away the key for his crimes against humanity. What a scumbag.

She closed her eyes, but it didn't stop reality from sinking in.

The way she'd responded to Harry...

The things she'd said...

The way she'd said them...

She'd overreacted. Big-time. Her pride had been stung, and she'd lashed out like a sulky kid. Yes, Harry could have been more diplomatic with his offer, but it had been made with the best of intentions—and she'd shoved it down his throat because she'd been embarrassed and angry. Embarrassed because she'd imagined the glint in his eye had been about her and not just because he was an inveterate ladies' man, and angry with both herself and Steve that she was in need of help in the first place.

She was the one who had frittered away her twenties working in bars and tourist hot spots in far-flung destinations, instead of planning for the future. *She* was the one who had chosen to give six months of her life to a man who had proven as deep as the nearest puddle and as reliable as a house of cards. Harry had nothing to do with any of that. He'd been kind and generous and noble—and she'd been a shrew. A crazy, irrational shrew.

She got out of the bath and reached for her towel. It was damp from the first time she'd used it, but she managed to blot up the bulk of the water before slipping into her robe.

She owed Harry an apology. Actually, she owed him a major grovel. On her knees, beseeching hands, the works. The sooner the better.

If Alice weren't sound asleep, Pippa would go to his place right now, before the memory of her behavior had a chance to solidify in his mind.

She sat on the end of her bed, regret making her toes curl into the carpet. She didn't consider herself a rash person, but every now and then she did something really stupid. Like take antibiotics then forget to use backup contraception, or blow up at a nice guy like Harry because he was being a decent human being.

She fell back onto the mattress, staring at the ceiling. She'd learned a lot about herself since having Alice. She'd learned that she was more resilient than she'd ever imagined she could be. She'd learned that if push came to shove, she could bear almost anything as long as her daughter was safe and well. She'd learned that she was stubborn—sometimes unattractively so—and more independent than she'd ever given herself credit for. And, apparently, she also had her fair share of pride.

She pressed her hands to her face, thinking about what she would say to Harry when she went to see him tomorrow. She hoped he'd at least hear her out. If he didn't… Well, she'd have to find some other way to make it up to him.

HARRY SLAMMED HIS way into the house, tossing his car keys onto the coffee table with so much force they skidded off the other side.

Perfect. Another thing gone wrong in what was shaping up to be an incredibly shitty day. Next time he felt the urge to get involved in someone else's life he was going to bite his tongue off and swallow it.

He went to the kitchen and grabbed a beer from the fridge, then crossed to the back door and let himself out into the yard. There wasn't much to look at out here, despite his sister's constant nagging for him to "do something" with the patch of lawn and jumble of trees, but he felt like he needed a bit of fresh air after his encounter with Pippa.

She'd been so angry. She was always so good-natured, such a good sport, he'd been taken aback by her fiery response to his offer. For the life of him, he couldn't understand where all that anger had come from. It wasn't as though he'd insulted her or gone out of his way to make her feel small. He'd simply wanted to help, to right one small wrong in her life because he couldn't fix the greater wrong.

I've gotten a raw deal and you feel sorry for me. Right? I'm the human equivalent of one of those plastic seeing-eye dogs that you slip a coin into at the supermarket.

He took a big swallow from his beer, shaking his head. He didn't see her as a walking-talking charity appeal. Far from it. He felt bad for her—and for Steve, for that matter. In a few years' time, he couldn't help but think that Steve would look back on how he was behaving now and feel about three inches tall. For sure that was how Harry saw him—as a man who didn't have the cojones to step up when it counted and own his responsibilities.

As for Pippa... Well, he'd tried. If she didn't want his help, if she was too proud to let an old friend lend a hand, that was her call.

It was probably just as well. The whole time they'd been talking—even when she'd been yelling at him—he'd been painfully aware that she was fresh from the bath or shower and almost certainly naked beneath her thin robe. The outline of her nipples had been visible beneath the fabric, her arms and legs pink and bare, her hair damp and clinging to her neck and shoulders... Every time she'd gestured or shifted her weight he'd caught a waft of something heady and floral that made him think of warm summer nights.

Stop thinking about her, man. This is not helping anyone or anything.

He took a pull from his beer, then paused with the can midair as it occurred to him that tonight was the first time he'd seen Pippa without her heavy-framed glasses. He'd always wondered how she'd look without them, and now he knew: too damned attractive for his peace of mind. Without them, the curve of her cheek had been revealed and there'd been nothing to distract him from the plushness of her mouth or the upward tilt of her small nose.

Which bought him full circle to tonight's argument being a good thing. The best thing, really.

He swallowed the last of his beer, then crushed the can and tossed it into the bin. He still didn't feel like watching TV, so he decided to drive to his parents' place. There was a fifty-fifty chance they wouldn't be home, given his mother's love of socializing, but the lights were on when he arrived.

He made his way up the path and gave a perfunctory knock before letting himself into the house.

"It's just me," he called as he shut the door behind him.

"In the kitchen." His mother's voice echoed down the hallway.

He found his parents seated around the table, the plates from their evening meal stacked neatly together, a half-empty bottle of wine and a handful of travel brochures on the table between them.

"Hey. What's up?" He pulled out a chair and dropped into it.

His mother looked at him for a long beat, her gaze unnerving in its intensity.

"What?" Harry said.

"I'm trying to work out why you're here."

"What do you think I'm doing? I'm visiting." He crossed his arms over his chest and stretched his legs out.

"It's Saturday night," his mother said.

"So?"

"When was the last time you stayed in on a Saturday night?"

"I have no idea. And I'm not in. I'm here."

"Which is even more strange." His mother stood. "Is everything all right?"

"Everything's fine. Why wouldn't it be?"

His mother carried the plates to the dishwasher. As usual, she wore a pair of jeans that most of the world would consider too tight for a woman pushing sixty. Her red tank top was equally tight, and the nails on her bare, tanned feet were painted a matching scarlet.

"Are you feeling sick or something?" she asked, concern wrinkling her forehead.

Harry resisted the urge to roll his eyes. "Mum, I'm fine. Change the record. How have you two been?"

"Same as we always are," she said.

His father shuffled the travel brochures together, crossing to the sideboard.

"What are you doing?" his mother said, a sharp note in her voice.

"Putting these away," his father said.

"But we haven't finished talking yet."

"Nothing's going to change, Val, no matter how many times we talk it over." He dropped the brochures into the drawer and pushed it shut.

Harry watched as his mother's mouth got thin, a sure sign she wasn't happy. "Maybe you can talk some sense into your father, Harry. He seems to think we should wait until we're completely fossilized before we start having fun."

"I have fun with you every day," his father said, sounding aggrieved.

His mother made a rude noise, clearly unmoved by the blatant flattery.

"What's the problem?" Harry asked, since it appeared to be expected of him.

"I want to go on a cruise. Libby and Dave up the road went on one and haven't stopped raving. But your father keeps coming up with excuses why we can't go."

Harry looked at his father, who shrugged eloquently. "I can't leave the business. You know what it's like."

Harry frowned. "What about Ben? Can't you leave him in charge for a few weeks?"

"Your mother wants to go for six weeks."

"Why fly all that way if you're not going to make the most of it?" his mother said.

Ben was his father's most senior mechanic, but there was no getting away from the fact he wasn't the most social bloke in the world. Great with an internal combustion engine, not so great with people. While the business might survive a week or two with him at the helm, six weeks was asking for trouble.

"What about Julian?" He was less senior than Ben, but more personable and sharp.

"He's too unreliable, especially now he's broken up with his girlfriend."

"What the business needs is a good senior mechanic with a smart head on his shoulders and a vested interest in the business," his mother said pointedly.

His father shot her a look. "Val."

"I'm just making an observation."

Harry contemplated the toes of his boots, aware that his mother's comment was a dig at him. When he didn't rise to the bait, she shut the dishwasher door so hard the plates rattled.

"Sometimes, Harry Neville, you really try my patience."

Harry sighed. It seemed his day was destined to suck no matter where he went. "Dad would be better off hiring a manager. I'm not cut out to run a small business."

It was the same argument he'd put forward the last time they'd had this discussion.

"Bullshit, Harry. God, it drives me crazy when you say that."

"It's true. I'm hopeless at admin stuff. I wouldn't have a clue how to hire and fire staff. Just because I'm family doesn't mean I'd be any good."

"You could do anything you put your mind to, and you know it. Don't think I've forgotten those straight A's you got in high school. The truth is you don't want to do it. That's all it is."

Harry met his mum's gaze. He was sick of pussyfooting around this issue. Maybe it was time to put it to bed once and for all.

"Okay. You want the truth? You're right, I don't want it. Dad's the one who had the burning desire to be his own boss, but that was never my dream. I like being a soldier ant. I like doing my hours and taking my wages and living my life without all the stress and crap I see Dad go through, worrying about taxes and superannuation and workers' compensation and whatever." Harry cut his gaze to his father. "No offense, Dad, but I don't want to be a slave to anyone or anything."

"Why do you think your father started the business? For exactly that reason. How are you not a slave when you're marching to the beat of someone else's drum, jumping when he says to?" his mother demanded. "Honestly, Harry, I don't understand how you can have this so backward."

Harry rose. If he stayed any longer, he would say something he'd regret.

"I'm going. Sorry for upsetting you." He glanced at his mother first, then his father. Then he headed for the door, shoulders tight.

He was descending the steps when he heard the screen door swing shut behind him.

"Wait up a minute."

He paused, giving his father a chance to catch up. He eyed him warily when his father joined him.

"I'm sorry, Dad, but I don't want to get into this now. I've had a crappy day, and this is pretty much the cherry on top."

His father's hand landed on his shoulder, heavy and warm. He squeezed once, firmly, before letting go and walking toward Harry's car.

"How's the Monaro running? You ever get around to switching out the fuel pump?"

It took Harry a moment to understand his father hadn't followed him to keep prosecuting his case.

"Haven't got around to it yet, but she's been running sweet lately so I might hold fire for a bit."

"Still thinking of replacing the shockers?"

"Yeah. Next month, maybe."

"Let me know and I'll help you out."

"Thanks."

They stopped beside the car. Even though it was his mother who had pursued the why-won't-you-come-

work-with-your-father line this time around, Harry
knew it was something his dad wanted. It was impossible to tell what his father was thinking or feeling,
however. He'd always had a good poker face and tonight it was utterly inscrutable as they both pretended
to inspect the Monaro.

"There must be some way you and Mum can take
that cruise," Harry said after a short silence.

"We'll work it out. Don't worry about it." His father
offered him a small, distracted smile and took a step
backward. "Everything turn out okay with your friend?"

It took Harry a moment to understand his father
meant Pippa.

"You could say that."

His father smiled properly this time. "Give you a
hard time, did she?"

"Something like that."

His father turned toward the house, still smiling.
"Thought she might."

He lifted a hand in farewell. Harry watched him walk
away, noting the gray in his father's hair. There had
been a time when his father's hair had been more pepper
than salt, but the ratio had reversed in recent years. His
father's shoulders were still strong and broad, though,
his arms still thick with muscle. To Harry, he seemed
as powerful and vital a presence as he'd ever been.

Unsettled, he got in the car. As much as his mother's
emotional appeal had made him uncomfortable, he dis-
liked his father's quiet acceptance even more because
he knew it hid a wealth of disappointment.

Harry thumped the heel of his hand against the steering wheel, feeling cornered and small and immeasur-
ably shitty as a result. Not once had he ever indicated
by word or deed that he was interested in taking over

the garage. In fact, he'd done the exact opposite, leaving his father's employ the moment his apprenticeship was finalized to avoid setting up expectations that would never be fulfilled.

He didn't want the responsibility, and he didn't want the worry. He wasn't the kind of man who craved big houses and expensive cars. He valued his freedom more than any material thing money could buy, and the thought of taking on the burden of the business, of being responsible for eight employees and his father's legacy... It made him feel like he was choking. As though the walls were closing in.

The Monaro started with a dull roar and he headed for home, where he probably should have stayed in the first place.

CHAPTER SIX

PIPPA WOKE TO Alice crying at five in the morning. She prepared a bottle and sat in the old armchair in Alice's room, watching her guzzle half a bottle before falling into a milky drowse. Smiling, Pippa put Alice to bed and went into the kitchen to make her own breakfast. It was still dark outside and she sat on the arm of the sofa in the sunroom, eating her toast and watching the dark sky turn gray and then pink with dawn.

Because Pippa didn't want to put off making her apology any longer than she had to, the moment Alice woke again at nine she dressed her and packed her into the car. Pippa swung by the bakery on the way to Harry's place, picking up a bag of doughnuts to sweeten her apology. When in doubt, bribe with food. It was a strategy that usually worked with Alice, and Pippa figured Harry probably wasn't that different.

She had an apology worked out. She'd started formulating it last night and perfected it this morning while she cleaned the house and waited for Alice to wake. She would tell Harry he was generous and kind and that she had spoken too hastily last night, letting her pride do the talking. She would tell him she appreciated everything he'd done and that she hoped he might one day forget she had been such a prickly, ungrateful cow. Then she would offer him the doughnuts and hopefully a miracle would occur and he'd smile and tell her it was okay, he didn't think she was a complete psycho-hose-beast.

The last bit was wishful thinking, but she figured she was in with a mild chance that he'd forgive her. Maybe.

She chewed her bottom lip as she parked in front of his house. Both his car and the old truck were in the driveway, a good sign he was home. This time she took Alice with her as she approached the front door. After knocking three times, she was forced to conclude that either Harry wasn't home, or he was so deeply asleep he was in a coma. She suspected it was option A, which meant she would have to delay her apology. Damn it.

She could leave the doughnuts on his doorstep, but they were covered with sugar and redolent of jam and the odds were good that the ants would find them before Harry did.

She drove home, set the doughnuts on the kitchen counter and told herself she would try again in the afternoon. Then she dragged out her textbooks to look for quotes to support the central argument in her essay.

She studied all morning and into the afternoon. At three o'clock she drove to Harry's place again, only to discover that his car was gone this time, a sure sign he was out.

She stared at his house, frustration welling inside her. She wanted this done, wanted to right her wrong, if that was possible, and get on with her life.

Fate had other ideas, because Harry still wasn't home when she tried again in the early evening, and he wasn't there the next day, either, when she'd be certain she would catch him after work. By that time the doughnuts were past their best—certainly they were past being used as a shameless suck-up. She ate three, then gave the remainder to the family next door in deference to the size of her backside.

Tuesday dawned gray and overcast, a perfect reflection of her mood. She worked a long shift at the gallery, picking up Alice from day care as the heavens opened and it began to pour. Pippa swung past Harry's place, feeling like a stalker, she'd been up and down his street so many times. Surely he must be home. Who went out in weather like this?

She swore under her breath when she saw that, once again, the black muscle car was missing.

What is wrong with you, Harry? Don't you like your home or something?

Where on earth could he be? Not surfing, which had been her explanation of choice on Sunday. Not in this weather. And even Harry couldn't hang out with the boys this much.

She frowned as it occurred to her that it was possible he was with a woman. As in a girlfriend. He hadn't mentioned that he was seeing anyone, but that didn't mean anything. It wasn't as though he'd ever been short of female companionship in the time she'd known him. Women responded like catnip to his hard body and the cheeky, knowing glint in his eye.

She was feeling more than a little disgruntled when she turned Old Yeller for home. She told herself she was frustrated because her attempt to do the right thing had been stymied. Definitely it had nothing to do with the idea that Harry might have a girlfriend. His love life had nothing to do with her. At all.

Perhaps it was time to give up on the notion of a face-to-face apology and move to Plan B. Not that she had a Plan B, but she could formulate one.

For instance, when she got home, she could compose

a written apology. She could then leave it on Harry's doorstep with a nice bottle of Scotch, ready for him to discover when he returned home. She had no idea if he drank Scotch, having only ever seen him drink beer, but she hoped that, like the doughnuts, it would be interpreted as a gesture of goodwill.

She liked the idea so much she drove home via the liquor store, purchasing a single malt Scotch with an appropriately Scottish name with lots of badges and coats of arms on the label and a hefty price tag. Between the beer she'd bought for Harry's dad and the bottle of Scotch, she'd pretty much annihilated her budget for the next couple of weeks, but it couldn't be helped. She needed to make amends.

She kissed her daughter's warm cheek as she left the shop. "We're in business, Alice. Once the letter is delivered, we—by which I really mean me—are home free. Sort of."

And hopefully the next time she ran into Harry in six months' time they would both be able to smile at one another the way they had last week.

The house was gloomy when she got home and she flicked on lights and even considered turning on the central heating. She made do with a shawl for herself and a blanket for Alice and sat with her laptop on her knees.

It took her an hour to compose a suitably friendly, regretful apology—not too formal, not too casual, not too sucky, not too flippant. She'd walked a fine line, but she was pretty sure she'd gotten there. Or thereabouts. She printed it, sealed it in an envelope and wrote Harry's name on the front with a sense of relief.

There. Almost done. Once it stopped raining, she'd deliver it and the Scotch. Problem solved.

Dusting her hands together, she stowed away her laptop, then registered the steady drip-drip-drip of water. She went into the hall, looking toward the bathroom. But the sound was coming from somewhere much closer. She frowned at the closed doorway to Alice's bedroom, then pushed it open. She flicked on the light. The room was illuminated for half a second before the bulb blew, but it was long enough for her to see a growing wet patch on the carpet.

The roof was leaking. Just what she needed.

She grabbed the flashlight from the kitchen cupboard and returned to Alice's room, aiming it at the ceiling. A dark stain marred the plaster, and water dripped down the wiring for the pendant lamp.

She didn't know much about electricity, but it struck her she had been extremely lucky she hadn't been electrocuted when she flicked on the light.

Thank God Alice hadn't been in her room during any of this.

She grabbed her phone and called the landlord, Peter. He was a master of excuses, but he had to do something about a leaky roof. If for no other reason than that it could cause permanent and expensive damage to his property.

The phone rang and rang before going to voice mail and she listened with growing outrage as her landlord explained he was on holiday and wouldn't be back for another two weeks.

Two weeks!

She was so busy reacting to the news she forgot to leave a message and had to call back to ask Peter to please phone her as she had an urgent repair that needed attention. Surely he must have organized for someone to keep an eye on things while he was away?

She aimed the flashlight at the ceiling again, studying the growing damp patch. The way things were
going, the plaster would come down in a sodden mess
unless someone took care of the leaky roof pronto.
Pippa made a rude noise as she imagined how long it
would take for Peter to get on to *that* repair. Judging by
his track record so far, a year or two. In the meantime,
she would have the privilege of living in a house with
a hole in the ceiling.

"Damn it."

Mouth pressed into a grim line, she changed into
yoga pants and a long-sleeved top, then tied her hair
back with a scarf. She made her way to the laundry
where the access hatch to the roof space was located.

She'd spent the week lamenting being a victim of
circumstances. She wasn't going to wait around for
someone to rescue her this time—she would take action herself.

The access hatch was above her washing machine.
Even standing on the machine she had no chance of
reaching it. She glanced around the room, her gaze falling on the storage unit she'd bought to hold her towels
and linen.

Perfect.

A bit of grunting and groaning saw the unit moved
into position next to the washing machine. She went
into the kitchen and gathered the stack of old ice-cream
containers from under the sink. Alice was playing with
her Fisher Price toys again, but to be safe Pippa put
her in her playpen. Then, armed with the flashlight
and her stack of containers, she prepared to do battle
with the roof.

It took her a full minute to clamber onto the washing

machine, then onto the storage unit and finally through the access hatch.

It was very dark in the roof cavity, despite the flashlight beam. Unease trickled down her spine as she balanced on a rough wooden rafter on her knees. What were the odds that there were rats and mice up here? She shone the torch around the roof cavity, noting the thin layer of fiberglass fluff masquerading as insulation. No wonder the house was so hot in summer and cold in winter. She aimed the light toward the front of the house. Something glinted in the far distance. It took her a moment to realize it was the flashlight beam reflecting off the stream of water coming in from the roof.

Well, at least she knew which way to crawl.

She made her way slowly forward, shifting from rafter to rafter on her hands and knees, the flashlight clenched between her teeth. Every few feet or so she tossed the ice-cream containers ahead of herself to keep her hands free. She was well aware that any slips would see her crashing through a thin layer of plaster into the room below, and she concentrated fiercely on where she put her knees and hands.

Every now and then she looked up to gauge how much farther she had to go. By the time she'd entered the space above Alice's bedroom, her knees were aching and her nose was itching from all the dust and fiberglass. She sat back on her heels and located the leak with the flashlight beam. Fortunately there was a rafter directly underneath and she was able to place the largest of the containers on a stable footing.

"Thank. God."

She was desperate to make her way back to the access hole, but she forced herself to inspect the surrounding space while she was there. She groaned with dismay when she saw another flash of light on water. Another leak. Above her bedroom, if she hazarded a guess.

"This is ridiculous."

She sighed heavily and clenched the flashlight between her teeth again and crawled, slow painful inch by slow painful inch, toward the second leak. It was close to the front wall where the roof sloped and she had to crouch low and slide the container into position.

"I am so asking for a discount on my bloody rent for this," she muttered as she swiveled on one knee to face the way she'd come.

This time she didn't scan for more leaks, even though she had one remaining container. She was over the dank darkness, her hands and chest felt itchy, her knees ached. She figured she'd done her bit, the rest was up to her landlord.

She was starting the homeward journey when the flashlight beam flickered dramatically.

"No. Don't even think about it." She froze, waiting for the beam to steady again.

When it kept flickering, she tapped it against her thigh.

"Come on. I only need a couple more minutes. Five, tops."

As if in response to her request, the flashlight flickered one last time before it steadied. She let out a grateful sigh.

Then the world went black.

"No. No way. Please don't do this to me," she pleaded as she fumbled in the dark, trying to find the switch on the side of the flashlight.

She flicked the flashlight on and off, then unscrewed the battery cap and jiggled the batteries around a little before screwing it back on.

No dice. The flashlight had deserted her. Leaving her stranded miles from the access hole in a very dark, potentially rat-infested attic.

Pippa swore vehemently, the worst four-letter words she knew. This was what she got for taking action and rescuing herself. Next time she was letting the stupid ceiling cave in.

Her knees screamed for her to move. Her heart in her mouth, she shuffled forward a couple of inches. The distant access hole was the only source of light. She could barely see her own hand in front of her face, let alone the detail of the rafters ahead of her.

Swearing repeatedly under her breath, she crawled forward another few feet. It wasn't as though she had a choice—it was shuffle forward into the unknown, or remain stuck in the dark with no hope of rescue. Especially since she hadn't been smart enough to bring her phone with her.

Her groping hands told her she'd reached a complicated part of the roof where the rafters changed direction, a mess that had been a whole lot easier to navigate with the help of the flashlight. Now, she groped and frowned and inched forward cautiously, flinching every time a splinter dug into her knees or hands but persevering because the only hope of relief was to reach that distant square of light.

A rustling on her left had her head whipping around. She froze, staring into the darkness, one knee balanced precariously on a rafter, the other midair.

Please let that not be a rat. Please.

She couldn't see or hear anything. Maybe it had just been wind. Maybe the noise had even come from *outside* the roof.

Her arms were starting to shake from supporting

the bulk of her weight. She put her knee down. She was lifting her leg to resume her journey when something skittered across her hand. Something sinuous and furry with a long tail and eyes that glinted in the dark.

Pippa didn't think. She simply reacted, screaming and rising up on her knees and flailing with her hands to beat off whatever rodent was in the vicinity.

Everything happened in a blur after that. Her head connected painfully with one of the rafters overhead, her knee slipped, and the next thing she knew she was off balance and toppling to her right. She hit the plaster sheeting with a resonant thunk. It gave instantly, cracking beneath her like too-thin ice and she shrieked as she plunged toward the floor and almost certain injury—only to land on something resilient and forgiving and springy.

It took her a few seconds to understand she was lying on her bed, fragments of plaster beneath and around her. She hadn't broken her leg or fractured her skull. She was alive and relatively well and incredibly, ridiculously lucky.

Her first impulse was to laugh, a great guffaw that spoke more of shock and relief than mirth. Then she rose onto her knees and did a quick body pat to confirm she really was in one piece.

She was. A minor miracle. Heart still hammering against her breastbone, she stood on distinctly shaky legs. Only then did she look up.

She silently mouthed yet another swear word as she took in the woman-sized hole in her bedroom ceiling. Bits of ragged plaster dangled from the hole, and insulation fluff and plaster dotted the bed and floor. She was covered in dust, plaster and cobwebs, with yet more insulation clinging to her clothes.

For a moment she was so overwhelmed she couldn't think. It was such a big hole. Then she remembered Alice and went to check on her daughter.

Alice was sobbing quietly to herself and Pippa guessed she'd probably been crying while Pippa had been stuck in the attic. She didn't dare touch her baby while covered in fiberglass, however, so she made reassuring noises before heading into the bathroom to shower. Barely two minutes later and wrapped in a towel, she lifted Alice into her arms.

"It's okay, sweetheart, Mummy's here. It's all right."

Holding her daughter against her chest and crooning reassurances, she returned to her bedroom doorway.

The hole in the ceiling seemed to have grown since she'd last seen it. She stared into it, cold water dripping down her back from her wet hair.

She needed to have it fixed, of course. She was no expert on home renovation, but she was pretty sure that would run into the hundreds, maybe even the thousands to repair.

For the second time in as many weeks she felt the bite of despair. She'd survived one financial crisis, only to find herself in the middle of another. All because she was an idiot. She should have let the stupid leaky roof destroy the ceiling. At least the repairs would have been the landlord's problem. Now, they were hers.

Even if she couldn't afford to replaster a matchbox, let alone a whole bedroom ceiling.

Pathetic, self-pitying tears pricked the back of her eyes. It was all very well to keep telling herself that things would be better in a year's time when she was qualified and teaching and earning a decent wage but right now, right this minute, she felt helpless and hopeless. It was the car all over again—she didn't have the skill to fix it on her own, and she didn't have the money to pay someone to do it. Not right away, anyway.

Alice stirred in her arms, hands grasping the edge of Pippa's towel. Pippa rocked her automatically, trying to push the horrible overwhelmed feeling to one side so she could think.

She didn't have to repair the ceiling immediately. She could simply sit tight and wait till she had the money to pay for the repairs, as she'd planned to do with her car before Harry had come riding to her rescue. Obviously, she wouldn't be able to use her room, since the thought of sleeping with a gaping hole above her head made her shiver. But there was a perfectly good couch in the sunroom. She could sleep out there until she'd saved the funds.

Even as the thought crossed her mind her mood dropped another notch. She didn't want to camp out in her own home. There must be some other way. Maybe she could patch the ceiling herself somehow or come up with some other kind of temporary measure?

She dismissed the notion after barely a moment's thought. She was about as handy as Ivana Trump—i.e. not very. Pippa had wreaked enough havoc without attempting to do some sort of half-assed, half-baked repair job.

She would simply have to suck it up, the way she'd sucked up everything else life had thrown at her in the past couple of years. Living with a dirty great hole in the ceiling wouldn't kill her.

Turning her back on the mess she'd made, she returned to the kitchen, telling herself that within a day tonight's events would be miraculously transformed into a hilarious dinner party anecdote thanks to a good night's sleep and a little perspective.

Here's hoping.

She was rounding the counter to turn on the kettle when her gaze landed on the bottle of whiskey she'd bought for Harry. She stopped dead in her tracks as a single, incredibly inappropriate thought hit her.

Harry would know what to do.

Hell, Harry could probably fix her ceiling with one well-muscled arm behind his back.

She shook her head. It was a dumb thought. She couldn't ask him to come running to her aid again. Not after the way she'd gotten all over him when he'd offered to fix her door. Any goodwill he might have had toward her had been well and truly worn out by her own stubborn, prideful behavior.

You are such an idiot.

She didn't flinch from her own self-assessment because she knew she deserved it. Not simply because of the way she'd reacted when Harry had so good-naturedly offered to help her out, but because even now when she had the opportunity to ask for help from someone who had always been kind to her, her pride demanded that she find some other way to handle the situation rather than throw herself at Harry's mercy. Even if that meant sleeping on the couch for weeks, and even if she knew in her bones that he wouldn't hesitate to help her, no questions asked.

The other night she'd asked Harry if her being a single parent meant that she wasn't allowed to retain any dignity. Standing in her self-sabotaged house, she couldn't help thinking that maybe she'd valued dignity a lot higher than perhaps she should have.

Maybe survival was more important. Maybe gracious acceptance of the fact that, at this particular moment in her life, she needed help held more weight.

Maybe she couldn't afford to be proud right now. Maybe that was what being a good mother and growing up was all about.

She stared at the bottle. Then, before she could talk herself out of it, she reached for the phone.

HARRY SPENT THE ten-minute drive from his place to Pippa's trying to understand why she'd phoned him. After the way they'd parted, he'd figured he'd be at the very bottom of her SOS list. Yet something bad had happened, and he was the person she'd turned to.

Even more confusing and mysterious to him was his reaction. He'd felt a definite thud of satisfaction when he'd heard her voice, a feeling that had only intensified when she'd confessed why she was calling. He'd been on the way out to play basketball with some friends, but he'd bailed on his mates rather than disappoint her. Because she needed him.

Crazy, confusing, messed-up stuff.

The porch light was on when he pulled into the driveway. He ran through the rain, his toolbox a heavy weight against his leg. She opened the door wearing a pair of old jeans and a sweatshirt, her wet hair in a messy ponytail, her glasses balanced near the end of her nose.

"You didn't have to come straight over, you know. It's not that kind of an emergency." She looked guilty, uncomfortable and sheepish.

He tightened his grip on the handle of his toolbox. It was either that or give in to the sudden urge to grab her by the shoulders and shake her till her teeth rattled.

She'd fallen through the ceiling. She could have broken her neck, her back, an arm, a leg.... She could be lying unconscious right now.

"Are you okay?" he asked.

"I'm fine. As I said on the phone, the bed broke my fall."

"You didn't knock your head or twist anything?" He didn't know why he couldn't take her at her word.

"I'm fine. Honestly. Apart from feeling like the biggest dick under the sun."

"Yeah, well. If the shoe fits…"

"Thanks."

He shrugged. She could have killed herself. He wasn't about to let her off the hook.

"If the flashlight hadn't gone out, I would have been fine."

"If the bed hadn't been there, you'd be in hospital."

"You sound like a parent."

He felt like one, too. Not a sensation he was particularly familiar with.

"Maybe you should show me the damage."

"There's something I need to give you first." She started down the hallway.

It took him a moment to follow her. He was too busy watching her ass as she walked toward the kitchen. He'd never seen her in jeans before. It was a revelation—and not a welcome one.

The soft denim hugged her full, rounded bottom. Her hips swayed from side to side. He found himself wondering if her panties were as colorful as the cherry-red bra she'd been wearing the other day and if she was a matching set kind of girl, or more the mix and match type. Then she stepped around the door she'd refused to let him fix and suddenly it was a whole lot easier to remember why he was here and why it was a bad idea for him to be staring at her butt.

His mind firmly on the matter at hand, he followed

her into the kitchen. She picked up a bottle of whiskey and offered it to him.

"This is for you. To apologize for the other night." She pushed her glasses to the bridge of her nose, a sure-fire giveaway she was nervous. "And this, too."

She offered him a crisp white envelope bearing his name in neat black handwriting.

He frowned. "You don't need to apologize."

"Harry, come on. We both know I do. I behaved like a petulant, spoiled schoolgirl."

He opened his mouth to deny it but she simply thrust the letter into his hand.

"Read it. Put me out of my misery."

"I don't need to read it. Apology accepted."

She gave him a pained look. "You can't just let me off the hook like that."

"Why not?"

"Because I deserve to squirm."

"Pippa, we're cool. Relax."

"Okay, if you won't read it, I'll say it. I was horrible the other night. I took all my frustration with Steve and my life in general out on you, all because you had the gall to offer to help me out. God forbid. Which was incredibly kind and generous and noble of you, by the way. In short, Harry, I'm unreservedly sorry for everything I said, and I hope you can forgive me."

"There's nothing to forgive."

She made a frustrated noise. "Sometimes you're too nice for your own good, do you know that?"

"I'm not nice." If she knew he'd been staring at her ass thirty seconds ago, wondering what color panties she was wearing, she wouldn't think he was nice. If she knew that he'd been thinking about the creamy fullness of her breasts for the past few days, and how good she'd felt when she'd embraced him, baby and all, she'd know exactly how down and dirty he could be.

"Well, I've yet to see any evidence of that, so we'll have to agree to disagree on that one."

She smiled at him, a cheeky, challenging smile that reminded him of all the smart-ass wisecracks she'd thrown his way. He felt a sudden, almost overwhelming surge of affection for her. He liked this woman. He liked her honesty. He liked her attitude and her smarts—hell, he even liked her feistiness, though it meant he'd been on the wrong end of her tongue more than a few times.

If it hadn't been for Steve, if they'd met anywhere else, under any other circumstances...

"So where's this hole?" he said.

Because there was no point thinking about what might have been. Nothing would change who she was or who he was.

Anyway, she'd probably laugh in his face if she knew what he was thinking. She'd never said it, but she'd been slumming it when she went out with Steve. She was educated and smart and arty—he and Steve were blue-collar guys who worked with their hands for a living and only opened a newspaper to find the cartoons and the sports section.

"It's in my room."

He kept his gaze strictly on the back of her head as she led him to her bedroom. She gestured for him to precede her into the room. His gaze swept briefly over the bed and tallboy, and a pile of debris that had been pushed into the corner, before rising to the ceiling. He whistled when he saw the mighty hole she'd punched in the plaster and she gave him a nervous look.

"So, what do you think? Is it fixable? Or do I need to

call in a builder?" She pushed her glasses up her nose again, then crossed her arms over her chest.

"You ever thought about getting a pair of glasses that stay up on their own?"

"Sorry?"

"Your glasses. They're always falling off."

"Oh. Right. That's because they're vintage. Technically, they're probably too big for my face. But I love them." She shrugged, her eyes lifting to the ceiling, worry once again filling their depths as she waited for his assessment.

"Relax. It's fixable."

"Really? Honestly?"

"Yeah. It'll take a bit of patching and some paint, but it's not a big job."

"Really?" She sounded hugely relieved. As though he'd taken a massive weight off her shoulders. "I thought it would cost a fortune to fix. But if it's not that big a deal, maybe I should talk to a plasterer or a builder or whoever fixes these kinds of things."

"Save your money." He walked to the kitchen to collect his toolbox.

When he returned, Pippa moved to one side as he stood on her bed and reached up to assess the plaster more closely. Using the claw on his hammer, he dragged the dangling chunks of board free and tossed them to the floor.

"You've punched through two sheets of plaster. The easiest thing to do is to rip them out completely and replace them. Once the joins are patched and plastered and the whole lot painted, no one will ever know anything happened."

"Apart from the fact that it will be the nicest, newest, cleanest part of the house," Pippa said.

"If you say so." He glanced around her room, noting the embroidered cuff on the snowy-white sheets on her bed, the silky-looking robe hanging on the hook near the door, the many-hued floral patchwork quilt folded across the foot of the bed. Pairs of well-worn shoes sat along one wall, lined up like good little soldiers, and a chair in the corner was draped with colorful scarves and discarded pieces of clothing.

It was a feminine room, but not in a bad way. It was soft, comfortable and welcoming. The kind of room it would be easy to while away a lot of hours in. Unlike his own bedroom, which boasted a bed, one bedside table and precious little else.

"It'll take a day to get the supplies, then I'll start."

"It's not urgent. I can sleep on the couch for a few weeks," Pippa said quickly.

He glanced at the hole again. "Afraid there are rats up there, huh?"

"I *know* there are. Why do you think I fell through the ceiling?"

"Then I'll pick up some bait stations, too, while I'm at it. And I'll be here after work tomorrow. That okay with you?"

Pippa's warm brown eyes softened with gratitude. "Harry… Thank you. For coming so quickly. For being so bloody generous—"

"About that. I have a couple of conditions." Might as well get a few things straight up front.

"Conditions?"

"If I fix the roof, I also fix the door and the lock. It's a package deal."

She blinked, then a slow, grudging smile curved her mouth. "You've got a real thing about that door, haven't you?"

"It's a fire hazard."

She gave him an assessing look. "Okay. You can fix the door and the lock—on the proviso that I cover any and all expenses, and that you accept dinner from me every night you work here." She raised her eyebrows expectantly as she waited for his response.

"I don't eat salad," he said, tossing his hammer into his toolbox. "And I hate pumpkin."

"Then I definitely won't make you my roast pumpkin and feta salad." She was grinning, pleased with herself.

For some reason, he thought of Steve. His friend had had this woman with her infectious smiles and wit and creamy skin and colorful underwear in his life, and he'd let her go. Worse, he'd abandoned her when she needed him the most.

"I should go." He hefted his toolbox and headed for the door. He could feel her following him.

"Sure. I'll see you out," she said, brushing past him.

It was tempting, but he didn't say a word as she wrestled the door open. Her expression was wry as she stood to one side to let him pass.

"Very big of you."

"No point being a sore winner."

She laughed, low and throaty. He'd always liked her laugh.

"I'll see you tomorrow night," he said.

"Bring your appetite."

Like that was going to be a problem.

He stepped out into the rainy night. When he got to his car, he glanced over his shoulder. Pippa was silhouetted in the doorway, the hall light a golden nimbus around her head.

He had a sudden, stupid urge to climb the steps and ask her if she felt it, too—the sharp, insistent pull of desire and need and attraction whenever he was with her. Did she look at him and wonder what his mouth would feel like on hers? Did she think about his body, about how his skin would feel against hers? Did she wonder what it would be like to be naked, to have him slide inside her…?

He got in his car, started the engine and reversed into the street, not allowing himself another glance at the house. There was no way he was having that conversation with her. Steve might be behaving like an asshole of the highest order right now, but it didn't change the fact that he was Harry's oldest friend.

Pippa was taboo. End of story, nothing to see here, please move on.

Any second now he figured the raging hard-on in his jeans would get the memo. Any second.

CHAPTER SEVEN

SHE HAD OVER-PREPARED. She knew she had, yet it didn't stop her from peeling another potato and placing it on the baking tray.

Pippa couldn't afford to pay Harry in any conventional sense, but one thing she could do was ensure he never went home hungry while he helped her out. Tonight she was offering him roast beef, roast potatoes, fresh green beans and peas, homemade gravy and apple pie for dessert. She had beer in the fridge, and the moment she'd arrived home from university she'd showered and changed into her jeans and a T-shirt so that she'd be ready to act as his right-hand woman, should he need her.

A little voice pointed out that the shower part hadn't been strictly necessary, nor had the bit where she'd smoothed on lipstick and spritzed on perfume. She chose not to examine her motive for either too closely. Mostly because she was already more than aware she'd developed what could only be described as a crush on her ex-boyfriend's best friend.

She wasn't sure when she'd stopped kidding herself. Maybe it was the moment when she'd opened the door last night to Harry on her porch, rain glinting in his short dark hair, toolbox by his side, looking lean and mean and powerful in a black T-shirt and dark denim jeans less than fifteen minutes after she'd asked for his help.

Or maybe it was the moment in her bedroom when he'd insisted on striking a deal with her before he consented to helping out with the ceiling repair.

Maybe it was a combination of all of the above, along with the fact that when he was in the vicinity she was achingly aware of where his body was in relation to hers, of how wide his shoulders were, how deep his chest, how powerful his thighs. If she closed her eyes, she could summon the smell of him—warm skin and clean soap—and she could remember exactly how hot and hard his body had felt when she'd given him that impulsive, impromptu hug.

Your basic, garden-variety crush, really, complete with inappropriate sexual fantasies and sweaty palms and racing heart rate because he was due any second and she'd been both anticipating and dreading seeing him again all day.

The anticipation was for obvious reasons, the dread because she was terrified she would embarrass herself by doing or saying something over the next few nights to clue Harry in to her developing obsession. She was smart enough to know that nothing would ever happen between them. Not only was she the absolute antithesis of the bar bunnies he usually hooked up with, she was also Steve's ex-girlfriend. Harry might look like an outlaw, with his tattoos and his piercings and his burly build, but at heart he was a deeply honorable man with a very strict personal code. In his head, she was Steve's, even though the relationship had ended more than a year ago and they were about as estranged as two people could get.

Satisfied that dinner was more or less ready to roll,

she went to check on Alice. Sure enough, there had been action down south and she gave her daughter a quick bath after wiping up the mess. Dressing her daughter, Pippa reminded herself there were other reasons why her crush on Harry should remain only her private, dirty little secret.

Like Steve, Harry was a player. A sexy boy-man who treated life as though it was an extended long weekend. He lived for his mates, saw women as playthings and avoided responsibility as though it was contagious.

A woman would have to be crazy in the coconut to even consider going there.

Okay. We done with the protesting-too-much? Because it's getting wayyy *old and it's pointless. Nothing will happen with Harry for the very simple fact that you have learned your lesson where guys like him are concerned. Right? Right?*

Pippa's hands stilled on the snap fasteners on Alice's Onesie.

She didn't like thinking about the dark days immediately following her discovery that she was pregnant, but perhaps now was a good time for a reminder of how grim it had been. She had been alone and scared, and she had been bitter, angry and hurt after Steve's rejection. Most of that bitterness and anger had been directed at herself. She was the one who had chosen Steve, after all. She was the one who'd entrusted him with her body. It had been her decision to spend six months of her life with him. Her poor judgment. And the knowledge that her unborn child would be the one to bear the consequences of her choices had sent Pippa spiraling into despair.

Her mother's warm, practical support and her own innate fighting spirit had saved the day. She'd pulled herself together, gotten her life on track. Enrolled for her diploma, started saving in earnest for the hard months after the birth when she wouldn't be able to work. And she hadn't looked back.

Pippa closed the last snap, smiling as Alice gurgled her approval. The anxiety and excitement had all but faded in the face of her self-enforced reality check.

Harry might be roguish and hot, but he was not for her. Not in a million years.

The doorbell rang, and she hoisted Alice into her arms and went to answer the door.

"I do like a man who's prompt," she said as she swung it wide.

Harry's gaze swept over her before returning to her face. "Is that dinner I can smell?"

"Why, yes, honey, it is. Can I take your tool belt for you before I fetch your pipe and slippers?"

He didn't say a word, simply gave her a look before carrying his toolbox into the house. The moment he'd dumped it in the hall, he headed back out to his car. She tucked Alice into her crib for safety before joining him to help bring in the remainder of his gear and supplies. After several trips there were two sheets of plaster leaning against the hall wall, a ladder, a can of ceiling paint and a bunch of painting gear. Harry dropped a power saw beside it all and dusted his hands together, eyeing her expectantly.

She laughed. "All right, I'll feed you."

She waved him into a chair at the dining table, which she'd set for two, then crossed to the fridge for a beer for him.

When he saw it in her hand he shook his head.

"Not for me, thanks. Not while I'm working."

"Oh. Okay."

Nonplussed, she put the beer back. Steve had never said no to a drink. In fact, he'd never said no to anything that involved pleasure or excess.

She felt oddly domestic as she carved the roast beef and served the vegetables, very aware of Harry at the table, waiting for his meal.

She tried to think of something to say, but her mind steadfastly refused to come to the party. In the end, she fell back on convention.

"So, um, how was your day?"

"Busy. But it always is at this time of year."

She looked at him blankly.

"Summer, the lead-up to Christmas holidays," he elaborated. "Everyone suddenly remembers they should get their car serviced before they take off on the family holiday."

"Right. Of course."

She poured gravy onto both plates, then ferried them to the table.

"This looks great."

She gave him a quick smile to acknowledge his compliment. For some reason she was having trouble meeting his eyes. "Let me know if you want more gravy."

Right on cue, Alice's cry cut through the house. Pippa stood.

"Don't even think about stopping eating. I'll be back in a tick."

She returned with Alice in her arms, then sat and balanced Alice on her knee with well-practiced expertise.

"One-handed eating," Harry said. "Haven't seen that since Justine's kids were little."

"It's a life skill, that's for sure."

Silence fell as they both concentrated on their meals. Pippa tried to work out why everything felt so strained all of a sudden. She and Harry had never had trouble finding something to talk about before.

"How are your studies going?" Harry asked after a few uncomfortable minutes.

"I'm getting there. I have a killer assignment due before the end of the year, but then I'm free until March. Which will be a relief, because homework sucks as much as an adult as it did when I was in high school."

"I've been thinking about it, and I can't imagine you as a teacher."

"Why not?"

"I don't know. You don't look like any of the teachers I had when I was at school."

"I'm not sure if that's an insult or not," she said.

"It's a compliment. Trust me. I don't think we had a female teacher under fifty at our school."

"Poor you. Guess you had no distractions in class, then."

He grinned suddenly. "Oh, no. There were always plenty of distractions. Shannon Lewis, Carolyn Crosby, Nicole Townsend…"

"Even you didn't have that many girlfriends in high school," she scoffed.

"Define *girlfriend*."

She held up a hand. "You know what? I don't want to know."

He laughed. "Relax. I wasn't that much of a player."

She gave him a skeptical look. "When did you have your first kiss? Eleven? Twelve."

"How precocious do you think I was?"

"Very."

He shrugged a shoulder. "I was thirteen."

She pointed a thumb at her chest. "Sixteen."

"Late starter, huh?"

"Just picky."

"You think I'm not picky?"

She took a moment before responding, spearing peas with her fork. "Actually, I think you're very picky. Why else would you still be single?"

He sat back in his chair and frowned at her. She had surprised him.

"I'm single because I've tried it the other way and it didn't work for me."

Honestly, she couldn't imagine him all settled down and domesticated.

"What?" he asked.

"I'm trying to imagine you buying tampons and milk."

"I did it. Mowed the lawn and opened up a joint bank account, too."

"When was this?" Not in the past few years or she would know about it already.

"When I was twenty-three."

"Pretty young to settle down."

"Yeah."

"Do you still see her?"

"Deb? No. She wound up hating me." His gaze was distant for a moment.

Not a happy time, clearly. She felt bad for bringing it up. "Sorry."

He shrugged. "Why? It wasn't your fault. If it was anyone's, it was mine. I'm not cut out for that kind of life."

"So, what? You're just going to play the field for the rest of your life? A different woman every week?"

He looked amused. "I don't have a different woman every week."

She made a disbelieving noise. She'd seen the way women eyed him off at the pub.

Harry took a long swallow from his water. "I don't get around as much as you seem to think I do. And I'm always up front with women. Always."

She propped an elbow on the table and rested her chin on her hand, genuinely fascinated now. "*Up front.* Tell me what that means." She made a "gimme more" motion with her fingers.

"It means what it says. I tell them I'm looking for a bit of fun and that I'm no good at relationships. If they want to leave it at that, they can. But if anything happens afterward, they know the score."

Poor, poor women. The man should come with a health warning tattooed on his forehead.

"You realize that's like catnip for some women, right? The whole 'I'm no good at relationships' thing. Some women hear that and automatically add 'because I haven't met the right woman yet' in their heads. Which makes you a challenge, and them the transforming magical woman who convinces you love and marriage isn't so bad after all."

"I think you're making it far too complicated."

"I'm a woman. Being complicated is part of my stock in trade."

"At least you admit it."

She cocked her head to one side. "Why do men always think that being simple is a virtue?"

"Because it is?"

She pretended to think about it. "No. That's not it." He grinned.

She leaned across and collected his empty plate. "Hold that thought."

She dumped the plates in the sink, feeling unaccountably buoyant. She got a kick out of sparring with Harry. She always had.

Good for you—as long as you keep in mind what he just told you while you're getting your kicks.

It was a timely warning, but it was hardly needed. She knew the score with Harry. She always had. He was fun. Cocky and cheeky and sexy—and a terrible, terrible bet for any woman who was looking for more. As he'd admitted.

Only an idiot with strong self-destructive impulses would sashay into that particular dead-end alley, and she might be many things, but she wasn't *that* stupid.

She was simply enjoying herself. Enjoying a bit of harmless banter with a hot member of the opposite sex. For Harry this kind of thing was like breathing and sneezing—utterly instinctive. It meant less than nothing and was going nowhere—hence the reason it was so enjoyable.

They kept up the banter through dessert, then Harry took their plates to the sink and rinsed them.

"Time for me to meet my end of the bargain, I think," he said as he turned away from the sink.

"I'll try to settle Alice, then I'll be in to help."

She carried her daughter into the sunroom and set her in the bassinet. Harry entered as she was tucking the blanket in around Alice's feet.

"I put her in here so she won't wake up if we make noise," she explained, glancing over her shoulder.

He looked at Alice with an unreadable expression on his face. "I didn't notice before, but she's got your nose and jaw."

Pippa considered her daughter's face. "It's funny, but all I can see is Steve. She has his hair and hairline. And his eyes."

"She looks like you, too." He crouched beside Alice and ran a finger lightly over her downy hair.

Pippa wasn't sure what it was, but there was something about his large, work-toughened hand touching her daughter so gently, so tenderly... All of a sudden a lump formed in her throat and she blinked rapidly to dispel totally inappropriate tears.

As if he could sense her inner turmoil, Harry glanced at her. She pulled a face, trying to make light of her stupid emotionalism.

"Sorry. Mummy hormones. Steve has only seen her one time, the day she was born...." She sniffed mightily, willing her stupid tear ducts to dry up.

Harry's mouth settled into a tight line as he returned his gaze to Alice. They both watched her daughter in silence.

"He'll come round, you know," Harry said. "I know him pretty well, and he'll come round."

"It says a lot of good things about you that you believe that, Harry, but I can't live my life banking on that. It's not fair to Alice. And it's not fair to me, either."

He didn't argue with her. What was there to say, after all?

She slapped her palms against her thighs and forced a smile. "So. This hole we're supposed to be repairing..."

Harry led the way to the bedroom, surveying the area briefly before turning to her. "It's going to get messy. I've got some drop sheets, but I think we should put your bed in the hall, since you're sleeping on the couch anyway."

"Okay, sure. I'll get rid of the bedding...."

She'd done a cursory cleanup last night, removing the worst of the debris and vacuuming up the insulation. Now, she tugged the quilt and sheets free and dumped them in Alice's room. When she returned, Harry already had her mattress off the bed and was manhandling it through the door. She helped him lean it against the wall, then returned to the bedroom to move the box spring. Lifting it revealed the many small odds and ends she stored beneath the bed—a pretty keepsake box, stacks of books, a few pairs of old shoes, her radio—as well as dust bunnies the size of small ponies.

"What can I say? Vacuuming is not my forte," she said when Harry nudged one with the toe of his boot.

"Better be careful one of them doesn't crawl up and eat you in your sleep."

"Idiot. Everyone knows dust bunnies are vegetarians. As if."

They were both smiling as they shuffled the box spring into the hallway and leaned it against the mattress. When they returned to the bedroom she knelt on the floor and began collecting the books. Harry leaned down to unplug the radio. Out of the corner of her eye she saw him reach for the keepsake box and an alarm sounded deep in her brain, sending a spurt of adrenaline rocketing through her body.

If anyone should be moving that box, it was her. In fact, if she'd been thinking with even a single brain cell, she would have anticipated this scenario and hidden it deep in the closet hours before he was due.

Acting on instinct, she shot out a hand to intercept him, hoping to beat him to the box. "I've got it," she blurted.

Not her smartest move ever.

Her hand collided with the side of the box as Harry grasped it, knocking it from his hand. She watched with dawning horror as it tumbled to the floor. The lid popped off, and the contents fell out and rolled across the floor.

Shit.

For a moment they were both very still as they stared at her hot-pink silicone vibrator, complete with spare batteries—just in case—and a small tube of personal lubricant.

Heat roared into her face. For a moment she could do nothing but breathe. She didn't dare think of making eye contact with Harry. Instead, she reached out and ever-so-calmly popped the vibrator into the box, along with her other goodies. Standing, she crossed to the tallboy, opened the top drawer and stuffed the whole thing in amongst her underwear.

She pushed the drawer closed, her hand clenched around the knob, painfully aware that she needed to face Harry.

Pippa didn't move. She felt as though every muscle in her body was stiff with embarrassment. God only knew what he was thinking of her.

That she was a horny single mum.

That she lay in her bed at night thinking about sex and men. That she was gagging for it.

You've got to admit, some of those things are true.

Not all of them, and not all of the time. For example, she didn't lie in bed *every* night thinking about sex and men. And she wouldn't describe her desire for sex as *gagging,* exactly. But she did miss sex. She did miss the hard strength of a man's body. She missed the sweaty earthiness, the needfulness of the sex act. She missed the intimacy and simplicity and the rawness and the release of it.

She missed feeling desired, and the warm, languorous few seconds afterward when her body was loose and satisfied and her brain ceased to function and simply *was*.

She missed feeling like more than a mother, missed feeling like a woman.

It won't get any easier. Turn around, say something clever, move on.

She unclenched her hand, took a deep breath and turned around.

Harry was winding the cord around the body of the radio, his movements very neat and precise. He didn't look up, and he didn't say anything. She tried to think of something witty to say, but her brain was still ringing with humiliation. Instead, she resumed collecting the books. She transferred them to the hall. Harry followed, placing her radio alongside them. They returned to her bedroom together and stared at the empty space they'd created.

"Lots of women have one," she said suddenly. "Women have needs, too, even if we don't run around advertising them on billboards. I refuse to feel embarrassed about a perfectly natural act."

"Then don't." He sounded pretty matter-of-fact.

She looked at him out of the corner of her eyes. He appeared pretty matter-of-fact, too. He caught her looking and shrugged.

"In case you haven't worked it out, I'm the last person who will ever judge a woman for seeking a little pleasure."

Huh.

She thought about it for a second and decided she believed him. Some of the tension left her shoulders. So he knew that she occasionally got off in the privacy of her bedroom with the aid of a battery-operated device. Big deal. They were both grown-ups. He probably did…things in the privacy of his own bedroom, too.

She cleared her throat. "I guess you'll want to set up the ladder now, yeah?"

He did, putting down drop cloths first before positioning the ladder to one side of the hole. She stood clear as he donned a face mask, grabbed his hammer, climbed the ladder and started pulling down the remainder of the two sheets of plaster. Dust filled the air and she retreated into the hallway. Five minutes later, that job was done, the room was filled with what looked like mist and Harry was standing in the middle of it, his hair and face and body covered with plaster dust.

Any other man would look stupid, like a man-sized sugar-doughnut. Harry looked like a Greek statue come to life, hard and tough and perfectly proportioned.

She crossed to the window and opened it, then they put the debris into garbage bags. It wasn't comfortable—she was still way too self-conscious over the *reveal* to feel comfortable—but it was bearable, and the next hour flew by as Harry hauled the new plaster sheets up the ladder and screwed them in place. She helped by holding each sheet up with the aid of a broom to extend the reach of her arms, bracing her body beneath the handle and gritting her teeth until her arms and legs trembled with the effort. By the time he'd installed both sheets she was dripping with sweat and wrung out.

"Enough for tonight," Harry said, tossing his hammer into his toolbox.

"If you're stopping because of me, I can keep going."

"Sure you can, slugger."

She decided not to argue with him, since she really

didn't have the energy. She helped him pack his gear for the night then offered him a coffee.

He hesitated a moment before shaking his head. "Thanks, but I'd better make tracks."

She saw him to the door and waved him off, just as she had last night. The second she closed the door, the moment with her vibrator sprung out from the vault she'd confined it to in her mind. She'd managed to keep it at bay while they worked, but now there was nothing stopping her from reliving the whole debacle in vivid Technicolor.

She closed her eyes and moaned pitifully as the image of her hot-pink vibrator tumbling at his feet played over and over in her mind. Talk about humiliating. No, it was beyond humiliating. Someone needed to invent a new word to cover the level of embarrassment she was currently experiencing.

She didn't want Harry knowing such a personal, private thing about her. It was way too intimate. And they weren't intimates. At best, they were sort-of friends—*sort-of* because there were a bunch of things standing in the way of them ever being true friends, Steve being the major impediment.

Despite that, Harry now knew that sometimes, when the need took her, she spent some up-close and personal time with her hot-pink battery-operated boyfriend.

She moaned again and clenched her teeth. If she could, she would erase those few seconds from the history of the world.

But she couldn't. Harry knew what he knew, and she knew that he knew, and nothing would ever change that. And tomorrow night he would arrive at her house promptly at six o'clock and she would have to look him in the eye and pretend it was business as usual, as she had tonight.

This would be a really good time to run off and join the circus, in case you were wondering.

The phone rang, the sound startlingly loud in the quiet of the house. Pippa raced to get it before Alice woke.

"Pippa. Sorry it's a little late, but I've been meaning to call all day and check how you are," her mother said. "Did the money come through all right?"

Pippa had called her mum last night to explain about the ceiling and ask for a small loan to cover the building supplies for the repair. True to form, her mother had agreed immediately and the money had landed in her bank account this morning.

"It did. Thank you. You're a life saver."

"You sound a little rushed. Is this a bad time?"

"No, Harry was here but he's gone now. I ran to get the phone so Alice wouldn't wake up."

"Harry?"

"He's the friend I mentioned who was helping with the repair."

"Oh, that's right. He's clearly a good friend to have. Would I have met him?"

"No." Pippa could hear the stiffness in her own voice. She wasn't sure why, but she felt uncomfortable talking about Harry.

"Sorry. Am I being nosy?" her mother asked in her blunt, no-nonsense way.

"There's nothing to be nosy about." More stiffness, with a side order of defensiveness. What on earth was wrong with her?

"Okay," her mother said diplomatically. "How's my favorite granddaughter?"

They talked about Alice for a few minutes before her mother wound up the call.

"Speak soon, okay?" she said.

"Okay. Love you."

Pippa was about to put the phone down when her mother spoke up.

"Pippa…if you ever wanted to go out to dinner or a movie, I'd be more than happy to come down and baby-sit. You only have to ask."

Pippa was so surprised she took a moment to respond. "Um, sure. Thanks."

"I want you to know the option is there, if you need it."

"I appreciate it, but don't hold your breath." It wasn't as though her social life was exactly jumping these days.

"Being a mother doesn't mean you're not a person still. You know that, right?"

Where was all this coming from? "I know that."

"I hope so."

They said their goodbyes then and ended the call. Pippa tried to understand why her mother had suddenly decided to give her a pep talk on getting a life. Was she really that sad?

She thought about the vibrator incident and groaned. Certainly, Harry thought she was that sad.

Because it didn't bear thinking about—any of it— she went to bed. Tomorrow was another day, after all, full of fresh opportunities to humiliate herself.

PIPPA HAD A vibrator. Not just any vibrator, either. A hot-pink, generously proportioned device that would give plenty of guys a permanent case of performance anxiety.

She had spare batteries at the ready, too, as well as a

tube of lubricant. She kept it all in a neat little box beneath her bed, within easy reach should the mood take her. Any time she got the urge, she had only to reach her hand down to find instant satisfaction….

Harry pulled over to the side of the road with a screech of tires. He gripped the steering wheel, shut his eyes and tried to banish the images filling his head—Pippa, flushed and breathless, pleasuring herself with Mr. Pink a dozen different ways. In the bath, in the shower, on her bed…

"Stop it."

He was out of control. At least, his libido was. The rest of him was fighting a valiant rearguard action, but he wasn't sure how much longer he could hold out.

It had been bad enough that she'd been wearing those jeans again. He'd been half expecting it, since she'd made it clear she planned to help him, but he'd still had trouble keeping his eyes off her ass as she moved around the kitchen.

Then there'd been their conversation over dinner. With any other woman, he'd have called their light, teasing conversation flirting. With Pippa… He didn't know what it was. They'd always teased each other, going out of their way to coax a smile or a laugh. They'd always bounced ideas and insults around. Before, though, she'd been Steve's, and it had seemed harmless to enjoy that kind of verbal play with her. Now, it felt different. He'd never let himself see her as a desirable woman before, but after tonight and the incident with her bra he had all these pictures in his head and it was getting harder and harder to stop himself from doing something stupid.

Something that would probably get his face slapped and make it impossible for him to help her in the future.

The thought sobered him, not so much because he

was worried about getting his face slapped, but because he hated the idea of Pippa needing help and not being able to ask for it.

A car sped past, rattling the truck windows. He unclenched his hands from the steering wheel.

He wouldn't make a move on Pippa. She wasn't some girl at the bar looking for fun times. She was serious. She had a daughter she was raising on her own. She was studying and working part-time. Her life was complicated and intense and full of compromises and responsibilities.

He wasn't up for any of that, and she wasn't the kind of woman who would be interested in a no-strings roll in the hay. It was never going to happen.

Harry felt a little calmer, a little more in control as he signaled and pulled out into the road. All he had to do was survive a couple more nights of close contact, then he could bow out of her life and go back to being a distant friendly face she saw in passing every now and then. A friendly face who kept his thoughts above her neckline.

A familiar truck was parked out front of his house when he turned onto his street. His foot stilled on the accelerator for a split second before he got a grip on himself. He pulled into his driveway and watched in the rearview mirror as Steve stepped out of his truck and made his way up the drive.

In all of Harry's justifications and excuses and rationalizations over the past few minutes, not once had Steve figured in his thinking—yet his friendship with Steve should have been the primary reason preventing anything from happening between him and Pippa. It should have been the first thing that came to mind, not the last.

It didn't matter that they'd parted badly the other night. It didn't matter that they hadn't spoken since. He and Steve had a shared history that stretched back more than fifteen years—not something a man threw away because he had an itch to scratch. Even if that itch was approaching unbearable.

Steve's expression was masked by darkness as Harry joined him in the driveway.

"You been waiting long?"

"Long enough." Steve ground the words out, low and angry.

"What's going on?"

"I saw your truck at Pippa's."

There was an unspoken accusation in his friend's tone. Harry went still. "And?"

"I want to know what you're playing at." Steve shifted, his booted feet scuffing the cement.

Harry might not be able to see Steve's face clearly but he could read his body language just fine. He was squaring up. Spoiling for a fight.

"I'm not playing at anything. I'm helping her out."

"You think I'm an idiot? You think I didn't notice the way you used to look at her when we were going out?"

Harry's temper rose. He'd never so much as looked sideways at Pippa when she and Steve were an item.

"Think really carefully about what you're about to say, because I've had a long freakin' day."

"Are you, then? Are you screwing her?"

"You're an idiot." Harry brushed past him, heading for the porch.

"What's wrong? Can't look me in the eye and admit it?"

"Go home, mate," Harry said without turning around.

"If you're not doing her, then why were you over there at ten at night?"

Harry unlocked the door and swung it open, reaching inside to flick on the porch light. Only then did he turn toward Steve, taking in his friend's strained, unhappy face and tense posture.

"I told you, I was helping her out. She had some things that needed fixing around the place and she can't afford to pay for it."

"So she called you? Out of all the people in the known freakin' universe?"

"Yeah, she did. Because I offered to help. Because I could see she was doing it tough and I knew you weren't going to step up."

Steve's eyes narrowed. "What I do or don't do is none of your business. Just like Pippa and Alice are none of your business. Stay away from both of them."

Harry couldn't believe what he was hearing. Steve had burned Pippa when she'd gotten pregnant with his child, essentially abandoning her, and now he wanted to dictate who she had in her life? He never would have thought his friend was capable of being such an asshole.

"What's your problem? You don't want her but no one else can have her? Do you have any idea how big a dick that makes you?"

"So you do want her." Steve sounded triumphant.

Harry stared at his friend. Out of everything he'd said, *that* was the bit that stood out to Steve?

"What's going on with you, man? How can you not see that what you're doing is wrong? You have a daughter. A gorgeous little kid. Doesn't that mean anything to you?"

Steve laughed, the sound bitter and hard. "As if this is about the kid. You want in her pants, that's all this is. You always have, and all this bullshit is your way of justifying it to yourself." Steve threw a hand in the air, as though he was throwing something away. "Go ahead, screw her if it's that important to you. Do her every which way from here till Sunday."

He headed for his truck. Harry watched him, frustration and anger warring inside his brain. Part of him wanted to tackle Steve to the ground and pound some sense into him the way he would have when they were both fourteen, but he knew it wouldn't change anything.

He didn't understand where his friend's head was at. The way Steve had treated Pippa, the way he was denying Alice... It was messed up, and Harry couldn't reconcile it with the guy he thought he knew. Better yet, he didn't want to.

If someone had asked him a month ago to come up with a scenario that would threaten his friendship with Steve, he would have drawn an absolute blank. He hadn't thought it was possible—maybe because he simply didn't have the imagination required or perhaps because he was too freakin' naive for his own good. Certainly he never would have imagined that Steve could be such a jerk.

The way his mate was behaving was deal-breaker stuff. The kind of stuff that made a person reevaluate everything.

Harry stepped backward.

He didn't want to go there, even in his thoughts. In his heart, he still believed Steve would come around. Maybe not as unequivocally as he had earlier... But the hope was still there.

Harry went inside, but instead of stripping for the shower he'd been looking forward to, he headed out to the garage. He pulled on his boxing gloves then he zeroed in on the long bag, pounding the padded vinyl with everything he had.

He rained blows on the bag until he was breathless and shaky and covered with sweat. Gripping the bag with both arms, he leaned his head against it, sucking air into his lungs.

Everything was messed up—and for the life of him he didn't know how to fix it.

CHAPTER EIGHT

THE NEXT DAY, Pippa woke at five o'clock to a crying child, worked on her assignment till eight, dropped Alice at day care, went to university till lunchtime, then raced to the gallery for an afternoon shift.

It was delivery day, when all the artists delivered their latest works. As well as dealing with any customers, Pippa's job was to unpack and catalog the new pieces and enter them into the computer system. The gallery dealt with in excess of fifty local painters, sculptors, jewelry makers and other artists, many of whom weren't naturals at organization or administration. By the time she'd put out a few spot fires, soothed some ruffled feathers and listened to several life stories there was precious little time left to get the actual cataloging done and she wound up doing nearly an hour of unpaid overtime.

She didn't begrudge it, because Gaylene had always been so supportive of her, but she was aware of time ticking away as her fingers flew over the keyboard. The moment she was done she locked up and sped to day care, apologizing profusely for being so close to the final pickup time. Alice was pleased to see her, all bright-eyed and smiley, and Pippa spent more time than necessary strapping her into the baby seat, kissing her cheeks and tickling her belly.

As she let herself into the house, she was very aware

that Harry was due in under half an hour. Feeling more than a little frazzled and stressed, she warmed up a bottle for Alice and started the sauce for spaghetti bolognese. She was mixing garlic butter for garlic bread when the doorbell sounded.

She glanced at the clock. Harry was early. Just her luck.

Pippa sucked a smear of garlic butter off her thumb as she walked to the front door, trying to think of something suitably light and smart-arsey to say to him to smooth over the hump of what had happened last night.

She swung open the door, witty quip ready to roll—and stilled.

It wasn't Harry filling the doorway, it was Steve.

For a moment she was so gobsmacked words deserted her, witty or otherwise. She hadn't seen him, even in passing, since the day she'd given birth to Alice. Her stomach dipped unpleasantly. Her hand tightened on the door.

"Hi," she finally managed to say.

His face was expressionless as he flicked a glance up and down her body. "We need to talk."

Just as he was the last person she'd expected to find on her doorstep, those were the last words she'd expected him to say. She'd been trying to get him to talk to her—for Alice's sake—for more than a year.

Yet the thought of him being in her home made her deeply uncomfortable. She was so angry with him, so disillusioned. She didn't want to sit at her dining table and talk as though he hadn't tried to will their daughter out of existence for the past six months. If she was free to obey the dictates of her gut and her emotions, she'd screech at him like a fish wife and order him off her front porch.

She compromised by nodding and gesturing for him to fall back. "Okay. But out here, not inside."

He retreated to the top of the steps and she joined him on the porch. Even though she knew it would appear defensive, she crossed her arms over her chest. She couldn't help herself—she *was* defensive. This man had set himself up as her enemy, and now he was here, out of the blue. She didn't trust him and she had no idea what he was about to say to her... She'd be out of her gourd not to be defensive.

"So, what's going on, Steve?"

He looked exactly the same as he had when she'd first met him—slightly scruffy sun-bleached hair, deeply tanned skin, bright blue eyes, well-muscled body—but his undeniable good looks left her completely cold today. Knowing that beneath his happy-go-lucky, laugh-a-minute facade there was a scared, angry little boy who didn't have the backbone to shoulder his responsibilities killed any lingering appeal he might have had for her.

"I wanted to give you this," he said, pulling something from his pocket.

It took her a moment to register that it was a wad of cash, held together with a grubby rubber band.

"I figure the baby must have expenses. Things she needs."

Pippa blinked. "I beg your pardon?"

He gestured with his outstretched hand. "It's a couple of thousand. To help you out."

Her gaze dropped to the money almost against her will. Two thousand dollars would be a wonderful, luxurious safety net to have in her bank account right now. She wouldn't have to juggle her school fees with her medical insurance payments. She wouldn't have to take every shift that came her way. She could let down her guard enough so that her shoulders didn't feel as though they were permanently up around her ears with stress…

"I don't understand," she said.

Because it wasn't as easy as simply accepting his money. Child Support Services were investigating him. He'd lied and falsified his business books to ensure he didn't have to provide her with adequate child maintenance payments. It didn't make sense that he was suddenly on her doorstep, keen to help out with "the baby's" expenses.

Steve sighed and let his hand drop to his side. "I heard you'd had some car trouble and that things were tight. I figured this would help."

"It would."

"So?" He held out the money again.

The practical part of her brain screamed at her to take the cash and worry about the whys and wherefores later, but everything else in her baulked. Legally and morally, he owed her a great deal more than two thousand dollars. If she took his money now, she would be signaling to him that she was prepared to forgive almost anything as long as the price was right.

She wasn't. She couldn't. This wasn't the kind of relationship she wanted with Alice's father.

"Why now?"

"I told you, I heard you'd had car trouble."

"You didn't think we might have needed some help before now? Why do you think I went through the nightmare of dealing with Child Services, Steve?"

His face fell into the impatient, frustrated lines she'd become so familiar with after their breakup. "Look, either you want the money or you don't. I just figured you'd like to be in a position where you didn't have to accept favors to get stuff done. But what do I know?"

"Is this because Harry's been helping me out?"

It was a stab in the dark but the way his expression instantly shuttered told her she'd guessed correctly.

She stared at him, even more confused. Harry was Steve's friend. Why on earth would Steve be over here offering her money so she wouldn't have to *accept favors to get stuff done* from *Harry,* of all people?

Steve jammed the money into his pocket. "It's none of my business, but you know what Harry's like. He's a dog. If he hasn't tried to throw the leg over yet, it's only because he hasn't got around to it. This way, you can pay someone to help you out."

Steve watched her closely as he spoke and it struck her that he was trying to gauge her reaction.

He wants to know if I've slept with Harry.

The realization hit like a lightning strike. Suddenly it all made sense: the impromptu visit, the unexpected money offer, the sudden interest in Alice's expenses. All of it driven by jealousy. Or, more accurately, a proprietal, dog-in-manger sense of territory. After all, Steve had had her first. God forbid that anyone else want her now that he'd discarded her, especially someone he considered a friend.

A friend who'd called Steve on his poor behavior and made him feel small—Harry had all but admitted as much the night he'd shown up on her doorstep, determined to ride to her rescue.

For a second anger was a physical burn in her belly.

This man was the father of her child, and the only thing that had prompted him to make contact with her was pride. Big, fat, wounded male pride.

"Wow. That is— Wow." She gestured forcefully, unable to articulate her outrage. "You have got balls of steel, you know that? Big, dumb balls of steel."

As if he sensed the Vesuvius of fury welling inside her, Steve took a step backward.

"How *dare* you come over here pretending you give a shit about me and your daughter when all you want to know is if Harry's been in my pants. I have *begged* you to take some interest in Alice. I've offered you access despite the fact that you lied your ass off so you wouldn't have to support her. I pleaded with you to at least talk to me so we wouldn't have to go to Child Services, and you wouldn't even give me the time of day. But the thought that Harry might be sleeping with me brings you running with a big wad of cash in hand—"

She ran out of words, made speechless by the sheer, unmitigated gall of the man with his dumb surfer-boy hair and his thigh-hugging jeans and his striking aqua-blue eyes.

How could so much asshole be contained in one person? He was the worst mistake of her life, a catastrophic walking-talking failure of judgment. The thought that she'd once let him inside her body, that she'd slept beside him and showered with him and shared meals with him literally made her stomach turn.

And yet he'd given her Alice, and her daughter was the best thing that had ever happened to her. The jury was still out, but Pippa was almost convinced Alice had even been the making of her.

The thought punctured her anger and suddenly she simply felt tired and sad. "You know what? Just go. I don't have the time or the energy to deal with your bullshit."

She turned to re-enter the house but Steve stopped her with a hand on her arm.

"You think you're special? You think you're any different from all the other girls he's screwed and left behind?"

It was too much. She'd tried to take the higher ground, she'd tried to walk away, but Steve clearly couldn't let it go and she was only human.

Her chin rose. She looked him dead in the eye. "Oh, I know I'm different. Last night, Harry told me I'd ruined him for all other women—this is while we were still lying in the hall because we didn't make it to the bedroom. Most of the time we don't, actually. Not that it matters. Harry's pretty creative, if you know what I mean." She glanced at the hand that still held her forearm.

He released her, his mouth an angry line. She had no idea if he believed a word she'd said, but she didn't really give a damn. She just wanted him gone, out of her life.

Pippa stepped into the hall and shut the door firmly behind her. She held her breath, waiting for the sound of his boots on the steps. Only when she was sure he was gone did she lean against the door and take a deep, shuddering breath.

What a jerk. What a gold-plated, shameless, egotistical jerk.

She couldn't believe he'd come over here and gone through the charade of pretending he gave a fat rat's caboose about his daughter in order to safeguard the sanctity of his ex's vagina. That was what it came down to, after all. He wasn't interested in any other part of her. He certainly wasn't interested in Alice or whether Pippa had enough money to care for her adequately. He simply wanted to ensure that Harry didn't have what he'd once had.

Pathetic, ridiculous caveman stuff. And it made her

want to weep for her daughter. The other night she'd told Harry that she couldn't afford to hope that Steve might one day come around. It was a lie. In her heart of hearts, buried deep, was a foolish, naive dream that one day Steve would get past whatever was stopping him from having a relationship with his child and come looking for Alice.

It's never going to happen. Face it and accept it and let it go.

She returned to the kitchen and resumed mixing the garlic butter. It came as no great surprise that her hands were shaking. She concentrated with all her might on slicing the bread and slowly the shaky feeling subsided. It wasn't until she slid the foil-wrapped roll into the oven that it occurred to her that Harry must have really struck a nerve with Steve for him to be so bent of shape and angry about Harry possibly being involved with her.

She stilled as the implications of her realization hit home.

Harry and Steve had known each other for years. She didn't even know how long, although the stories and anecdotes they'd recounted to her had gone back into their early teens. They surfed together, they hung out together, they had each other's backs... And now they were at odds because Harry had been kind and foolish enough to pull over when he saw her stranded on the side of the road.

It didn't sit well with her, even though she knew that she had done nothing to create a wedge between the two men.

Apart from telling Steve that you and Harry were doing each other, you mean.

She winced. She'd been so busy spitting in Steve's eye she hadn't stopped to consider the repercussions of her hasty words. Whatever was going on between Harry and Steve would only be exacerbated by what she'd implied—okay, by what she'd blatantly rubbed in Steve's face.

Sometimes she wished she could uninstall her stupid temper like an underperforming phone app and get on with her life. This was the second time in as many weeks it had gotten her into hot water. And both times she'd ended up owing Harry an apology.

Right on cue—because apparently her life had become a French farce—the doorbell rang. She smoothed a hand over her hair, then made an impatient noise. Not only did she know, without a doubt, that she looked worn out and pale and definitely not at her best after a long day and a wrangle with her ex, she also knew it wouldn't make any difference to Harry. Especially once he'd heard what she had to confess.

Bracing herself, she went to answer the door.

"HEY. RIGHT ON TIME. Sadly, dinner is not, but it won't be long," Pippa said as she opened the door.

The moment Harry laid eyes on her he knew something was wrong. He didn't know how he knew, he just did.

Maybe it was the way she was smiling with only her mouth. Or maybe it was the way she held herself, as though expecting something bad or painful to happen in the next few seconds or minutes.

"What's wrong?"

She blinked. Then quickly shook her head. "Nothing. Why?"

"Bullshit. What's going on?"

She eyed him for a beat, and he guessed she was trying to work out how much effort it would take to convince him to believe her lie.

"Steve was just here."

Damn.

Last night, after Steve had taken off and Harry had finished pummeling his punching bag, he'd debated with himself over whether he should tell Pippa what had happened. His conclusion, after more than an hour staring at his bedroom ceiling, was that what she didn't know wouldn't hurt her. Whatever was going on, it felt like it was between him and Steve. He'd figured it would stay that way.

He'd figured wrong. Obviously.

He'd been silent too long and Pippa tilted her head to one side as she studied him.

"Why don't you look surprised?"

"He was on my doorstep when I got home last night. Saw my truck in your driveway, wanted to know why I was spending time with his ex-girlfriend."

She blinked again, but this time it read more like amazement at Steve's gall than surprise.

"He came right out and asked you that?" Her voice was a little on the high side, her eyes wide.

"Not in those exact words." He wouldn't repeat what Steve had said. It wouldn't do anyone any favors.

Pippa's chin lifted and he had a feeling she didn't have many illusions about the flavor of the conversation they'd shared.

"I'm sorry you had to go through that, and I'm sorry that helping me has made trouble between you and Steve."

"You've got nothing to apologize for. It's not your fault Steve's acting like a dick."

"But it's because of me. Because of our history."

"It's because of Alice and because Steve has got some shit he needs to deal with. Neither of which places you in the firing line."

Her expression softened. "You're a nice guy, Harry. Sometimes too nice."

"I wish you'd stop saying that."

"Tough luck." She smiled. Then she lifted a hand and pushed her glasses up her nose and he knew there was more.

"What else do you need to tell me?"

This time her look was incredulous. "Have you been taking mind-reading pills or something?"

He gestured with his index finger around his own eyes to indicate her glasses.

"You muck around with your glasses when you're nervous."

"I do not." Her hand lifted to adjust her frames again. She caught the action midair and returned her hand to her side, but her expression was rueful.

"There goes my career as a covert double agent," she said.

Harry crossed his arms over his chest and propped a shoulder against the door, letting her know that they weren't going anywhere until she came clean.

She sighed, tweaked her glasses again, then shook her head in frustration at the gesture.

"Okay. Fine. The truth, the whole truth and nothing but the truth. But you won't like it. And this is definitely my fault."

He made a winding motion with his finger, encouraging her to stop tap-dancing and start talking.

"Okay. I'm getting there. In case you haven't noticed, I have this ridiculous temper. Sometimes it takes the wheel and dumb-ass things come out of my mouth.

Like the other week when I gave you a hard time for offering to help out when it was really myself and my stupid feckless life I was angry with."

He raised his eyebrows, waiting.

"Steve pretty much wanted to know the same thing—what you were doing over here last night—but he offered me money for Alice before going there. When I told him I didn't want his money under those circumstances, he warned me off you, told me I was stupid to think I was special and you would treat me exactly the same as all your other women."

Her face and chest were pink but she didn't look away. Harry had to school his own features to keep a lid on the anger growing inside him. Last night Steve had been an asshole, but tonight he'd stepped over the line. Big-time.

"He made me so angry, pretending he gave a toss about Alice when all he cared about was whether you were sleeping with me or not. Whatever you said to him, you must have really pissed him off."

She stared at him expectantly, inviting him to fill in the blanks, but he simply shrugged. He wasn't about to start telling tales. Somehow he'd gotten stuck between his oldest friend and Pippa, but he wouldn't stay any longer than he had to.

He'd barely finished shrugging before Pippa held up a hand.

"Forget I asked that. What happens between you two is your business."

"Tell me the rest of it, Pippa." Because it was becoming clear to him that she'd be happy to prevaricate all day long if he let her.

"Okay. But I might not be able to look at you while I say it."

"All right."

She scrunched up her face like a kid about to swallow a mouthful of cod liver oil. "After he made that crack about me not being special, I, um, may have given him the impression that his suspicions were more than grounded. There, uh, may even have been a reference to us doing it on the hall floor and you being very creative…" She swallowed. The sound was audible, like a cartoon gulp. Confession over, she relaxed her face and made eye contact with him, waiting for his reaction.

Clearly she thought he'd be angry. Maybe he should be, given the state of play between him and Steve, but as he'd said earlier, it wasn't her fault Steve was acting like an asshole. Harry figured he'd have been pretty damn provoked, too, if someone had thrown the same kind of crap at his head.

And maybe he was warped, but he couldn't help admiring her chutzpah.

"The hall floor?" he asked after a short pause. "What's wrong with the bed? Apart from the fact that it's leaning against the wall, of course?"

"We didn't make it to the bed. Too impatient."

"Ah."

"I'm really sorry." Her hands gripped each other tightly at her waist. "I know I should have turned the other cheek, and if you like I'll call him and explain I only said it to get a rise out of him. I'm pretty sure he didn't believe me, anyway, because I'm about a million miles away from one of your usual bar bunnies. Plus there's Alice. If he'd stopped to think about it for half a second, he'd have known that he was definitely barking up the wrong tree in the wrong forest in the wrong country."

"Define *creative* for me."

She stared at him, arrested. "You're not angry."

"Why would I be angry?"

"Because I've made things even more difficult between you and Steve."

"Nope. He did that by coming over here being offensive and insulting you."

"Harry... You have to stop letting me off the hook."

"Deal—if you stop trying to take responsibility for stuff that isn't yours to own." He pushed away from the door frame. "Is that garlic I smell?"

"Yes." She appeared distracted, a worried frown creasing her forehead. "But I'm not sure we should be doing this anymore. Even if Steve is totally out of line, I hate the thought of you two fighting because of me and Alice."

He laid a hand on her shoulder. What he really wanted was to pull her into his arms, but that was never going to happen. He could feel her distress vibrating through her frame like a low-voltage current.

"I'm here because I want to be. No other reason."

He was a little surprised to realize it was true. He'd started helping Pippa because he'd felt for her situation. He'd kept helping her because someone had to step into the breach left by his mate's irresponsibility. But beneath all of his good intentions there had always been a rock-solid foundation of liking, pure and simple. Pippa was good people. He wanted to make her life better.

And he was fast developing an obsession with getting her naked—but that was a whole other ball game.

"If you keep being nice to me, I'm going to cry. And then I'm going to have to kill you, because I pride myself on never crying in public."

He squeezed her shoulder lightly before releasing his

grip. "Okay. Where's my dinner? That mean enough for you?"

She blinked rapidly a couple of times. "Yeah, that'll probably do it."

He dumped his toolbox in her bedroom before following her down the hallway. She wore one of her retro dresses today, this one a red-and-blue striped sundress with little red strawberries scattered across it. The fabric swished around her slim calves as she walked, flirting with the backs of her knees. She had nice legs—shapely without being too skinny or too muscular. As Goldilocks would say, they were just right.

But you won't be sleeping in that bed, Goldi. Remember?

He forced his gaze away from Pippa's body as they entered the kitchen. Alice was playing on a mat beneath a colorful plastic toy frame, batting at a bright yellow star. Because he didn't trust himself to keep his eyes to himself, he crouched down beside the baby.

"How are you doing, Miss Alice?"

Predictably, all Alice did was stare at him, wide-eyed. Then her small mouth curved into a gummy smile and he couldn't resist the urge to touch one of her tiny-nailed hands. Her skin was incredibly soft. Harry watched, fascinated, as her hand curled around his index finger. He smiled. This kid definitely had a thing about woman-handling men.

"We're having spaghetti with garlic bread, but I'm running a little late getting it all together," Pippa said from behind the kitchen counter.

He slipped his finger from Alice's grip and stood. "It's cool. I haven't got anywhere else I need to be."

She nodded and rummaged in the kitchen drawer for

something. She still looked agitated. Steve's visit had rattled her more than she wanted to let on.

"Don't suppose you've got any wine?" he asked.

"I do. A Semillon sauvignon. It's a little fruity but okay."

She sounded surprised and he knew she was remembering that he didn't drink while working.

"You look like you could use a glass of wine," he said.

She puffed her cheeks out. He got the feeling she was trying to decide between being amused or offended. After a few seconds she smiled.

"That obvious, huh?"

"Only to the trained observer."

"Right. Remind me again what you're trained in observing?" She opened the fridge as she spoke, pulling out the wine.

"Women."

She laughed. "I guess you are."

She poured two glasses. He accepted his with a murmured thanks when she passed it over.

"Cheers, Mr. Observer," she said, lifting her glass in a brief toast before taking a healthy mouthful.

He took a smaller sip, barely managing to stop his mouth from puckering at the grassy acidity of the wine. He was more of a beer and red wine man generally speaking, but if sharing a glass of white wine with Pippa meant she'd happily have one, he was prepared to suck it up.

"So. How was *your* day?" she asked with forced brightness.

He told her about an incident with a customer at work, exaggerating the personalities to make her laugh. By the time they sat down to eat, she'd finished her glass of wine and the tightness had left her face. She lifted the bottle, asking silently if he wanted a second glass, but he shook his head.

"I'm good for now, thanks."

She hesitated a moment, then shrugged as if to say "what the hell" and poured herself another.

He asked her questions about her university course for most of the meal, watching the emotions chase themselves across her face as she first enthused about a particular lecturer and then condemned a narrow-minded education department policy that she was convinced was all about bureaucracy and nothing about education.

"You sound pretty passionate about this stuff," he said.

"Do I?" She looked surprised.

"Yeah, you do."

She considered for a moment. "Maybe I am a little passionate." She laughed. "I never thought I'd say that. When I signed up for the diploma I was just being practical. But there are definitely parts that I really enjoy."

"Like?"

"The kids. Their energy. I've done two lots of teaching rounds now and the things kids say…man, they're funny. The way they view the world is refreshing." She poked her fork in his direction. "What about you? Do you love your job? Are you passionate about it?"

"About cars and engines? Can't think of anything else I'd rather be doing. But I wouldn't call it a passion, as such. But I like solving problems, making things work."

"You know what that is? Your white-knight complex, in its career form."

"I don't have a white-knight complex."

"Sure you do. Running around helping people. Riding to the rescue."

It was on the tip of his tongue to tell her she was the only person he'd rescued lately, but at the last minute he decided it might be a little too revealing.

"I think of it more as an adult form of playing with Lego," he said.

"And the people you work for, they're okay?"

Harry helped himself to another slice of garlic bread. "Leo's okay. Loses his cool a little too much for my liking. But he's not the worst boss I've ever had."

"Let me guess—that was your dad, right?" She looked pleased with herself, as though she'd just aced her Psychology 101 exam.

"Actually, Dad was a good boss. Good teacher, too, which was weird, since he just about throttled me when he was teaching me to drive. When it came to work, though, he knew what he was talking about and I listened."

Pippa sat back in her chair. "So why aren't you working for him, then? Why doesn't the sign above the door say Porter and Son instead of Village Motors?"

"You sound like my mum."

"It comes with the territory." She glanced toward Alice, gurgling happily in her bassinet, before nailing him with a look. "You going to answer my question or not?"

"I'm thinking about it."

She huffed out a laugh and planted an elbow on the table. "Thinking about it?"

Pippa leaned toward him, all amused outrage and mock-challenge. Her warm brown eyes were alight with interest, and the wine had put color in her cheeks. He found himself thinking for the millionth time about her cherry-red bra and creamy, full cleavage.

"It's not what I want," he said.

"Your own business?"

"The long hours. The responsibility. Everyone looking to me when things go wrong. Why take on all of that when I can pull down a good wage and go home at the end of the day, put my feet up and forget about everything?"

"You're not ambitious? No big life plan?"

"What more do I need? I've got my own place. I've got a truck and one of the best vintage muscle cars Australia has to offer. There's not a lot of stuff that I want that I can't get."

"You make it sound pretty good."

"But?"

"But nothing. Like I said, you make it sound pretty good."

Pippa was sincere. He sat back in his chair. He hadn't even realized he'd moved toward the edge of his seat until then, the better to counter the argument she hadn't made.

"What's wrong?" she asked. "You look surprised."

"I don't know. Guess I was expecting more resistance."

Definitely he'd been expecting more judgment.

"Because I sounded like your mother before?"

"Because the consensus from the rest of my family seems to be that I'm copping out."

Pippa drained the last of her wine. "You know what? Everyone should just live their lives and let you live yours. You're not hurting anyone. You're happy and healthy and content. What's not to like about any of that? There are plenty of people with six-figure incomes, huge mansions and garages full of cars who can't say the same."

"So teaching's going to do that all for you? Keep you happy and healthy and content?"

She flashed him a rueful smile. "That's a whole different ball of wax."

Pippa started gathering the plates. He stood and took them from her hands, stacking the cutlery and their water glasses on top.

"Why?"

"Because I have Alice. I don't have just me and what I want to consider. My life isn't only mine anymore."

He frowned, even though she hadn't made it sound like a complaint, more as though she was simply stating the facts.

"That sounds pretty grim."

Pippa was folding the place mats, but she stopped and looked at him, a startled expression on her face.

"Does it? I didn't mean for it to. Having Alice, thinking of Alice and what she needs is the best thing that's ever happened to me. It's sort of…I don't know…opened my heart. Made life less about me. And I mean that in a good way. Loving someone and wanting them to be happy is a pretty great mission to have, in my book."

She gave him a small smile before slipping past him to stow the place mats away. He dumped the plates in the sink, her words echoing in his head.

He wasn't sure why, but they made him feel…unsatisfied in some way. Unsettled.

"I'll go get changed. We're plastering and painting today, yes?"

"Yeah. Old clothes."

She laughed. "All my clothes are old."

He dried his hands on a tea towel as she left the room.

Then, because he didn't know what else to do, he ran water into the sink and washed the dishes.

And all the time he thought about Pippa, about the glow she'd gotten in her face and eyes when she talked about her daughter.

She was a special woman. Funny, smart, self-aware, sexy. He liked the way she looked at the world. Liked the way she kept surprising him.

Maybe after he'd finished fixing her ceiling he could swing by and see her every now and then. Have a beer, maybe, catch up. He didn't have any women friends, unless his sisters counted—and he suspected they didn't. Maybe he and Pippa could be friends, Because he was starting to feel as though it would be hard to not have her in his life.

CHAPTER NINE

PIPPA KNELT ON the cold tile in the bathroom to tie the laces on her runners. The two glasses of wine she'd drunk with dinner had worked their way through her system, warming her belly and taking the edge off her anger with Steve. Or maybe it was Harry's easy good humor that had done that.

He'd been so calm and understanding, even when she'd confessed that she'd dumped him in it with his best friend. He could have been angry—very angry—with her. But he wasn't, and he hadn't packed up his stuff and gone home. He'd eaten her dinner and done his best to distract her.

Beneath his rugged, take-no-prisoners exterior was an incredibly decent man with a good heart.

A wave of gratitude washed over her. If only there was some way she could repay him for all his many large and small kindnesses. She stared at the wall, trying to think of something—anything—she could do or buy that would let him know how much she valued his efforts and support.

Maybe she could buy him some new tools when money wasn't such an issue. She'd noticed his screwdriver set was pretty beaten up. Maybe she could save up and get him a new one.

It felt so feeble in the face of his generosity, but it was all she could come up with.

Sighing, she stood in front of the mirror, quickly brushing her hair back into a ponytail. She'd pulled on an old man's shirt she'd bought a while ago and her oldest yoga pants and she finished her ensemble with a scarf tied over her hair to protect it from paint spatter. Not her most attractive look, but tonight was about practicality. Hell, at the moment, her whole life was about practicality.

She set Alice up in the sunroom with the baby monitor once again, then headed for the bedroom. Harry was already up the ladder, a trowel and a bucket of ready-mix plaster in hand. She tilted her head back and watched him smooth a thin coat along the joins between the old and new plaster sheets, impressed by his expertise and trying not to notice the muscles in his chest and arms ripple as he worked.

"For a mechanic, you make a pretty good plasterer."

"Did a few summers on building sites when I was a kid. Picked up a few tricks along the way."

"Is there anything I can do to help?"

"Not right this second." He glanced down at her, quickly returning his attention to the ceiling.

"Do you want something else to drink? A coffee, maybe?" She felt so superfluous, standing around watching him work.

"Coffee would be good, thanks."

She half suspected he'd only said yes to give her something to do, but she headed into the kitchen to put the kettle on. By the time she returned with two mugs, he'd shifted the ladder across the room and was smoothing plaster over the last join.

"That was fast."

"It'll dry fast, too. Thirty minutes and we should be able to sand and get a coat of paint on."

"Here." She held up his coffee, the handle turned toward him so he could grasp it easily.

He glanced down at her as he slid the coffee from her hand. "Thanks."

He frowned as he took a sip of his drink.

"If it's too strong, I can add more milk," she said quickly.

The least she could do was give the man coffee how he liked it.

"The coffee's fine." He flicked another quick look at her before once again focusing on his mug. "But you should probably know I can see right down your top from up here. Might want to do up another button."

Pippa glanced at her shirt. It was old and baggy with several buttons missing and she'd never given a thought to whether it was decent or not when she'd pulled it on. Sure enough, however, she could see lots of décolletage, along with a generous amount of bra.

"Sorry," she mumbled, retreating from the ladder to fumble with the neck of her shirt.

"I wasn't complaining. But I figured you'd probably want to know." He said it casually, as though it was no big deal to him whatsoever.

It probably wasn't, given the amount of breasts and bras he'd seen in his lifetime.

She couldn't help but be aware that this was the second time she'd offered him all-areas access to the goods. Both times he'd been incredibly matter-of-fact about revealing her exposure but it didn't stop her from feeling self-conscious as she double-checked that she was now decent. From now on, she was wearing turtlenecks when he was in the vicinity.

She glanced at him when she turned around. He'd set his mug on top of the ladder and was smoothing plaster across the final corner join. Her gaze slid down his chest and caught on something below his waist. Something pretty substantial and difficult to ignore.

He had a hard-on.

She blinked, but it was still there when she opened her eyes again—a very defined, very impressive bulge in his jeans.

Pippa looked away, her thoughts scattering like birds.

Harry was turned on. Aroused. Hard.

Because he'd seen down her top?

Surely not.

But the more she thought about it, the more it didn't seem that big a stretch. In fact, unless the man had a serious thing for plaster or ladders or DIY in general, there wasn't really any other explanation for what she'd seen.

Her breath caught in her throat as she considered the implications.

Harry wanted her. Pretty badly, if the size of that bulge was anything to go by.

Illicit, indecent excitement licked along her veins. She pressed a hand to her belly, trying to hold back the tide of arousal that washed through her.

Because Harry was a bad bet. Harry was good times and no-strings sex and no tomorrows. Better yet, he was closely connected with the father of her child.

He was the last person she should want.

Didn't stop her from wanting him, though. Hadn't stopped her from noticing his body for the past few weeks, either. Hadn't stopped her from remembering how it had felt when he'd held her, or how he'd smelled, or how firm and hot his chest had been when she'd pried her daughter's hands off him.

Oh, boy.

She stepped backward, recognizing the impulse to-ward recklessness rising inside her. Two years ago, she would have allowed that impulse to take over. She would have thrown caution to the winds and let Harry know in no uncertain terms that the attraction he felt was more than reciprocated.

But she had Alice now. Her life wasn't about im-pulse and whims. Every decision she made these days came with a price.

She would be mad to get involved with Harry. A true glutton for punishment after what had happened with Steve.

Even if Harry was incredibly hot. Even if she could feel herself growing wet and warm as she contemplated what it would be like to be skin-to-skin with so much raw masculinity.

She was a mother now. She was training to be a teacher. Life wasn't about what felt good or right in the moment. Life was about the future. About playing it safe and making smart, good choices.

Her body felt hot beneath her hand. She swallowed and took a deep, calming breath.

She would not sleep with Harry.

The decision felt as final as a door closing. Some of the tension drained out of her body. She smiled faintly.

Phew. Crisis averted.

She felt almost giddy with relief that she'd managed to subvert her worst impulses. It had been close for a minute there, but she'd held out.

Pippa snuck a look at Harry, feeling a little wistful as she eyed his erection again. In another time, in another place, she had no doubt that he would be a wonderful lover. Fun, intense, powerful… But it wasn't going to happen.

"Done." Harry descended the ladder. "We should be ready to sand by eight-thirty." He dumped the trowel and plaster bucket onto the drop sheet, then collected his mug. Lifting it to his mouth, he drained the last of the coffee. Pippa stared at the tanned column of his throat, mesmerized by the uniquely masculine bob of his Adam's apple. He sighed his appreciation as he lowered the mug.

"Good coffee. Thanks." He stepped toward her, offering her the empty mug.

Her gaze slid down his broad chest and flat belly to his crotch.

"Is that for me?" The words slipped out of their own accord, born of too many nights alone and bone-deep curiosity and need.

It had been so long, and she was only human.

Harry's gaze tracked hers to his groin. She held her breath, waiting for him to respond, aware of the pulse of desire between her legs.

A slow smile curled Harry's lips. "This, you mean?"

Pippa watched with dawning horror as he reached into his pocket and drew out a tube of filler.

His smile grew into an outright grin, his eyes dancing with mischief and amusement. "I'm not sure whether to be flattered or intimidated, to be honest," he said, eyeing the tube assessingly.

Pippa opened her mouth to say something to rescue herself but the only sound that came out was a small, choked cough. Heat flamed its way up her chest and into her face.

Harry was watching her, grin still in place, amused and entertained. In a moment of blinding clarity, she saw herself through his eyes—frumpy single-mum

Pippa, down on her luck, a bit quirky and needy in her pill-covered yoga pants and baggy old man's shirt.

A million miles from the kind of woman that would inspire a hard-on the size of a tube of spackle.

God, what had she been thinking? What on earth had made her say something so bold and stupid?

She spun on her heel, aware that retreat would only make her look more foolish but unable to stem the impulse to run and hide. She reached the hall and looked around wildly before bolting into the bathroom. She shut the door with a teeth-rattling slam then dropped onto the edge of the tub.

She was literally sweating with embarrassment. If she checked, she was sure even her toenails would be blushing. This was far, far worse than the incident with her vibrator. Never in a million years did she think she would ever say that, but here she was, redder than Rudolph's nose and desperate to somehow take back her rash, revealing words.

A knock sounded on the door. "Everything okay in there?"

She closed her eyes. Great, now he was worried about her.

She couldn't think of anything to say so she simply sat there, radiating heat and humiliation.

"Pippa?"

"Go away."

There was a short pause, then the door handle turned. Pippa slid along the side of the bath, retreating, as he opened the door.

"Go away. Just…leave me alone a minute."

He studied her intently for a beat. "You were serious."

He sounded surprised. Stunned, almost. It hit her

that if she'd only stood her ground and come up with something smart to say, she could have pulled it off as a joke, because clearly that was the way he'd taken it—until she'd run from the room and hidden out in the bathroom like a ridiculous teenager.

Something else to regret later.

"Five minutes. Give me five minutes," she said miserably.

He frowned, then entered the room fully. She slid farther away, instinctively wanting as much distance between herself and the source of her humiliation as possible, only to overbalance and slip backward into the tub. Her head hit the wall behind the bath with a thunk and she wound up with her ass in the tub and her legs bent over the side. She pressed her palms to her face.

If the world exploded in a ball of fire right this second, she would be grateful and happy. She wanted to die.

"Pippa."

She spoke through her hands. "Harry, for the love of God, please just give me five minutes."

"I thought you were joking. You're always such a smart-ass...."

"I got that. Now can you go?"

"Did you hurt your head?"

She moaned. He wouldn't go. He would stay and be a nice guy and let her down gently.

"Can't you leave me to my misery?"

She heard him move closer, then she felt his hands close around her upper arms.

"Come on." He hauled her upward.

She let him drag her to the edge of the bath, mostly because she didn't have a choice. She dropped her hands into her lap as he stepped back, defeated by his persistence.

"It was a mistake. Can we just forget I ever said anything?" she asked, steeling herself to meet his gaze.

There was no sympathy in his clear gray eyes, however. No amusement, either, or discomfort or unease or any of the other emotions she'd expected. Instead, he was oddly intent as he studied her face.

"It wouldn't work. You know that, right?" he said after a long moment. "Nice as it would be."

It took a second for meaning to sink in. Was he saying what she thought he was saying?

"You've thought about it?" she asked cautiously.

Because no way was she jumping to a conclusion where he was concerned ever again.

"Yeah." There was a wealth of revealing frustration in the single word.

She sat a little straighter. "Oh."

So she wasn't completely deluded, then. There *had* been something happening between them. An energy. An interest.

Harry's expression was rueful. "But like I said, it's a bad idea."

"Because…?"

"You really need me to answer that?"

She didn't. She knew the reasons as well as he did. Alice, Steve, who she was, who he was…

"You're right. It's a stupid idea."

"Not stupid. Complicated. Messy."

"Yeah. I know." She could hear the regret in her own voice.

What the hell—she *was* regretful. For a few seconds there she'd indulged in the fantasy that the sexy, hard-bodied man in front of her could be her lover. It had been heady and incredibly appealing.

But it wasn't going to happen and she needed to accept that.

She met his eyes. "Thanks, anyway."

"What for?"

She shrugged self-consciously. "For the ego boost, I guess."

He quirked an eyebrow. "Your ego needs boosting?"

"Sometimes, yeah. I'm a woman. I've been trained since birth to worry about anything and everything."

His gaze traveled down her body, lingering on her breasts. This time there was no mistaking the very male, very obvious appreciation. "You've got nothing to worry about. Believe me."

She tried to stop herself from smiling and failed. "Thanks, Harry."

She might not be able to have him in her bed, but she would get a lot of mileage out of that look. A lot.

Pippa stood. "Better get back to it, I suppose."

"Yeah."

He followed her into the bedroom and they both considered the ceiling for a beat.

"Think it's dry yet?" she asked.

"Probably needs another ten minutes."

"Right."

He stood beside her, just inches away. It was probably an illusion, but she was sure she could feel his body heat. She stole a peek at his big, tattooed arms. What would it feel like to have him on top of her, his weight bearing down…?

"You want another coffee while we wait?" she asked.

"Sure."

He sounded frustrated. Almost annoyed. She glanced

at him and caught him looking at her. She saw lust and need and desire and frustration in his face.

He wanted her. He really wanted her. Despite all the sensible things he'd just said.

"Harry—"

"Screw it."

He reached for her at the same moment she closed the distance between them. Her breasts hit his chest as his arms closed around her and she tilted her head for his kiss. Harry's mouth found hers unerringly, his tongue sliding into her mouth in a heated rush.

He tasted like desire. She moaned her approval as her body went up in flames. Dear God, it had been so long, and this man knew how to kiss.

His tongue stroked hers sensuously, demandingly, while his hands roved over her back before settling on her backside. He grabbed a cheek in both hands and pulled her toward him. She moaned again when she felt how hard he was.

Definitely not a tube of filler this time.

Pippa gripped his shoulders, pressing her hips against his, tilting her pelvis to find the best fit. He pivoted, somehow moving her at the same time, and suddenly the wall was behind her and his hands were beneath her shirt. He cupped her breasts, his hips holding her against the wall, his thumbs teasing her nipples through the lace of her bra. She slid her hands from his shoulders to his hips, then around to his ass. She lifted a leg and wrapped it around his waist, using her grip on his backside to pull him closer.

For long seconds they kissed and groped each other through their clothes, pulses racing. Pippa could feel how hard he was and the thought of having all that hardness inside her made her weak at the knees.

Then Harry pushed her shirt up and pulled her bra down and lowered his head to her breasts and she lost the ability to think coherently. He didn't just kiss her breasts, he consumed them—tonguing her nipples and drawing them into his mouth and shaping her breasts with his hands. He feasted, eyes tightly shut, utterly obsessed with the task at hand.

She panted and held on to him as her body turned molten with need. She had never been so turned on, so desperate to have a man's weight pressing down on her. She wanted to feel his skin on hers. She wanted to taste him. She wanted to wrap her legs around his hips and invite him into her body.

Hands shaking, she found the stud of his jeans and popped it open. The zip was warm from his body heat and she pulled it down before sliding her hand beneath the elastic of his underwear. His whole body jerked as she wrapped her hands around warm, silken steel. She stroked her hand up and down his shaft, reveling in the thick length of him. Her thumb found his head, gliding over the velvety skin. He shuddered again, then suddenly his hands were at the waistband of her yoga pants and he was pushing them and her panties down her hips. She assisted him by toeing her shoes off and then kicking her clothes away.

She gasped as his hands glided over her naked ass and thighs, big and warm and slightly roughened. He kissed her again as his palm smoothed down her belly and into the curls between her thighs.

"Damn," he groaned when he discovered how wet she was.

She tightened her grip on his erection and tilted her hips forward, craving his touch so badly she ached. He accepted her invitation, sliding a finger inside her.

She sobbed as her body tightened greedily around his invasion.

He felt so good and she needed this so badly.

"Now, Harry," she panted, pushing his jeans down his hips.

He slid a hand from her breasts to help her, freeing himself. She heard the crinkle of foil and realized he'd pulled a condom from his pocket. He handed it to her, his gray gaze heated. She bit down on the side of the packet and tore it open, then sheathed him with trembling hands. The moment he was safe he reached for her backside, lifting her. She wrapped her legs around his hips and reached between them to guide him to her entrance.

He slid inside her, big and hot and long, and she was gone, just like that, her body throbbing around his in a breathtaking climax.

He started to thrust, his body hard with need. She pressed kisses to his neck and shoulder and finally his mouth. He plunged in and out of her, every muscle tense. She gripped his shoulders and inhaled the smell of sex and felt herself climbing again.

"Yes," she panted.

Harry's fingers pressed into her hips and ass as he intensified his efforts. She arched her back and tilted her hips...and then she was there again, his name on her lips as she came and came and came. He lost it, burying himself deep and staying there. She throbbed out the last of her climax as he shuddered into her.

He remained still for seconds afterward, his face buried in her neck. Then he loosened his grip and she unlocked her ankles from around his hips and he withdrew from her. The next thing she knew she was standing on shaky, uncertain legs. She expected Harry to move away, but he remained close, his body still pressing hers against the wall. He turned his head and pressed a kiss to her neck. She felt him exhale on a long, shaky sigh.

"Pippa," he said.

There was a world of regret and wonder in the single word, because what had just happened had been amazing, utterly mind-blowing—and they both knew it had been a stupid mistake.

His hands smoothed down her sides to her thighs, skating over her backside warmly before finally settling on her hips. Only then did he pull away from her, and then just enough to allow him to look into her eyes.

His cheeks were flushed, his eyes bright. His mouth looked slightly swollen from her kisses. She reached up and laid her hand on his cheek, feeling the rasp of stubble against her fingers. She felt dazed and bemused and wholly, utterly satisfied.

A smile tugged at the corners of his mouth, then he lowered his head and kissed her. She felt her body stirring yet again. He broke the kiss and she let him step backward.

"Five seconds," he said, turning away.

She leaned against the wall, eyes closed, as she listened to him walk down the hall to the bathroom. Her whole body was one big satisfied throb, warm and wet and soft.

Until this second, she hadn't realized how much she'd missed sex. The swept-away craziness. The closeness with another person. The raw simplicity of it. And sex with Harry... God, if she'd known how good sex with Harry would be, she'd have ambushed him weeks ago.

She heard the tap run in the bathroom and stirred. Any second now Harry would return and she'd be standing here half-dressed with a blissed-out smile on her face. Quickly she collected her yoga pants and stepped into them. She was tugging her bra back into place when Harry filled the doorway. They looked at each other for a long beat.

"Don't even think about saying you're sorry," she said.

"Last thing on my mind."

She lifted her chin. "What's the first thing?"

His gaze drifted down her body. "That we're kidding ourselves if we pretend that won't happen again."

She grinned, aware of a rush of triumph sweeping through her body. "You're pretty confident."

"And you're hotter than a bike seat in summer, Pippa White." He said it with a dirty, cheeky smile and she laughed. She felt lighter than air, better than she had in months. Maybe tomorrow this would all seem crazy and wrong, but right now it felt right. It felt like it was exactly what she needed.

Every waking moment of her life was devoted to work or study or being a mother. She deserved a few seconds for herself—a little oasis of hedonism that was about her and nothing else.

She wasn't an idiot—she knew there was an unspoken caveat to what Harry was suggesting. This wasn't a relationship in the making. This was about sex and sex alone. Great, earth-moving, body-on-fire sex.

From where she stood right now, it seemed like a pretty good deal.

"I guess it's probably good that you were planning on fixing my bedroom door, then," she said.

Harry's gaze did a slow tour of her body again. "Maybe we should take care of that now."

She laughed. "Maybe we should."

The baby monitor chose that moment to come to

life with Alice's plaintive wail. Harry looked a little startled, as though he'd forgotten she had a child. She turned for the door.

"I won't be a moment."

It took her twenty minutes to change Alice and feed her a bottle. She smiled to herself as the electric sander started up. Trust Harry to just get on with it. He was such a man of action.

Her body grew warm as she relived those few, breathless minutes against the wall. She couldn't quite believe it had happened. That Harry had wanted her as much as she'd wanted him. That it had been so good between them.

Once Alice was asleep she returned to the bedroom. Harry was dusting white plaster off his shoulders and out of his hair.

"Sorry that took so long," she said.

Harry glanced at her. "She okay?"

"Yep. Back to sleep again."

"We're ready to paint in here." He indicated the roof.

It only took a few passes with the roller to cover the patched part of the ceiling, but the fresh white stood out starkly against the old ceiling so Harry insisted on doing the whole thing. Pippa used the ladder to paint the cornice, then they worked together to clear away the building debris. The whole time they worked she was acutely aware of him, of his body, his scent, the way he moved. She always had been, of course, but she'd given up the pretense that she wasn't interested in him the second he'd pushed her against the wall and kissed her.

Half an hour later, they dropped her mattress on top of her bed base. Pippa stepped back and brushed her hands together.

"Done." Although she still needed to vacuum away the remaining plaster dust.

"Yeah. Except for the door and the front lock."

"Right." She tugged on the hem of her shirt and met his gaze. "I was thinking maybe you could do them tomorrow night. I could make you dinner again...."

"Sounds good." She didn't know how he did it, but he managed to imbue the two words with a world of meaning.

"Well. Good," she said. She could feel a pleased, smug little smile tugging at the corners of her mouth.

"I'll get out of your hair now, then," Harry said.

"Okay."

She watched as he collected his things, enjoying the play of muscle and sinew, then followed him to the front door. He exited to the porch and looked at her.

"Tomorrow?" he said.

"Yes. Definitely."

He smiled and she wondered if perhaps she'd sounded a little too fervent. She shrugged. So what? He'd just given her the ride of her life. She wouldn't pretend he hadn't rocked her world.

"Sleep tight, Pippa."

He leaned toward her, surprising her as he dropped a kiss onto her mouth. For some reason she hadn't expected him to kiss her goodbye. Which was a little crazy, since they'd just had wild animal sex against the wall.

Pippa hovered on the doorstep watching him walk to his car until it occurred to her that it might look a little needy. As though she was regretting letting him go.

She gave him a cheery wave and stepped back into the house. She collected Alice from the sunroom and settled her into her crib, then went to the bathroom and shed her clothes. There was a faint suck mark on her right breast, and when she turned she could see five small, pale gray circles near her left hip from where he'd gripped her. She turned on the shower and stepped beneath the water, letting it wash over her.

A slow smile spread across her mouth.

She had a lover.

She had no idea for how long, but it didn't matter. She would enjoy what he had to offer for as long as it was good, and she wouldn't feel bad or guilty about it. She would revel. She would luxuriate. She would make hay while the sun shined.

A less welcome thought intruded: Steve, with his offensive offer and warnings. Her smile faded. He'd predicted this would happen.

Pippa shook off the thought. Steve was not a part of her life—through his choice, not hers. She owed him nothing, and she certainly wouldn't start worrying about what he thought or did. What went on with her and Harry was none of his business.

She lifted her face to the spray and focused instead on tomorrow night. A far more enticing subject.

CHAPTER TEN

HARRY LAY IN his bed, his body still damp from the shower. He couldn't get Pippa out of his head.

The feel of her body beneath his hands. The pale, soft skin of her breasts and inner thighs. The taste of her.

"Man."

He was hard for her again. Unbelievable.

He folded his arms behind his head, thinking about tomorrow night, what he wanted to do to her. Strip her naked, for starters. He wanted to see all of her, wanted to lick and suck and touch every inch of her pale, smooth skin. He would take his time, too, no rushing into things like a bull at a gate the way he had tonight. Not that she'd seemed to mind too much, since she'd climaxed the second he was inside her, but still. A guy had his pride. He wanted to make her feel good. He wanted to make her soft and pliant and slightly dazed again. The look in her eyes afterward had been better than any praise any woman had ever thrown his way.

Great. She's hot. You want to sleep with her again. What about Steve?

He pushed the thought away but it kept circling back to the front of his mind. He'd made a liar out of himself tonight. He'd turned his back on years of friendship because Pippa had looked at him with lust in her eyes and he'd realized that if he wanted to, he could have her.

God, how he'd wanted her. More than he'd thought

possible. But it wasn't just about sex and lust and desire. Pippa was a great person. He liked her—a lot. This wasn't simply a matter of his own libido or being seduced by a soft, sexy body.

Still, he was pretty sure that Steve wouldn't see it that way when he found out.

If he found out.

Harry winced. He had no idea how long this thing with Pippa would last—a week, a month—but the idea of lying to Steve for the duration didn't sit well. The up-front, adult thing would be to let Steve know what was happening and let him deal with it. But it wasn't only about him and Steve, it was about Pippa and Alice, too. Harry didn't want to make her life more difficult than it already was.

As he'd said to her before reason had taken a flying leap out the window, the situation was messy and complicated.

Yet if he had the chance, he wouldn't take back what had happened tonight. That first slide of his body inside hers…

He would never regret having had that experience with her. No matter what.

Harry rolled over and punched his pillow into a better shape. He needed to stop thinking and start sleeping. Whatever was going to happen would happen, whether he worried about it or not.

He fell asleep with thoughts of Pippa still in his mind and woke with a hard-on that only a cold shower could cure. He spent the day at work with one eye on the clock, feeling like a fifteen-year-old eager to meet his girlfriend at the school gate.

Not that Pippa was his girlfriend. She was a woman, for starters. Definitely she was a woman. But the friend part was accurate, he realized. He'd enjoyed every minute he'd spent with her in recent weeks, even when she'd been giving him hell and driving him crazy.

He left work at five on the dot and went home to shower and shave. Last night he'd left whisker burn on her breasts. Tonight he wanted to give her nothing but pleasure.

He was showered and dressed again by five-thirty. Way too early to head over to Pippa's place. She'd think he was desperate to see her again.

He distracted himself by dropping in on his sister, Mel. She buzzed him through the automatic gates at the entrance to the Summerlea estate and he parked out the front of the rambling Edwardian farmhouse that she'd restored with her husband over the past two years. Her dark curly hair bounced around her shoulders as she descended the porch steps to greet him.

"Hello. This is a surprise."

She kissed his cheek and smiled. She did that a lot these days. Harry figured it was due to Flynn, which was why he would do pretty much anything under the sun for the man.

"I was driving past."

"You drive past all the time."

"If you want me to go…" He turned toward his car.

She laughed. "Don't be an idiot. You want a Coke? I was about to walk down to the orchard, see how the apples are going. We're fighting an ongoing battle with the birds. Can you believe those sneaky Rosellas burrow in under the nets and then just stay under there and pig out?"

"They're a protected species. You know that, right?"

"Lucky for them, that's all I can say."

He followed her to the kitchen and accepted a drink.

Talking easily, they left the house and walked into the garden. The Summerlea estate encompassed six acres of beautifully laid-out gardens, originally created by esteemed landscape designer Edna Walling more than fifty years ago. Over the past two years Flynn and Mel had brought it back to life, renewing and reimagining the design.

"Looking good," Harry said as they passed the beautifully constructed wooden rose arbors he'd helped install recently.

"It is, isn't it?"

She sounded smugly satisfied and he gave her a fond look. He'd always been closer to her than to Justine, who took the whole older sibling thing a little too much to heart. Mel had always been more interested in being his friend than the boss of him, and he valued her opinion.

"I've got a bit of a situation on my hands," he heard himself say.

"Yeah? What's up?"

He hadn't come here intending to confide in her—not intentionally, anyway—but clearly some part of his brain wanted another perspective on what was happening with Pippa.

"Did you ever meet Steve's ex, Pippa White?"

"She's the one who fell pregnant, yes? I think I met her at the pub one night. Dark hair? Glasses?"

"I've been helping her out lately. A few repairs around the place she's renting. Anyway, last night…" He paused, unsure how much to reveal.

Mel rolled her eyes. "Don't bother trying to find a delicate way to phrase it. I can imagine what happened. You're such a dog, Harry."

She nudged him with her shoulder, breaking his stride and making him lurch to the side. Like himself, she'd inherited the Porter shoulders and tall build and could pack some punch when she put her mind to it.

"It's not like that. Pippa is... It's not like that."

"Okay. If you say so." Mel shot him an appraising look. "How's Steve feel about all this?"

Harry frowned at the Coke in his hand. The bottle had grown slippery with condensation and he moved his thumb across the slick surface.

"He's not happy. He doesn't want anything to do with Pippa or Alice, but he doesn't want me near her, either."

"Sounds messy. Steve's got a shitty temper."

Steve had been a familiar face at the Porter house over the years and Mel knew him—and his temper—well.

"Yeah."

"Have you tried talking to him?"

Harry remembered how belligerent his friend had been last time he'd seen him. "I'm not sure that will work."

They'd reached the orchard and Mel stopped and regarded him solemnly. "You've been friends with Steve for more than fifteen years."

"I know."

"Lots of other women in the world, Harry."

The words were out his mouth before he could stop them. "Not like Pippa."

His sister looked surprised. "You like her."

He gave her a look. He'd slept with Pippa. Of course he liked her.

"I don't mean sexually. I mean you *like* her. Don't you?" Mel watched him very intently.

He shrugged, suddenly self-conscious. "I'm just looking for a way to sort this out without someone getting punched in the face."

Mel didn't say anything for a beat as she studied his face. "I only met her that one time, but she seemed nice. But if you're going to do this, Harry, you have to be serious. She's got a kid."

He frowned. "I'm not 'doing' anything apart from helping her out and spending some time with her."

"Does she know that?"

His sister sounded disapproving, which was typical. In his experience, women always circled the wagons when it came to certain subjects.

"She knows me."

Mel nodded. "Good. Because you're too charming for your own good sometimes. You big lug." She glanced around the orchard, her narrowed gaze scanning the net-shrouded trees. "Aha! Look at that—they've pulled up the net again. Little buggers."

She strode away to pull up one of the tent pegs that had been placed in the ground to secure the nets, re-fixing the net once again to protect the tree. Harry watched her patrol the rest of the orchard, a scowl on his face.

He hadn't laid it out in black and white for Pippa last night, but he'd been pretty sure she understood that whatever was happening between them was about great sex and a bit of fun, no strings, no stress. He didn't want to hurt her, but he wasn't about to kid himself, either— when it came to long-term, he was a bad bet. He didn't do domesticity, and he figured it was pretty unlikely he was about to start now, even if he did like Pippa more than he could remember liking anyone in a long time.

"Quit looking so worried, Harry. It's called growing up," Mel said as she rejoined him. "Every man meets his match eventually."

He gave her a sardonic look. "Keep hoping, and I'll keep living my life my way."

Mel laughed and reached for his Coke, taking a swig before handing the bottle to him. "Let me know when you're ready for us to meet her."

He made a rude noise.

She laughed again. "Oh, this will be fun."

"You done here? I need to get going."

"Sure. I've made you squirm enough."

They turned toward the house.

"Whatever happens, you should sort things with Steve," she said after a short beat of silence. "You guys have been mates too long to let this come between you."

"Yeah."

The easiest thing would be to simply walk away from Pippa, but Harry suspected that at least half of Steve's anger was because Harry had called him on his poor behavior. If Harry backed off from Pippa and turned a blind eye to Steve's crappy decisions, no doubt their friendship would be just dandy.

Harry scowled at the graveled walkway. He'd never considered himself a moralist before, but apparently even he had standards. Now he knew Steve was short-changing Pippa, he couldn't simply turn a blind eye to it. Couldn't stomach it.

As for the walking-away-from-Pippa part…

Mel's hand landed warmly on his shoulder and he realized they were standing in front of the house.

"You know, I almost feel sorry for you."

He let out a frustrated sigh. Why did women see romance everywhere?

"Quit trying to make this into something it isn't."

She held up both hands. "You're the one striding around like Heathcliff, scowling at rocks and whatnot."

"And women wonder why men don't talk about their feelings more."

Mel smiled and punched his arm. "Keep me posted."

"As if."

Harry walked to his car. Mel climbed the steps to the porch and stood watching him reverse out of the drive. She waved goodbye as he pulled into the street. He gave the horn a quick blast and took off.

Five minutes later he parked in Pippa's driveway. He didn't get out of the car immediately. Instead, he sat and thought very deliberately about what he was about to do: go inside and get down and dirty with Pippa again.

If he was going to call a halt to this, now was the time. He could go in, rehang her door, fix her front door lock and keep his hands firmly to himself. It wouldn't fix things with Steve in and of itself, but it would go a long way toward calming things down. Maybe once he was out of the picture, Steve would come to his senses regarding child support for Alice.

Maybe.

And it would definitely ensure that there were no crossed wires with Pippa regarding what had happened between them.

Harry got out of the car and climbed the three steps to the front door. He knocked and rubbed his suddenly-damp palms on the thighs of his jeans. Footsteps sounded inside the house.

Pippa answered the door, hair a damp tangle down her back, face flushed from the shower. She was wearing a black-and-white polka-dot drop waist dress that looked as though it was made from silk and her feet were bare, her toenails painted a pale pink. Her smile was both chagrined and a little apologetic.

"Sorry. Alice just threw up everywhere and I'm running late again. But I've got some nibbles to keep you going until dinner."

He breathed in vanilla-scented perfume and watched as she pushed her glasses back to the bridge of her nose. The need to shove her against the wall and kiss the smile off her lips swept over him. She looked so soft and warm and friendly and sexy, he just wanted to get her naked and make them both a little crazy all over again.

Harry stepped over the threshold and reached for her, aware that in doing so he was choosing the more difficult, complicated path, opening himself up to a world of potential drama, misunderstanding and recrimination.

Funny thing was, it didn't feel as though it was a choice, not when Pippa was standing there, ready to be kissed. More like an imperative, as undeniable as the need to breathe.

And he was in no mood to deny anyone anything.

PIPPA STARTED A little as Harry's big, warm hands closed over her shoulders.

"Wha—" she said, then her back was against the wall and Harry's mouth was covering hers.

He kissed her deeply, his tongue by turns coaxing and demanding, his hands roving from her breasts to her hips to her backside and back again. Her body instantly became more liquid than solid. She had to concentrate on staying upright as her knees started to shake.

This man… This man was a master of the art of kissing.

She was ready to slide to the floor by the time he lifted his head and looked into her eyes.

"Where's Alice?"

"In bed, but not asleep yet."

"But you've got a baby monitor, right?"

"Yes."

"Good."

He wove his fingers with hers and towed her into her bedroom. She gave a passing thought to the frittata in the oven. Maybe she should go turn down the heat....

Harry let go of her hand to haul his T-shirt over his head. Her mouth went dry as she stared at his bare chest. Rational thought evaporated as he popped the stud on his jeans, his eyes never leaving hers.

She hadn't exactly led a sheltered life, but she had never had a man look at her or kiss her or touch her the way Harry did all those things. It was intoxicating, heady and such a huge turn-on...

He shucked his jeans and underwear in one smooth, decisive move. Her gaze fell to his erection, bold and proud against his belly. Her sex tightened instinctively as she remembered what it had felt like to have him inside her.

And it was about to happen again.

Belatedly she realized that he was naked and she still fully clothed, mostly because she'd been standing there like a dodo, gawking at him as he undressed. She reached for the zip on the side of her dress, dragging it down with what could only be described as indecent haste. She was pretty sure she'd never wanted to be naked as much as she wanted to be naked right this second. She wrenched the dress over her head and reached for the clasp at the back of her bra.

"Whoa, whoa, whoa," Harry said, holding up a staying hand. "Slow down a little."

She stared at him. "You're the one who's naked already."

"Yeah, but I don't look like you."

The admiration in his tone sent her self-esteem soaring. Pippa glanced down at her best underwear, dark green silk with bright pink trim.

"You like this?"

"My favorite part of Christmas is unwrapping the presents."

He tucked a finger into the waistband of her panties, encouraging her forward. She stepped into his embrace, only to find herself falling toward the bed. She barely had time to bounce before he was crawling on top of her, grinning like an idiot.

"Very smooth," she said drily.

"Wait till you see my next move." He ducked his head and used his teeth to graze the curve of her breast along the edge of her bra cup. She shivered, running her hands across the firm muscles of his shoulders. He caught the lacy edge of the cup in his teeth and dragged it down. Then his mouth was closing over her nipple and she was doing her best not to come on the spot.

Maybe it was because it had been so long. Maybe it was because he was so good. Maybe it was something about her and him together—whatever it was, one touch from this man was enough to make her breathless and mindless.

She let her head fall back against the mattress, giving herself up to his touch.

"You have very sexy breasts, Pippa," he said after a few minutes, his breath warm against her skin.

"Th-thanks," she panted. Her hands were clamped to his shoulders as she hung on for dear life.

He lifted his head and grinned at her. "How you holding up? Doing okay?"

She didn't even try to pretend she wasn't a warm, gooey mess. "Don't gloat, it doesn't suit you."

Harry pressed his smile into her cleavage. She shuddered again as he started to kiss his way across her rib cage. When he went farther south, her heart started racing with excitement. Deep in her secret, dirty, dark heart, she'd always imagined this—Harry, between her thighs, a knowing glint in his eyes.

She held her breath as he circled his tongue around her belly button, her hips lifting involuntarily as she encouraged him lower. She felt him smile against her skin. She fisted her right hand and thumped him on the shoulder.

"Smugness is also unattractive."

He didn't say anything, simply slid lower, gripping the elastic of her panties in his teeth. She moaned as he inched her panties down, licking the exposed skin between her hip bones. Her belly muscles quivered as he pulled her panties lower again, his breath feathering through her pubic hair.

"God," she hissed, her whole body trembling with anticipation.

He glanced up at her, his gray eyes full of smutty intent. "I can stop now if it's too much."

"Stop now and I'll kill you."

He laughed. She lifted her hips as he tugged her panties down her legs. He smoothed his hands up her thighs, pushing them wide. She bit her lip, waiting.

"So pink and pretty," he murmured.

He lowered his head. She lost track of time after that. There was only the wet, firm warmth of his mouth between her thighs, a delicious, slippery friction that made her forget how to breathe and think and speak. He slid his hands beneath her hips, holding her in place as he tortured her.

"Harry, please," she begged, twisting in his grip.

She wasn't even sure what she was asking for, but

he knew. He slid a finger inside her, then another. She arched off the bed, her climax rippling through her. For long seconds he kept her at her peak, his tongue and mouth deft, subtle and knowing.

Then she collapsed back onto the bed, limp and sated and dazed.

Harry kissed her thighs, then her belly, working his way back up her body. She could barely lift her head as he reached her face. He was smiling again when he kissed her mouth.

"Still breathing?"

"Barely."

"Roll onto your side."

She felt his erection against her backside as he tucked in behind her. She waited for him to find his own satisfaction, but he seemed more interested in her belly and breasts, smoothing his hands across skin.

"You feel so good," he murmured near her ear. "So soft."

Even though she'd just climaxed she was painfully aware of his erection, pressed against the curve of her ass. He felt hard and hot and she kept remembering what it had been like to have him stretching her, filling her. Almost without being conscious of it she pressed her backside into the cradle of his hips. He continued smoothing his hands over her breasts, apparently oblivious to her invitation.

"Harry…"

"Shh."

He slid his hand between her legs, stroking her with two fingers. She could feel how wet she was, could feel, too, that he liked that because his hard-on surged against her. He pushed a knee between her thighs, encouraging her to open to him more.

It struck her then that he was determined to please her, that her pleasure turned him on. The knowledge heightened her sensation, bringing every brush of his fingers into tight focus.

Pippa was ready to roll over and take what he wasn't giving her when she heard the telltale crinkle of a condom being opened. He moved away for a second. When he came back he surged inside her in one smooth, slick stroke.

She sighed her relief, clenching her hands in the sheets as he started to move.

At last. Finally. Thank God.

Neither of them spoke for a few minutes, the only sound their breathing, the susurrus of their bodies against the sheets and the wet sound of him moving inside her. He felt so good, so big and hard... And she was so ready for him. Every stroke of his body inside hers brought her closer to completion, a gentle, gradual build.

"Yes, yes," she whispered, arching into his thrusts.

She could feel her climax bearing down on her. So close. Harry slid a hand over her hip and between her thighs. She bucked against him as he found her, and then she was gone. Utterly gone.

She'd barely come back down to earth when she felt him tense. His hips ground against her backside as he found his release. Then he relaxed. They lay side by side, sweaty and breathless.

"Open your eyes," Harry said after a few beats.

She did so, only to find his face inches from hers.

"I love the look in your eyes after you come." He sounded satisfied, very pleased with himself, but she figured he'd earned it.

And then some.

And all she'd done was cook him dinner.

"The frittata!"

She bolted upright, scrambling toward the edge of the bed. She was about to slide off when he grabbed her ankle.

"Hey!" she said.

"The frittata can wait."

"It's probably a burnt crisp by now."

"Perfect." He tugged on her ankle, trying to lure her back to his side.

She laughed, delighted and flattered and silly over the idea that he wanted her again so soon.

"A compromise—I'll turn the oven off then come right back."

He released her ankle. "Don't make me come get you."

There was something in his eyes, a primitive possessiveness that made her almost want to test his threat. She grabbed her silk robe off the hook on the wall and shrugged into it as she slipped from the room. The silk felt cool against her heated body as she made her way to the kitchen.

By some miracle, the frittata was merely very golden instead of black and crispy. She pulled it out and left it to cool on the stovetop. She was about to head back to the bedroom when Alice began to cry.

Tightening the sash on her robe, she went to check on her daughter. Face red, eyes filled with tears, Alice howled out her misery, arms flailing against the coverlet.

"It's okay, Ali bear, Mummy's here." She lifted Alice into her arms, tucking her against her body.

Alice continued to sob as Pippa rocked her gently. She checked Alice's diaper—dry—and rocked her back and forth. Alice continued to cry. Pippa smoothed a hand over her daughter's head and made soothing noises. She glanced at the doorway, wondering what Harry was thinking.

Probably nothing good. Or nothing she'd want to know about, anyway. He was used to girls who partied all night, not women who stayed up trying to coax a teething baby to sleep.

She pictured him on the other side of the wall, sweating bullets and wondering how quickly he could make his excuses and head for the hills.

She grimaced, aware of the push-pull of almost-embarrassment versus indignant defiance within herself. Like most women, she wanted to be seen as sexy and desirable, one of the reasons Harry's intense, focused lovemaking had struck such a deep chord within her, and a crying baby was pretty much the opposite of sexy. But there were also the realities of life to consider, and the reality of her life was that she was a mother. She couldn't disappear Alice conveniently when it suited her. Alice was an integral part of her world. She cried. She demanded attention. She needed feeding and petting and playtime. Alice was utterly dependent on Pippa, and if listening to her daughter cry made Harry break out in hives and want to shimmy out the window on a rope made of sheets…well, this was going to be the shortest-lived inappropriate affair in the history of the world.

Which was probably a good thing, when it came right down to it.

"Anything I can do?"

She whipped her head around. Harry stood in the doorway wearing nothing but jeans and a concerned expression. Her gaze scanned his chest before dropping to his flat belly. In the back of her brain, a part of her punched the air and hooted with triumph that this hot, sexy, built man had just been in her bed.

"I might try a bottle. Sometimes that settles her. She's just started teething...."

"Okay." He glanced around the nursery as though looking for something he could physically move or fix.

She smiled. "Thanks for asking, though."

He lifted a shoulder, brushing off her gratitude as he always did. "Have you got a bottle made up already? Can I stick it in the microwave or anything?"

"I'll have to mix some formula." She eyed him assessingly, trying to work out if he was simply being polite or if he was sincere with his offer to help. She decided to take him at his word. "I could talk you through doing it if you were up for it...?"

That way she wouldn't have to put Alice down, something she hated to do when her daughter was so distressed.

"Sure. Figure it can't be harder than overhauling a fuel injector rail."

She watched him carefully, but there was no sign of twitchiness or discomfort. Apparently he wasn't about to grab his car keys and make a run for it, after all.

"Well, okay."

He followed her into the kitchen and she talked him through taking a bottle from the sterilizer and mixing the formula. She had a strange out-of-body moment as she watched him shake the bottle. This was Harry, after all. Mr. Sexy, Mr. Footloose. Standing in her kitchen, mixing formula bare-chested and barefoot.

If I wake up right now and find out the past two days have been a dream, I am going to be really pissed.

The thought made her smile. No way could she have

dreamed what had just happened in her bedroom. Her imagination wasn't that good.

As for Harry making up Alice's bottle... It simply wouldn't have ever occurred to her to put the two things together, not even in her subconscious.

Harry screwed the top on the bottle. "Now what?"

"We sit it in some hot water for fifteen minutes so it can warm up."

"Don't know if you've read about this crazy new invention called the microwave..."

"Nice in theory, in practice a big no-no. Lots of babies with mouth and throat burns."

"Okay. No microwave. Got it."

She watched as he sat the bottle in a saucepan full of hot tap water.

"The world's a minefield once you have a baby. Every corner hides a peril," she said.

"No kidding."

Alice was still grizzling, grasping at the front of Pippa's gown sporadically and occasionally hiccupping.

"Must kill her not being able to tell you what's wrong," Harry said.

He moved closer so he could peer into Alice's face, his eyes soft with sympathy. Pippa's gaze dropped to the inky blackness of his tattoo, tracing the lines across his shoulder and down on to his broad chest. She wondered how long it had taken and if it had hurt. And she wondered which of his many tattoos had been his first, and if he regretted them at all.

She couldn't imagine him without them, they were such an essential part of who he was, but there was no denying that a lot of people must look at him and see nothing but a lot of tattooed muscle. They'd never know how funny and smart he was, how kind. How gentle he could be. How playful.

Harry's arm brushed her sleeve and he glanced at her. He stood so close she could see the tiny stars of darker gray radiating from his pupils and the shadow of tomorrow's beard beneath his skin. She had an almost irresistible urge to lean forward and press her lips to his cheek, a physical expression of the sudden upswell of affection she felt for him. She resisted—barely— but she couldn't stop the impulsive words that spilled from her lips.

"I'm really glad you pulled over to help me the other week."

Harry didn't move a muscle, but something shifted in his eyes. After a few seconds he put some distance between them, circling back behind the kitchen counter to check on Alice's bottle.

"How do we know when this thing is ready?"

"You test it on the skin inside your wrist. It should feel warm, but not hot."

He took the bottle from the water and shook a few drops onto the inside of his wrist. He frowned, then shook his head.

"I have no idea if that's even close to being right."

He passed her the bottle and she managed to juggle both it and Alice enough to sprinkle a few drops on her wrist.

"It's perfect. Thanks."

She slipped the teat into Alice's mouth and felt her daughter's small body slowly relax as she gave her attention to the bottle. Harry crossed to the sink and tipped the water from the saucepan down the drain. He was frowning when he turned to face her.

"I should go see to that door."

"If you give me ten minutes, I'll be able to help you. She's worn herself out so much she's already falling asleep."

"It's not really a two-person job, but thanks."

He left the room. Pippa stared at her daughter's face and tried to understand what had just happened. One minute they'd been fine, then all of a sudden he'd gone cold on her.

She thought back over their conversation, remembering the way his eyes had grown distant when she'd said she was glad he'd pulled over to help her.

Suddenly she got it. She pressed her lips together and stewed on her conclusion for as long as it took Alice to finish half the bottle and slip into sleep. She walked carefully to Alice's bedroom and settled her, then she went to find Harry.

CHAPTER ELEVEN

HE WAS PRESSING some kind of foul-smelling pink putty into her bedroom door frame with a plastic spatula.

"What's that?" she asked, momentarily diverted.

"Builder's filler. The door frame is so damaged there's nothing to screw the hinges back into. This stuff will set in about five minutes and I can redrill the holes."

She nodded, then fixed her gaze on his. Very directly, because there was no other way to do this.

"What I said before, about being glad you stopped to help me—it didn't mean anything apart from the fact that I was glad you stopped. Okay?"

His gaze shifted to her briefly before returning to the door frame. "Okay."

He wore his poker face and she couldn't tell what was going on in his head.

"I'm not an idiot, Harry. I know what this is. I'm not making room for your clothes in my closet, if that's what you're worried about."

He looked at the smelly pink putty on the end of the spatula. "Good. Because I'm a bad bet as far as any-thing else goes."

Something inside her recoiled as he fed her the same line she was sure he'd used dozens of times before. Steve's words echoed in her mind. *You think you're going to be different from all the other girls he's screwed and left behind?* Not for a second had she ever believed that this thing between her and Harry had the possibility of becoming anything more than what it was—hot sex and a bit of fun—but the notion that she was simply yet another woman whose expectations Harry felt he had to manage stuck in her craw.

In that one respect she *did* want to be different from Harry's other women. She wanted him to respect her enough to be honest with her. She didn't want the easy line or pat response.

"Harry, on what planet do you think any rational woman would think that you're a *good* bet? You change women like you change socks. Your life is one big adventure playground. You said it yourself—you want an easy, no-stress, no-muss, no-fuss life. You've never said anything other than that, and I got the message, believe me. I let you into my bed with my eyes wide open, so don't go getting wiggy on me because I said something nice to you. In case you hadn't noticed, I *like* you. I enjoy spending time with you—hence the fact that I was recently horizontal with you, breathing hard and making funny noises. But none of those things mean I have designs on your prized bachelor status. Not unlike yourself, I am able to separate sex and love and romance and friendship. Okay?"

"Okay."

He appeared relieved. Surprise, surprise. Despite what she'd said to him, it would be easy to be offended. But she refused to be. She had no illusions where he was concerned, and he'd never made her any promises—except, perhaps, the promise of a good time.

Pippa checked the sash on her robe and flicked her hair over her shoulder. "Good. We're all sorted, then. Do you want some dinner while that stinky stuff sets?"

"Sure."

They ate standing at the kitchen counter. There was still a faint air of constraint between them and Pippa didn't know how to relieve it. She snuck glances at him from beneath her eyelashes, studying his face, his body, wondering what he was thinking.

Even though they'd both agreed they were on the same page, there was the very real possibility that by being so frank and forcing a confrontation she had killed the buzz between them.

Damn, but it would be a shame if the best sex of her life was over before it had really started.

"Relax, Pippa," Harry said after a few minutes.

She peeked at him.

"I can practically hear your brain whirring," he said.

There was no good answer to that, so she didn't say anything. He slipped her almost-empty plate from her hand, then plucked the fork from the other. She watched as he placed them both on the counter before moving to stand in front of her.

She lifted her chin, meeting his gaze. He lowered his head and kissed her, the fingertips of one hand touching the curve of her jaw. He stood close enough that she could feel the heat of his body through the silk of her gown. She pulled him closer, tilting her hips into his. He was hard already, his arousal a firm pressure against her belly.

He tugged on the sash of her robe, pushing it off her shoulders. She let her head drop back as he kissed his way down her neck to her breasts. Her nipples were already hard for him, begging for his attention. Warmth pooled between her thighs as he drew a nipple into his mouth.

Amazing how quickly he could turn her on. Amazing, too, how good he felt beneath her hands. She ran her palms across his chest, teasing his flat, male nipples with her thumbs, raking her nails down his belly. She slid a hand into the front pocket of his jeans, pleased to find the small square of a condom beneath her fingers.

She pulled it free and made short work of his fly. Wordless, he lifted her, placing her on the edge of the counter. She sheathed him and guided him to her, wrapping a leg around his hips as he slid inside her.

She braced her arms behind her on the counter as he drove into her—long, slick, needful strokes. His gaze roved her body, from breast to breast, down her belly, until he was watching himself slide in and out of her body. The avid intensity of his gaze thrilled her and she dropped her gaze, too. The sight of him moving in her body lit something inside her. His tattooed chest, the stud in his ear, the hardness of his body, the length of him filling her...

She gripped his shoulder, needing the anchor as her climax hit. She closed her eyes and let it roll over her. *So good.*

Harry became more frantic, less controlled as he pumped into her. She opened her eyes and watched his face and body tighten as he approached his own climax. She wrapped her other leg around him and locked her ankles behind his back, lifting her hips in time with his thrusts.

"Pippa..." he groaned.

He drove himself deeply inside her and stayed there, veins showing in his neck as he closed his eyes and got swept away. She watched him ride out his climax, loving that she'd given him so much pleasure.

He opened his eyes and looked at her. His gaze was still cloudy with desire, his face soft with satisfaction.

For the second time tonight she was hit with the urge to press an affectionate kiss to his cheek or lips or chest. He'd given so much to her. But she knew better than to do that, especially after the conversation they'd just had.

Instead, she slid off the counter and pulled her robe across her body again.

"I suppose you want dessert now."

He smiled, as she'd hoped he would.

"Thought I just had it."

"Well, you thought wrong, mister, because I have chocolate and raspberry brownies."

She crossed to the fridge.

"I'll go check on the door frame, see if the putty is dry yet."

She watched over her shoulder as he left the room. Then and only then did she press her forehead against the cool white metal of the fridge door.

She'd talked a good talk, so good she'd almost convinced herself, but the truth was that being with Harry, making love with Harry, spending time with Harry was something she could get used to very easily.

Which would be a big mistake. Really, really huge.

For a moment she wondered if she was fooling herself, entering into a no-strings fling with him. She'd had her fair share of lovers and a handful of one-night stands over the years, but what she had going on with Harry felt like a new thing, entirely different from either the serious or the casual relationships of her past.

It felt…addictive. Compelling. Magnetic.

She pushed away from the fridge, shaking the thought off. She'd just outlined to Harry exactly where she stood regarding what was happening between them. She had no illusions—in a week or two or three, she and Harry would be parting ways. Only a very foolish woman would let herself lose sight of that fact.

IT WAS NEARLY MIDNIGHT when Harry left Pippa's place. He'd fixed her bedroom door before moving on to her front door lock. Then he'd spent fifteen minutes in the shower coaxing her to a climax again with his hands and mouth.

He smiled to himself as he hefted his toolbox into the back of his truck. Three times in one night. He hadn't been this horny since he was a kid.

But there was something about Pippa's soft, pale skin and lush breasts... And the noises she made when she came, soft, needy and desperate... And the way she walked and talked and laughed...

He glanced toward the house. He could see a Pippa-shaped shadow moving behind the curtain in her bedroom. He recalled what she'd said to him tonight. She had been very clear about what they were about. Her words—very straightforward and up-front—had wiped away any misgivings he had about continuing to see her. As long as they were both on the same page, there was nothing to stop them from having a good time together.

He hadn't been out with a single mother before—he wasn't in the business of raising expectations. He'd be lying if he said it hadn't been a shock when Alice started crying tonight. From the moment he had set eyes on Pippa this evening, he'd been so intent on getting her into bed that he'd forgotten everything else. Alice's cries had brought him back to reality, quick smart. Lying on Pippa's bed listening to Alice's screams, he'd had visions of the night becoming one big cry-fest, with Pippa pacing and feeding the baby bottles and whatever else mothers did to comfort their babies while any chance he had of getting her naked again evaporated into thin air.

Then a strange thing had happened. Alice's crying had changed, kicking up a note, and he'd heard the raw misery in her voice and her very real distress. She'd sounded so lost. So inconsolable.

Without really thinking about it, he'd pulled on his jeans and gone to see if he could help. Not exactly the way he'd imagined the evening panning out, but not the end of the world, either.

Surprisingly.

Harry started his truck and reversed into the street. He was about to drive off when he saw a set of headlights flick on a few houses down. An engine started, a robust V8. It was dark, but he was pretty sure he could make out the shape of a high, square truck cabin.

Jaw set, he headed for home. The truck fell in behind him. Harry pulled into his driveway five minutes later, the truck still on his tail. He braced himself for a fight as he exited his own truck, walking to the head of his driveway and waiting for Steve to pull up. He didn't. Instead, he cruised past at speed, engine roaring.

It was impossible to see inside the cabin in the dark but Harry didn't need to—he could feel his friend staring at him as he passed.

The truck turned the corner and the sound of the engine faded into the distance.

How long had Steve been sitting out front of Pippa's place? All night?

Harry thought back to the silhouette he'd seen in Pippa's bedroom as he was leaving. While not explicit, it had been revealing enough. How much had Steve seen tonight? Enough to know that Harry was no longer simply helping out around the house?

Guilt bit at him. He tried to shrug it off but it wouldn't go away. Mel had told him to settle things with Steve, and she was right. They needed to clear the air. Say whatever needed to be said. The last thing Pippa needed was an angry ex loitering outside her house and Harry didn't want to burn a friendship that had meant a lot over the years.

He rubbed his forehead. He'd known this would be messy going in, but he'd still shoved Pippa against the wall and kissed her last night, and he'd done it again tonight.

It wouldn't be the last time, either. Maybe it made him a selfish asshole and a bad mate, but he couldn't stay away from her.

For some reason, his sister's words echoed in his head. *Every man meets his match eventually.*

He made a rude noise and walked toward the house. His sister was deluded. Just because she was happily settled with Flynn didn't mean that Harry was about to succumb to the lures of coupledom. He could still remember how he'd felt when he'd been living with Debbie. As though he was suffocating. As though his world was shrinking. He never wanted to feel that constrained again.

Mel didn't seem constrained by Flynn, though, and if anyone had reason to fear commitment, it was his sister. Her marriage had been unhappy, bordering on abusive, something he'd only found out after the divorce papers were signed. If anything, Mel had blossomed since Flynn came into her life. She'd shaken off the past and embraced the world—and herself—again.

Maybe, if the right person came along and a man was at the right stage in his life, the white picket-fence dream wouldn't be such a nightmare. Maybe.

Harry winced, imagining how triumphant his sisters would be if they could hear his thoughts. They'd think their constant drip-feed of monogamy-pushing had finally started to bear fruit.

There was something sitting on the doorstep when he reached the porch. He couldn't make it out in the dark. He touched the screen on his phone to bring it to life and aimed it at the object. The cold blue light reflected off the shiny gold of a football trophy. He crouched and picked it up. He had one just like it inside somewhere, a souvenir from 1996 when the Frankston Rovers had won the grand final. Steve had played full-forward that season, Harry ruck-rover. The parties had lasted all weekend and they'd felt like kings for months afterward.

Harry stared at the trophy. He needed to talk to Steve. Properly this time. Calmly.

His gut told him it wouldn't be pretty, but he had to try.

Shoulders tense, he let himself into the house.

PIPPA WOKE IN sheets that smelled of sex and Harry. Memories from last night flashed across her mind as she lay in the early-morning light.

She was thirty-one years old, but she'd never had a man so hot for her that they'd made love three times in one night. It was heady, seductive stuff.

But it wasn't only memories of Harry's attentiveness and passion in the bedroom that revisited her. She recalled the way he'd offered to help settle Alice, and the sympathetic warmth in his eyes as he'd watched Alice in Pippa's arms. She thought about the way he'd tugged her robe across her body and tied the sash for her before she'd walked him to the door to say goodbye.

Be very careful, madam.

She deliberately called to mind the conversation they'd had about where they both stood and what they both wanted. None of that had changed overnight.

She threw back the covers. She had a busy day ahead. A full eight hours at the gallery, then a night of watching Alice and Becca's boy, Aaron, while Becca worked, her part of their reciprocal child-minding arrangement. She didn't have time to lie about second-guessing herself.

Pippa showered, dressed and ate breakfast in the gaps between changing Alice and dressing her and preparing her bottle. Predictably, her thoughts drifted to Harry as she started a load of washing before dashing out the door.

She had no idea when she would see him again. He'd finished repairing her ceiling and the other minor tasks he'd wanted to take on so they were officially all out of excuses for him to visit. Any future interactions would be because they wanted to see each other, pure and simple. Yet he hadn't made any reference to the future before he left, and neither had she.

It was possible she wouldn't hear from him for a while. She had no idea what his social life was like. For all she knew, he might have parties lined up for the next two months. Women, too.

She stilled in the middle of putting detergent into the dispenser, a dart of pure, possessive jealousy shooting through her at the thought of Harry with another woman.

Nowhere in their conversation last night had they covered other people. He'd made it clear he wasn't looking for a relationship. She'd told him that was more than obvious and that neither was she. She hadn't thought to

ask if their short-term, just-for-fun-and-orgasms fling
was to be exclusive for its duration.

Probably she should have, because the idea of being
one of many women that Harry serviced on a casual
basis made the gorge rise in her throat. She wasn't stupid, she knew the man had a past. Hell, she had a past,
too—probably not as prolific and high-rotation as his,
but she was no nun. No amount of experience would
ever reconcile her to sharing her lover like a bicycle in
a public lending scheme.

Pippa went to work feeling vaguely anxious and unsettled. As the day wore on her unease only grew. She
kept checking her phone to see if Harry had called,
then catching herself and giving herself yet another
mental lecture.

So much for being "able to separate sex and love and
romance and friendship." Every anxious minute that
ticked by made a mockery of her bold, emancipated
words last night. She'd been riding her very highest
horse, smugly pointing out to him that she understood
exactly what the parameters of their relationship were.
Determined to prove to him and herself that she wasn't
like his other women.

And yet here she was, not even twenty-four hours
later, fretting over if he was going to call and if he was
hers exclusively.

Not good. Distracting, undermining and draining.
This was why she'd warned herself off Harry in the first
place. Her life was already a crisis waiting to happen.
She needed less drama, not more.

By four in the afternoon she'd almost convinced herself that it would be a good thing if Harry never called
again. Then she looked up from taking a phone call
and found Harry walking toward her, his stride long

and confident, big shoulders dipping from side to side with each step. She was powerless to stop the delighted smile that curved her mouth.

"What are you doing here?" She'd mentioned she'd be working at the gallery last night but he hadn't appeared to pay particular attention to the information. Clearly, however, he'd filed it away.

"I wanted to see if you and Alice felt like dinner at the Brewery tonight?"

Pippa's smile dimmed a little. The Mornington Brewery was a local bar that offered boutique beers, wood-fired pizzas and live music. She would have loved a night there with Harry.

"I can't. I'm looking after another little boy. I have this reciprocal arrangement with a woman from university...."

She braced herself for Harry's disappointment. No doubt this was the first time he'd been turned down in favor of a night with two six-month-olds. He was used to shaping his life to suit himself, not bending himself around responsibilities and obligations.

"How about I bring pizza and beer to you, then?"

He said it easily, utterly accepting. A surge of wholly unwarranted relief swept through her.

"You heard the bit about me babysitting the kids, right?"

"Will there be a chance of me getting you naked?"

Pippa shot a glance to the side to make sure no one had overheard his question. An older couple were examining some jewelry in a nearby showcase but they didn't appear to be listening.

She returned her focus to Harry. "I'd say your chances were good to very good. Becca's picking Aaron up at nine."

"Then I'll see you at seven with beer and pizza. Any requests?"

"No anchovies. Extra olives."

"Done." He turned to go, then swiveled back. "You still have that lacy red bra?"

"Yes."

"Think you could wear it tonight?"

"Um, sure."

"Good."

His gaze swept down her body. She was wearing a striped shirtwaist dress with her black eyelet boots—hardly siren stuff—but the expression in his eyes made her feel like Pamela Anderson, Sophia Loren and Marilyn Monroe all rolled into one. Heat bloomed between her thighs. She swallowed a lump of pure lust. Harry's mouth tilted into a knowing smile. He knew exactly what he did to her.

He turned to exit again but there was something she needed to ask him before this thing between them spun into another night.

"Harry…" She slipped from behind the desk and made her way to his side, acutely aware of the older couple and how echoey the space was.

Harry raised his eyebrows, waiting for her to speak. She tried out a few phrases in her mind, but she'd always been a direct person, and—to date, anyway—Harry had always seemed to appreciate her forthrightness.

"Are you sleeping with anyone else at the moment?"

He blinked, then a slight frown wrinkled his forehead. "No. Are you?"

She snorted her amusement. "Right. That's why I have a spare set of batteries under my bed."

His frown disappeared. "I'm a one-woman-at-a-time kind of man."

"Okay. Good to know."

It *was* good to know. A huge relief, actually. She could consign those visions of him with other women to the dustbin in her mind.

Until their fling had run its course, naturally.

"I'll see you later," she said, stepping away from him.

She didn't have eyes in the back of her head, but she knew he watched her walk all the way back to the desk. She loved that she turned him on so much. She loved the way he looked at her. And the fact that he remembered what bra she'd been wearing weeks ago… Yeah, that was pretty hot, too.

It was her turn to watch him walk away now, and she did so with gusto, mapping his broad shoulders and back with her eyes before lavishing her attention on his backside.

If she was a poet, she would write an ode to his butt. She'd talk about how muscular and round and perfect it was, and how she wanted to sink her teeth into it, it was so damned sexy…

"Excuse me, miss?"

She tore her gaze from Harry's derriere to focus on the elderly gentleman who had approached the desk.

"Um, yes?" She smiled and pushed her hair behind her ear, feeling flushed and more than a little caught out.

"We were wondering if we could take a look at the opal rings in the cabinet?"

"Sure. Yes. Absolutely. Let me grab the keys…."

She cast one last glance toward the door as she tugged open the drawer in her desk to find the keys, but Harry was gone.

Well. She would see him again tonight. Hugging the knowledge to herself, she went to open the cabinet.

HARRY TAPPED HIS hands on his steering wheel, gazing out the side window at the stucco facade of Steve's town house. Where the hell was he?

He knew via Macca that Steve had been finishing up a job today, but Steve never worked past five on the weekends. It was nearly six-thirty now, and Harry had been waiting over an hour.

He glanced in the rearview mirror. It was possible Steve had seen Harry's car parked out front and kept on driving. Or maybe he was being paranoid, and Steve simply had other plans for the night.

Harry let his head drop back. He'd worked himself up to this all day and he wanted it done. Not that he had high hopes they would resolve anything, but he had to at least try. Fifteen years of friendship demanded it.

He went over what he'd decided to say in his head for the tenth time. He'd apologize for getting in Steve's face about Pippa and Alice. As much as Steve's behavior made him grind his teeth, at the end of the day it was none of Harry's business. He wasn't Steve's conscience, and he'd said his piece on the subject. The rest was up to Steve.

That just left Pippa. He didn't fully understand why Steve was so cut up about Harry's interest in her. It wasn't as though Harry had even looked sideways at her while she was with Steve, and it had been more than a year since they'd broken up.

Harry thought back to the days immediately following Pippa's announcement that she was pregnant. Steve had been furious, white-hot furious. Harry had thought then and still thought now that it had a lot to do with what things had been like for Steve as a kid. Jack Lawson had been a hard bastard and he'd taken his nasty temper out on Steve and his brothers and sisters on a regular basis. Many was the time Steve had slept on the floor in Harry's bedroom to avoid going home.

Harry figured that the prospect of becoming a father scared the living crap out of Steve. Added to the fact that his mate had a pathological need to always be in charge of his own destiny, it had made for a pretty potent knee-jerk reaction to Pippa's pregnancy.

But Steve had had plenty of time to freak out. He needed to stop being an asshole and start being the guy Harry knew. The guy who was the first to offer a lending hand to a mate and the first to reach into his pocket for a good cause. Punishing Pippa and Alice for the shortcomings of his own childhood was pure crazy. As was burning a friendship that had endured fifteen years of ups and downs.

Harry stared at the roof-lining of his car, wondering how in hell he would deliver all of the above in a way that would make Steve stop and listen. No brilliant ideas came to him.

He checked his watch. He needed to go get pizza. He picked up his phone and dialed Steve's number. It went straight to voice mail—surprise surprise.

"We need to talk. Call me, okay?"

He tossed his phone onto the passenger seat and started the car, knowing that the chances of Steve returning his call were less than zero.

Fifteen minutes later, the car was redolent with super supreme fumes and he was heading back up the highway toward Pippa's place. He had a six-pack of pale ale and the heady expectation of Pippa in a lacy bra to look forward to. He was turning on the radio when his phone rang. He punched the radio off again and took the call.

"Yo."

"Harry. It's me. Where are you? You sound like

you're in a wind tunnel." Mike Porter's voice sounded too loud over the hands-free speaker.

"I'm in the car, and you say that every time, Dad."

"That's because you sound like you're in a tunnel every time."

"Yeah, yeah. What's up?"

His father was not a chitchatter, and neither was Harry.

"Wanted to give you a heads up, in case you heard anything through Leo or one of the guys at work. I've been talking to a business broker about putting the workshop up for sale. The ad should go out next month."

It was so out of left field that for a moment Harry was speechless.

"You still there?" His father's voice echoed around the car.

"Where the hell did this come from?"

"Your mother and I have been talking about it for a while. She wants to see the world while we still have our own hips and teeth. I figure she's put up with enough lost weekends and late nights."

"So you're selling up your life's work because she wants to go on a cruise?"

"Gotta loosen the grip sometime. Might as well be now as later."

Harry ground his teeth. His father wasn't saying it outright, but this was about him, about his refusal to step into his father's shoes.

"Look, I know you're pissed with me, Dad, but don't cut off your nose to spite your face."

To his surprise, his father laughed.

"I know this will come as a shock to you, Harry, but you're not the center of my universe. This has been a long time coming."

Harry frowned at the road ahead. "It's your business, Dad. You can do whatever you like with it."

He didn't say it, but his tone said the rest: it's yours to screw up, too.

"It is. It definitely is. You got a big night planned?"

"Dinner with a friend."

"Well, have a good one."

"Yeah. You, too."

The phone went dead. Harry felt as though someone had walked up behind him and smacked him on the back of the head with a piece of four-by-two.

His father was selling his workshop. The business he'd sweated over for decades.

Harry almost drove past Pippa's place, only realizing that her house was approaching at the last second. He made a sharp turn into her driveway and then simply sat staring blindly at her house.

His mum must have been pressuring his father. That was the only explanation. Because his father lived for that workshop.

After a few minutes the porch light came on and the front door opened. Pippa peered out at him, a bemused smile on her face. He collected the pizzas and beer and climbed out of the car.

"It *is* you. I thought maybe Knight Rider had come to visit," Pippa said as he approached the house.

"Just me." He forced a smile.

She tilted her head as he climbed to the porch, her gaze scanning his face.

"Is everything okay?" She was wearing the same striped dress she'd had on at the gallery earlier in the afternoon. Her feet were bare, her hair loose around her shoulders. Her heavy black glasses framed her warm brown eyes.

She looked good—familiar and sexy and relaxed.

"Yeah." He offered her the pizza boxes. "I got super supreme with extra olives and no anchovies, and Hawaiian."

She hesitated a second before taking them. "I love Hawaiian. Good choice. Come and meet Aaron, who hasn't slept a single wink since Becca dropped him off."

She led him to the kitchen where he found Alice and another baby with a profusion of dark hair lying together on a quilted throw rug.

"Isn't she a little young to be dating?" he asked.

Pippa laughed. "She's well chaperoned. And Aaron has trouble sticking his thumb in his own mouth. I think we're good for another decade or so."

The table was already set with paper napkins, plates and cutlery. Pippa flipped the lids back on the boxes and handed him a bottle opener for the beers. He knew from experience that she was a drink-her-beer-from-the-bottle kind of woman—his kind, in other words—and he flipped the cap off a beer and passed it across to her.

"Fantastic. I've been thinking about this all afternoon," she said.

The moment the words were out of her mouth her cheeks turned pink. He eyed her as he took a mouthful from his own beer. It amused him no end that she was so quick to blush out of the bedroom and so shameless within.

"Me, too."

She pressed her lips together and gave a rueful shake of her head. "Giving away the game again, White. When are you ever going to learn?"

He laughed. His shoulders dropped a notch. She was easy company.

"I'm about to eat my body-weight in pizza. Close

your eyes if you're easily grossed out," she said, reaching for her first slice.

She asked him about his day at work, then told him about hers, making the ordinary entertaining with her witty observations. They were both on their second beer when she pushed her plate away and drew her foot up so that her knee was against her chest and her heel rested on the seat of her chair.

"You going to tell me what's wrong now or do you need to stew on it a little longer?"

He looked down at the half-eaten pizza on his plate. Pippa didn't need to know about his dad's crazy decision. What did it matter to her if his father was making a huge mistake? She had enough of her own stuff to deal with.

"Okay. More stewing it is. I'll have another slice, then," Pippa said lightly.

He poked a finger at a piece of pineapple. "My dad wants to sell the workshop."

"I take it this is a surprise to you?"

He huffed out a laugh. He was aiming for wry but it came out sounding a little bitter.

"You could say that. He's poured his lifeblood into that place. It's his dream—his own place, his rules, his way."

"Did he say why he wants to sell?"

"He and Mum want to travel, start winding down."

"How old is he?"

"Fifty-nine."

She shrugged. "Not out of the question for retirement."

"You've seen him. He's hardly on his last legs. He loves that place, Pippa."

She cocked her head. "Are you sure that this is about him?"

"I know Mum's been campaigning to go on a cruise. I figure she's cheerleading him on this one."

"I meant are you sure this isn't about you? Since you're not interested in taking on your father's business, he was bound to have to sell it at some point. Or simply shut it down."

"No way. He's built it up too much to just walk away from it."

"So if you don't want it and he can't sell it or shut it down, what should he do with it, then? Keep working until he falls over?"

He stared at her for a beat, then dropped his gaze to his plate. She was right. He'd left his father with nowhere to turn.

"I still don't think this is what he wants."

"I've only met your father once, but he didn't strike me as the kind of man who does anything he didn't want to."

He ran a hand over his head.

"This was always going to happen, Harry, right?" she said, her voice soft with sympathy.

"I hate the thought of him giving it up."

She reached across the table and curled her fingers around his. "At the end of the day, you have to live your life. He can't live his for you, and you can't live yours for him."

Harry straightened in his seat. "You want the last slice of Hawaiian?"

She gave him a small smile. "Did we just reach your deep and meaningful threshold?"

He lifted a shoulder. "Talking won't change anything."

"Sure. But sometimes it can make you feel better."

She stood and collected their empty bottles. She dropped a hand on his shoulder and gave it a warm squeeze before heading for the sink. Harry watched the sway of her hips, thinking about what she'd said. He was still pissed and frustrated, but not anywhere near to the degree he'd been when he arrived. Talking to her, having her listen, had taken the edge off.

"Thanks," he said.

She smiled at him. Pippa was so down to earth and funny and honest. She never pulled her punches. She drank beer out of the bottle. And he was pretty damned sure he'd just caught a glimpse of a red bra strap at her neckline.

He pushed back his chair and stood. Her eyebrows rose in silent question as he walked toward her. He reached for the neckline of her dress, pulling the fabric away from her skin so he could inspect her cleavage. His gaze fell on creamy breasts cupped in lace.

She was smiling a secretive, pleased smile.

"You wore it," he said.

"You asked me to."

"You're making me think of a whole bunch of other things I could ask you to do."

"Maybe you should try your luck."

"Maybe I should."

He lowered his head and kissed her. She tasted of beer and the sweetness of pineapple. He slid a hand into the hair at the nape of her neck, angling her head, deepening the kiss. She had such a great mouth. He could kiss her for hours.

She made a small approving noise and he moved forward, pressing her back against the sink with his hips.

Her hands slid to his rear, sliding inside the pockets of his jeans and curving into the muscles of his ass.

White-hot need burned through him. She was so damned sexy. The snap in her eyes. Her full, soft breasts. The way she reached out and took whatever she wanted. If there weren't two six-month-olds watching their every move, he'd throw her over his shoulder and take her to the bedroom right now.

He broke their kiss and pulled away enough to look down into her face without going cross-eyed. "What time is your friend coming to pick up her kid?"

"Nine."

A whole hour away. He grasped her elbows and gently tugged her hands free from his jean pockets, stepping away from her. She grinned, getting the message.

"Probably a wise decision." Her gaze dropped to his crotch, her mouth tipping down regretfully. "Seems a shame to waste that, though."

He looked down at his hard-on. "I'll have another just like it in an hour. Trust me."

She laughed, the sound low and dirty and knowing. He couldn't help it, he had to kiss her again. He leaned forward and captured the last of her laughter with his lips. Her hands found his shoulders, her fingers digging into his muscles, holding him close.

Man… If they were alone.

But they weren't.

He stepped back. "You want to watch some TV?" he said, his breathing a little ragged.

"Okay." She wasn't smiling now, her cheeks pink, her mouth wet from his kisses. "I might text Becca to make sure she's on time."

It was his turn to laugh then. He crossed to the table and collected the pizza boxes. It was only as he was folding them into the rubbish bin that he realized the tension he'd been carrying since talking to his father had slipped away. Pippa had eased it, with her patience and sympathy and sexiness.

It hit him suddenly that it was going to be hard to walk away from her when the time came. Despite all the complications.

For a second he allowed himself to contemplate the alternative: not walking away, not turning his back on her and the way she made him feel. A possible future shimmered in front of him, full of diapers and night feeds and laundry and Alice's gummy smile and small, soft hands and Saturday nights in front of the television instead of down at the pub. Nights in Pippa's bed, mornings with her beside him when he woke. Lawns that need mowing and bills that needed paying and holidays for three instead of one.

None of it seemed too awful, not with Pippa at his side.

Then he blinked and the vision was gone. He shook himself. Clearly, great sex was messing with his head. He was years away from wanting to take on any of that stuff, if ever. He had a great life right now. No way was he ready to give it up to embrace domesticity, no matter how much he liked Pippa.

CHAPTER TWELVE

IT WAS STILL dark outside when Pippa woke. A warm, solid arm pressed against hers, and when she shifted her leg she felt the roughness of a hard, hairy male calf against her own. She smiled, remembering what had happened after Becca collected Aaron. Alice had been tetchy, crying off and on, her teeth obviously painful. Pippa had tried everything, rubbing gel onto her daughter's gums, offering her various soft objects to chew on. Then she'd handed Alice to Harry while she mixed a bottle of formula, only for Alice to pipe down almost immediately.

She'd looked around to find her daughter gnawing on Harry's thumb, a deeply satisfied expression on her round face. She'd expected Harry to balk, or at the very least hand Alice back after a token few minutes, but he'd settled on the couch with her and let her gum away until she'd fallen into a fretful sleep. Then he'd carried Alice to her room and stood to one side as Pippa tucked her in.

Pippa would be lying if she pretended there hadn't been a moment—maybe even two or three—when she'd glanced across at him holding her child and let herself imagine.

She'd caught herself every time. Harry was a good-natured guy, and Alice was a novelty to him. No doubt he'd been won over by her wide-eyed adulation and fascination with him, the only male in her orbit. Pippa was sure that a few sleepless nights, foul diapers, rashes and sick-ups would fix that. This was Harry, after all, the ultimate Peter Pan.

After Alice had fallen asleep, she and Harry had showered together before he'd massaged her shoulders and back…and then other parts of her that hadn't been so much tense but more hot and very ready for him. By the time he'd finished she'd been panting and desperate and she'd pushed him down onto the mattress and climbed on top and taken them both for a long, slow, crazy ride. She'd pushed him to the brink and over and watched him come, his body racked with pleasure. Then she'd smoothed a palm down her belly and between her thighs and found her own climax with him still inside her, his gray eyes glinting up at her through half-closed lids.

He'd fallen into a doze afterward and she'd pulled the covers up and curled into his side, telling herself it would only be a few minutes before he woke again and got dressed to go home.

Now, she peered at the clock on her bedside table. It was nearly four. She squinted to make sure she was reading the numerals correctly, then lay frowning into her pillow as she tried to work out how she felt about Harry staying the night.

On the surface, it was no big deal. He didn't steal the quilt or drool or snore. And it wasn't as though she was worried about what the neighbors might think. But there was something very seductive about waking to find a big, warm, hard body beside her and hearing someone else's soft breathing and knowing she wasn't alone in the night.

While she'd had Mr. Pink and an emergency stash of batteries to stop her from climbing the walls in the past year, there was no substitute for this kind of intimacy. And no, a pillow didn't come even close to cutting it.

The sensible thing to do would be to wake him. Allowing herself to get used to him sleeping in her bed was the first step down a very slippery slope. She reached out to touch his shoulder, intending to shake him awake. Her fingers slid over warm, smooth skin. She shaped her hand to the curve of his muscles, feeling how strong he was, how solid. She slid her head closer, pressing her nose to his shoulder and inhaling deeply. He smelled so good, like sunshine and warmth.

Pippa didn't want to kick him out of her bed. The second she admitted as much, she started making excuses for herself. It was nearly morning, anyway, and she wasn't an idiot. She knew him staying didn't mean anything more than that he'd been comfortable and that he'd fallen asleep. She wasn't about to weave fantasies based on his presence between her sheets for a few extra hours.

She let her eyes drift closed again and woke three hours later to the warm tug of his mouth on her breasts. She murmured her approval as he rolled on top of her and made slow, languid love to her in the gray morning light.

Afterward, she lay and watched him pull on his clothes, feeling drowsy and lazy. He had a lovely body. Following the play of his muscles as he dressed was a very, very pleasant way to start the day. He sat on the end of the bed to pull on his boots and shot a glance at her.

"Keep looking at me like that and you'll be in trouble," he said, a glint in his eye.

"What kind of trouble?"

"Guess."

She smiled and stretched her arms above her head, self-satisfied as a cat.

"What have you got on for the day?" she asked idly as he pocketed his phone, car keys and wallet.

"Maybe a surf. Should probably do some Christmas shopping. Get it out of the way." He strapped on his watch. "Thought I might drop by and talk to Dad, too."

"Sounds good." Especially the bit where he would talk to his father.

"Oh, yeah. Sounds riveting." He glanced at her. "Busy next week?"

"Yep. My assignment's due, and I've got an exam on Friday. Plus the usual."

He leaned down to kiss her, his lips soft and warm. "I'll call you."

A little dart of pleasure shot through her at his words.

She propped herself up on one elbow. "Maybe *I'll* call *you*." There was no reason why he should be the only one calling the shots, after all.

He grinned. "You do that. Anytime."

He slipped out her newly-hung door. She expected to hear the front door closing in short order, but instead he walked up the hall in the other direction, toward the kitchen. At first she assumed he must be using the bathroom, but the toilet didn't flush. Then she heard his voice come over the baby monitor, low but perfectly audible.

"That's right, little lady, keep snoozing. Get your beauty sleep so you can be as pretty as your mummy one day. I'll see you later, okay?"

Pippa pressed a hand to her heart, an instinctive, ridiculously clichéd gesture. But there was no denying she was touched by his interest in Alice. That he'd taken time to say farewell to her daughter spoke volumes for the sort of man he was.

She heard his footsteps in the hall again, heading for the door this time. She flopped back onto her pillow as she heard it shut behind him, aware that the tide of emotion rising inside her was as much about Steve's neglect as it was about Harry's casual warmth and affection for her baby daughter.

She swallowed the lump in her throat. She had a sudden vision of how she would look to an outside observer—the recently-sated single mother, lying in bed getting all dewy-eyed because her casual lover had deigned to toss a kind word in her child's direction.

Pippa pushed the covers back abruptly. She wasn't that stupid or desperate or sentimental. It was nice that Harry had spared five seconds to think of her daughter, but that was all it was. It didn't mean anything, just as his having accidentally stayed the night didn't, either. This thing between them would work only if she kept the parameters front and center.

"Sex, Pippa. It's all about the sex."

Maybe she should get a T-shirt made—and maybe a cap, for good measure. And maybe she should draw up a few ground rules for herself, starting with not allowing him to stay the night in her bed again. It was too cozy, too domestic, having him here in the morning.

It felt too real, as though it meant something. And it didn't.

She stood, feeling empowered by her decision. She'd gone into this thing with her eyes wide open, and she would keep them that way.

HARRY DECIDED TO DRIVE past the workshop on his way to his parents' place. Even though it was Sunday, it

wouldn't be unusual for his father to have put aside
some of his morning for all the paperwork he hadn't
got around to during the week.

A shiny red truck turned the corner ahead of Harry
as he drove into the Village. It reminded him that Steve
had yet to return his phone call and he grabbed his
phone and dialed Steve's number.

It went through to voice mail, as it had last night.
Harry pictured Steve checking caller ID and leaving
Harry to swing in the breeze. Idiot.

It went against the grain to be cast in the role of sup-
plicant, but he left a second message anyway.

"Steve. Call me, okay? Just… Call me."

Like last night, he didn't hold out much hope for a
return call. He figured he would run out of patience
with the little game Steve was playing sometime soon.
They were both too old for this shit. With a bit of luck,
Steve would see sense before then.

He spotted his father's car in front of Village Motors
and pulled in beside it. His father was seated at the desk
in the reception area, a takeout cup of coffee in front of
him as he studied the computer screen, fingers hunting
and pecking their way across the keyboard. He glanced
up as Harry entered.

"Morning." He didn't sound too surprised by the
impromptu visit.

"Morning." Harry sank onto one of the visitors'
chairs. He crossed his arms over his chest and sat back,
watching his father tap away.

The silence stretched, the only sound the rhythmic
clickety-clack of the keyboard.

"If you've got something to say, Harry, you should
spit it out. Staring at me like that is just plain creepy."
His father didn't look away from the computer screen.

"I've got a deal for you. I'll talk to Leo, see if he'll give me six weeks' leave. Let me know when you and Mom want to go on that cruise and I'll pitch in here for the duration so you know the home front is covered."

His father stopped typing, letting his hands drop into his lap. He swiveled the chair to face Harry, his face calmly neutral. "So you take leave and come work for me temporarily so I can take leave?"

Harry lifted a shoulder. "Gets you out of a jam, and I'm happy to help out."

His father stroked a finger down one side of his horseshoe mustache. "Nice idea, but there's not much point to it. You can't take leave every time I want to have a break from the business."

"Then hire someone to manage the place."

"That's just delaying the inevitable." His father shook his head decisively. "If I'm making the cut, I'm doing it cleanly."

Harry swore under his breath. This was nuts. His father lived and breathed this place.

"You'll go stir-crazy sitting around at home. What are you going to do, take up golf?" The idea of his father in pastel pink polo shirts and plaid pants was laughable.

"I told you. Your mother wants to travel. She's got enough trips planned to cover the next ten years."

Harry stood, frustrated. "If you think this will make me change my mind, you're wrong. I've told you how I feel, what I want."

"I know. And I listened. That's why I'm doing this." His father's voice was tinged with resignation.

It hit Harry that his father was deadly serious about this sale. This wasn't a gambit or a tactic. This was for real.

He sat down again with a thump. For a long beat they

simply stared at each other, then his father shrugged one big shoulder.

"It was never your dream. I get it. I won't lie, it's disappointing. I kind of liked the idea of starting a dynasty." He smiled faintly. "But it was never meant to be a choke hold."

Harry shifted in his seat. "That's not the way I see it."

"A bear trap, then." Another faint smile from his old man.

Half a dozen explanations and justifications for the way he'd chosen to live his life marshaled themselves at the back of Harry's throat. Stuff about valuing his freedom and not being able to stand being hemmed in or pinned down. Stuff about not being good at all the i-dotting and t-crossing that came with being the boss. He didn't utter a word, because even in his own head it sounded lame.

Like the complaints of a little kid who'd been asked to finish his chores.

It was an uncomfortable realization. Harry glowered at the toes of his boots.

"Relax, Harry. You're officially off the hook, and so am I."

Harry looked up. His father shrugged. Harry stood, his guts churning.

"I've got to go."

He walked out to his car and slid behind the wheel. He had no idea where he was going until he found himself wending his way through the back streets toward his favorite beach, a tucked-away cove surrounded by sand dunes and weathered wooden walkways. It had no official name but the locals called it Mt. Steep, after the tallest of the sand dunes. He parked in the sandy visitors' lot and hiked along a twisty-turny gravel track for ten minutes before he emerged at the beach. A flight of silver-timbered stairs took him down to the sand. It was still early—barely ten—and the beach was empty. He sat on the sun-warmed sand and tried to understand himself.

All his life he'd been restless. Maybe because he was the youngest of three, he'd always felt as though there was stuff going on that he was missing out on. Adventures and challenges he was considered too young for. When he got old enough to concoct his own adventures and challenges, he'd set forth with a vengeance and never looked back. Footy trips with his mates, surfing holidays, backpacking through Asia, fast cars, fast women, tattoos and piercings and trouble... Then he'd met Debbie and fallen hard and spent the next three years trying to mold himself to her dreams and failed miserably.

It was an experience that had left a bad taste in his mouth, not least because he was painfully aware that he'd behaved badly. He'd hurt her. Not something he was proud off all these years later.

He'd decided then that he wasn't cut out for serious. He hadn't liked feeling obligated, and he'd deeply resented being in a situation where his choices were so limited. He'd pretty much arranged his life since to avoid all of the above. He'd chosen a job that was low-key, bought a house that required the minimum mortgage, sidestepped any woman with the gleam of forever in her eyes. Every time his father or mother had raised the idea of him taking over the workshop, he'd told them the same thing: thanks, but no thanks. When his sisters had hassled him, questioning his stance, he'd told them to butt out.

He'd trumpeted his easygoing, no-muss, no-fuss philosophy to anyone who'd listen, including Pippa. And yet he'd never thought through the logical consequences of his decision regarding his father's workshop. Pippa had asked him last night what he'd expected his father to do with the business if Harry wasn't going to take it over. The truth was, Harry had never thought that far ahead. He simply…hadn't.

When he pictured his father in his mind's eye, he saw him leaning over an engine, hands grubby with grease and oil, an absorbed, patient expression on his face as he puzzled out a problem. His father was ageless in his imagination, the setting never changing. His father's work and, by extension, the workshop, were who his father was. Always had been, always would be. It had never occurred to Harry that his father would opt out at some point.

But his father *was* opting out, and his decision had forced Harry to recognize something he'd kept well hidden from even himself: deep in his heart of hearts, he'd believed that the workshop would always be there, equal parts opportunity and obligation, ready for him if and when he ever decided he wanted to take the plunge. In the same way that he'd always imagined that he might meet the "right" woman and settle down sometime in the hazy, distant future, he'd imagined that there might come a time when the moon and stars aligned and the partying was over and he'd surfed enough beaches and raised enough hell that he'd be ready to step into his father's shoes. And that when he chose to do so, those shoes would simply be waiting for him, ready to be filled.

It was an arrogant, careless, childish belief for a man of thirty to hold. It was a young man's imagining of the future, nebulous and utterly self-focused.

He squinted his eyes against the glare of the sun on the water and dug the heels of his boots deeper into the sand.

He didn't like thinking of himself as childish or selfish. He owned two cars, paid his bills and turned up to work every day he was expected to be there. If he said he'd do something, he did it, no questions asked. He wasn't afraid of a challenge or a dare. He liked to think that he didn't hold back in life.

Yet he'd been holding back in the most basic possible way for a long time now. He'd been living the life of Riley, keeping his father's expectations and hopes at bay, telling himself he was choosing freedom and individuality over obligation and restriction—and yet all the time he'd had his little fail-safe measure tucked away, ready to deploy if and when it suited him.

And now his father had called Harry's bluff, called bullshit on his claims that he wasn't interested in the business. After all these years, his father was laying it on the line. Giving Harry the choice to put up or shut up.

He inhaled deeply through his nose, breathing in the scent of hot sand and salt and the faint tang of seaweed. The wind raised the hairs on his arms and cooled the back of his neck.

There was no question in his mind what his decision would be. Funny that after all these years of stalling the answer felt so certain. So unequivocal.

He wouldn't stand by and watch something his father had built up from nothing pass on to a stranger. It simply wasn't going to happen.

He waited for the heaviness of his decision to settle over him. He would be saying goodbye to the last remnants of his youth, after all, when he took over the reins of Village Motors.

Harry's gut felt tense, but—surprisingly—it was adrenaline that was tightening his belly, not dread.

A part of him was ready for this. Maybe even wanted it. The next stage of his life. The next challenge.

He pulled his phone out and dialed.

"Hello?" Pippa's voice came down the line, drowsy and distracted. He pictured her still lying in bed, shoulders bare, her hair dark against the pillow.

"It's me."

"Oh, hey." She sounded pleased.

"Are you still in bed?"

"No such luck. I'm working on my big assignment. It's due on Thursday."

"I won't keep you then." He wasn't even sure why he'd called, and he didn't want to hold her up.

"You're not keeping me. Did you talk to your dad?"

Something inside him relaxed as he heard the sympathy in her voice. "Yeah."

"Did it go okay?"

"I'm going to take over the business."

She exhaled in a rush. "Oh. Harry."

He couldn't tell if she was surprised, disbelieving, approving or disapproving. It was a little alarming how much he hoped it wasn't the latter.

"You think it's a bad idea?"

"I think it's a great idea if it's what you want. If you're doing it for the right reasons and not because you feel obligated."

"I'd be lying if I said there was no obligation. But it's not just that. I guess I always figured I'd get around to stepping into the business at some point."

Despite what he'd advertised to the world and himself.

"Kind of like I always imagined I'd do something with my degree sometime, huh?"

He didn't need to see her to know she was smiling self-deprecatingly.

"Kind of like that."

"Funny how life sneaks up on you sometimes."

He stared at the glittering blue of the ocean, suddenly wishing he was there or she was here. He wanted to see her. He wanted to touch her. And it wasn't just about sex.

"Your dad must have been pretty happy, huh?"

"I haven't told him yet."

There was a small pause. "Then why are you talking to me?"

"Because I wanted to."

Because the moment he'd made the decision he'd wanted to tell her about it. To hear her opinion. To have her approval.

"Talk to me later. Go put your father out of his misery." She sounded stern. No-nonsense.

"Is that your teacher voice?"

"It will be, one day. I hope. If I can get this assignment done."

"I'll let you get back to it."

"Call your father."

He smiled. "I will."

"Good."

He ran his thumb over the screen on his phone after he'd ended the call, thinking about Pippa. Thinking about the future.

Harry stood, dusted off his ass and started up the hill.

HE CRUISED PAST the workshop but his father's car was gone, so he went to his parents' place. The roller door to the garage was up when he arrived, a sure sign his father was in there, tinkering on his current pet project. Ever since Harry could remember his father had had a restoration project on the go in the garage. Over the years he'd returned more than a dozen cars to their former glory, always selling them at a good profit.

The current work in progress was a left-hand drive 1976 Mustang. His father was at the workbench contemplating the carburetor when Harry entered.

"How's it looking?" he asked.

His father glanced over his shoulder. "Like a forty-year-old carbie. In other words, shit-house."

Harry joined his father at the bench, running a practiced eye over the part. The carb float was dark with fuel residue, the bowl equally coated in crud. "Got your work cut out for you there."

"Thanks, Captain Obvious."

Harry smiled.

"Your mum's in the garden if you're looking for her."

"I wanted to talk to you. About the workshop."

His father frowned and picked up a small open-ended spanner, loosening the nut on the carbie. "No offense, but I don't see the point in going over it again. Let's just let sleeping dogs lie, eh?"

His father shot him a look from under his eyebrows, seeking Harry's agreement. Harry leaned his hip against the bench.

"I want in. I'll give Leo six weeks' notice, give him time to find someone to replace me. You can take off whenever suits you, come and go as you please. But I want at least a year of handover. And I'm buying in. You're not just handing it to me on a platter, and you and Mom will need some money to fund this lifestyle you've got planned."

It was something he'd thought about on the way over. He didn't want to be a freeloader. He wanted to be invested. If he was going to do this thing, it would be all or nothing. It would mean increasing the mortgage on his house, but he figured he could handle it.

His father's hands stilled for the briefest of moments before resuming their work. His face was utterly impassive. "It's a nice gesture, mate. But like I said this morning, it was never meant to be a choke hold."

Harry tugged the spanner from his father's hand. "It's not a gesture."

His father turned to face him squarely. "That's not how you felt this morning."

"Let's just say it took a while for me to see past my own bullshit."

Harry shifted his weight, self-conscious. Very aware that what he was about to admit didn't reflect well on himself. "Turns out that maybe, in the back of my mind, I figured the garage would always be there as an option." It was embarrassing saying it out loud to his old man, on par with admitting he still dreamed of being a rock star or a superhero or something equally juvenile.

His father nodded, once, then lowered his gaze to his hands. Harry waited for him to say something else, but he didn't. It took him a few seconds to register that his father's mustache was trembling as his father worked to suppress strong emotion.

In thirty years, Harry had never seen his father cry. Mike Porter prided himself on his self-control, always had. But here he was, fighting back tears because Harry had finally pulled his head out of his own ass. It made Harry's chest and gut tight. Made him wish he'd been smart enough to see through his own bullshit years ago.

"Dad…"

His father shook his head, lips pressed together, eyes

swimming. Harry's own eyes pricked with tears and he blinked rapidly.

"Bloody hell," he said.

He flung an arm around his father's back and hauled him close. After the barest second his father reciprocated, squeezing him so hard Harry was sure he heard a rib pop. They stayed like that for long seconds, both of them fighting back tears. His father thumped him on the back a couple of times, then released him, taking an abrupt step backward. There was a beat of silence as they both avoided one another's eyes. For some reason Harry imagined what Pippa would say if she could see them both playing so tough and stoic, and a small laugh escaped him. His father looked askance at him, checking that Harry wasn't laughing at him. He must have been reassured, because after a second he smiled, too.

"You got any beer?" Harry asked.

"Screw that. This is champagne territory. The fancy stuff. Your mother's been hoarding a bottle in the back of the fridge. Let's go commandeer it."

Harry was more than happy to go celebrate, but there was something he needed to say first.

"I'm sorry for mucking you around for so long, Dad."

His father shook his head. "No need for apologies. You're supposed to live your life, not mine."

Harry grimaced. His father was being generous. But he always had been.

"Come on, let's go thrill your mother."

Together they walked into the house.

PIPPA KNEW WHO it was the moment she heard the doorbell. Even though she was still knee-deep in her assignment, she couldn't stop the smile from spreading across her face as she made her way to the front door.

"Mr. Porter. This is a surprise," she said as she swung the door wide.

He held a bottle of champagne and his gray eyes smiled at her. "Five minutes, tops, then I'll let you get back to it," he promised.

She gave him a rueful look. As if. There was no way she was sending him away after just five minutes and he knew it.

"I'm guessing your father took it well?" she asked as she led him to the back of the house.

"Yeah."

There was a wealth of meaning and emotion in the single word. She cast a look at him over her shoulder. He met her eyes, his face filled with the emotion of the day. She stopped, turning to face him. She pressed a kiss to his cheek, then his lips, then the corner of his jaw.

"For what it's worth, I think it's a great decision. For all of you."

"Thanks."

He seemed pleased and sheepish all at once and she knew he was thinking about all the things he'd said to her about loving his carefree life and how he had it all worked out. She'd said the same sorts of things about her life, too, before Alice came along.

"Like I said earlier, life has a way of creeping up on you," she said, reaching out to touch his forearm.

"No kidding."

There was a light in his eyes as he looked at her. Something swooped in her stomach. Fear or excitement—it was hard to tell which. Then he blinked and the light was gone and he simply looked happy.

She was happy for him, too. As she'd said, this was a great thing for him.

They entered the kitchen and she grabbed some

champagne flutes. He popped the cork and poured two foaming glasses. They clinked their flutes together.

"To the next big adventure," she said.

"To late nights, debt and premature gray hair."

She laughed. "Amen!"

They were both smiling after they'd taken their first mouthful. She asked him about the conversation with his father and he gave her a rundown of what had been said. He got a little choked up as he talked about his father's reaction and she had to blink away sympathetic tears. He made her laugh, though, when he described his mother's ecstatic response to the news. After twenty minutes he looked at his watch and put his glass down, his gaze flicking across to the table where she had her laptop and textbooks set up.

"I should leave you to it. I know your assignment is due."

She shot a rueful look at the dining table. "Yeah. It is."

It was so tempting to say "to hell with it" when he was standing there looking so sexy and happy and buoyant, but her assignment was not going to write itself. As attractive and compelling as Harry was, he was not her future, and teaching was.

"Call me when you're done?" he said.

"Straight to the bat phone."

Because she couldn't help herself, Pippa stepped forward and kissed him. His arms came around her, his hands smoothing over her back before sliding to her ass and pulling her closer, snugging her hips more firmly against his. She made an approving noise when she felt his hard-on, all thoughts of study flying out the window. She curled her fingers into the muscles of his back and pumped her hips against his, inviting him to play. He deepened the kiss, hungry, demanding.

Then suddenly she was grasping thin air as he slipped away from her.

"Call me when you're done, okay?" he said again. He was a little breathless, his eyes dark with need.

It took her a second to understand he was being as good as his word and leaving her to study, despite the blatant invitation she'd just issued. Even as her body protested, her heart expanded with warmth at his consideration. He knew how much this diploma meant to her, what a difference it would make to her future.

"Thanks, Harry," she said softly.

He dropped a quick kiss onto her forehead before backing off. "Later."

She followed him with her eyes as he made his way to the front door, not trusting herself to keep her hands off him if she went with him. He raised a hand in farewell as he opened the front door, then he was gone.

Pippa stared down the length of the hall at the closed door. Over the years, men had brought her flowers, chocolate, jewelry and sexy underwear. Harry's respect and consideration topped them all easily. Hands down.

"It's just sex. Just sex, just sex, just sex," she said out loud.

Except it didn't feel that way.

CHAPTER THIRTEEN

IT DIDN'T FEEL that way when she called him at ten on Tuesday night, either, to let him know she'd written the five thousandth word and he told her he'd be there in ten minutes and made it in eight. It didn't feel like just scx when he pressed her against the hall wall when he arrived and kissed her and kissed her until she was hot and wet and pliant and ready for anything.

It didn't feel like just sex when he wrapped his arms around her afterward and fell asleep in her bed. Which was why she didn't wake him and send him on his way, in line with her own self-ruling on the matter.

She didn't send him home on Thursday night, either, when he took her and Alice out for dinner, or on Friday night when he came over with a DVD to help her baby-sit Aaron again. She told herself that she had a grip on things, but it wasn't until Saturday night that she realized exactly how deluded she was.

She'd planned to take care of her Christmas shopping in the morning, but Harry suggested breakfast at Lilo Café down on the Mornington foreshore and before she knew it she was watching him feed pureed apple to Alice and enjoying French toast with raspberries and vanilla mascarpone while looking out across clear blue water. They drove back onto the main street afterward and Harry followed her from shop to shop as she agonized over how to spend her meager Christmas dollars.

She bought luxury soaps and hand cream for her mother, an inveterate self-pamperer, then some gourmet sauces and jams for Gaylene, a small token of her appreciation and affection. Alice was next on her list and she led Harry into the toy store, expecting him to send up a protest at any second. They'd been walking around for over an hour and she kept waiting for him to start getting twitchy, but so far he was holding up well. A minor miracle.

She searched his face. "Are you secretly going stir-crazy and looking for the exits?"

He raised his eyebrows. "Sorry?"

"Shopping. You men are supposed to hate it."

"I do. Normally."

"But today it's okay?"

"Yeah, it is. I know you're wearing black lace under that dress." He shrugged as if this explained everything.

She smiled, ridiculously flattered. He was so easy and fun to spend time with. He made her feel sexy and clever. Best of all, he made her forget that when he wasn't around, her life was an obstacle course of stress, lack of sleep and not enough hours in the day.

She left him with the stroller while she went to investigate options for Alice. Her daughter was so young that any gifts for her were nonsensical, really, but Pippa was acutely aware that this would be her daughter's first Christmas. She didn't want to shortchange her little girl or cut corners—but there was also only so much money to go around.

After ten minutes she'd narrowed her choices down to a big, cuddly bear that looked as though it would be a long-lasting childhood companion and a set of beautifully made children's cutlery. Then her eye was caught by a dollhouse display across the aisle. She drew closer, unable to stop herself.

"Oh, wow. The chandeliers even have little wooden candles," she said, peering inside the house.

A classic two up, two down model, it featured a central staircase, peaked roof and Victorian fittings. She took in the self-striped wallpaper, the wainscoting, the perfectly proportioned settee and armchair and mantelpiece and shook her head in wonder.

"I think this is nicer than any real house I've ever lived in," she said, awestruck by the attention to detail.

Harry gave it an assessing glance. "No garage, though."

"Shocking, I know."

A saleswoman zeroed in on them, professional smile in place. "Beautiful, isn't it? They come in kit form and you can pick and choose which accessories you want. We even have a selection of wallpapers for you to choose from."

Pippa smiled and took a step back. Even before the woman had opened her mouth she knew that she would never in a million years be able to afford to buy a dollhouse like this. Harry, however, ran an assessing hand over the rooftop. He ducked his head to inspect the inside more closely.

"How much did you say it was?" he asked, glancing across at the saleswoman.

"The kit itself is four hundred. The furniture starts at twenty and goes up."

Pippa raised her eyebrows. Good God, did people really spend that much money on a kids' toy that would be bashed around, drawn on and abused for a few years, and then disdainfully ignored as its young owner outgrew it?

"Alice is a little too young for that kind of thing yet," she said diplomatically.

Harry circled the display to check out the rear of the house and Pippa gave the stroller a little push to keep Alice pacified.

"If your husband is the handy type, we have plans for dollhouses, too. Not quite as elaborate, but still very nice."

Pippa blinked, taken by surprise by the woman's words. She glanced across at Harry to see if he'd heard, an embarrassed laugh rising in her throat. He was busy reading the back of one of the accessory packs, apparently oblivious to what the woman had said.

"There are also some less elaborate dollhouses in the next aisle, if he's not handy. Although he looks as though he might be." The saleswoman gave a little titter.

Pippa opened her mouth to explain that Harry wasn't her husband—far from it—but the phone rang at the front of the store and the woman laid a hand on Pippa's arm apologetically.

"Excuse me, will you, but I need to get that."

Pippa shut her mouth with a click as the woman bustled off, stifling the urge to go after her and force the truth on her. It was no big deal, after all, if some nameless woman in the local toy store made a mistaken assumption about her and Harry. No one would ever know, it didn't mean anything.

Pippa stole a glance at Harry, worried he might have overheard the conversation after all and thought she'd deliberately let the woman maintain her assumption. He'd moved on to inspect the Nerf gun display, looking like a big kid as he considered the colorful boxes and brightly colored guns. She couldn't help smiling at his absorption. Boys and their toys.

Her smile faded as she imagined how they must have looked to the sales assistant—her and Alice and Harry, gathered together like a little unit. It wasn't impossible to see them as a family, even though Alice was blond and blue-eyed and Harry and she were so dark.

For a dangerous few seconds the image held in her mind. Then she shook her head and it dissolved and reality reasserted itself.

"Sex, sex, sex," she muttered under her breath, turning away.

Maybe she did need to get those T-shirts made, after all.

After a moment's determined concentration, she settled on the teddy bear, deciding that cutlery was too dull a present for Alice's first Christmas. The saleswoman gave her a bright smile as they approached the cash register.

"He's a lovely bear, isn't he? Is it for your little one?"

"Yes." Pippa bit her lip anxiously, dreading the woman making another reference to Harry as her husband. This time Pippa would leap all over her the minute the word was out of her mouth. She didn't want Harry thinking she was starting to get ideas. God, that was the last thing either of them needed.

She was on tenterhooks for the full two minutes it took the other woman to ring up the sale, but the h-word didn't pass the saleswoman's lips again and soon they were stepping out into the bright afternoon sun. Lifting her face to the warmth, Pippa let the tension go.

Stupid to get so wound up over an easy mistake that was essentially meaningless.

She put the incident behind her and managed to get almost all her shopping done before they returned home midafternoon. Harry amused Alice while Pippa did some laundry, then she found herself inviting him to stay for dinner. By ten they were dozing on the couch, tangled in one another's arms while Alice slept on her rug on the floor.

Pippa wasn't sure what woke her—a noise from Alice, a dog barking outside—but she stirred, rubbing her cheek against Harry's T-shirt-covered chest. He smelled so good. Felt so good, too. Like a big, warm rock.

She smiled at the image, then turned her head and pressed a kiss to his chest, aware even as she did so that she wouldn't have dared such a purely affectionate gesture last week. Somehow, she'd dropped her guard where little things like that were concerned. In the same way that she'd never quite got around to kicking him out of her bed every night this week, either.

She frowned, but before she could start to over-analyze things Harry stirred, his chest expanding as he took a deep breath and stretched his arms overhead.

"What time is it?"

"Just past ten."

"Hmmm. Why are you still dressed?"

She snorted out a laugh and let her concerns slide away. She could worry later. Right now, she had bigger, hotter things to occupy herself with.

"It's a good question. I could ask the same of you."

His hands closed around her upper arms as he pulled her higher on the couch so he could kiss her. She lifted her leg and draped it over his hip, arching her back so her breasts pressed against his chest.

"I haven't made out on the couch since I was a teenager," she murmured as he broke their kiss.

"The way I remember it, there are rules for the couch. Hands outside clothes, in case your mum comes in."

"Like you respected that rule," she scoffed.

His laugh was a rumble in his chest as his hand slid onto her breast. He caressed her through the fabric of her dress, plucking at her nipples then soothing them with his palm. She rode his knee and rubbed her hand along the hard length of his erection through his jeans.

After twenty minutes she was feeling more than a little frustrated and horny.

"I don't remember it being this frustrating," she said.

"That's because you know what comes next now. Back then it was a voyage of discovery."

He slid a hand under her skirt and up her thigh, fingers gliding over her skin. She gave a little moan of appreciation as his fingers dipped between her thighs. She knew what he'd find there—damp silk and lots of heat. She pressed herself into his hand shamelessly, urging him on.

"What if your mum comes?" he whispered against the soft skin of her neck.

"Oddly, not really thinking about my mum right now. And if anyone's going to come…"

He laughed again, his fingers stroking her through her panties. She shuddered her approval.

"You've done this before, haven't you?"

"Not like this." There was a serious undertone to his words.

She wondered what he was implying. That sex was different with her? Or was she reading too much into three little words? Was he simply playing along with their silly, nostalgic little game?

Her breath caught in her throat as he slipped his fingers beneath the elastic of her underwear.

"You are so hot…" he murmured.

The sound of glass smashing nearly sent her rolling

off the couch. Harry pushed her to one side and shot to his feet, instantly on the alert.

"What was that? Was that out in the street?" she said, dragging her dress down.

He grabbed his boots and jammed his feet inside. "Yeah. That was out in the street."

His face was tight, his jaw set as he straightened and headed for the hall. Alice started to cry, startled by the sudden activity. Pippa scooped her up and went after Harry, alarm making her movements tight and jerky.

"Harry... Don't go out there. I'll call the police if there's a problem."

Frankston was a tough neighborhood, with more than its fair share of problems. Street violence was common, especially on the weekends when the young men of the area had been drinking heavily. Every week there was a report in the local paper of property damage or a bashing or stabbing.

Harry was already flinging the front door open and flicking on the outside light. He stepped onto the porch, an intimidating silhouette. Pippa ran the last few meters, Alice clutched to her chest.

"Harry—"

The rest of her warning died in her throat as she stepped onto the porch and saw the man standing on her front lawn, baseball bat in hand.

"You know what you are? You're a freakin' liar," Steve yelled.

He strode toward Harry's Monaro, arms swinging back. The baseball bat came down in a crushing arc, smashing into the rear passenger window. The sound of glass breaking echoed around the street, as loud as a gunshot.

Pippa reached out with her spare hand to grip the

back of Harry's T-shirt. His back was as hard as a rock and she could feel the adrenaline surging through him.

Dear God. This would not be good.

Harry twisted to face her, resting his hand on her shoulder.

"It's okay. I'll calm him down and send him home."

She transferred her grip to the front of his T-shirt. "He's drunk. He could do anything, Harry."

"I can handle him." He eased away from her, forcing her to let him go.

He dropped a quick kiss onto her mouth before descending the stairs.

Steve smiled in triumph when he saw him coming, resting the bat on his shoulder. "Ready to spin more bullshit for me, Harry?"

"I never lied to you."

"You said you hadn't touched her."

"When I said that, I hadn't. You need to put the bat down and go home, mate. Before someone calls the cops."

Lights were starting to turn on in the street. The neighbors came out onto their front porch in their dressing gowns, faces concerned. Pippa spared them a quick glance before returning her focus to Harry.

"You threatening me?" Steve lifted the bat from his shoulder, his expression belligerent.

Pippa held her breath, terrified things were about to spiral out of control. This was so horribly crazy. Like a scene from a movie.

"How many people do you think heard you smash the car window?" Harry gestured toward the street, indicating the rubbernecking neighbors.

Steve glanced around, taking in their growing audience, his brow furrowed. He was very drunk, Pippa realized. It was probably a miracle he was still standing.

Steve aimed the end of the bat at Harry, sighting down the length of wood as though it were the barrel of a rifle. "You're supposed to be on my side. You're supposed to be my mate, you disloyal prick."

"I *am* your mate."

Steve shook his head. "No. You sold me out, you bastard. You sold me out."

"What is this, high school? No one's taking sides. You're just too pissed to see it."

Steve jabbed the bat in the direction of the house. "She stitched me up. You know she did. She stitched me up and you don't give a shit because she wiggled her ass at you and all you can do is think with your dick."

There was so much anger in his voice. Pippa tightened her grip on Alice, instinctively resting her hand on the back of her daughter's head, as though the small gesture could protect Alice from her father's rage.

"She got pregnant. It was an accident. You think you're such a catch she'd go to all that trouble for you?" Harry countered.

Steve swayed on his feet, his angry snarl dissolving into confusion as he tried to process Harry's words.

"Mate, go home," Harry said quietly. "Better yet, I'll take you home."

Pippa tensed as Harry held out his hand for the bat. When Steve didn't immediately object, Harry risked taking a step closer. He was about to close his hand around the end of the bat when Steve took a jerky step backward, snatching the bat away, his chin coming up. Pippa forgot to breathe again.

"I'm not going anywhere with you, you lying asshole."

Pippa caught the faint, far-off sound of a police siren in the distance. One of the neighbors must have called the police. Something she should have done the minute she realized what was going on.

Harry glanced toward her and she knew he'd heard the sirens, too, and understood what they meant.

Steve would end up in court over this.

Shame and grief and anger churned in her belly. How on earth had she ever lain down with this man? What was wrong with her that she hadn't seen the ugliness and weakness that was on rampant display here tonight?

Her gaze shifted from Steve's tense form to Harry's. Any second now things were about to get physical. She could feel the violence in the air, like the crackle of electricity. Adrenaline and fear coursed through her. Harry might be hurt. Steve wasn't even close to being rational. If he got worked up…

Alice squirmed in her arms and Pippa realized she was holding her too tightly. She relaxed her grip a little and let out her breath and reminded herself that Harry knew Steve. They'd grown up together. Gone to school together. Come of age together. If anyone knew how to handle Steve when he was like this, it was Harry.

They were practically twins under the skin, they had so much in common.

Pippa stilled as the thought echoed in her mind. Her whole body tensed as realization washed over her, chilling in its awful clarity.

Because she'd done it all over again—fallen for the wrong man. It was such a sudden, startling, brutal revelation she closed her eyes.

She'd been so determined to never be that woman again—that stupid, delusional, self-defeating woman. It had all been so clear in her mind in those first, ugly days when she'd understood that she would be raising her unborn child on her own. She'd thought it was a lesson that had been etched in her bones. Hard-won self-knowledge that would serve her a lifetime.

And yet she'd spent the past month flirting and laughing and having sheet-searing sex with a man who was Steve's spiritual brother in more ways than she cared to count. Worse than that—if that wasn't bad enough—she'd sold herself on the relationship by telling herself it was all about sex and fun, while secretly she'd been harboring white-picket fantasies about Harry.

Treasuring those small moments when he was gentle and attentive with Alice.

Basking in his easy, ready affection.

Allowing him to invade every corner of her life. Her house, her bed, her mind.

Allowing herself to imagine she and Harry and Alice as a family, a little unit, the three of them against the world.

All of this with a man who was roguish and charming and utterly, utterly incapable of being the kind of man she needed him to be.

Just like Steve.

You idiot. You stupid, stupid, foolish woman.

Down on the lawn, the standoff came to a crashing end as Harry feinted to the left, then lunged forward and grabbed the business end of the bat. He yanked on it, hard, and Steve staggered off balance. Quick as lightning Harry pulled the bat from his grasp, tossing it behind him, well out of Steve's reach.

"Now—" Harry said.

Pippa screamed a warning, but it was too late, Steve's swinging fist had already connected with Harry's right cheek. His head snapped back on his neck and he staggered. Dumb instinct told Pippa to go to him and she actually took a step forward before she caught herself. She had Alice to think of. She couldn't go throwing herself between two angry men.

She quickly saw that Harry didn't need her to throw herself anywhere; he easily dodged Steve's second punch, shoving the other man in the side to send him sprawling. Steve scrambled to his feet and came at Harry again, swinging wildly. Harry sidestepped him, pushing him as he passed and sending him to the ground a second time.

Steve pushed himself to his feet, swearing black and blue. The police sirens grew in intensity. Pippa willed them to arrive *now* so this nightmare could be over.

"Cops'll be here any second…" Harry warned as Steve wove on his feet.

Steve came at him again, a desperate, almost frenzied attack. Harry dodged and blocked and absorbed the blows, never once going on the offensive. The moment Steve showed signs of flagging, Harry wrapped his arms around him, hugging him close, effectively immobilizing him.

He got his leg behind Steve's knee and pushed him backward, knocking him off balance. He went down to the ground with him, grappling Steve onto his belly and levering Steve's arm up behind his back. Steve howled in protest as Harry planted a knee between his shoulder blades and let his weight rest on the other man. After a few seconds of struggling and swearing, Steve finally gave up, resting his forehead on the grass.

Pippa let out a shuddering breath. It was over. This part of it, anyway. There was still the police to be dealt with, of course. And the neighbors.

And Harry.

Because after her moment of clarity there was no
place for him in her life. He was a folly she couldn't
afford. A mistake she refused to make.

Something cold dripped onto her chest. She touched
her cheek, noticing her own tears for the first time.
Alice stirred against her breasts. Light and sound filled
the street as a police cruiser swung around the corner
and came to an abrupt halt in front of her house.

Harry looked up at her, checking to see if she was
okay.

She wasn't okay. She was foolish and self-destructive
and enormously self-deceptive.

But she was about to take steps to remedy that.

HARRY SPARED A QUICK glance for the police cruiser before leaning close to Steve's head.

"Don't be an idiot," he warned as the police exited
the car.

He shifted his weight, removing his knee from the
other man's back and standing. He kept his movements
slow and careful, because he was more than aware what
the police saw when they looked at him—six foot two
of tattooed muscle. In their lexicon: trouble. He'd had
enough unwarranted attention from them as a younger
man to know the drill.

He held his hands out from his sides to show he was
unarmed and kept his posture relaxed as the first policeman approached warily.

"One of you gentlemen want to tell me what the
problem is?"

Steve pushed himself up onto his hands and knees.
The stink of booze and cigarettes rolled off him.

"A domestic situation. No one was hurt." Harry
glanced across at the porch, worried about Pippa.

He caught a quick glimpse of her pale face before the policeman blinded him with his flashlight. Harry flinched away from the brightness.

"You look like you copped a hit," the policeman said.

"No one was hurt," Harry repeated.

Steve was already in enough trouble. At the minimum he would be arrested for drunk and disorderly, along with property damage. He wanted to shake his old friend for the way he'd scared Pippa, but Harry couldn't help thinking that if he'd made a bigger effort to hunt Steve down and clear the air in the past week, tonight might have been avoided. Maybe.

Not that he hadn't tried. After Steve had ignored his phone calls, Harry had swung by his place one final time. Steve's car had been in the drive, but he'd ignored Harry's knocking. Fed up to the back teeth, Harry had left one final, pissed-off message letting Steve know the ball was in his court.

Apparently this was Steve's response.

"Maybe you should walk me through this from the beginning. Do you have any ID on you, sir?"

Harry reached into his pocket and handed over his wallet. He turned to check on Pippa again. She was halfway down the steps, her expression tight as she braced herself for the hoopla that was about to unfold. Harry felt a fierce surge of protectiveness. If he could, he'd make this all go away for her and Alice. He'd fix things with Steve and manage the police and ensure that all the messy loose ends and small hurts in her life were healed.

He couldn't do any of that, but he could offer her comfort.

He held up a hand to stall the policeman.

"I just need to talk to my friend," he said.

He'd barely taken a step when the cop moved to block his way.

"If you don't mind, Mr. Porter, I'd like to clear this up first."

Harry shot the man an irritated look, then returned his gaze to Pippa.

"You okay?" he called.

She nodded, the movement stiff and jerky. Her cheeks were shiny from tears. The need to comfort her made him flex his hands.

"I take it you don't reside at this address, Mr. Porter?"

Harry sighed and gave the cop his full attention. Clearly, he wasn't going to get what he wanted until the other man was satisfied.

The next half hour was spent going over and over the night's events. Steve was moved to the other side of the lawn where the second policeman presumably went through the same routine with him. Another cruiser arrived after ten minutes and Pippa disappeared inside with a female officer.

The whole time he answered questions and repeated himself, Harry's mind was with her. He needed to know she was okay. Needed to hear it from her own lips. Needed to dry her tears and assure her that she and Alice had never been in any danger and that Steve would never try something like this again. Ever. Not if Harry had any say in it.

It was another twenty minutes before the police were satisfied they had enough information. Most of the neighbors had given up on the floor show by then, although there were a few stragglers watching from a distance. Steve was cuffed and pushed into the back of a cruiser. Harry watched him, torn between guilt and righteous anger.

What a freaking mess.

"We'll need you to come down to the station tomorrow to sign your statement, okay, Harry?" the policeman said.

Somehow, over the past hour, they'd progressed to first-name basis.

"No problem."

The policeman offered his hand. Harry shook it and turned toward the house, eager to get to Pippa. He took the steps two at a time and was bounding onto the porch when Pippa emerged from the front door, seeing the policewoman out.

"Hey. How you holding up?" Harry asked, ignoring the policewoman as she brushed past him on her way to the steps.

"I'm fine."

She wasn't fine, anyone could see that. He reached for her but she took a step backward. He stilled, studying her face. Her cheeks were pale, her glasses smudged, making it hard for him to see the expression in her eyes.

"They're taking Steve away now. They'll probably hold him overnight."

She nodded tightly. "They explained that."

He was aware of the police car starting up behind him and pulling away from the curb. It was all over.

Except Pippa wouldn't look him in the eye.

"Let's go inside. I'll make you a cup of tea," he said.

It was his mother's cure-all for most traumas. White, with lots of sugar and a plate full of biscuits.

He stepped toward the door but she shifted, blocking the entrance. It happened so quickly he knew it couldn't be anything but an instinctive reaction.

He frowned. "Pippa—"

"I need you to go, Harry."

His frown deepened. "Pippa. What's going on?"

She crossed her arms over her chest. "I don't want to sleep with you any more."

Not what he'd been expecting. By a long shot. It took him a moment to get his thoughts together enough to respond.

"Can I ask why?"

"Because I don't want to make the same mistake twice."

He flinched. "You think I'm like *Steve?*"

He was insulted by the comparison, especially after what had just gone down.

"Look, it doesn't matter, anyway. You were only in this for the fun, and tonight it stopped being fun. So let's just call it quits before it gets any messier than it already is."

He was starting to get pissed now. Barely an hour ago, he'd had his hand up her skirt on the couch. Things had been good—great—between them. Now he was being given his marching orders?

"Who said I was only in this for the fun?"

She looked him dead in the eye. "You did, Harry. Repeatedly. Remember?"

Right. That stupid conversation they'd had after the first night. The one where he'd told her he wasn't a good bet. At the time, it had seemed like the right thing to do and say, because he hadn't wanted to lead her on or hurt her. But things had changed since then. He'd felt it. He knew she had, too. This thing between them had become about a lot more than sex very quickly.

He reached for her again, determined to prove as

much to her but she kept her arms crossed tightly, her body stiff and unyielding.

"Could you please just go?"

He wanted to protest. He wanted to demand she tell him what had suddenly changed, why she was suddenly pushing him away. But there was something about the way she held herself, the way she looked at him that told him she was close to losing it. She'd had a bad night. The father of her child had just been led off in handcuffs. The last thing she needed was him demanding anything.

"I don't think you should be on your own tonight."

"Harry—"

"Is there someone I can call for you? A friend? What about Becca? Or the woman from the gallery?"

She stared at him. She blinked rapidly for a few seconds, combating welling tears, then pushed her glasses up the bridge of her nose.

"I'll be fine on my own. I'm used to it."

She was so determined, despite the threatening tears. Or maybe because of them.

"Can I come tomorrow to talk?"

"I don't think there's much point, do you?" She straightened, squaring her shoulders and lifting her chin. "You've been really terrific, Harry. With the car and the ceiling and everything else. I'll always be grateful for what you've done for me and Alice. But I can't afford to muck around anymore. My life is serious. I've got Alice. I can't afford to screw up."

"You think what happened between us is a screw-up?"

Somehow she dredged up a smile. "It was fun. While it lasted. And now it's over."

She turned and slipped inside the house. He caught

one last glimpse of her as the door closed between them. She looked distant and closed off, all her vibrancy clamped down. Then the door was in his face, black and solid and unequivocal.

He stared at it for long seconds, trying to understand what had just happened. He'd wanted to comfort her, reassure her—and she'd kicked him out.

No, not just kicked him out, she'd given him his marching orders. She didn't want to see him again. They were over.

It didn't feel over for him. In fact, it felt the exact opposite of over.

He turned and walked to the edge of the porch, sinking onto the top step. He stared at the empty street and the night-dark houses and felt like the biggest fool under the sun.

Because what kind of an idiot only worked out that he was in love with a woman when she shut the door in his face and told him she never wanted to see him again?

It had been under his nose for weeks. The way he'd kept coming up with excuses to see her—the car, the broken door, the ceiling repair. The way he'd bent over backward to ensure she was happy. The way he hadn't been able to keep his hands to himself, though he'd known right from the start that getting involved with her would be complicated.

He loved her. Her scent. Her smile. Her warm eyes. Her self-deprecating humor. Her soft, smooth skin. Her stubbornness. Her temper. Her vintage dresses and old-fashioned shoes and big glasses and bright underwear. He loved all of it, because it was all Pippa, and he couldn't get enough of her.

Harry shook his head as he remembered that first

kiss in her half-repaired bedroom. He'd been so stupid, so slow. He should have known then. The moment his lips touched hers, he should have known.

Instead, he'd told her he was a bad bet for anything more than a good time, and he'd brought violence and rage to her doorstep because he'd failed to clear the air with Steve.

He'd bumbled through this whole relationship like a stupid kid who'd didn't know his arse from his elbow.

Was it any wonder—really?—she'd shut the door in his face? Was it any wonder she thought he was a mistake waiting to happen?

Way to go, dickhead. Really well played.

Heaviness settled in. He ran his hands over his head, trying to think. Everything in him wanted to hammer on her door right this second and lay his heart at her feet in a big, unscripted blurt. He'd tell her she was wrong about him, that he wasn't like Steve. That he loved her, and that what had happened between them had never been just about fun.

It was such a strong impulse it pushed him to his feet. He barely managed to stop himself from approaching the door. Despite his own sense of urgency, he understood instinctively that now was not the time to declare himself.

Pippa had had a shock tonight, and she was holding herself together through sheer willpower. She'd been scared and shaken by Steve's out-of-control rage and confusion. She wasn't used to drunken idiots showing up on her front lawn with baseball bats, yelling the house down and smashing stuff up. She wasn't used to having the police arriving on her doorstep, lights and sirens blazing.

She'd asked for time. She'd asked him to go. The least he could do was honor her wishes. For now.

He headed for his car. He had to use an old T-shirt from the trunk to clear the broken glass from the driver's seat. He drove home with the cold night air rushing into the car. Once there he wrapped a bag of frozen peas in a damp towel and pressed it to his face and lay on his bed thinking about Pippa and Alice and how much he wanted to be with them and how stupid he was not to have realized it sooner.

He must have fallen asleep at some point because he woke in the morning to a soggy pillow and a bag of defrosted peas beside him. The whole right side of his face ached and he approached the bathroom mirror warily. Sure enough, his right eye socket was purple and gray. A lovely memento of a shitty night.

He wanted to drive straight over to Pippa's place, but he sucked it up and did what needed to be done first. He went to the police station and signed his statement, then he waited over an hour on a hard wooden bench before Steve was released from the holding cells.

He looked like utter crap, seedy and greasy, with grass stains on the knees of his jeans. He stopped in his tracks when Harry stood to meet him in the foyer. Neither of them said anything. After a beat Steve walked past him and out through the automatic double doors.

Harry followed and found Steve waiting for him on the small patch of grass in front of the station, his brow furrowed as he squinted against the brightness of the morning sun. Harry took up his own position a few feet away, eyeing him neutrally. Early-morning traffic buzzed past and the smell of cooking oil drifted across from the nearby McDonald's. After a beat Steve spoke up.

"How bad is the Monaro?"

"Nothing that can't be fixed."

"Send me the bill and I'll take care of it."

Harry shrugged impatiently. "Like I give a shit about the car."

"You love that car."

"Mate… This is bigger than the Monaro."

Steve's gaze dropped to the grass. "Out of all the girls you could have gone for…" He shook his head.

"I love her."

It was the first time Harry had said it out loud. He was surprised how good the words felt in his mouth. How right.

Steve's head jerked up. His gaze was searching as he stared at Harry. After a few seconds he nodded. They were old enough friends that he took Harry at his word. They'd both thrown a lot of four-letter words around over the years, but never that one.

"So, what? You and Pippa are going to do the whole white picket fence thing…?"

"I don't know," Harry said.

For all he knew, Pippa might shut the door in his face again. He was hoping she wouldn't, and he planned to put his foot in the way and state his case if she did, but he wasn't about to make any bold predictions at this early stage.

"I suppose you're going to keep hassling me about her," Steve said.

"Nope."

Steve raised his eyebrows, clearly not convinced. Harry shrugged.

"I'm not your keeper. You want to be an asshole for the rest of your life, go right ahead."

Steve's jaw twitched.

Harry eyed him, wondering what to say to get through to him. "Look. I don't know what's going on in your head where Pippa is concerned, but you have to know she didn't get pregnant to try and trap you. But you know what? Even if she did, Alice had nothing to do with any of that. She's your kid, man, and you haven't even seen her since she was born. She's got your eyes and your hair and Pippa's nose and the most amazing smile. She's freakin' gorgeous, and she's yours. How can that mean nothing to you?"

Steve's nostrils flared. He ducked his head, kicking at a bare patch in the lawn. Harry was reminded forcibly of the inarticulate, messed-up kid who used to gravitate to the Porter house in search of sanctuary from an ugly home life.

"Mate…" Harry said, moved by the pain he could see in his friend's face.

"I never wanted to have kids. Made myself a promise I never would." The words came out as though they hurt. "Knew I'd be shit at it…"

"You're not like him, if that's what you're worried about."

Harry had wondered if that was the problem, but he'd never dared express the thought before. Maybe he should have. Maybe they wouldn't be standing in front of the police station having this conversation if he'd voiced his thoughts earlier.

Steve shook his head.

"You're not," Harry insisted.

"What I did last night, that was a classic Jack Lawson move."

Harry reflected for a second. It was true. There was no point denying it.

"So don't let it happen again."

Steve frowned, shooting Harry a quick, searching look. "That easy, huh?"

"Why not? I know you, mate. I've seen you at your best and your worst. This stuff with Pippa… So what if having a kid with your ex-girlfriend is not what you had planned? Life throws crap at you all the time. You roll with the punches and get back up again. It's the only thing you *can* do."

Harry pulled his car keys from his pocket. "Come on. I'll give you a lift home. You'll have to clear the glass off the passenger seat, but it's better than walking."

Steve's mouth kicked up into a sheepish almost-smile at the reference to the broken glass. Harry started for the parking lot, Steve falling in behind him.

"How's your eye?" Steve asked.

"Awesome. Thanks for asking."

"You could have ducked."

Harry glanced over his shoulder. Sure enough, Steve was smiling.

"Just for that you can buy me breakfast."

CHAPTER FOURTEEN

PIPPA WOKE EARLY and pulled on jeans and a T-shirt. Alice was fretful, no doubt responding to Pippa's jangled nerves. Pippa fed her and rocked her and as soon as it was light outside put her in the stroller and went outside to clean up the broken glass from the driveway.

It was a small thing, but she didn't want any reminders of what had happened last night. It wouldn't stop the neighbors from glancing askance at her for the next little while, but it would make her feel better. As though she'd done something to move on. Fortunately the police had had Steve's car towed last night, so she didn't have to deal with that this morning, too. She still couldn't believe he'd gotten behind the wheel so drunk. But she couldn't believe a lot of things about the way he'd behaved last night.

She swept the glass into a pile and used her dustpan and broom to transfer it to the bin. She felt marginally better as she wheeled Alice back into the house.

She spent the morning tidying, putting the house to rights in an attempt to do the same thing with her mind. She was contemplating what to have for lunch when a knock sounded at the front door. Her gut told her it was Harry and for a few seconds she considered not answering. Then she reminded herself that she was a grown-up, not a sixteen-year-old, and that Harry deserved more from her than silence.

She gasped when she saw him. His right eye was black and blue, the skin swollen. It took a real act of will not to reach out and touch him.

"Is it okay?" she asked, gesturing with her chin toward his eye. "I mean, is your vision all right...?"

"I'm fine. How are you? Did you sleep okay?"

She shrugged. She'd slept badly, but it was neither here nor there.

"Can I come in?"

She bought some time before responding by jiggling Alice and glancing down into her face. She was afraid of what he might be about to say to her. Afraid of how appealing she found him. Of how weak she was.

"Pippa... I just want to talk."

He could only hurt her if she let him. If she was stupid enough to put her trust in him.

The thought gave her strength. She stepped to one side, tacitly inviting him in, then turned and walked to the kitchen. She sat at the table, Alice in her lap, eyeing him across the scrubbed pine tabletop.

"I want to start again," he said.

As an opening gambit, it wasn't what she'd been expecting.

"I'm sorry?"

"I want to start from scratch. No get-out-of-jail-free cards. Just you and me."

Despite everything—last night's revelation, this morning's grim determination—something lurched in the pit of her stomach. She was very afraid it was hope.

"It's a nice idea, but it wouldn't work," she said.

"Why not?"

"Because we want different things from life, Harry."

"You don't know that."

She gave a small smile. "I do, Harry. I know you."

In a way, she wished she didn't. She could have indulged herself for a few more weeks. But the outcome would have been the same. She would have been left high and dry once the fun times wore out.

"Maybe you don't know me as well as you think you do. Or maybe you're confusing me with someone else."

He meant Steve. She held his eye.

"I'm flattered, Harry, I won't lie. But I've played this game before."

"I'm not him, Pippa."

"I know that."

"Do you?"

He was utterly focused on her, his gray eyes demanding a response. Yesterday, she would have been thrilled to hear him saying these things. She would have been over the moon.

Yesterday she had been living in a fantasy land.

"I know you're not Steve. You don't have his temper. You're funnier. I like spending time with you a whole hell of a lot more. You're a better lover. You're sweet with Alice. You're generous with your time…"

The furrows in his brow deepened with every word she said.

"But?"

"But you don't do serious, Harry. You said it yourself. You're a bad bet romantically speaking. You're not looking for a mortgage and 2.5 kids. You want to surf and hang with your mates and kick back."

He started to speak but she held up a hand to stop him.

"There's nothing wrong with any of those things. At all. But they make you pretty much a disaster from where I'm sitting. I have a little baby girl who looks to me for everything, Harry. *Everything*. I am her world.

If I fall over, she falls over. If I have a bad day, she has a bad day. She wears the consequences of all my mistakes. I can't afford to make a mistake with you."

He shifted in his chair, leaning forward. Before she realized what he was doing, he'd captured her hand. He held it in his, his gaze locked with hers.

"What if it's not a mistake? What if the mistake is pushing me away?"

She tried to ignore the warmth of his hand, the strength of his fingers.

"Sadly, Harry, that's a mistake I *can* afford to make, because I know what that looks like. That's my life now. That's the gallery and university and Alice. But I can't afford to go on a fishing expedition with you. I can't afford to believe in you and start building a life around you and then have that all pulled out from beneath me when you realize that playing house and playing daddy aren't all they're cracked up to be."

His chin jerked back and she knew she'd offended him.

"You think I'm a kid, that I don't get it, Pippa? That I'm not serious? That this is some kind of game?"

God, he was saying all the right things. Doing all the right things, too, sitting there looking so earnest and sincere and gorgeous, his hand gripping hers, his body leaning toward hers. If this were a movie, she'd be in tears by now, flinging herself into his arms and into the life he was offering.

But this wasn't a movie. This was real life—her life—and she didn't have the luxury of finding out how far the novelty of her situation would carry Harry. One month? Two? Six? How long before he started to slip off to the pub on Friday nights for a "boys' night"? How long before he resented the time and love and attention she devoted to Alice? How long before he started weighing his lost freedoms against the everyday domestic tedium of family life and finding one far greater than the other?

She reached out and laid her hand over his, steeling herself to say what needed to be said. A little amazed that she was able to find the strength, frankly, when he was offering her what was pretty much her secret fantasy: Harry, for always, in her bed, in her life, walking through the door each night, telling her stories and making her laugh and giving her daughter the love, attention and adoration she deserved.

But something had shifted in her last night. Hardened. Maybe she'd taken the last, final step into full, responsible adulthood.

Or maybe she was simply running scared, absolutely terrified by how much she wanted what Harry seemed to be offering.

Either way, she'd learned a vital lesson last time she'd gone down this road with a charming man: she'd learned how to protect herself.

"Harry, you're a great guy. I have loved my time with you. But you have spent the last ten years avoiding exactly this situation. Am I supposed to believe that I'm the exception to the rule? That I'm the one woman who makes you want to give it all up?"

"I don't see it as a sacrifice, Pippa. Don't you get it? I love you."

She sat back in her chair, jerking her hand free from his grip.

"No."

"It's not a yes or no proposition, Pippa."

She stood, clutching Alice to her. "I'm, um, flattered, Harry, but it doesn't change anything. You should g-go...."

She trailed off as her treacherous voice betrayed her. A light came into Harry's eyes and she knew that he'd seen into the secret heart of her in that one, revealing moment. He'd seen something that she'd kept so well hidden that she hadn't even acknowledged it to herself.

He stood and rounded the table. She retreated, matching him step for step as he approached. It took three steps for her back to hit the wall. Harry stopped, leaving only inches between them.

"Tell me you don't love me, too, Pippa."

"I-don't-love-you." She said it very quickly, the words running together.

He should have looked disappointed. She'd said it, hadn't she?

He smiled. She swallowed nervously as he moved closer still. His face lowered toward hers. She turned her head, offering him her cheek instead of her mouth.

She wasn't stupid. She wanted him too badly, even now, to be able to keep him at arm's length if he kissed her.

His lips brushed her cheek, then moved to her ear. "Fibber." The single word slid across her skin like a caress.

She opened her mouth to deny him again but he kissed the sensitive spot below her ear, his tongue darting out to taste her skin. She closed her eyes, reminding herself that she was holding her daughter and that she was fully clothed and that there was no way he could know how much his touch affected her.

His lips nibbled the lobe of her ear. A shudder went through her. Hard to believe they'd made love only yesterday. She felt as though she'd been starving for his touch for years. Decades.

"Pants on fire, Pippa."

He pulled back enough for her to see the glint in his eyes. He was so charming, and so confident in that charm. It was his stock in trade. The honey he'd used to lure many a woman over the years. And she'd been so determined to be different from them all....

She looked down at Alice, reminding herself of everything that was at stake. Alice stared back at her unblinkingly.

So much trust. So much faith. So much vulnerability.

She lifted her gaze to Harry again.

"My pants don't figure into this," she said.

Some of the confidence leaked out of him.

"At least give me a chance, Pippa. Let me prove that I love you and Alice. Let me prove how much I want both of you in my life."

"No."

"Why not?"

"Because I think it's best if we just end things and go our separate ways."

"Because you're afraid you'll cave? Because you want me as much as I want you?" His eyes held hers. "Because you love me?"

"Because I made a promise to myself. And to Alice."

She didn't wait for him to respond, slipping away from him. She put a good bit of distance between them, shifting Alice's weight from one hip to the other.

Harry eyed her from across the room. "I'm not giving up."

There was a determined note underpinning his voice that both thrilled and scared her.

"I was never yours to give up."

"Yes, you were, Pippa. At least be honest about that."

She couldn't hold his gaze, letting it slide down his chest.

"I'm not giving up, Pippa," he said again.

He left the room. She remained where she was until she heard the click of the front door. She walked into the sunroom and sank onto the couch. She laid Alice carefully on her play quilt on the floor, then pulled her legs up onto the couch and backed into the corner, resting her forehead on her knees.

Then and only then did she let herself cry.

Because of course she loved him. How could she not? He'd ridden into her life in his shiny black car and rescued her and infuriated her and seduced her. He was larger than life, warm, generous, charming, sexy, clever...

And not for her.

So not for her.

Did you hear what he said? He loves you. He loves Alice. He wants both of you. What is wrong with any of that?

She pressed her forehead harder into her knees, trying to keep quiet so Alice didn't pick up on her distress.

She wanted to believe in Harry's love so badly. She wanted to believe in him so much she ached.

But what if she got it wrong again?

She gave up on being quiet then, letting her tears fall, sobbing helplessly into her knees.

She was afraid. That was the truth of it. Afraid she wasn't enough. Afraid she wouldn't be strong enough to survive another abandonment. Afraid of letting down her daughter again.

There. She'd admitted it. It didn't change anything, but she'd admitted it.

Now she had to remain strong and hold her ground.

HARRY FOUND Mel and Flynn in the herb garden, both of them sporting garden gloves and tans and hats to protect them from the harsh midday sun.

"Harry, hey— Oh, wow. What does the other guy look like?" Mel said as she noticed his eye.

"I need to talk."

Her welcoming smile faded. "Is everything okay?"

"No."

She shot a glance at Flynn.

"I'll go grab us all a drink," Flynn said diplomatically.

He headed for the house. Mel moved closer and lifted a hand as if to touch his face. Harry flinched away from her.

"It hurts, if that's what you're wondering."

"Who hit you? Steve?"

"Yeah. But that's not why I'm here."

"Okay." Mel looked confused.

"Pippa doesn't trust me, Mel. She thinks I'm going to freak out like Steve and leave her high and dry. She says she can't afford to take a risk anymore because she's got Alice." He paced in front of his sister, frustration spilling out of him. "She loves me. She denies it, but I know she does. I can see it in her eyes. But she won't even give me a chance."

Mel reached out and caught his wrist. "Harry, you are seriously making me dizzy. Stand in one spot for five seconds, okay?"

He planted his feet and regarded his sister. "I don't know what to do."

He was fully aware of the irony of his own words. From the moment he'd looked at girls and liked what he'd seen, he'd known what to do with them. He'd made them laugh and stolen kisses. When he'd grown older, he'd talked them out of their underwear and stolen a whole lot more. Now, here he was at thirty, asking his sister for advice on how to get through to the woman he loved, the one woman who wanted nothing to do with his charmer's bag of tricks.

"You love her." It was a statement, not a question.

"Yes." More than he could articulate. So much it scared him if he thought about it too much. He loved her, and he loved Alice because she was a part of Pippa, and because when she looked at him or grabbed his sleeve or his finger or laughed up into his face, he felt as though he was a part of something real and good and worthwhile.

"Tell me what she said."

He sighed impatiently, but Mel made him go over his conversation with Pippa. Then she made him tell her about last night. After he'd answered all her questions, she bit her lip, her expression pensive.

"What?"

"She's scared, Harry. And she's got every reason to be. Steve really did a number on her, didn't he? She must have been terrified, finding herself pregnant, and with him telling her he wanted nothing to do with her or her child."

He stared at the ground, burning with shame and self-directed anger as he remembered how he'd distanced himself from the whole situation. It had been messy and emotional—and he didn't do messy and emotional. He'd told himself it was none of his business and

assuaged himself with visiting Pippa in hospital once
Alice was born.

"She thinks I'm like him, but I'm not Steve." He
could hear the defensiveness in his own voice.

Mel touched his arm. "I know that, Harry. You'd
never walk out on your responsibilities. She probably
knows that, too. But that doesn't stop her from being
scared. Far, far easier to batten down the hatches and
lock the world out than take a chance."

She said it ruefully and he knew she was thinking
about her relationship with Flynn.

"I told her I wasn't going to give up on her. I want
this, Mel. I want to make her happy. I want to watch
Alice take her first steps and I want to teach her to
ride a bike and I want to scare boys off when they start
sniffing around. I want to give her a brother or sister.
Maybe one of each. I want to get them out of that dump
of a house. I want—" His voice broke and he stopped,
swallowing a lump of emotion.

Mel's eyes were full of sympathy. "Harry. My God,
this is a big sister's wet dream, hearing you say all this
stuff after all your years of messing around. And I can't
take any pleasure in it because I hate seeing you this
unhappy."

"I don't know what to do," he said, aware he'd come
full circle.

He gazed at the toes of his boots and waited for his
sister to offer some insight. When she didn't immediately offer up a pearl, he glanced at her. She shrugged.

"I don't have a magic wand, Harry. I can only tell
you what worked with me and Flynn. Patience. He hung
in there and waited me out."

Harry frowned at his boots. It wasn't bad advice. It
wasn't what he wanted to hear, because he wanted to

be with Pippa *now*. He wanted to start the rest of their lives *now*.

But he'd heard what his sister had said. He got it. He'd seen the fear in Pippa's eyes.

If she needed time, he would give it to her. But he wasn't going away, and he wasn't giving up.

PIPPA WOKE ON Sunday to find an old-fashioned paper shopping bag on her doorstep when she went to collect the morning paper from the front porch. She opened it and discovered a jar of homemade preserves, a pat of Danish butter and a loaf of crusty sourdough from the boutique bakery in Mount Eliza.

She walked to the top of the steps and looked out into the street. She couldn't see Harry's car or truck, and she turned back to the house.

She took the bag into the kitchen and considered it.

She'd ended things between them. The fair and honest thing to do would be to drop the bag back on his doorstep, with a polite yet firm thanks-but-no-thanks. She made the mistake of peeking in the bag again then, and discovered that the jam he'd chosen was the same one she'd selected for Gaylene's Christmas present. She'd made a comment as she selected it, confessing how much she loved raspberries and joking that it was good for your soul to give someone something that you coveted yourself.

He'd remembered. A silly, throwaway line, one of many she'd made as they browsed the shops that day, and he'd remembered.

It wasn't the first time he'd held on to the small, inconsequential things she said. He was always attentive. Always interested.

Because he loves you. Remember that small, incon-sequential thing he *said?*

She pushed the jar of jam back into the bag, but every time she walked past the kitchen counter her eye was drawn to it. The smell of fresh-baked bread seeped into the room and her willpower gave out midafternoon. She'd just put Alice down for her afternoon nap, and she returned to the kitchen, looked at the bag for the fiftieth time that day and something snapped inside her.

Pippa pulled out the bread and cut herself two thick slices, slathering them with butter and raspberry jam. She sat at the dining room table and ate Harry's offer-ing and thought about how early he must have gotten up to buy the bread, jam and butter and leave them on her doorstep without being seen. She thought about him lying in bed last night, planning his strategy. She thought about him selecting the jam for her from amongst all the jams on offer in the store.

The need to call him was like an ache in her bones. She didn't, though. She put the jam and butter in the fridge and wrapped the bread so it would stay fresh and unpacked her books to study.

She'd made her decision. She was playing it safe.

The following Wednesday, she arrived home to be enveloped by the smell of fresh-cut grass the moment she got out of the car. She frowned. Then it hit her—someone had mown her lawn. Instead of a knee-high mess, it was now neatly clipped, the edges crisply fin-ished. The garden beds had been weeded, too, and the dangling flap on the back of the letter box repaired.

She stood and stared for long minutes. Then she turned and got Alice out of her baby seat. Once she was inside, she poured herself a glass of wine and stood on the front porch and surveyed her neat, tidy yard as she drank it. With every sip, something loosened inside her. Warmth spread through her belly and down into her legs. She thought about Harry pushing the mower through the jungle of her yard. She thought about Harry on his hands and knees pulling weeds.

All that thought and consideration. All that energy he'd put into looking out for her. Showing her that he wasn't going away. That he wasn't giving up.

Because he loved her.

It was heady stuff. Intoxicating, really. She stared at her phone as she finished the last of her glass of wine, tempted. So tempted.

It would be so easy to call him and give in. To throw herself on his mercy.

She called up a blank text window on her phone and tapped in a message. She read it twice before she hit send.

Harry, the bread and jam were wonderful, the garden a godsend. Please don't do anything more.

Pippa didn't hear from him for the rest of the week and all of the weekend. She told herself that she was relieved, but the truth was that every time she came home and found no sign of Harry, she felt a small, dull throb of disappointment.

You're such a pathetic hypocrite, she told herself as she turned into the driveway on Monday night, painfully aware that her heart rate had picked up at the prospect of coming home.

Just in case there was something from Harry.

She spotted the large, rather substantial-looking box on her porch immediately. It wasn't until she was halfway up the steps, Alice a heavy weight in her arms, that she registered that the box had a peaked roof.

"No. Harry, you didn't."

But he had. It was the same style of dollhouse as the one in the shop, but he'd chosen different colored wallpaper and arranged the furniture to suit himself. When she circled it she saw he'd installed an addition— a neatly made garage, fixed to the side of the building.

"You idiot," she said under her breath.

It would be years before Alice was old enough to appreciate this. And it was so expensive. Ridiculously so. It was a crazy, impulsive, silly thing to have done.

And it made her giddy with suppressed joy. It made her want to sit down and cry and throw back her head and laugh at the same time.

He'd wallpapered a dollhouse for her and built a toy garage. He was mad, utterly mad.

And he loved her. He really loved her.

She pulled out her phone and thought for a long time before sending him a message.

You shouldn't have. She will love it forever. I don't know what to say.

Although she did. She simply wasn't sure she was ready to say it yet.

That night, Pippa dreamed of a small, perfect house filled with small, perfect people. The next morning she ate her breakfast while examining all the exquisite details of the dollhouse interior. Harry must have put in hours and hours to make it so beautiful.

The thought made her want to call him, but she still wasn't ready so she got dressed for work instead. She got a call from day care midafternoon to let her know that Alice had a mild fever and she needed to come pick her up. Pippa took her straight to the doctor, who assured her it was nothing to be worried about and sent her home with some baby aspirin. She didn't notice the large envelope sticking out of the letterbox until she was locking up the car. She tucked it under her arm with the rest of Alice's paraphernalia and concentrated on settling her fractious daughter.

Even when she finally turned her attention to the mail, she didn't understand what she was looking at until she pulled the thick sheaf of papers from the envelope and saw the impressive letterhead.

She read the covering letter with growing incredulity. By the time she'd finished she sat back on the couch and stared blankly at the wall, utterly stunned.

Steve had had a trust created in Alice's name and deposited ten thousand dollars into it. He was proposing that Pippa be the sole trustee, in charge of disbursing funds as she saw fit. The letter said he would be adding to the funds on a quarterly basis as well as making regular child support payments.

She reread the letter twice, then flicked through the paperwork to make sure she hadn't misunderstood.

Steve had stepped up. He'd finally acknowledged his daughter. Not exactly in the way that Pippa might have hoped, true, since there was no mention of his personal involvement in her life, but it was a stupendous start when they'd started from less than zero.

She knew who she had to thank for the tectonic shift in his attitude, too.

Harry.

Harry, with his strong moral code and principles. Harry, with his determination to right the wrongs in her life. Harry, who had never ceased riding to her rescue.

The thought of him being her advocate with his friend even while she held him at arm's length made her chest ache.

He was a good man.

Something expanded inside her as the thought echoed in her mind.

He *was* a good man. He had only ever behaved honorably toward her, even when he'd been slipping into a relationship that was way out of his comfort zone. He was hardworking and respectful and considerate, in and out of the bedroom. He was funny and irreverent, too, but he stepped up when he needed to, as he had with his father's business.

As he wanted to with her—except she'd sent him away.

Pippa pressed her fingers to her lips, striving to contain the strong emotion rising inside her. After a few seconds she decided it was useless, so she let the tears flow as she stood and went to collect Alice from her room. She sobbed as she strapped Alice into the car and wiped tears from her cheeks for the entire ten minutes of the drive to Harry's place. She had the hiccups by the time she got Alice out of the car and approached his front door.

Harry flung open the door before she could knock, barreling out onto the porch in nothing but a pair of well-worn jeans.

"Pippa. What's wrong? Is it Alice? God, please tell me it's not Alice." He reached for them both with a fierce urgency, gathering them close protectively.

"I love you," she hiccupped, looking up into his beautiful face. "So much. I'm sorry I've been such a big chicken. I'm sorry I made you wait. I was so determined not to screw up again, Harry, but you were right.

Letting you go would be the big screw-up. The biggest screw-up of my life."

The confused, worried look faded from Harry's face. "So you're okay? Nothing's wrong with Alice."

"No." She sniffed and used the back of her free hand to wipe her cheeks. "No. I just love you. That's all."

Harry closed his eyes for a beat, resting a hand over his heart. "Bloody hell, Pippa… When I saw you crying—"

She cut him off with a kiss, standing on her tiptoes and hooking a hand behind his head to drag his mouth down to hers. She kissed him fervently, desperately, pouring all of her pent-up feelings into the meeting of their mouths. His arms stole around her body, hauling her and Alice closer. She felt the press of his big, hard chest against her breasts and knew that she'd come home.

Finally.

They kissed until she was breathless, until her knees were weak and her thighs on fire. They kissed until Harry was trembling with suppressed need, his hands curling into her back.

There was no telling where it might have ended if Alice hadn't started crying. Pippa opened her eyes and drew back enough to look down at her daughter. Alice stared up at her, an outraged expression in her wide blue eyes.

"I'm not sure, but I think we just shocked her," she said.

"Figures. I could never stand it when Mum and Dad got busy when we were kids. No one wants to think of their parents having sex."

He said it so easily. So naturally. *Parents.* As in family. As in the three of them. A ripple of fear, closely followed by excitement, washed through her.

"You want that, Harry? You really want that?" she asked.

She already knew the answer. She wouldn't be here if she didn't. But she wanted to hear it. She needed to hear it.

"I want you," Harry said, without hesitation. "I want you and Alice. I want the bottle sterilizer and the stinky diapers and you pulling your hair out over assignments and me pulling my hair out over the accounts and weekends pottering around the house doing nothing except being with both of you. I want you, Pippa White. I want you forever."

Pippa's smile was so wide it physically hurt. No one had ever told her that happiness could feel both sharp and sweet at the same time. But she knew now. Thanks to Harry.

"You've got me, Harry. You've got me."

Harry lowered his head and kissed her again—and this time Alice didn't make a sound. Smart girl.

* * * * *

THE LARKVILLE LEGACY

A secret letter…two families changed for ever

Welcome to the small town of Larkville, Texas, where the Calhoun family has been ranching for generations.

Meanwhile, in New York, the Patterson family rules America's highest echelons of society.

Both families are totally unprepared for the news that they are linked by a shocking secret.

For hidden on the Calhoun ranch is a letter that's been lying unopened and unread—until now!

Meet the two families in all eight books of this brand-new series:

THE COWBOY COMES HOME
by Patricia Thayer

SLOW DANCE WITH THE SHERIFF
by Nikki Logan

TAMING THE BROODING CATTLEMAN
by Marion Lennox

THE RANCHER'S UNEXPECTED FAMILY
by Myrna Mackenzie

HIS LARKVILLE CINDERELLA
by Melissa McClone

THE SECRET THAT CHANGED EVERYTHING
by Lucy Gordon

THE SOLDIER'S SWEETHEART
by Soraya Lane

THE BILLIONAIRE'S BABY SOS
by Susan Meier

Dear Reader,

I was excited when my editor invited me to participate in THE LARKVILLE LEGACY, an eight-book continuity series centred around two families, a secret and a ranch in Larkville, Texas. I've read many romances set on ranches, but I had never written one. I figured it was time. Imagine my surprise when I discovered the hero in my book wasn't a cowboy but a famous movie star! And the story doesn't take place in Texas, either.

Megan Calhoun, the youngest of the Calhoun siblings, is an aspiring costume designer. She's interning on a film set in Hollywood, far away from friends, family and Larkville. The last person she expects to befriend her is Adam Noble, a handsome stuntman turned leading man.

Setting a story at a movie studio (aka "the lot") and in the world of filmmaking was fun, but it offered a few challenges.

The first was Megan's costume designer occupation. My family says I'm "fashion-challenged." I prefer to say I dress for comfort. One of the perks of being a writer! Fortunately a friend is a designer and Irish dance dressmaker. Knowing her and how she works gave me some much-needed insight into my heroine.

The second challenge was my lack of moviemaking knowledge. Thankfully a friend from college, who lives in the Los Angeles area and has worked on films, offered not only to help me but also to put me in contact with a producer and a costume designer, who were happy to answer my many questions.

I hope you enjoy Megan and Adam's story and THE LARKVILLE LEGACY series.

Melissa

HIS LARKVILLE
CINDERELLA

BY
MELISSA McCLONE

First published in Great Britain 2013
by Mills & Boon, an imprint of Harlequin (UK) Limited,
Eton House, 18-24 Paradise Road, Richmond, Surrey TW9 1SR

© Harlequin Books S.A. 2012

Special thanks and acknowledgement are given to Melissa McClone for her contribution to The Larkville Legacy series.

ISBN: 978 0 263 90075 0
ebook ISBN: 978 1 472 00428 4

23-0113

Harlequin (UK) policy is to use papers that are natural, renewable and recyclable products and made from wood grown in sustainable forests. The logging and manufacturing processes conform to the legal environmental regulations of the country of origin.

Printed and bound in Spain
by Blackprint CPI, Barcelona

With a degree in mechanical engineering from Stanford University, the last thing **Melissa McClone** ever thought she would be doing was writing romance novels. But analyzing engines for a major US airline just couldn't compete with her "happily-ever-afters." When she isn't writing, caring for her three young children or doing laundry, Melissa loves to curl up on the couch with a cup of tea, her cats and a good book. She enjoys watching home decorating shows to get ideas for her house—a 1939 cottage that is *slowly* being renovated. Melissa lives in Lake Oswego, Oregon, with her own real-life hero husband, two daughters, a son, two lovable but oh-so-spoiled indoor cats, and a no-longer-stray outdoor kitty that has decided to call the garage home.

Melissa loves to hear from her readers. You can write to her at PO Box 63, Lake Oswego, OR 97034, USA, or contact her via her website, www.melissamcclone.com.

For Alison Thrasher

Special thanks to Julie Adams,
Mary Church, Roxanne Coyne,
Jay at Zuma Jay Surfboards in Malibu,
Terri Reed and Jennifer Shirk.

CHAPTER ONE

MALIBU, California, was a long way from her family's ranch in Larkville, Texas.

Tension bunched Megan Calhoun's shoulder muscles. She would be impressed with the exclusive gated beach community if she weren't under so much pressure. She exited her car, parked on the driveway of a beachfront mansion. The breathtaking Mediterranean-inspired villa belonged to an award-winning film producer.

A breeze rustled the palm tree fronds. Gray clouds made it look more like winter than springtime, but the temperature was warm. Or maybe she was working so hard she didn't have time to feel cold.

Interning for a film costume designer in Hollywood was supposed to be a dream come true. So far this first week on the job had been nothing but sixteen-hour-long days filled with driving, picking up and delivering things and running countless other "errands."

Intern and *indentured servant* seemed to mean the same thing with production to begin next week. Sleep was now considered optional. If this was life before filming, she couldn't imagine what working on an actual movie set would be like.

She jammed her car keys into the front pocket of her jeans, then grabbed the large leather portfolio from the backseat of her car. Eva Redding, the woman who held the fate of Megan's internship and possibly her future career, had left the studio this morning with the wrong portfolio. That delayed a meeting with a couple of Hollywood's heavy hitters. Now everyone was waiting for Megan to arrive with the correct designs so they could continue discussing costume concerns with the proper visuals.

Hurrying toward the villa's entryway, her comfortable tennis shoes felt more like cement blocks encasing her feet.

No way would she let her nervousness about coming face-to-face with the producer and director get the best of her.

Failure wasn't an option. She was not returning to Larkville. Her family might be there, but no one else. Not even Rob Hollis, her best friend for as long as she could remember; he had taken an engineering job in Austin, Texas. Her fingers tightened around the portfolio.

She stepped onto a large, tiled entryway. In the corner, a green leafy potted plant stood as tall as her. A hanging vine with fuchsia flowers scented the air. A wrought-iron tiered shelf held terra-cotta pots filled with various flowering plants.

What if film costume design wasn't where she belonged, either? Her stomach churned as uncertainty threatened to get the best of her.

No. She had a job to do. Megan's father had always told her to do the best job possible no matter what.

She felt a pang of grief. If only her dad were here so he could give her a much needed confidence boost. She took a deep breath to calm herself and jabbed her finger against the doorbell.

As melodic, multitoned chimes rang inside the villa, she remembered the instructions given to her by the costume supervisor.

"Hand Eva the portfolio and get out of there without saying a word."

That would be no problem. Megan excelled at being silent and fading into the background. She'd been doing it most of her life. She'd never fit in at the ranch. Her dad had been the only one who seemed to get her and really care, but he was…gone.

A lump burned in her throat. Her dad, the larger than life Clay Calhoun, had died of pneumonia in October, seven months ago. She was on her own in more ways than one now.

The ten-foot-tall wooden door opened.

"About time." Eva snatched the portfolio away. In her early forties with a flawless ivory complexion and jet-black hair styled into a French twist, the woman wore a black tunic, pants and heels. African-inspired jewelry added a funky and unexpected twist to the stylish and elegant clothing. "What took you so long?"

On Megan's second day in Tinseltown, she'd learned one of the only acceptable answers for being late. "Traffic."

Her boss's hard, assessing gaze ran the length of Megan. Eva's red-glossed lips pursed with disapproval. "You're slouching. Stand straight."

Megan did.

"Is this how you dress on the ranch?"

A plain pink T-shirt, faded capri jeans and comfy tennis shoes weren't going to put Megan on any of Hollywood's best-dressed lists. But her clothing wouldn't draw any attention to her, either. Well, except for now. But she imagined nothing she wore would live up to Eva's exacting expectations. "Yes."

The word *ma'am* sat on the tip of Megan's tongue. She'd used the term with Eva on Monday, the first day of the internship. Megan wouldn't make that mistake again.

"I don't suppose you have any other clothes in your car," Eva said.

Megan had grown up on a ranch in middle-of-nowhere Texas and graduated college less than two weeks ago. All her clothing was casual except for a few of her own creations she'd never had any reason—or courage—to wear outside her bedroom. Not after being made fun of freshman year at high school for the way she'd dressed. After that happened she'd adopted Rob's and his friends' geek look as her own style. "No."

"Then let's go." Eva motioned her inside. "Everyone's out on the patio."

Panic rocketed from the brown hair piled on top of Megan's head to the tips of her canvas sneakers. She wasn't supposed to speak, but she wasn't supposed to stay, either. "I'm, uh, supposed to head back to the studio."

"Not anymore."

The cartwheels turning in her stomach would have made Larkville High's Cheer Team proud. Not that any of those girls had ever given Megan the time of day except when they were trying to fundraise for new uniforms or a competition. "My car..."

"...isn't going anywhere without you," Eva said. "Come on."

Megan stepped inside the villa. The door closed behind her with a thud.

Goose bumps covered her skin.

Trapped, except she wasn't standing in some dark, musty, Gothic manor. This mansion was bright with big windows and gleaming floors. The air smelled fresh, flowery with a hint of citrus. The temperature was cooler than outside. Air-conditioning. That explained the goose bumps.

Glancing around the foyer, she pressed her lips together to keep her mouth from gaping in awe. To the right, an elaborate wrought-iron chandelier hung over a huge dining table that seated twenty. The living room on the left was filled with expensive furnishings and fancy artwork with huge windows that showed the breathtaking ocean view.

Eva strode across the gleaming wood floor at a rapid clip, an amazing feat considering the high heels on her shoes. "Don't dawdle."

Megan quickened her pace. She had no idea what was going on. Pretty much if it wasn't illegal or immoral, she would do what was asked of her. Anything to secure a full-time position.

Eva glared back. "Don't talk unless someone addresses you directly."

Megan nodded. That suited her fine.

She followed her boss through glass doors out onto a massive deck overlooking the beach and ocean. A breeze carried the salty scent of the sea. The sky looked like yards of gray flannel spread out to the horizon.

The patio stretched across the backside of the house and was decorated as nicely as the interior. Seating arrangements had been set up with comfy pillow-covered chairs and chaise longues. One corner had a built-in barbecue and a bar with stools. There was even a hot tub.

Two men, who she didn't know, sat at a table. Both wore light-colored short-sleeved shirts, slacks and dark sunglasses even though the sky was overcast.

Another man and woman, both wearing sunglasses also, stood at the railing. She recognized them from the wardrobe department. The man looked all business in his dark, tailored pants, white long-sleeved dress shirt and multicolored silk tie. The cut and line of the woman's salmon-pink above-the-knee skirt and cap-sleeved jacket reminded Megan of a designer from Milan she'd written a paper on at college.

No one acknowledged her presence. Megan wasn't offended or surprised. Invisible could be her middle name.

Most people had been calling her "hey, you" or "new intern" since she arrived at the studio on Monday morning. She was, in a word, forgettable. Nothing special, as her late mother continually reminded Megan, whereas her three siblings— Holt, Nate and Jess—defined the word. Megan wondered if their new two half siblings, the Patterson twins, fathered by her dad before he married her mom, were more like Megan's brothers and sister than her.

"I finally have the designs." Eva's tone made the delay sound like Megan's fault. "We can get started now."

"Hey, you," a male voice said. "Girl in the pink T-shirt."

Megan looked at one of the men sitting at the table. He was handsome in a distinguished-gentleman sort of way. His tan skin and sun-bleached hair made her think he spent a lot of time outside. She guessed he might be the producer who lived here.

"Go get Adam," the man said.

Adam? The blood rushed from Megan's head. She had no idea who the guy was talking about.

Eva laughed. "Megan is new in town, Chas. She's from Texas and my latest intern. One of her former professors is a very close friend of mine who has an eye for raw talent. Emphasis on *raw*."

The man and woman standing at the rail looked at Megan for a nanosecond, then returned to their conversation.

Megan tried to let it roll off her. The way she used to do back in Larkville.

Here in Hollywood, she had no choice. Getting your foot in the door was all about connections. A few people managed positions on their own, but it wasn't easy. Professor Talbott had secured this internship for her. But nothing was guaranteed. She would have to prove her worth or she would find herself back at the ranch before the annual Fall Festival in October. Who was she kidding? She might be home by Fourth of July, or worse, Memorial Day.

A heavy weight pressed down on her. She struggled not to let her shoulders droop.

"Texas, huh?" the blond man Eva had called Chas said.

Megan nodded.

He gave her the once-over, but with his sunglasses on she couldn't tell what he thought about her. "Dallas or Austin?"

"Larkville."

"Never heard of it."

"You're not missing anything unless you like pickup trucks, cowboys and the smell of cow manure," she replied.

Her comment drew a wide smile full of straight, white teeth. "Sounds like lyrics to a country song."

"Megan," Eva said sharply. "Run down to the water. Tell Adam it's time for him to join us. That's Adam Noble, our star actor. I'm sure even a small-town Texas girl like you knows who he is."

Megan had seen some of his movies, action-adventure flicks that required him to take off his shirt as many times as possible. Adam had a killer, athletic body still toned from his college quarterback days and a classically handsome face. The guy also had a habit—perhaps a hobby—of having flings with his leading ladies. Or so the grocery store tabloids reported.

She nodded.

Most women would call the actor hot, but she preferred guys who were more…cerebral. Guys like her best friend, Rob. Her Mr. Right, if ever one existed. All she had to do was wait it out until he realized she was his Ms. Right.

A squawking noise sounded overhead. She looked up to see two seagulls. Their white feathers were almost lost against the cloudy sky. Very cool. She couldn't remember the last time she'd seen this type of bird.

"We don't have all day," Eva said.

Megan ran down the deck's staircase to the beach.

Eva's cackling laughter followed Megan onto the sand.

Her cheeks burned. Compassion and understanding didn't seem to exist in Hollywood. No one cared if she felt like the proverbial fish out of water, overwhelmed and exhausted. They only cared that she got the job done. If she couldn't, ten others were waiting to take her place.

Not. Going. To. Happen.

She would do whatever it took to succeed in this business. Not that she had seen any costume designs other than those hanging on the walls, storyboards and drafting tables at the work space at the studio. She'd touched only clothing and fabric bolts needed by the staff. But she knew how each coworker took their coffee or tea, what they ordered for lunch and that "Firebreather," Eva's nickname, wasn't an exaggeration.

Megan's tennis shoes sunk into the sand.

Her internship was nothing like she thought it would be. Girl Friday seemed too glorified a term for what she did. That was run errands, emphasis on the running. Gophers got more respect than she did. And she was doing this all for free…for the experience.

But paying her dues was required in the film industry.

Costume designers worked their way up in the food chain.
She had to start somewhere. Whatever she was doing here was
better than being stuck back in Larkville and using her sewing
ability to make alterations at the nearest dry cleaners. If only
Rob had wanted her to move to Austin instead of encouraging
her to take this internship…

She stumbled over a piece of seaweed. Sticking her arms
out to keep her balance, she managed to stay upright. No doubt
she looked like an idiot. As usual. She was all limbs and hair.
Always had been.

A few people stood at the water's edge. In spite of the gray
sky, women wore tiny strips of fabric that showed off their
toned and honey-gold tanned bodies. Megan would never have
the nerve to wear a bikini like that even if the temperature had
been warmer and the sun shining.

Men wore board shorts and no shirts. Muscular physiques
abounded. One thing was certain. The beach was a magnet for
attractive men. But she'd still take Rob over any of them, even
if he were thinner with not so many muscles. He wanted to
spend time with her. He was always there to give advice, offer
support and hang out with. Guys like him were hard to find.

She looked at each of the men. None had Adam Noble's
trademark tousled brown hair and loose curls.

Megan dug the toe of her shoe into the sand.

Where could he be?

She noticed everyone was looking at the water. A lone surfer
rode a massive wave. He did a fancy move with his board. She
thought he might wipe out, but he somehow stayed on his feet.

Two women cheered. Another clapped. One man whistled.

A different woman sighed. "Adam is so hot."

Megan studied the surfer, who wore some sort of wet suit.
It didn't take her long to realize Adam Noble was the one riding the wave. He cut back and forth on his board, across the
rolling wave, doing tricks and inspiring oohs-and-aahs from
the captivated crowd.

Show-off.

She wasn't impressed. Okay, she would give him a few props for making the women drool and the men stare at him with envy. But Adam could have ridden the wave without doing so many risky moves. The guy had a starring role in a new feature film, one she would work on as part of her internship. He should be more careful, not out there endangering himself and possibly the entire production so he could perform for his adoring fans on such a big wave.

Talk about an idiot.

He reminded her of those cowboys back home who risked their lives for an eight-second ride on some bucking bull named Diablo. The guy was all brawn. He didn't have a brain cell in that handsome head of his.

No wonder his costars slept with him. They probably couldn't find anything to talk about with him and figured sex was an easy way to fill the time between scenes.

Thank goodness Adam was riding the wave to shore. The sooner she could get him to the villa, the sooner she would be able to get back to the studio.

Megan might be a lowly intern with only more errands to run, but she had better things to do than stand around and wait for a self-indulgent, stupid movie star like Adam Noble.

As Adam walked to the beach with his board tucked under his arm, waves lapped around his calves. Water dripped off his hair and ran down his lite three/two full suit. He couldn't wait until summer, his favorite season of the year, when he wouldn't need protection from the cold water.

He smiled at the small crowd watching him. Being a star meant putting up with fans wherever he went. He didn't mind. Fans were the ones who paid to see his movies. Without them, he'd still be doing stunts and going home with sore muscles and bruises.

He'd gotten used to the invasion of privacy except for the paparazzi. Those vultures lurked everywhere with their digital cameras and high-powered lenses, waiting for a chance to

capture him looking or doing something stupid. He always had
to be on guard and make everything he did appear effortless.

Like surfing.

Even if he thought he would wipe out. Twice.

Adam would hate to see a picture like that plastered over
the internet and tabloid covers with a "shocking" headline
blaming alcohol or drugs or some mysterious woman for his
fall. The tabloids exaggerated and blew everything he did out
of proportion. But not this time.

He'd stayed on his feet. Once again. And gotten a much
needed rush. He loved surfing on the Fish, a light and maneu-
verable surfboard. Few things in this world beat taking a risk
whether it was with surfing or acting, and succeeding.

As he hit the sand, three women thrust out their chests
barely covered by bikini tops and sucked in their stomachs.

His gaze ran along the line; the blonde had a pretty smile,
the brunette had exotic looks and the auburn winked at him.

One thing he could say…his job didn't suck. But he wondered if any of the three women didn't use the word *like* in
every other sentence and could have a conversation that lasted
more than five minutes.

Men extended their arms to shake his hand. Other women
said breathy hellos, tilted their heads coyly and touched his
arm.

He continued through the crowd, acknowledging each person. Okay, the women. He preferred more of a challenge than
many female fans offered, but he was still a man.

Nothing wrong with looking.

He could invite a couple women to Chas's villa, but he
doubted the producer would want the meeting turned into a
party. It had been delayed long enough due to the costume
designs not being here. He should get back and see if they've
arrived.

His gaze left a zebra-striped bikini-clad *Sports Illustrated*-
swimsuit-issue-worthy body and saw pink. He jerked to a stop
so hard he thought he might get whiplash. Instead of soft skin

and delectable cleavage, he saw a baggy pink T-shirt hiding every feminine curve he might want to check out. Jeans— baggy, as well—covered her legs except for white calves. Not the hint of a tan—or even a fake one—on her legs or arms.

Allergic to the sun? Unless she was one of those vampire types.

She looked to be in her early twenties. Her shoulders hunched, as if she were trying to hide or maybe had bad posture. Light brown unruly hair was clipped haphazardly on the top of her head. Corkscrew curly strands stuck out every which way. Unglossed lips pressed together in a thin line. But her eyes drew his attention.

Dark, thick lashes surrounded pretty brown eyes. The color reminded him of a cup of espresso. Dark and rich with subtle hints of something more, something deeper, spicier.

A funny feeling took root in his stomach.

He stared, captivated.

Warm, expressive…and not happy to see him.

He did a double take.

Disdain filled her eyes, making him feel like a piece of trash washed onto the sand by the tide. He knew the feeling all too well and didn't like it one bit.

Adam forced his feet to move and walked past her.

At least she wasn't one of those rabid stalker fans who stared at him in awe, saw his movies at least three times on opening weekends, slept on a pillowcase bearing his image and believed he was truly the character Neptune, his most successful role to date, and wanted him to impregnate her with a half human, half deity fetus. Those women scared him.

"Mr. Noble." A feminine voice with a slight twang called his name.

Adam stopped. People rarely called him mister. He kind of liked it. He wondered which of the scantily dressed beauties the Southern accent belonged to. He wouldn't mind playing Rhett Butler to a Scarlett O'Hara, especially one who showed the same strength as the Georgia belle. He turned.

The girl with the messy hair and pink T-shirt took a step toward him.

Her? He was usually luckier than that, except she did have beautiful eyes.

On second look, she wasn't as plain as he originally thought. She reminded him of a Midwestern tourist or one of those nerd types who attended schools like Cal Tech or MIT and recited lines from *The Lord of the Rings* without a moment's hesitation. Kind of cute if you liked geeks. "Yes?"

She looked at the sand, as if meeting his gaze would turn her into a block of stone. "The meeting is about to start. They would like you to come back to the, er, house."

Funny, but he would have never expected her to be in the business. She didn't look like any personal assistant he'd seen running around a lot or set. Someone's daughter or niece? Maybe the housekeeper or nanny. "You were sent to get me?"

As she nodded, hair fell out of the clip. Curly strands framed her face. Her high cheekbones, a nice straight nose and full lips were attractive. But she wore no mascara, eyeliner or foundation. Not a hint of lipstick. He was used to women wearing makeup and going to great lengths to play up their assets and look their best. This girl seemed to have missed that memo. Or maybe she didn't care what people thought about her. He found that idea very attractive.

"Duty calls, ladies," he said to the women in bikinis.

As they walked away with promising smiles, the girl before him shook her head. She'd yet to smile.

Her attitude amused him. He wondered what it would take to turn her disapproval into acceptance.

"Who are you? A PA?" Adam asked her.

She tilted her chin. "I'm Megan Calhoun. An intern."

Aha. So she was at the bottom of the food chain. But that didn't explain the way she was acting. Her attitude and her looks wouldn't help her move up the ladder.

"We should get going, then." He wanted to get her to crack

a smile. "I wouldn't want to be responsible for getting you into any trouble."

No smile, but her features relaxed. Gratitude shone in her eyes. "Thanks."

Interesting how she let every emotion show. The girl must never have heard the expression *poker face* before. Adam could have some fun with that. In fact, he would.

"You're welcome." He handed her his surfboard. "Here."

She inhaled sharply. As her fingers gripped the wet board, she struggled to hold on to it. The Fish weighed ten pounds or so, but it was half a foot taller than her. "You want me to carry this thing?"

The indignation in her voice made him bite back a smile. Not quite a modern-day Scarlett, but as close as he'd find on a beach in Malibu. "You're the intern."

"In costumes," she clarified.

Now that surprised him. Costume people tended to dress the part. They didn't wear their best clothes when working on the set because they could get dirty. But they usually looked good. Stylish, even in their grubbies. Megan dressed like one of the tech crew. Maybe she liked being comfortable, not stylish and fashionable.

"You're still an intern." Adam wanted to get a response out of her. This should do it. He grinned wryly. "And I'm the star."

CHAPTER TWO

MEGAN'S full lips narrowed into a thin line. Pink colored her cheeks. Resentful, offended, annoyed, angry, put out. Her feelings flashed across her face brighter than the neon lights on the Las Vegas Strip.

Adam had wanted a reaction. Looks like he got one.

He fought the urge to laugh. Someone who didn't know how to control her emotions was rare in a town where showing any weakness could mean you were shark bait. He liked it. "I suppose I can carry the board myself. If it's too much trouble for you."

Megan didn't say a word. But the determined set of her chin and the gold flames flickering in her eyes told him to back off.

He did. Playing with her was more fun than he thought it would be. He didn't want her to get angry and storm off. Not that any intern would do that if they had half a brain. Truth was, he was the star and could get away with…a lot.

She maneuvered the Fish awkwardly, as if she'd never held a surfboard before. Given the way she tried to carry it, she probably hadn't. She looked like she might tip over.

He reached toward her, but she shrugged off his assistance. Interesting. Many women liked playing the damsel in distress to his knight in shining armor. Not this one.

Megan readjusted the board, nearly losing her balance again. She walked toward the villa.

Adam's respect inched up. She was tougher than she looked.

He liked rooting for the underdog. He'd been one himself until recently.

He lengthened his stride to catch up to her. "Being an intern sucks. But you have to start somewhere in this business."

He waited for her to say something. She didn't.

"I was a stuntman and a stand-in before becoming an actor," he continued.

Still nothing. That was…odd.

Something had to be wrong with her. People sucked up to him no matter what he did. Women would kill to be in her spot right now. Not carrying the surfboard, but having his undivided attention.

"Long hours." Adam wasn't sure why he was trying so hard. Maybe because most women liked him, flirted with him, wanted him. He wasn't used to it when they didn't or how to feel about that. He settled on amused. A challenge was always nice. "But it paid off in the end."

Megan stared at Chas's patio about a hundred yards away, as if Adam didn't exist. He might as well be talking to a brick wall. That was both annoying and intriguing. Women didn't ignore him. Okay, a few did because they were playing hard to get. Megan didn't look like that type, but he'd never put anything past a woman. He'd grown up watching his mother do some crazy things to get a man.

"Let me guess," Adam said, not ready to give up. "You're interning in costumes, but you really want to be an actress."

Megan stared at him as if he were a wild animal let loose from its cage at the San Diego Zoo. A V formed above the bridge of her nose, making her look strangely attractive. "Do I look like someone who wants to be an actress?"

Her harsh tone matched the annoyance in her eyes. "Honestly, no. But you could be a method actor and deep in character at the moment."

The V deepened. "What character would that be?"

He studied her—curly, messy hair, slumping shoulders,

two-sizes-too-big clothes that could be hiding some delectable curves. Or not. "Insecure girl desperately seeking a boyfriend."

Her icy glare would have frozen the equator.

He'd been a little too honest. Next time he'd stick to being polite. "O-kay, not an actress."

As she walked—almost marched—away from him, heading toward Chas's place, Adam's curiosity grew. No rings on her fingers. Hooking up with her could be a possibility. Though she wasn't his type. He preferred athletic women who were tan, lithe and straight-to-bed sexy. Still he wouldn't forget those eyes anytime soon.

"So…" he said.

"I'm here doing my job, Mr. Noble," she said. "You don't have to go out of your way to talk to me."

Her straightforwardness surprised him.

"Call me Adam. I'm just messing with you about carrying my board. A little Hollywood hazing of the intern." He waited to see if she was amused. Nope. He almost regretted making her carry the board. "I'll take it now."

She tightened her grip on the board and sped up.

Stubborn. Adam had to admit he was impressed by Megan Calhoun's total lack of sucking up to him. He wanted to know more about her. "You sound like you're from the South."

No reply.

"You must be new in town," he tried again.

Megan glanced his way again, only this time her gaze was wary. "Why do you say that?"

Her pale skin and clothing were dead giveaways. Not to mention her ignoring him. Most people no matter what their job title and status in the industry would leech on to him, like barnacles on the hull of a boat, in hopes of getting a boost to their own careers. "Just a hunch."

"I've been here six days."

"A newbie."

She nodded.

"First time in Malibu?" he asked.

Another nod.

A breeze toyed with the ends of her hair. Adam wouldn't mind twisting one of those curls around his finger. He imagined her hair loose, flowing past her shoulders in long ringlets. The temptation to remove her hair clip was strong.

Nah, better not try it. She would drop the Fish. Or hit him with it. The mousy ones could be a lot stronger than they looked. Megan might not have the posture of a ballerina, but he was showing some backbone.

"They call this weather the May Gray," he explained. "The June Gloom follows."

"I thought the beach would be sunny."

"Don't let the clouds fool you, you can still get sunburned. Always wear sunscreen." That was what his mom had told him. He bet Megan's nose would be a little pink soon. Her cheeks, too. "How do you like Los Angeles?"

"I haven't seen much," she said. "No time."

It would be hard to sightsee and make friends with the hours interns worked. No pay. No sleep. Zero respect. "If you're ever lonely and want me to show you around town…"

The offer escaped before he realized what he was saying.

Her pursed full lips looked as if they'd been specially made for slow hot kisses. Maybe she would say yes. He wouldn't mind a kiss. He was curious whether she tasted sweet or bitter.

"Thanks," she said. "But I'm not that lonely."

Most likely bitter.

But her dismissive tone only piqued his interest. Chasing Megan could be interesting. Catching her, too. He winked. "At least not yet."

She stumbled.

Adam grabbed hold of her, wrapping an arm around her waist, and the surfboard, to keep both from hitting the sand. Her body tensed beneath his hand. "Relax. I've got you."

She stiffened more. "I'm okay now."

Better than okay, actually. He expected the baggy clothes to be hiding a soft, lumpy body. But that didn't seem to be the

case. Megan Calhoun, intern, was full of surprises and much
thinner and fitter than she looked. "Let go of the board."

"I'm fine."

"Let go or I won't let go of you."

Her hands released the board as if it were on fire.

He liked her doing what he said. Playful images of the things
he wanted to tell her to do to him ran through his mind. He
could think of a few ways to put a big smile on her face. He
wondered how her eyes expressed attraction, desire, passion

Megan accelerated her pace.

Adam kept up with her. "What's the hurry?"

"My boss is watching us."

He glanced up at the deck. Chas, who was producing Adam'
new film, stood next to Eva Redding, the costume designer
Adam hadn't known which of the three costume people Megan
would be working for, but she didn't seem the type to get along
with Eva. Not that many people got along with her. "You're
interning with Firebreather?"

Megan nodded.

Damn. Adam should have made the connection before. He
still wasn't sure why he'd been included in today's costume
meeting, but at least they'd told him to go surfing while they
waited for the designs to arrive. He probably shouldn't have
surfed for so long. He wanted to give his input and make this
film the best it could be. Maybe then he'd get the recognition
he wanted for his acting. "I'm sorry."

And he was. Not only for having Megan carry his board
Someone who wore her heart on her sleeve would never stand
a chance with Firebreather. Eva Redding wowed people with
her talent, but also intimidated them with her take-no-prisoners
personality. She went through interns like bubble gum. Rumor
had it the last one, a young woman he'd met during a costume
fitting, was let go on her fourth day.

"When did your internship start?" he asked.

"Monday."

Three days ago. The clock was winding down for poor Megan.

Adam felt like a jerk for treating her the way he had. She must be under a lot of pressure. He hadn't made a great impression, either. Having Eva see him holding Megan could make things worse for the intern.

He knew what it was like to work your way up from the bottom. It would be hard enough to succeed with Eva Redding as a boss. He didn't want to do anything to screw up Megan's internship. Best to back off so she didn't get in trouble.

As Adam rinsed off in the villa's outdoor shower, Megan stood by the stairs with his surfboard, something he apparently called the Fish. She hadn't been sure what to do when they arrived at the house. She decided to wait for Adam, figuring it might be considered bad form to go up to the deck without him given he was "the star."

The guy had some nerve.

She was surprised he hadn't wanted her to walk four feet behind him, as if he were royalty. But Adam Noble was no Prince Charming. Not like Rob, who would never allow her to carry a shopping bag, let alone a surfboard. Well, if he surfed. Rob didn't like the water. He was into mental challenges, not physical ones.

Still she couldn't deny Adam's attractiveness. His eyes shone brightly and he could carry a conversation, suggesting he wasn't as stupid as she initially thought. But it was weird that a movie star of his caliber had bothered talking to her at all.

If you're ever lonely and want me to show you around town...

Yeah, right. The man had gorgeous half-naked women throwing themselves at him. No way would he want to spend time with someone like her.

Insecure girl desperately seeking a boyfriend.

Surprisingly he'd gotten it half right.

She might be insecure. Who wouldn't be in a brand-new

place doing a brand-new job and after a lifetime of being told she didn't fit in? But she wasn't looking for a boyfriend. Far from it.

She knew the man she wanted. All she needed was for her best friend to come to his senses and realize friendship was the perfect foundation for a serious, committed relationship. Marriage would follow. Then a dog, cat and kids. A happily ever after, the kind she'd grown up watching in the movies and dreamed about for years.

The shower stopped.

Adam's wet suit hung over the swinging door. Megan saw his bare feet underneath. He stepped into a pair of blue-and-white board shorts.

A lump formed in her throat. Had he not been wearing anything underneath the wet suit? Not that it mattered one way or the other.

The shower door swung open. Adam stepped out.

Her breath caught in her throat.

He wore board shorts. No shirt. His hair was wet—so was the rest of him.

She swallowed.

Water rolled off his wide shoulders, down his muscular arms and chest, past his six-pack abs to his narrow hips....

What in the world was she doing?

Heat flooded Megan's cheeks. She forced her gaze up to the patio. Eva no longer stood there. Thank goodness. Megan didn't want her boss to think she was ogling the film's star.

Yes, Adam Noble was handsome and had a killer body if you liked that all-American athletic look. But *she* would never be interested in *him*.

Adam sauntered over, his wet hair pushed back off his face. Water dripped from the ends.

Her pulse kicked up a notch. Maybe two. She understood why he'd been named one of the Fifty Most Beautiful People.

"Thanks." He took the surfboard from her. "After you."

She motioned him ahead of her. "They're not waiting for me."

Adam opened his mouth as if to speak, but didn't. He climbed the stairs. She followed.

On the patio, the others sat around the table. People greeted Adam. He gave each person his full attention, focusing his gaze on them, the way he'd done with her on the beach.

Her father had been called "larger than life." Adam Noble was like that, too. His charisma captivated people. Herself included.

Adam joined the five people at the table.

"Hey, you," Chas said to Megan. He motioned to the bar where a stainless-steel coffee carafe and several glass pitchers containing various colored beverages sat. "Refill everyone's drinks, Texas."

Megan cringed at the nickname. She wanted to forget where she was from. But Chas was the producer so she assumed that meant he could call her what he wanted. Given the choice, she preferred "hey, you" to "Texas."

She headed to the bar, resigning herself to the fact her internship wouldn't give her much costume design experience, but she'd end up with great waitress and driving skills. She picked up the requisite pitchers and refilled the glasses on the table.

"We are on schedule." Eva had the costume sketches displayed. She must have started the meeting without Adam. "Based on our last meeting, Damon, I made the alterations to Calliope's costumes. I'll need Krystal and Adam for a final fitting, then we'll be ready to shoot."

Megan had loved Krystal Kohl's most recent movie. The tall, willowy and gorgeous actress was so talented. Though Krystal had a reputation for being difficult on the set and everywhere else.

Adam held one of the sketches. "This is the new gown for the dinner scene."

Eva nodded. "Krystal will look divine next to you in the Dior tuxedo."

He nodded. "Excellent work."

Eva's sincere smile made her look nice. Maybe there was more to the designer than her bright red lipstick and severe personality. "Thank you, Adam."

Chas removed his sunglasses. "Great work, Eva. As usual."

Damon nodded. "That's exactly the look I was going for. And I appreciate the effort you put into the new designs, but there's been a slight change. That's why we've asked all of you here today."

Eva's gaze bounced between the producer and director like a Ping-Pong ball during a championship match. "Define *slight change.*"

Chas leaned forward. "Krystal Kohl is at a rehab facility in Tucson. Her role is being recast."

No one gasped. No one said a word, but an uncomfortable silence fell over the table.

Eva stared at the costume designs with a blank face.

The two wardrobe people looked at each other, but their expressions didn't change.

Megan stood at the bar arranging glasses and pitchers, trying to appear disinterested. She might be a "newbie," as Adam had called her, but this couldn't be good news with filming scheduled to start next week.

She looked at Adam to see his reaction.

His posture hadn't changed. He sipped from his glass of water, as if the news of his leading lady being replaced at the last minute wasn't a big deal. It didn't seem to be except…

A muscle pulsed at his jaw.

Not as immune as the others appeared to be. He wasn't happy about the role being recast.

"A lot of work went into casting Krystal as Calliope," Adam said. "This isn't some summer blockbuster flick, but a serious drama."

Chas nodded. "We know the caliber of talent needed for the role."

Adam leaned back in his chair. "Who are you thinking about as a replacement?"

"Lane Gregory," Damon said. The award-winning actress was the only child of two movie stars and America's sweetheart. "We've worked together before. Very professional. She can step in at the last minute without a lot of prep."

"She's older than Krystal," Adam said.

"Yes," Damon admitted. "Lane brings a different level of maturity to Calliope."

Adam straightened. "She's accepted the role."

It wasn't a question. The tension lacing each of his words surprised Megan. She loved Lane Gregory, way more than Krystal Kohl. Lane had the reputation of being nice and down-to-earth. Maybe those qualities weren't what Adam wanted in his next movie-set fling.

The thought of him with the talented actress left a bitter taste in Megan's mouth. Lane was too sweet for a man like Adam. But what happened between the two actors was none of Megan's business. Neither was the discussion they were having now. She wiped the bar where condensation had dripped off the pitchers.

Damon nodded.

Tight lines bracketed Eva's mouth. "Krystal is tall and thin. Lane is short and curvy. We're going to have to rethink everything, including the dinner gown."

"You have until Tuesday," Damon said.

Eva's startled gaze darted from the director to Chas. "What?"

"We have no leeway in the schedule," the producer admitted. "Adam is committed to another project after this."

Adam nodded.

"The other talent has commitments, too." Damon flashed the designer a big smile. "No worries. You've done this before, Eva. And won awards."

"I have." Eva shot a pointed look at the two wardrobe people, who pulled out their cell phones and started texting furiously. "I will again. But it's either going to kill the costume department or they'll want to kill me."

"Don't they already?" Adam teased.

Chas and Damon smiled. The two wardrobe people pressed their lips together as if not to agree with the actor. Megan felt herself nodding and ducked behind the bar to grab some napkins before Eva saw her.

"Tell us what you need," Chas said to the designer. "It's yours."

"You don't have the budget for what I need," Eva said.

Megan stood.

Adam waved his empty glass at her. "Refill, please."

She grabbed the water pitcher with lemon slices floating on top. As she stood next to Adam refilling his glass, awareness hummed through her. All that bare skin and muscle was hard to ignore. She wanted to touch him and see if he was as strong as he looked.

No, she didn't.

The guy needed to put on a shirt. And pants. Long ones.

She tightened her grip on the pitcher's handle.

"There goes your weekend," Adam said to her. "Mine, too."

Megan stared at him, confused. His clear, warm green eyes weren't helping matters. He had to be wearing contacts. She realized he was still talking to her. "What?"

"There will be a mad dash to get costumes for Lane. That means extra fittings and alterations," he explained. "Some of my clothes will change, too, since they were designed to go with Krystal's."

"Oh." Not the most intelligent response, but that was the only thing that came to mind as she looked at him. Darn the man with his hard, hot body, killer smile and amazing eyes. "I didn't think I'd have a lot of free time until after filming ended."

If she was still here then…

That burst of reality helped her regain her focus. She checked everyone's glasses so Eva wouldn't think she was slacking off. Or worse, swooning. No one else needed more to drink.

"You won't have much time," Adam said. "But the experience you gain during the shoot will be worth it."

Megan didn't know why he was talking to her. He must be bored because the others were busy. Unless he'd taken a fall out on the water and whacked his head on his surfboard. That was the only other logical explanation for the attention he was giving her. "Do you want me to get you anything else?"

Wicked laughter lit his eyes. "I can think of a few things…"

Megan inhaled sharply. She opened her mouth to speak, but no words came out.

"Be careful with what you offer around here, Texas." Adam spoke with a low voice so others wouldn't overhear.

The nickname bristled again. She was happy to have escaped Larkville, but she didn't hate the town. Okay, maybe a part of her did. But she missed a few things—her nephew, Brady, the yummy chocolate milkshakes and greasy fries at Gracie May's Diner, her dad's horse Storm and, of course, Rob. Megan missed him the most.

"Someone will take you up on it," Adam continued.

What was going on? He'd made fun of her on the walk to the house. Now he was cautioning her. That made zero sense. Then again, maybe things in Hollywood weren't supposed to add up the way they did back home. "I'll be more careful."

And she would be. Especially around him.

Megan wasn't a flirt or fan girl. She didn't dream of being swept off her feet by the gorgeous movie star or some other good-looking guy for that matter. Her heart belonged to her best friend. Or would once Rob realized they belonged together. He hadn't expressed any romantic interest in her and hadn't appreciated when she'd expressed hers in him. But that was okay…for now.

Her dad always said good things came to those who waited. She'd learned patience at a young age. This would be no different.

Parlaying this temporary, unpaid position into a permanent, salaried one was her priority. Rob was in Austin trying to get his own career going. But true love knew no bounds. The distance would make him realize how much she meant to him. Once she gained experience, she would be more employable, could live in Austin and work on location. She had it all planned out.

"I was talking about refreshments," she clarified.

"I know, but not everybody is me."

He sounded genuine, as if he cared what happened to her. That was odd, but she had to admit nice. Maybe there was more to Adam Noble than a pretty face and great body. "I'll remember that."

A cell phone, lying on the table, rang. He picked it up, looked at the number on the display screen, then stood. "Excuse me."

As he walked down the stairs to the beach to take his call, Megan carried the pitcher back to the bar. She didn't look back at Adam, though she was tempted. He was the first person who seemed to care about her beyond what errand or task she could do for them. Unless he was being nice as a ploy to get her in the sack.

No. She didn't think that was Adam's angle. He wouldn't waste his time on her. Not with so many beautiful women wanting to hop into his bed.

That was why his friendliness surprised and unnerved her.

Megan preferred honesty to flash. That was how she'd been raised back at the ranch. She wished her dad could have known he had two other children. She had no doubt he would do the right thing by them, whether they wanted it or not.

But Hollywood wasn't like that. It was full of flashy people. Total strangers whose strange world she'd step into. And that begged a question. Of all the people she'd met since arriving in Los Angeles, why was Adam Noble the one being so nice to her?

Adam stood on the sand in front of Chas's villa with his back to the water. He was far enough from the patio so no one would overhear his conversation with his agent, Sam Tomlinson, who once again showed impeccable timing with his phone call. "Lane Gregory is the new Calliope."

"She must have sweet-talked her fiancé into getting her the role," Sam said.

Lane's fiancé was Hugh Wilstead, the wealthy and powerful studio head backing the film. This movie was supposed to be a game changer for Adam. Instead of his typical action-adventure film, this new film was a serious drama piece. Not quite an indie production, which would have increased his award chances, but close enough to get him recognized for his acting ability. "Damon thinks she'll be good in the part."

"Definitely. But I'm more concerned what's going to happen when the cameras aren't rolling."

Lane's acting talent would help Adam in his pursuit of an award nomination. But she was also a costar man-eater, who would aggressively try to sleep with him in spite of her fiancé. "I'm not going to be her next boy toy."

"If Hugh finds out anything went on between the two of you outside of shooting..."

"I know." Rhys Rogers, Lane's costar in *The Island's Eye,* saw his burgeoning career come to a screeching halt after a fling with the lovely actress. She hadn't been engaged to Hugh then, only dating. "Rhys can't get hired for a reality TV gig now."

"Stay away from her," Sam cautioned.

"Hard to do when she'll be playing my wife." Some actors had no trouble figuring out where a role ended and reality began during shooting, but Adam sometimes did, especially if he felt a spark or connection with a costar. "Unless the script has a major rewrite this weekend, there are love scenes."

"Love scenes are fine as long as you're not rehearsing in private," Sam said. "Might be a good time to give celibacy a try."

"No reason to go crazy. I'll tell Lane the truth. I don't go out with engaged or married women."

"She may not be swayed so easily."

"She won't have a choice when I find someone else to help me relax during shooting."

"Please not another actress on the set," Sam said. "Catfights will be counterproductive."

Adam remembered the last time two actresses had gotten into it over him outside the Château Marmont. It had been flattering, but a mistake on his part. The publicity and negative vibe on the set easily could have been avoided if he hadn't been on such an ego trip back then. He enjoyed female companionship and seduction, but he had to be smart about it or he became nothing more than tabloid fodder. No one would take him seriously then. "I'll find a woman not on the cast list."

He noticed movement on the patio. He caught a glimpse of a pile of curly dark hair. Megan, the intern from Texas. That explained her slight twang.

A smile tugged on his lips. At least one good thing would come out of the casting change. Her internship would continue for at least another week. Eva would be too busy getting new costumes ready to fire Megan.

The thought of her sticking around longer made him happy. That was a little bizarre given she was a total stranger. But something about her appealed to him. Her eyes, yes, but he couldn't quite put his finger on what else it might be. Maybe her apparent dislike of him.

He looked up on the patio again, but didn't see her. No doubt she'd been ordered to do something else for someone.

Megan should make the most of her internship and time in Hollywood. She might have received a reprieve from being sent home in the next day or two, but she wouldn't last. Her quiet personality and self-conscious demeanor weren't cut out for Hollywood, but Adam hoped she would be here long enough to figure that out herself.

It was better for a person to change their dreams than have them stripped away. That had happened to his mother. His father had broken her heart when he took off. Since then, Adam had watched her chase pipe dreams and men. Nothing mattered to her except grabbing the golden ring—another wedding band. She would give up everything, including him, to find her one true love. Adam didn't want a broken dream to have that same kind of effect on anyone else, especially someone so quiet and shy, like Megan Calhoun.

CHAPTER THREE

THREE days later, Megan opened the hatchback of her car. Shoes and shoeboxes were strewn everywhere. She swallowed the sigh threatening to escape. She'd been sighing too much the past few days.

Besides, she had only herself to blame for this latest mess. She'd put down the backseats to give her more room to transport items. That hadn't worked out so well with the shoeboxes.

Megan tucked the car keys in the front pocket of her jeans.

She must have taken a few curves too fast. Not surprising, she'd been running late. Again. Driving was where she could make up time, if, and it was a big if, there wasn't any traffic on the road.

But standing here staring at all the sandals, pumps, flats and boots wasn't getting it done. She needed to put the shoes back into their boxes and carry them inside before Lane Gregory's fitting. That was the reason Megan had been given strict instructions with an impossible time frame.

Eva must want her to fail. Megan matched up boxes with lids. That was the only explanation for being stuck in interning purgatory. A headache threatened to erupt.

She rubbed her temples. It didn't help. More caffeine might. That stuff had been keeping her going the past two days. What she needed was a sit-down meal with fresh vegetables and a decent night's sleep. Neither looked likely in the near future.

Megan arranged the boxes so she could see what was missing what. Gathering the pieces for today's costume fittings had meant killer hours, irregular meal times and little, if any, sleep. Not just for her, but everyone working wardrobe and costumes on the film.

Talk about an insane schedule.

But she couldn't give up. That wasn't the Calhoun way. Her dad might not physically be here any longer, but his spirit and memory lived on. She wanted him to be proud of her.

She picked up a shoebox with a single silver slingback sandal inside. The matching shoe had to be here somewhere.

As she sorted through the shoes, putting them into the correct boxes, she imagined what awful task they—okay, Eva—would assign next. A long list of horrible, degrading tasks ran through Megan's mind. She half laughed.

Hard to believe she was working so hard for free.

Not only working, but driving.

She'd put a couple hundred miles on her car running errands around town for Eva and company. Granted Megan would be reimbursed for mileage and gas, but hazard pay for being forced to drive on the L.A. freeways should be included.

Something silver near the left passenger door caught Megan's eye. The sandal. She grabbed hold of it. Her cell phone vibrated in her back jeans pocket.

Unbelievable. She grimaced. As soon as she was close to finishing an errand, a text would arrive telling her what to do next. It was as if a camera followed her every move so she would never have a spare moment. Coincidence, yes. She didn't think Hollywood was that wired, but it was still weird.

She removed her phone from her pocket, but hesitated looking at the display screen.

Please don't make me go back to the warehouse clear across town. The one I just came from.

That had happened twice yesterday during bumper-to-bumper traffic on the 405. She'd had to drive from Santa Monica to Van Nuys and back again.

Talk about a total nightmare. She shivered.

But if asked to make that drive again, Megan would. She would smile and drive wherever they asked. She would do whatever it took in the hopes of gaining real costume design experience with this internship.

However unlikely that looked at the moment.

She placed the shoe in the box with its match, put the lid on top, then read the name on the cell phone's display screen.

Rob.

Finally.

Usually a thrill shot through her each time she heard from him, but today she felt a sliver of annoyance. She'd been sending him texts all week, but he hadn't replied to any of them. No doubt he'd been as busy getting settled in Austin and starting his new job as she was here in Los Angeles. But she didn't see why he couldn't take two minutes out of his day—thirty seconds even—to text her back.

Megan read his message.

How's showbiz?

She thought about everything she'd been doing, from driving all over L.A. to meeting Adam Noble. The guy, or at least images of him wearing only a pair of shorts with water dripping down his tanned skin, had taken up permanent residency in her thoughts. She chalked it up to him being nice to her. But she'd much rather think about someone else.

Someone like Rob.

Her perfect guy. Even if he wasn't the best at keeping in touch with her.

She typed a one-word reply summing up her first week in town.

Exhausting.

Everything about her internship tired her out. But in spite of the exhaustion, she honestly couldn't think of anywhere else she'd rather be than here in Hollywood. Well, except Austin with Rob.

"So you can smile."

The familiar male voice startled her. She glanced up from her phone display to see Adam Noble standing next to her. He wore a pair of khaki cargo shorts with a button-down, light blue, short-sleeved shirt and hi-tech-looking sports sandals. His brown hair was casually yet artfully tousled. His easy smile showed a gleaming row of straight, white teeth. He looked...good.

Not that she cared how he looked outside of him wearing one of the costumes. She slid her cell phone into the back pocket of her jeans. "Everyone can smile, Mr. Noble."

"Adam."

Oh, yeah. He'd told her to call him by his first name. She stared at the shoes scattered in her car. She needed to get busy.

"You didn't smile at Chas's place," Adam said.

She put a pair of black ankle boots into a large shoebox. "I was working."

"You're working now."

"Trying to work," she mumbled.

Her cell phone beeped. Rob. Anticipation at his quick response to her last text surged—the way it did on the day her copy of *Vogue* arrived in the mail. Maybe absence *was* making his heart grow fonder. Megan fought the urge to whip out her phone, but that would be rude with Adam here. She didn't want to get in trouble for texting when she should be delivering the shoes. Not that Adam would tattle. Or maybe he would...

Not worth the risk. She matched another pair of shoes.

"I know why you're smiling."

Adam's playful tone drew her attention away from the shoes and on to him. "Why?"

His green eyes twinkled with mischief. "I saw you with your phone. Your boyfriend is texting you."

In her dreams.

Okay, Rob was a boy. He was also her friend. But he wasn't

her boyfriend. Not yet, anyway. Sometimes—a lot of times lately—he frustrated her. But she hoped once he realized how good they would be as a couple everything would fall into place.

Still, who she exchanged texts with was no one's business, especially Adam's. "I'm sorry, but I need to get these shoes sorted and inside before the fittings begin."

"You're discreet."

His charming smile sent her pulse skittering. She chalked up the reaction to tiredness.

"I like that," he added.

His compliment made her straighten. She wasn't used to being complimented. Most people in Larkville had pegged her as an oddity years ago. Being friends with Rob, who might be a geek but was also the mayor's grandson, was the only thing that kept her from being an outcast.

Megan reached for another pair of shoes. Her hand trembled.

Uh-oh. She couldn't let herself be affected by Adam. The guy was an actor, a player who had more lines than a pad of graph paper. The realization irritated her. "I don't have time to talk right now. I'm running late."

"You have a mess on your hands."

Captain Obvious seemed as fitting a name for him as Adam. She searched for a red leather pump. It had to be here somewhere. "Yes."

"I'll help."

"That's not…"

Her cell phone vibrated again. Rob.

Adam held up the missing red shoe. "Where does this go?"

Okay, maybe she could use the help. The sooner she finished this task, the sooner she could get back to Rob. "In the brown box."

Adam helped her sort the rest of the shoes. Having his assistance made the task go faster. She put on the lids, then stacked the boxes. "Thanks so much. I won't have time to grab lunch, but I won't be in too much trouble for being late."

"You haven't eaten?"

The concern in Adam's voice surprised her.

"I've eaten. Well, not today. I've been living off pizza, fast food and coffee. I was hoping to have a sit-down meal. Maybe tomorrow." Megan picked up five boxes. The different sizes made balancing difficult, but she managed. "I'd better get these inside."

Boxes slipped.

Adam straightened the stack with one hand while his other rested on the small of her back. "Be careful."

No kidding. The jersey knit fabric of her T-shirt kept their skin from touching, but awareness seeped through her. Heat, too.

The imprint of his large, warm hand left her tongue-tied. She took two steps back. "Th-thanks. I've got them."

"You have a lot of boxes," he said. "I'll carry some in."

Megan's brow knotted. "But you're the star…"

"I was trying to get a rise out of you by saying that."

"It worked."

"And now you're not going to let me forget I said that."

"You are the star."

He shook his head, but looked amused.

"Don't worry," she said. "I won't be able to remind you about it too much. I doubt our paths will cross much after filming begins."

"They call it shooting, not filming."

"I didn't know that. Thanks."

Not seeing Adam would be kind of a bummer. He was the only person who had not only been nice but also offered to help her. That made Adam Noble the closest thing to a friend she had in Los Angeles. Not that she had anything in common with him.

His eyes darkened. "I was a jerk to you at Chas's place."

Megan drew back, careful not to let any of the boxes fall. She never would have expected Adam to own up to his behavior. She wasn't sure what to make of it. Him. *Hollywood*

A-lister and *all-around nice guy* seemed to be contradictory terms, yet he appeared to be both. "I'm figuring out that's how things work here when you're new."

"That's not how things should work." Adam picked up several of the shoeboxes, enough to save her two trips. "Let me make it up to you."

Once again, Adam had done—make that said—the unexpected. His display of chivalry confused her. He seemed so different from everyone else she'd met this week. She wanted to know how he thought things should work in Hollywood, but he didn't need to make anything up to her. Not really. "You are, by helping me."

"This is nothing," Adam said. "Let me buy you lunch after the fitting. We can have a sit-down meal in the commissary. No eating on the run or in your car."

She hadn't known what he'd meant by making it up to her, but a lunch invite hadn't been it. A part of Megan wanted to accept. She could use some company and conversation. Both were sparse around here. Not to mention she was hungry. But his reputation as a ladies' man made her wonder if he had an ulterior motive. Maybe he was the type of man who always wanted women to like him. "You don't have to do that."

"I want to."

"I might not finish at the same time as you."

"I'm not in a hurry."

"I might be sent on another errand."

"You might not."

His attention flattered her. Until Megan remembered how he'd focused on each person at the table in Malibu. Maybe Adam was the kind of person who didn't like to feel under obligation.

"What do you say?" he asked. "Give me your number and I'll text you when I'm finished."

If Adam felt he owed her, her accepting his invitation would make things square between them. If he had asked her out for more nefarious reasons, she could handle it. Him. Nate had taught her a few self-defense moves he'd learned in his military training. But she honestly didn't think she had to worry about that with Adam.

Truth was, having lunch with him appealed to Megan. Eating her meals on the go and alone was getting old fast. She was figuring out the people you knew in the business were as important as what you knew. Being on good terms with a movie star of Adam Noble's stature couldn't hurt her, especially when it came to finding a permanent position. She would need people to give her recommendations. His name would carry weight.

"Sure," she said. "I'd like that."

Two hours later, Adam stood in one of the dressing rooms in the wardrobe department. People, mainly women, scurried in and out, buzzing around him like bees as they scribbled notes.

He was nothing more than a living, breathing mannequin. Clothes came off. Others went on. His white boxer briefs were the only item that remained on his body the entire time.

A mix of perfumes wafted in the air. Adam recognized the scent of one, Chanel No. 5. His mother wore that.

He preferred the way Megan smelled—like springtime. Light, sunny, a little flowery. Not a chemical scent manufactured in a lab, but the real deal.

He was looking forward to having lunch with her. She was different from the people he normally came in contact with, so unaffected.

She'd disappeared after they'd brought in the shoes. He kept hoping she'd breeze into his dressing room.

The costumer, a woman in her early thirties named Kenna, straightened the shoulders of his tuxedo jacket. "I'd forgotten how well this tuxedo fits you. Forty-two long, right?"

Adam nodded. He'd worked with her before on the Roman gods epic blockbuster that had made him a bankable star. Her hair had been blond then, not a flaming red. The new color suited Kenna as did the vintage clothing she always wore. "Thanks to you."

With a grin, she adjusted his sleeves. "I wish all actors had wide shoulders like yours. Suits and tuxedos look so much nicer."

Adam would wear the tux during the first turning point when his character, Maxwell Caldecott, became the scapegoat for his wealthy father-in-law's illegal activity and was arrested. But the tux made him think of something other than that pivotal scene—award season. He was banking on this drama, a character piece with big emotions, to catapult him into an award nominee and winner.

He winked. "I bet you say that to all the actors."

The set costumer, a woman in her late twenties named Rosie, tied his bow tie. "Only the hot ones."

"The truth comes out," he teased.

The women smiled at him. These weren't flirtatious come-ons, but genuine grins.

Adam appreciated their good humor. He couldn't imagine the past few days had been easy on them. They both had the same dark circles under their eyes as Megan. He wondered what she was doing right now.

"Turn," Rosie said.

He did.

"Now for the accessories." Kenna glanced at her clipboard. "We've changed a couple of things so they wouldn't clash with Lane's costumes. She's not a big fan of gold."

Rosie glanced in a marked container. "Speaking of which, where is the new wedding band?"

"Eva had it earlier," Kenna said.

Rosie sent a text. "We'll have it in a minute. Once we get Eva's approval on this ensemble, you can go."

Kenna nodded. "We'll tag the items, then it's time for a much needed lunch break."

Her words made him think about Megan again. He thought she would say no to his invitation, but he was pleased she hadn't. Buying her lunch would make up for the way he'd teased her at Chas's house.

As if on cue, Megan entered the dressing area with a small ring box in her hands. She didn't look at him.

All business. Adam's grin widened. Well, except for her casual clothes. She'd removed her jacket. She was wearing the same baggy pink T-shirt and jeans she'd worn at the beach. Her wild, curly brown hair was piled and clipped on top of her head once again. But the earrings were new. She hadn't worn jewelry before. Add a pair of smart-girl glasses and she really would have the geek-chic look down. Her cheeks were flushed pink, as if she were exercising. Most likely running errands.

"You have Maxwell's ring?" Kenna asked.

Megan nodded. "Eva said there are extra cuff links if you need them."

Kenna glanced at the clipboard. "We're using the silver ones with the diamond chips."

Adam noticed Megan seemed more comfortable here than at the beach house and less agitated than at her car earlier. Not only her demeanor, but her posture and voice. Except for the way she was dressed, she fit right in.

"Show Adam the ring," Kenna instructed.

Megan shuffled forward, her feet encased in white canvas sneakers. She looked a little pale, more tired than when he'd seen her earlier. No doubt hungry, too.

"Our paths cross again, Texas," Adam said.

Lines creased Rosie's forehead. Her gaze bounced between them. "You two know each other?"

"We met at Chas's house a few days ago," Adam explained.

Gossip spread like wildfire on sets. He watched what he said around the crew. Not that anything was going on with the intern. Or any other woman at the moment. Unfortunately.

"I had to take Eva the right portfolio," Megan explained.

Rosie sighed. "The day our lives ended."

Kenna nodded.

Megan removed a platinum-and-diamond ring from the box. Light reflected off the row of diamonds, sending colorful prisms dancing on the walls and ceiling.

Whoa. Adam wouldn't wear that kind of ring in real life, but he could see his character Maxwell wanting something flashy like that. "That's fancier than the original gold band I was going to wear."

"Lane picked it out," Kenna explained. "She felt since she's playing the role of your wife, she should decide what kind of wedding band Maxwell wears."

"So Maxwell is into bling now," Adam teased.

"He will be once you're wearing it," Kenna said. "Put it on his left ring finger, Texas."

Megan's eyes widened at the nickname, and not in a good way. Oops.

He expected her to say something to Kenna, but Megan didn't. Damn. She couldn't. Not as an intern. She didn't dare risk stepping on toes around here.

One more strike against him. More to make up to her. Adam would force her to order dessert. Something chocolate. Most women, even chronic dieters, loved chocolate.

Megan held the ring between her index and thumb. "Left hand, please."

Her serious expression, coupled with her slight Texas twang, made Adam bite back a laugh. She was trying so hard to be professional when it looked like what she really needed was a decent meal, a big hug and a comfy pillow to rest her head. He'd offered the first. He wouldn't mind providing all three.

Adam extended his arm and flexed his fingers to make it easier on her.

As she reached toward him with the ring, her hand trembled ever so slightly.

Her nervousness tugged at Adam's heart. So sweet, the quintessential girl-next-door. He'd bet she wasn't from a big town in Texas. She had small town written all over her both in her dress and mannerisms. Hollywood and Firebreather could eat her alive. He hoped that didn't happen.

The cool metal of the ring touched his fingertip. A slight shock jolted him. Must be static from the carpet.

Megan slid the ring the rest of the way onto his finger. Her skin, soft and warm, brushed his. She tensed, pressing her lips together.

He wanted to lighten the mood and see her smile again. Having her breathe wouldn't be a bad idea, either. She wasn't the type to be easily charmed. He'd tried only to crash and burn. Humor might work. "Do you know how many women would love to trade places with you right now?"

Those beautiful brown eyes of hers mesmerized him with their intensity. Something flickered in them, flashed. "Oh, I don't know. A star of your caliber? I suppose…millions."

Her lighthearted tone matched the mischievous smile gracing her lips.

Objective achieved. He liked her sense of humor. Adam grinned. "At least that many."

Kenna laughed. "But none of us."

Rosie nodded. "Not unless we want to face Firebreather's wrath."

That familiar V formed above the bridge of Megan's nose. "We're not allowed to be fans?"

"Oh, we can be fans. Just not a certain kind of fan," Kenna explained with a pointed look.

"That's a big no-no," Rosie added.

Megan looked genuinely confused. "I have no idea what you're talking about."

As far as Adam knew, there weren't any firm rules about relationships on film sets as long as they didn't interfere with the production schedule. He'd had his fair share of them. His only requirement was when the shoot ended so did the fling. "What's a big no-no?"

"Set romances happen all the time, but Eva won't allow us to get involved with the lead actors," Kenna said.

Adam flinched. He was a lead actor. "Seriously?"

Kenna nodded. "Eva thinks the entire crew should keep their distance from the talent, but she has no say over what they do."

"Nothing personal, Adam." Kenna stuck her pencil behind

her ear. "But some actors wouldn't hesitate to have a crew member fired if they didn't want a person around any longer. That's why Eva tells us to stay away from the leads. It isn't worth losing our jobs over, and it's too big a pain for her to replace us."

Megan exhaled on a sigh. "That makes sense."

Maybe to her, but not to him. Adam was offended lead actors had such a bad rep with crew members. Not that he'd ever gotten involved with one, but there was always a first time.

His gaze rested on Megan, who wasn't his type and likely had a boyfriend, the person she'd been texting.

But, on second thought, when had he ever let minor details like that stop him?

Never.

In the costume workroom, Megan sorted through the scarves that hadn't made the final cut during Lane Gregory's fitting. Megan tried to focus on the task at hand, but all she could think about was Adam.

What was he doing? His costume fitting had ended twenty minutes ago, but he hadn't texted her about lunch.

Thinking about him sent her pulse skittering. He had looked so gorgeous in that tux. Suave and debonair. A perfect leading man, yes. But he'd also reminded her of a...

Groom.

Megan swallowed.

When she'd approached him with the ring, she'd thought he looked a lot like a husband-to-be waiting for his bride at the altar.

A silly thought. No doubt due to sleep deprivation and lack of healthy food.

But when she'd slid the wedding ring onto his finger she'd felt a slight shock, a prick of static electricity. Thank goodness the ring had been over his finger or she would have dropped it.

But she hadn't. She'd held on to the ring and done her job. End of story.

No reason to turn this into something it wasn't. She was tired. Nothing else would explain why, for a moment in the dressing room, she'd forgotten everything and everyone.

Kenna, Rosie, even Rob.

Rob.

Megan's stomach dropped to her feet. How could she forget her best friend? Her future boyfriend and husband? She'd never checked his text message after bringing in the shoeboxes with Adam.

Guilt coated her mouth. She'd been distracted. That was all. As soon as she finished with the scarves, she would not only reply but also give Rob a quick call, if only to leave a voice mail.

That was if Adam didn't text her in the meanwhile.

She reached for a lime-green scarf. Her fingertips brushed across the soft fabric. Cashmere. But not even the luxurious fabric made her feel better.

Agreeing to have lunch with Adam had been a big mistake. Especially after hearing Kenna and Rosie's warning about Eva wanting them to stay away from lead actors.

Okay, eating lunch with Adam wasn't a date. He was simply paying her back, righting a wrong, evening the score. But after seeing how hot he looked in that tux and how she kept thinking about him, spending any time with him seemed like a really bad idea. She couldn't afford to mess up this internship. Nor was there room in her life—her heart—for a crush on a movie star.

Megan glanced at her watch. Two o'clock.

Maybe he'd changed his mind or forgotten about lunch.

She ignored a prick of disappointment. Not getting together with him would be for the best.

Footsteps sounded in the hall.

Adam.

Anticipation made her glance toward the doorway.

A short woman with spiky bleached-blond hair and a tight black miniskirt and purple blouse hurried past.

Megan exhaled the breath she'd been holding. She put away the scarves.

Whether Adam blew her off or not, she needed to focus on the positive—the costume fitting. She was still running errands and delivering items to people here at the lot, but she hadn't been asked to get anyone food to eat or a beverage to drink. This was the longest time she'd spent in the department since arriving on Monday. Maybe things were changing. A satisfied smile settled on her lips.

"Ready for lunch?"

Megan dropped two scarves onto the floor. She glanced over her shoulder.

Adam leaned casually against the door frame, making her wonder how long he'd been standing there. His shoulders looked wider than normal, even though he no longer wore the tux, but the same T-shirt and shorts she'd seen him wearing earlier.

Darn the man. He looked just as hot dressed casually. She cleared her dry throat. "I thought you were going to text me."

"I decided to come by instead."

"I need to put the scarves away."

"I'm in no rush, Tex."

She sighed. "Please don't call me that."

He grinned. "It's cute."

Her heart did a little two-step. "It's not my name."

"No, but it's memorable."

That was the problem. The name reminded her of Larkville, the place she wanted to forget. Sure, she loved her family, the way you were supposed to love your brothers and sister, but they were so wrapped up in their own lives they didn't need her. They never had.

A weight pressed down on the center of Megan's chest. "This might take a while. Go to lunch without me."

"I can't imagine seven scarves taking that long to put away."

Were there only seven? She made a quick count. Seven. Guess it was too late to hope Eva would appear and demand

Megan run another errand or do some other task. "I've been thinking…"

"That can be dangerous."

Especially when it came to him. She mustered her courage. "I thought about what Kenna and Rosie said during your fitting."

"About lead actors and the crew."

Megan nodded. "Us having lunch probably isn't a good idea."

"I invited you out to eat, not to have sex in my trailer." Desire flared in his eyes and made her mouth go dry. "Though if you'd rather pay a visit there…"

Heat burned her cheeks. She tried to think of a witty response. Tried and failed. All she could think about was his trailer and what might happen during a visit. Her entire face must be as red as the cherry preserves her mom and sister, Jess, used to can.

Laughter danced in Adam's eyes. "No trailer today. Just the cafeteria for an innocent lunch."

He emphasized the last two words, but Megan doubted he knew the definition of *innocent*. The guy was wickedly charming. Regular guys—the kind who didn't star in movies and ooze sex appeal 24/7—rarely gave her the time of day. Granted, she never encouraged male attention because the only man she spent time with was Rob, who didn't notice any of her encouragements. But she couldn't understand why Adam was acting this way. He could do much better than her.

"You have to be hungry," he added.

Her shrug gave way to a nod. She was starving. As if on cue, her stomach growled.

He stepped closer and held her hand.

Warmth seeped through her fingers and hand and up her arm. His skin felt rough, calloused like her father's and brothers' hands. But there was nothing familiar about the heat rushing up her arm and the way her pulse accelerated like a thoroughbred out of the starting gate. The urge to bolt for the nearest exit was strong.

Adam gave a gentle tug. "It's just lunch. No big deal."

Maybe not to him. Megan wasn't so sure. She liked Adam holding her hand. Liked it a lot. And that was oh-so-wrong. On many levels. A funny tingling sensation settled in the pit of her stomach.

Pulling her hand away and giving him some excuse why she couldn't have lunch today was the smart thing to do. That was what she should do.

He squeezed her hand. "Come on. Let's go."

CHAPTER FOUR

So much for doing the smart thing.

Sitting across from Adam at a table in the studio's cafeteria, Megan's nerves threatened to get the best of her. Her foot tapped uncontrollably. She pressed her toe against the tile floor. It didn't ease her jitters.

Megan knew better. She should have never agreed to lunch. But when he squeezed her hand in the workroom, she'd caved like a house of cards built on a wobbly teeter-totter. Resolve and common sense had disappeared faster than the hush puppies served at Nan's Bunk'n'Grill out on I-38.

Done in by a pretty face, warm skin and tingles.

Pathetic.

Except the tingles were out of this world. She'd never felt anything like them.

The din of customers' conversations rose above the instrumental music playing from hidden speakers. Using her fork, she pushed around the baby greens, Gorgonzola, pears and candied walnuts. She didn't know why she'd ordered a salad in addition to a sandwich, fries and dessert.

Adam's plate contained a roast beef sandwich and steamed veggies. "So what do you think of the place?" he asked.

As she ate a forkful of baby greens, she surveyed the cafeteria. It was more like a café with modern decor and not one pastel-colored tray in sight. People filled the tables, whether for a late lunch or midafternoon snack she couldn't tell. Coffee mugs and water glasses seemed to be in a race for the drink of choice. No doubt the low calories appealed to the masses.

"This is nothing like we have back home where greasy fries and hash browns reign supreme. Gracie May calls them Texas Taters. Not to be confused with the ever popular Texas Toast." The knot in Megan's stomach tightened. "I'm rambling, aren't I?"

Adam wiped his mouth with a napkin. "No, I like hearing you talk."

He would be the first. Well, next to Rob and her dad.

"Thanks. But being at a film studio is a little surreal." Megan lowered her voice. "I recognize a few people. Actors I've seen on TV and in the movies."

Adam smiled at her. "You'll get used to it."

"I don't know about that." She pushed her salad plate to the side and scooted the plate with a Reuben sandwich and French fries in front of her. "I keep wanting to pinch myself to make sure I'm really here, in Hollywood, and not dreaming. Though they're not always good dreams. I sometimes feel like I'm sitting on a chair covered with thumbtacks pointy side up."

"Ouch." He raised his water glass. "You need to relax. Loosen up."

"I don't think that's possible." At least not when he was with her. Something about Adam Noble put Megan on edge, made her nerve endings stand at attention and her senses shift into overdrive. She toyed with the napkin on her lap. It ripped in half. She needed to calm down. "Was today a typical fitting?"

"Fairly typical. More rushed due to Lane joining the cast so late. But last-minute changes are nothing new. Cast. Crew. Costumes. Script." Adam took a sip of water. "How did you like the fitting?"

She leaned forward with excitement. "It was so awesome."

"That's a strong adjective."

With a shrug, she sat back. "You wouldn't understand."

He raised a piece of broccoli with his fork. "Try me."

Rob supported her interest in fashion, but he had zero interest in talking about clothing. Adam sounded interested. But for all she knew he was being polite. "Really?"

"Yes."

Not saying anything would be rude. He had invited her to lunch. What's the worst that could happen? She'd been teased and taunted her entire life. Adam might tease, but his ribbing could never cut her down like the people back home.

Truth was, she was bursting at the seams to talk to someone about her internship. She'd been going over things in her head, but that wasn't much fun or helpful. If Adam wanted to listen she was more than willing to spill. "Well, up until today's fitting I've spent my time driving all over Los Angeles and doing the jobs no one else wants to do."

"The life of an intern."

"I get that's what I'm supposed to be doing," she admitted. "But during the fitting I finally saw what working with costumes was like. I was allowed to help, too."

He set his fork on his plate. "That would be pretty awesome."

She nodded. "It was eye-opening and showed me how much I have to learn."

"What do you mean?"

"I dressed characters in theater throughout college. I thought I had a good eye when it came to clothes, but today when the costumers and dressers pointed out things that need to be fixed or changed I realized how much I'd missed."

"They pay attention to minute details."

"I know," she said. "I felt like I was watching an episode of *What Not to Wear,* except the show was on steroids with a warehouse-size closet of clothing and accessories to choose from. Then each piece was put under a fashion microscope. A little overwhelming, but I learned a lot listening to Lane talk about how Calliope would dress."

"Some actors like to involve themselves in the costume process."

"Lane sure does. Do you?"

"Yeah. I usually have a good idea about what my characters would wear. Think about what's in your closet. A lot of pieces have stories behind them. A character's wardrobe is no different."

Wow. Megan had no idea a guy would see clothing that way. At least not a straight one. She was impressed. "I didn't think it would be so much of a collaboration. I thought it would be more one-sided with the costume designer deciding everything."

Someone waved at Adam. He acknowledged them with a nod. "It's give and take between actor and costume designer. The camera people can also get involved if they have lighting or color concerns."

"Was the tux one of your suggestions?" she asked.

"The scene called for formal wear. Eva and I agreed on the designer because of Maxwell's background and need to fit in with his wealthy in-laws. But when push comes to shove Eva has final say. Though she's pretty good about letting the talent think we're in control."

Megan remembered something Eva had said to Lane. "Aha."

"You saw it in action today."

"Yes, but I don't think Lane realized that's what Eva was doing."

"I'm sure she didn't." Adam waved to someone calling his name. He seemed to know everyone. "One thing I have to say about Eva. She understands actors as well as she does costumes."

"The woman is meticulous." Changes were made to a costume—color, accessories or something new altogether—until Eva deemed the outfit acceptable. Then photographs would be taken, items tagged and stored. "I can't wait to see how it looks on film."

"Sometimes directors show dailies on Fridays. Keeps morale high among the crew. Damon's pretty good about doing stuff like that."

Megan dipped a French fry in ketchup. "I can't believe filming, I mean, the shoot starts in a couple of days."

"No reason to be nervous."

She stared down her nose at him. "What makes you think I'm nervous?"

"I was my first time on a film set," he admitted. "I am a little anxious with this shoot. I have high hopes for this film."

His openness made her feel less self-conscious. "Okay, I'm nervous. Though I'm sure I'll spend all my time running errands and won't be able to see any of the shoot."

"They might need your help on call days with lots of background artists."

Kenna had told Megan that extras on movie sets were often called background artists. "I hope so. I need some real experience if I'm going to find a permanent job out here once my internship is finished."

His gaze narrowed. "You want to stay in L.A."

"Yes." She didn't plan on returning to Larkville until October for her father's memorial celebration at the Fall Festival. Even then she would only stay for the weekend. "It's the best place to build up my résumé. It's rather light at the moment."

"Your family..."

Her chest tightened. "My sister, Jess, her five-year-old son, Brady, and my brother Holt still live in Larkville. My other brother Nate is in the army. But cattle and ranching aren't my things. I don't really fit in. The town caters to livestock and cowboys, not the arts and fashion. I have different interests and felt stifled creatively. Even the way I dressed made people uncomfortable."

Adam's brows slanted. "Jeans, T-shirts and sneakers made people uncomfortable?"

"This was before I, um, started dressing like this." She shifted positions in her chair. "Anyway, people thought...they still think I'm...different."

"Nothing wrong with being different."

That was what Rob always told her. Easy for him to say since everyone liked and accepted him. "True. But when you're a Calhoun people in Larkville have certain expectations, especially about fitting in."

Including other Calhouns. Her appetite disappeared.

Adam stared at her. "That's gotta be hard."

He had no idea. But no sense dwelling on things she couldn't change. "That's one reason I didn't go back after I graduated college. If everything works out like I've planned, I'll be here for a while."

"You've got plans."

Big ones. She nodded.

"A planner?"

She raised her chin. "Yes."

Amusement gleamed in his eyes. "I wasn't slamming you. Just asking a question."

"Sorry, I'm a little defensive about a few things."

"People back home didn't like your plans, either."

"You'll never amount to anything if you pursue costume design. Forget about working in the film industry. You'll never cut it. You won't be able to support yourself, either. And I'm not about to give you money to live on while you chase some ridiculous dream."

Her late mother's words echoed through Megan's head. She stabbed her fork into a slice of pear. "No, but that hasn't stopped me."

"Perseverance is the key to success."

"I've heard it's all about having the right connections."

"That's a part of it, too, but if you give up it doesn't matter who you know." He picked up his sandwich. "How's your plan working out so far?"

"Too early to tell."

"Cautious. I like that."

"I've learned being too cocky about the potential success of a plan can lead to big disappointment."

"Sounds like there's a story there."

"I tried to run away from home," Megan admitted. "I had it all planned out, but I didn't count on one thing."

"Common sense kicking in," he joked.

"I was fourteen."

"That explains it," he said. "So what didn't you count on?"

"My best friend, Rob. I told him my plans. He wouldn't let me go on my own. Told me he was coming with me."

"Sounds like a good guy."

"A great guy and also the mayor's grandson." Thinking about Rob made her feel all warm and cozy, the exact opposite to how she felt around Adam. "We got as far as the bus station, then the chief of police showed up."

"That's a plan-buster."

"No kidding." Only now could she laugh at the horrified expressions on her family's faces. Her mother had been mortified that Megan had dragged a fine, upstanding young man like Rob into her teenage rebellion. "I was *so* grounded after that. My parents took away my sewing machine. I was devastated. But I'm much better at planning things now."

He grinned. "And who you tell about those plans."

She smiled. "Exactly."

"Remember, you can't plan everything," Adam said. "Some of the best moments in life just happen."

"For some people, yes. But I'm not really into spontaneity and surprises." That was one reason she was relieved to be in California, not home having to deal with two unexpected half siblings. Her half sister, Ellie Patterson, was now living in Larkville and dating the town's sheriff, Jed Jackson. "I like to know what's coming."

"Not knowing what's around the corner is half the fun."

Megan shrugged. "I still have fun."

"I hope so." Adam winked. "All work and no play makes Megan…"

"And Adam," she joined in.

"A dull girl."

"Boy," she said at the same time.

He smiled at her.

She smiled back.

Something seemed to pass between them, as if an invisible cord suddenly connected them. A ball of heat ignited in her stomach.

What was going on? Okay, he was gorgeous. Nice. And…

Time to chill. She took a sip of her lemonade to cool her down. "Though I can't imagine you ever being a dull boy."

"I prefer excitement and keeping the adrenaline pumping to dullness."

"That's why you surf."

"And backcountry snowboard, skydive, bungee jump and BASE jump, too."

"An extreme-sport aficionado."

"Guilty as charged."

"Your family must worry about you."

As he stared into his water glass, his green eyes darkened. "It's just my mom and me. She's not that much of a worrier. At least not about what I'm doing."

Adam sounded resigned, not bitter. Good for him. Megan wasn't quite there yet. "Do you see your mom a lot?"

"No," he said. "She lives in Beverly Hills, but keeps herself busy. She enjoys traveling. She's on a cruise now."

"She must be proud of you."

"My mom likes having a famous movie star as a son." A touch of bitterness now crept into his tone. "It sure beats working two jobs and having to move to a new apartment every six months or so."

"That would be tough. For both of you."

He raised his water glass. "You learn how to make new friends fast."

"An important skill to have." One she didn't possess. Making friends was as hard for her as fitting in. She hadn't shared the same interests as other kids. Her dad had said she was a city girl stuck in a Podunk cow town. That had always angered her mom. But Megan appreciated how her dad understood her longing to get away. But she had to admit that so far she hadn't fit as easily into Hollywood as she thought she would, either. "I've lived in the same house my entire life except for four years of college and coming here."

"There's something to be said for that kind of familiarity."

Maybe if they'd moved around she would have found a place she fit in. But her dad's heart had always been in the land and the cattle. Hard to take those with him. "I suppose."

"Your parents must like Larkville or they would have moved away."

Her insides twisted at the reality of her new world.

"My parents are...dead." Saying that felt weird. Wrong. "I'm sorry to say it so bluntly. I'm still getting used to my dad being gone. He died in October. Pneumonia. My mom died of a heart attack three years ago."

Adam reached across the table and covered Megan's hand with his. "I'm so sorry."

His skin was warm, but rough. The touch was meant to comfort, but heat shot up her arm. She focused on his face. "My dad told me we're never given anything we can't handle. I keep reminding myself of that."

And if she wanted to handle her internship the right way, she'd better pull her hand away right now.

Megan did. She immediately missed Adam's warmth. But it was better this way. Safer.

"Are you close to your siblings?" Adam asked.

"No. But we never have been. Holt is thirty, Nate is twenty-eight and Jess is twenty-six. I've always been seen as more of a pest than an equal in their eyes even though I'm twenty-two now."

Megan ate another French fry.

As if that explained why none of them had showed up to her college graduation a couple of weeks ago. Jess had been too busy with her new husband. Holt was away dealing with a friend who was terminally ill. Nate hadn't even called to say he wasn't coming. Megan had no idea where he was, if her soldier brother was alive or dead. If not for Rob and his family she would have been on her own after the commencement service. Without her best friend, she wouldn't have anyone who cared about her.

"My dad was the one who'd kept the family together after Mom died. Now that he's gone, it's been...different." Megan might have three siblings and two half siblings, but she felt so alone, an orphan in every sense of the word. "But what am I going to do?"

"Move to Los Angeles and make a new life for yourself."

She appreciated that Adam understood. He was so easy to talk to. "My dad knew the ranch wasn't where I belonged. He wanted me to pursue my dreams. That's one reason I hope I succeed. To show him he was right about me."

And that her mom was wrong.

Three women sashayed down the aisle with swaying hips and expert hair-flipping skills, but Adam never looked in their direction even though they were supermodel gorgeous. Instead, he kept his attention focused solely on her. "I'm rooting for you."

"Thanks." One of the women glared at Megan. As if she were any kind of competition. Still she appreciated how Adam made her feel special when she was so obviously out of her league. "I have a feeling I'm going to need all the help I can get."

As they ate and talked about their favorite baseball teams and vacation spots, she realized Adam hadn't mentioned his father. "You said it was you and your mom. Your dad—"

"Was a total jerk," Adam interrupted. "He took off when I was a little kid. Haven't heard from him since. But I don't want to talk about that."

Megan didn't blame Adam. Her heart hurt for him and what he must have gone through as a kid. At least she'd had two parents when she was a kid, even if one hadn't liked her much. "What do you want to talk about?"

Adam pushed his plate away. Not a bit of his roast beef sandwich remained. Someone else had been hungry.

He leaned back in his chair. "You."

The way he looked at her sent her temperature inching upward. "I'm all we've been talking about."

"I want to know more."

"There isn't much more to tell." She lowered her voice. "In case you haven't figured it out, I'm boring."

His smile crinkled the corners of his eyes, sending her pulse into overdrive. "Any woman who orders a salad, French fries, a Reuben sandwich and a slice of chocolate layer cake could never be called boring."

"You were buying. I was hungry," she said. "I really like food."

"So do I."

They had something in common. Two things if you considered their dependency on oxygen. They also didn't have dads. Three things. She could probably find a few more.

What was she doing? And then she realized…

Adam Noble might appear to be a brainless surfer dude with an arrogant streak as wide as the Texas panhandle, but he wasn't. She was attracted to him. Not only his looks, but also the way he listened and talked to her. It wasn't the same as with Rob, but nice. Almost…better.

Not better, she corrected. Different. Still…

Falling for him would be a disaster of epic proportions.

She had to keep reminding herself that.

Over and over again until it sunk in.

There wasn't room in her life or her heart for someone like Adam Noble.

Walking Megan back to the wardrobe department, Adam couldn't remember the last time he'd enjoyed a meal so much. Not the food, though it wasn't bad, but the company. Something about Megan Calhoun put a big smile on his face. Being with her made him feel good. Not that he'd been down, but something seemed to be missing in his life lately. He couldn't quite explain it, except when he was at lunch with Megan he hadn't felt that way.

He glanced at her. She was the definition of low maintenance, something rare in this town. He appreciated that she ate real food and didn't seem concerned about calories or making sure she had the perfect forty-thirty-thirty percentages of protein, carbs and fat on her plate. Yet she wasn't overweight, though her baggy clothes suggested as much.

If he were looking for a girlfriend...

Whoa. A girlfriend was the last thing he needed. Wanted. A fling during a shoot was all he would commit to. Would a small-town girl be interested in a no-strings relationship? Given what her coworkers had said, probably not.

Unfortunately.

Megan's gaze bounced from one thing to the next, taking mental pictures. She was like a sponge soaking up the objects around her. Her interest and her excitement at the buildings, equipment and people they passed were palpable.

Very cute.

Adam couldn't believe she thought she was boring. Someone who was boring would never have accepted an internship so far from home. If anything, she wanted to be swept into an adventure, though she'd deny it. After all she'd been through, she deserved one.

The V between her eyebrows had returned during lunch and remained there. That bothered Adam. He wanted her to relax, not tense up around him. "You okay?"

"Full after such a big lunch, but otherwise fine." Megan stared at a photo shoot. The photographer's assistant rearranged lights. "Everywhere I look I see something new. This studio is a world unto itself."

Her wide-eyed wonder appealed to Adam. "It's like living in a bubble during a shoot. The set becomes your entire life."

"I suppose there are worse places to be."

He thought of some of the apartments and trailer parks he'd lived in as a child. "Much worse."

She spun, looking up, down, all around. "It's almost as if you can feel it."

Megan was so much fun to watch. He'd been as excited as he was nervous when he worked on his first film, but he hadn't wanted others to know that. "Feel what?"

"Movie magic."

The awe in her voice wrapped around his heart like a hug. "Some of that magic will get lost once you see what goes on during a shoot. It doesn't seem quite so real with all the lights, cameras and equipment around."

"Maybe, but I'm sure when I see it on the screen I'll feel the same way."

"You like movies."

She nodded. "I love them. Nothing better than losing myself for a couple of hours in this world or another universe."

"You'll have to go to Mann's Chinese Theatre. A perfect place for a movie buff."

"It's on my list of sights to see."

He remembered her saying she was a planner. "That's one way not to miss anything."

She stared up at him. "Let me guess. You're a shoot-from-the-hip kind of guy."

He nodded.

"Most guys are."

He wondered what kind of guys she knew, who she had dated or was dating. None of his business. "I have an agent, a manager and an assistant who make lists. Two are men."

"An entourage of list makers, huh?"

Megan sure had a pretty smile. "Entourages are important in this town. Lots to keep track of with me."

"I'm sure keeping track of you is a full-time job," she teased.

His agent might agree with her. "Don't believe everything you read. At least half of what they print is a lie or exaggeration."

She raised a finely arched brow. "Only half?"

He grinned. "Three-quarters."

"The juicier, the better, I assume."

"Scandalous headlines sell better," he admitted. "The stuff

they write is unreal. I haven't lived like a monk, but I'm not some dog chasing after every female in heat."

"You're nicer than I thought you would be."

"Thank you. I think."

"It's a compliment."

That was something. "I can be nice, but I'm a big flirt, too. You know guys. We always have to try."

Megan stopped walking. "Always?"

The V deepened. Something was bothering her. "Pretty much."

"Hypothetically, if a guy doesn't try…"

"Then he's already got a girl or…"

Megan stared up at him with rapt attention. "Or?"

She had to be talking about herself. Adam cocked a brow. "Hypothetically?"

"Not exactly." She bit her lip. "Maybe you could help me understand this. Him."

Knew it. And Adam didn't like it. Territorial? Maybe, even if it made no sense. He wanted to know who the guy was. Someone she'd known a long time or someone she just met. Whoever he was sounded like a fool. Megan wouldn't have to ask Adam twice to fool around with her. "Sounds like you've been banished to friend zone."

"*Banished* is the right word. I could walk around naked and he wouldn't notice me."

Adam would notice. But her words made him wonder what kind of friend this guy was. "Have you walked around naked in front of him?"

She drew back, as if horrified by the question. "Of course not."

Good. Adam didn't want her to be taken advantage of. "I've got to be honest with you. Most guys will fool around with female friends if given the opportunity."

Her shoulders slumped. She blew out a puff of air.

Adam didn't like seeing her look so deflated. "Not what you wanted to hear."

"Nope."

"There are two other possibilities," Adam offered.

Megan perked up.

"The guy could be superconservative and religious."

"He goes to church only for funerals and weddings."

If Megan knew that much about him, he couldn't be a new guy. "Then he's gay."

She glared at Adam. "Rob is not gay."

"So this hypothetical has a name. The same name as your best friend from high school."

"Yes, and trust me, Rob likes girls. Women. He's dated several. Just not me." She sighed. "Forget I said anything."

Her dejected tone bothered Adam. "I can't forget now that it's out there."

"You're an actor," she countered. "Pretend."

"I can do that for you. Or…"

She sighed. "I'm not sure I'm ready to hear more. Why don't we say goodbye here? I can find my way back."

He wasn't about to let her get away from him that easily. "A gentleman always escorts his date home."

"I'm not your date."

"I thought you were going to say I wasn't a gentleman."

The corners of her mouth lifted. "The thought may have crossed my mind."

Good. She was back to joking. "You, Megan Calhoun, are one of a kind."

"Next you'll say I have a great personality."

"I don't know you well enough to say that." Even if he was thinking it. "But I will tell you if your best friend, this Rob guy, has stuck you in friend zone, you're better off without him because he's got to be a total idiot."

She started to speak, then stopped herself. "Rob is smart. He's an engineer."

Adam wished she wasn't so quick to stand up for the guy. She deserved better than to wait around for some bozo, one that lived in another state, to wake up. There were plenty of men here in L.A. to choose from. "Being book smart doesn't apply here. Find another guy. Someone who'll appreciate you. Spoil you. Kiss you until you can't see straight."

Her lips parted.

With another woman he might think that was an invitation for a kiss. With Megan, he couldn't be sure of anything.

She eyed him suspiciously. "Exactly where am I going to find a guy like that?"

"He could be right under your nose," Adam said. "But if you keep waiting to get out of friend zone with Rob, you'll probably miss him."

CHAPTER FIVE

On Sunday afternoon, Adam returned to the lot. The studio was the last place he needed to be, but he wanted to check out his trailer.

He glanced around seeing his favorite things that would help him relax in between takes and during downtimes—weights, a pull-up bar and video game consoles. "Looks good. Thanks."

Veronica Tully, his personal assistant, stared at her tablet. She was the definition of efficiency. "You've been invited to two parties tonight as well as a special event at the Wilshire. If you're going to show up, no worries, but if not I'll send your regrets."

With his first call on the set early Tuesday morning, Adam should make the most of tonight. But the thought of hanging with the usual crowd didn't appeal to him.

Parts of his character, Maxwell Caldecott, must be rubbing off on Adam. Forget clubbing and partying. Hardworking, idealistic, family man wannabe, Maxwell attended formal events, the kind that required tuxedos or jackets and ties. Anything to prove his worth to the high-society wife he loved more than life. Too bad she was going to end up making the Wicked Witch seem more like the tooth fairy.

Staying home didn't appeal to Adam, either. He'd spent last night working on lines. Still…

Sometimes he had to show up at events and parties because that was expected of him due to starring in a certain role or wanting to be cast in an upcoming project. He'd "dated" costars because the producer or studio wanted to drum up publicity. It was all business, all the time. "Any reason I should attend?"

Veronica scanned her tablet. "No."

"Send my regrets," he said without any further hesitation.

"I'll book a table for you for dinner. Seven-thirty," Veronica said with the same competency she'd shown since she started working for him a year and a half ago.

Adam didn't want to be tied into any plans. He'd have enough of that during the shoot. "Thanks, but I'll figure out something myself. Take the rest of the day and tomorrow off. It'll be crazy around here starting Tuesday."

"Thanks, boss." She walked toward the door, then glanced back. "If you need me…"

"You're only a text away."

So was someone else, Adam realized. Megan. As Veronica exited the trailer, he whipped out his cell phone and typed.

Working today?

He didn't know why Megan kept popping into his mind. No, he knew. Someone different and new was more fun than the same old same. She was probably out and about, checking off sights she wanted to see on her list. He'd bet she had actual lists, either on paper or her computer. No doubt a copy on her cell phone.

A beep sounded. A text had arrived. He checked his cell phone. A reply from Megan.

Yes, but almost finished.

Too bad. Adam was hoping she'd been able to have fun today. He typed.

Running an errand or at the lot?

Lot.

Her reply was almost instantaneous. He smiled. If they were so close, they could be talking instead of texting. An idea formed in his head. He typed another message.

All work and no play...

Hahaha.

Laughter wasn't the reply Adam wanted. He wanted her to say she was up for some playtime. Fun. He'd try again.

Let me show you some sights when you're finished.

No reply came. That was weird considering how quickly he'd answered back before. He typed some more.

Lived in L.A. area my entire life. I like playing tour guide.

Time dragged. He checked out the shelf full of video games. Some good titles.

His cell phone beeped. Finally. He read the text.

Too tired. Not up for fighting freeways and crowds.

Adam knew she must be tired, but he didn't like the idea of her being alone. He remembered what being the new kid was like, whether at school or at a studio. It could be lonely, even if others were around. People had helped him when he first went to work on movies. He wanted to do the same with Megan. Tonight was the perfect time, possibly the only time, to do it. And being with her this evening beat any of his alternatives.

His thumbs tapped the touchscreen.

Understand. But I know the perfect place. Very relaxing. We can make it an early night.

As Adam waited for a reply, anticipation built. Must be the challenge. Few women kept him waiting. Most simply fell at his feet, seeing him whenever he wanted to see them. Having women willing to revolve their lives around him was convenient, but it made Adam uncomfortable because that was what his mom did for her man of the moment. He couldn't picture Megan doing that.

The seconds ticked into minutes. He imagined her weighing the pros and the cons, the V between her eyes deepening into almost parallel lines, as she made a list. Perhaps a mental one, or she might even be jotting one down. He wouldn't put it past Megan. But he still hoped she said...

Another beep. He glanced at the screen.

Sure.

Adam pumped his hand. "Yes."
Another message immediately followed.

Where do you want to meet?

Picking her up would be easiest, but that might seem like too much of a date. Like it wasn't a date, a voice mocked. Ignoring it, he typed.

Griffith Park Observatory parking lot. Five o'clock.

Okay. See you then.

A satisfied feeling flowed through Adam. He couldn't wait to see Megan. Once the shoot started, things would be hectic for both of them. He wanted to make the most of tonight.

And he would.

The sun dropped lower toward the horizon, filling the sky with satiny tendrils of yellow and pink. Megan sat on a blanket on the lawn area of the Griffith Observatory. Adam sat next to her. In his jeans, long-sleeved red shirt with a surfer logo on

he front and an L.A. Dodgers hat with the brim pulled low,
ie still didn't look like an average guy. But no one walking
passed them recognized him.

The scent of the grass filled the air, mingling with the smells
from the delicious dinner Adam had brought. A good thing
hey'd taken a short hike through Griffith Park when they ar-
ived. She didn't think she could do it now after eating fried
chicken, corn on the cob, sweet potato fries and the flakiest
buttermilk biscuits she'd ever tasted.

Megan stared at the view of Los Angeles, including the
iconic Hollywood sign. "I always thought everything in L.A.
was flashy and loud. Glad to see I was wrong."

"This is an oasis in the city. My mom and I used to come
here when I was younger."

She wondered what Adam was like as a kid, probably a daredevil even then. "Thank you for suggesting we come here. It's
so nice. The park. The view. The food."

"The company."

She smiled up at him. "That, too."

And so romantic. Better not go there. They were friends.
Only friends.

Except being with Adam wasn't the same as hanging out
with her friends. A strange undercurrent kept things from feel-
ng comfy and cozy like when she was with Rob. With Adam,
she felt kind of prickly and off balance. She had no idea what
might happen next. Funny, but that didn't bother her as much
as she thought it would.

Megan put her arms behind her so she could lean back and
support her weight. Her hand brushed Adam's. Heat and tingles
erupted from the point of contact. She straightened. "Sorry."

"No worries."

Megan was worried. She couldn't control her body's reac-
ions to him. Even the slightest touch sent her insides aquiver.
Not good.

He removed a white cardboard box from the picnic bas-
ket, then opened the lid. "I hope you saved room for dessert."

Megan peeked inside to see two big chocolate cupcakes with fluffy white icing. The mouthwatering scent added two more inches to her hips. She took one, anyway. Focusing on dessert was better than thinking about Adam. "No matter how full I am, there's always room for a cupcake."

Laughter filled his eyes.

"What?" she asked.

"It isn't often I meet a woman who enjoys food the way you do."

Megan shifted uncomfortably. She wanted to fit in with everyone else, find where she belonged, but she wasn't about to starve herself to do it. Especially when cupcakes were involved. "It's a love-hate relationship. Most women enjoy food but they hate the calories."

"You don't seem worried about calories."

"I'm not," she admitted. "I might have been a size zero for about a week when I was twelve. But as long as I'm fit and healthy why not eat?"

He held a cupcake. "I agree completely."

She bit into hers. The vanilla frosting, creamy and sweet, filled her mouth. So tasty. The cake was light and chocolaty. Perfect, like Adam.

Megan stiffened. He wasn't perfect. Okay, maybe physically. She'd concede that much. But other things considered— stability and respectability—not even close. Adam might not be as big a show-off as she'd first thought, but he was reckless and a daredevil. Totally wrong for her. She stared at her cupcake.

"You look a million miles away," Adam said.

She turned her head. The intensity in his green eyes made her breath catch.

"I'm back." She took another bite of the delicious cupcake. "You said you came here with your mother."

He nodded. "We didn't have a lot of money when I was growing up. This was one place we could afford. Admission is free except for the planetarium show."

"A bargain for the beautiful views."

"Wait until you see inside and look at the sky through a telescope. I used to…"

The wistful look in his eyes intrigued Megan. She leaned toward him, eager to hear what he was going to say. "What?"

"Dream about being an astronaut."

More adventure and thrills. Not surprising. "You wanted to fly the space shuttle."

"No." Now that surprised her. "I didn't want to be a pilot, but a mission specialist. A scientist."

To be a scientist meant he had to like science. Her first impression of him being a dumb jock had been way off base. This only reaffirmed how far off.

Megan imagined Adam wearing a white lab coat. He would look good no matter what he wore. "You would have been the hottest scientist ever. Every female research assistant would have wanted to work on your project."

On him!

Adam grinned. "Thanks."

"But I'll be honest, you would look even hotter in a space-suit."

"I've worn one before. I played an astronaut in a movie. The best part was experiencing zero gravity during a parabolic flight. Talk about wild. You would have liked it."

"I suppose doing somersaults in midair would be fun as long as you didn't hit something while you were floating around."

"Everything is controlled. Very safe."

Being an actor gave Adam the opportunity to experience unique things that an average person like herself didn't get to do. That had to be fun for him. "Playing an astronaut in a movie would be a lot safer than actually being blasted into space."

Mischief gleamed in his eyes. "Nothing wrong with a little danger."

"Says the surfer who rides the biggest wave out there."

He raised his hands in the air like he had won a close race. "And conquers the biggest wave."

"Long-term, my money's on the wave."

Adam shrugged. "The rush is worth the risk."

"I'll take my chances on dry ground."

"There's rock climbing."

"Not my thing," she admitted. "I'm not a big fan of heights."

"So no skydiving or BASE jumping."

"Nope." She'd never done anything like that, nor did she plan on it. "I like to keep my feet firmly planted on the ground. I'm addicted to breathing, not adrenaline."

"Come on, you can't tell me you're totally risk adverse."

"It's true."

"If it were, you wouldn't be here."

Megan drew back, feeling suddenly exposed. Most people took what she said without looking deeper. Even Rob. She might not have known Adam long, but the things she kept hidden from the world seemed somehow visible to him. She didn't like it. "You mean here with you?"

"I'm not dangerous."

Oh, yes, he was. She swallowed.

"I was talking about your internship," Adam continued before she could say anything. "You left your family and friends to move to Los Angeles. That's not exactly taking the safe path."

Moving to a new town wouldn't kill or injure her the way his risks would. At least she hoped not. "There aren't many job opportunities for costume designers in Larkville. None unless you count the annual Christmas pageant at the community church. They've used the same costumes for years."

"What about another city like Austin? They're well-known in filmmaking circles."

She'd had this discussion with Rob. "Nothing beats being in Hollywood if you want to be in the film industry. Lots more opportunities."

"That's true," Adam said. "A great place to gain experience."

Maybe that was why Rob had encouraged her to take the internship. Once she had experience, she would be able to move

o Austin. "But relocating for a job isn't the same as risking
my neck trying some extreme sport."

"Maybe not, but it still could be life changing."

She stifled a yawn. "Time will tell."

"You're tired."

Nodding, she wiped her mouth with a napkin and put the
cupcake wrapper with the other trash. "It's been a long week."

"Let's relax and watch the sunset before heading into the
observatory."

With her stomach full and her eyelids heavy, Megan
stretched out her jean-clad legs and leaned back on her elbows. "Sounds like a plan."

"That doesn't look comfortable." He moved back until he
was behind her, his legs outstretched alongside hers. "Lean
back."

Her heart lodged in her throat, as if she'd swallowed an entire box of cupcakes whole. This didn't seem like a friendly
gesture, but a come-on. "I…"

He slipped his hands under her arms and scooted her against
him so her back rested against his chest. "This has got to be
more comfortable."

Only slightly better than walking on hot coals. Every single
muscle knotted. Should she pull away or…?

"Relax." He kneaded her shoulders. "You're so tense."

Warmth and more tingles pulsated through her. If Adam decided to give up acting, he would make a fortune as a masseur.

"That's a little better," he said.

Yes and no. The man had magic hands. The tightness in
her shoulders loosened, quickly melting beneath his skilled
fingers, but his touch heated the blood flowing through her
veins. Uh-oh. She could not allow herself to make a mistake
here. "Much better. Thanks. You can stop now."

"In a minute."

A minute, huh? Megan could handle that. She started counting. One-Mississippi, two-Mississippi, three…

* * *

Megan was asleep. Her entire body was finally relaxed. He chest rose and fell evenly.

With his left arm around Megan, Adam felt an odd sense of contentment. He'd never brought a date here before. This had always been his and his mom's favorite place, but bring ing Megan felt right. Special.

One of her curls tickled Adam's nose. He inhaled the scen of her shampoo, fruity and sweet.

"Wheeeeee."

A little boy squealed as he toddled across the grass while his mom chased after him. Beyond them, on the path, an olde couple walked hand in hand. A teenager jogged to catch up to his friends heading toward the observatory.

Megan shifted in his arms. He glanced down at her. She wa wearing lipstick, a natural-looking pink shade. He'd never no ticed her wearing makeup before.

A serene smile graced her full lips. Was she dreaming' Of him?

This morning he would have said no way, but he wasn't sure now. She'd agreed to spend the evening with him and didn' protest his massaging her shoulders. She might be a little more dazzled than she would admit, but that didn't stop her from acting naturally around him. She didn't try to impress him Nor try to seduce and flirt with him. She was herself and le him be himself. A rare occurrence. One he liked very much.

Adam didn't think Megan was as practical as she claimed to be. Planners could have an adventurous streak. He would like the chance to bring hers out. He wanted to see her face light up with joy, to hear her laugh from the gut. If only she would let him…

He brushed a corkscrew curl off her face. Her pale skin contrasted with her brown curly hair.

A modern-day Sleeping Beauty or Snow White.

All she needed was a kiss.

Bad idea.

Each time they touched, Megan about jumped out of he

kin, suggesting she was attracted to him. But she was denying her interest in him. She was trying to banish him to friend zone because she had her sights set on another guy.

Adam could overcome her resistance. He had no doubt about that. Yet even if he was tempted to brush his lips against hers and steal a kiss, he wouldn't.

Adam might be charming, but he wasn't a prince. He was more like the huntsman. Megan's heart wasn't safe with him. She might not be his normal type, but the more time he spent with her, the more he liked her. One kiss might lead to more and that could take them to the wrong place. The last thing he wanted to do was hurt Megan.

Listening to her talk about her feelings for Rob, hearing about her plans, told Adam that she was a forever type of woman. He wasn't that kind of guy. Kissing her was out of the question. Even if he might want a…taste.

She shifted positions, turning so her cheek rested against his chest. Her soft-in-all-the-right-places curves pressed against him.

A flame ignited deep within him.

Adam swallowed around the lump in his throat. Better there than in his jeans. That would be hard…difficult to explain if Megan woke up.

He focused on the other people around them. It didn't help.

He thought about the scene he'd been working on earlier that day. He'd kept screwing up one line. He repeated the words in his head, messing up again. But at least his temperature hadn't skyrocketed into the danger zone. He went over the line in his head. Again and again. He spoke the words aloud.

Megan stirred.

Damn, he should have been quieter. At least he'd managed to stave off being embarrassed by his attraction to her.

A gasp escaped her parted lips. Wide eyes stared up at him.

He smiled at her. "Sleeping Beauty awakes."

Her cheeks turned a cute shade of pink. She bolted upright. "I fell asleep."

He missed the feel of her warmth and softness against him

"You were tired."

She wouldn't meet his eyes. "I'm sorry."

"Don't apologize." He didn't want her to be embarrassed

"I'm sorry I woke you. I was practicing a line."

To stop himself getting too turned on. *Real classy, Noble*

A good thing Megan didn't need to know that piece of info.

"Do you need help?" she offered.

Yes, he would love her help, but not with the line. "Another time."

"Just tell me when." She brushed strands of hair off her face. "That's the least I can do to thank you for being my bed while I napped."

If only they could be in bed together… Nope. Not going there. "You're welcome. I'm happy to oblige anytime."

"Anytime Eva's not around," Megan clarified.

She would bring that up. Adam wished he could put her at ease about her internship. He enjoyed flirting with her whether it went anywhere or not. "Even if Eva strolled by, what could she say? It's not like we're naked with our legs and arms tangled amid the sheets and each other."

The images had been rolling around in his head ever since she'd mentioned the word *bed*.

Megan cleared her throat. "No, you're right. It's not like that at all."

Too bad, Adam thought. That image held a certain appeal

"A good thing or I'd be out an internship," Megan continued

"True," he said.

But what a way to go.

Forget movie magic, Megan had gotten a taste of real magic tonight with Adam. She stood next to him by her car in the parking lot, feeling rested and content.

Above her in the night sky, stars twinkled, the same stars she and Adam had stared at through the telescope at the observatory. "I thought that was a shooting star."

"Shooting star. Satellite," he said. "Not a lot of difference."

"You can't wish upon a satellite."

The lights from the parking lot combined with the brim of his baseball cap cast shadows on his face. The proverbial tall, dark and handsome. "You can make a wish on anything you want."

"No, you can't," she countered. "You need a coin and a fountain or wishing well. Birthday candles or…"

He grinned wryly. "I didn't know there was a wish rule book."

Megan gave him a look. "You can't make up your own wishing rules."

"For your information I've made plenty of wishes up here," he said. "Granted, they were on stars, but none were shooting across the sky."

She wondered what Adam would wish for. He had looks, money, fame and a great career. Nothing was missing from his life. "Have any come true?"

"Yes," he said without any hesitation. "So there's nothing from stopping you from making a wish now."

"Only if you make one, too."

"I'm always up for making wishes," he said to her surprise.

Megan thought he would put up more of a fight. She hadn't taken Adam as the fanciful type, but the more time she spent with him, the more she realized how much she didn't know about him and wanted to know.

"Close your eyes," Adam said.

"You implied there isn't a rule book."

"Now is not the time to be logical." He tapped the tip of her nose with his fingertip. "Close them."

She did. "Are yours closed?"

"Yes," he said. "Now make a wish."

I wish I could spend more time with Adam.

Wait. The words sounding in her head had come out of nowhere. Her eyes sprung open. Spending time with Adam wouldn't be smart if she wanted to impress Eva. Megan grimaced.

She knew what she should have wished for—a permanent costume design job. Or Rob to see her as more than a friend. Or finding the place she belonged. Or... Her shoulders sagged.

Instead, she'd made a stupid wish. For something she didn't want or need. For someone who wasn't a part of her life and never would be. A do-over wish was definitely in order.

Adam's eyes opened. She realized he'd taken a long time to make his wish.

"Did you make one?" he asked.

"Yes." Even if it was a total waste of a wish. Oh, well. Her wishes had never come true. This one wouldn't, either. "You?"

"I made a good one."

He sounded happy. She was tempted to ask him what he wished for, but realizing he'd want to know hers kept Megan quiet. No way was she admitting her wish to him. To anyone.

This seemed like a perfect time to say good-night. They couldn't stand here for hours, making wishes or staring at each other. She needed sleep and clarity. "I should get going. Thanks for tonight."

"It doesn't have to end."

Megan's pulse kicked up a notch. She didn't want the night to end. Being with Adam made her feel special, as if for the past couple of hours the universe revolved around her. She knew it was the way he treated everybody—making her feel like the most important and only person in the world—but she didn't care. It felt so good. Her dad had made her feel so unique and special. With him gone, she'd wondered if she would ever feel that way again.

"There are plenty of other sights to see at night," Adam added.

His trailer? Her pulse sprinted as if she were running a hundred-yard dash.

Uh-oh. Time to slow down. No sense getting carried away over a pleasant evening. Adam had admitted to being a flirt, but she shouldn't go too far hanging out with him. Definitely time to call it a night.

As she removed her car keys from her purse, metal jingled.

"I have an early call time tomorrow morning." The words sounded flat even to her ears. She needed to sound more enthusiastic. She had come to Hollywood for her career, not to be crushing on a movie star who had millions of women lusting after him. She forced a smile. "Lots to prepare for Tuesday's call."

"Strong work ethic. I like that."

"Something my dad instilled in us. Me."

"It's an admirable trait."

Megan couldn't drum up any excitement over Adam's compliment. He may have been interested in her enough to flirt, but she wasn't hot enough for him to put in more effort and pursue. Being friends seemed to be okay with him.

Disappointment shot through her. Foolish, she knew, because friends were all they could be given her internship. And Rob. Megan couldn't forget about Rob. But spending time with Adam tonight gave her a glimpse of what being a princess must be like. Usually she felt like one of the ugly stepsisters, not Cinderella. Megan didn't want the feeling to end even if it were for the best. "Thanks again."

He wrapped his arms around her in a big bear hug. "Thank you for tonight."

The scent of him filled her nostrils. Musky and spicy and oh-so-male. Her cheek pressed against his chest, his heart beating in her ear. She hugged back, wanting to soak up his warmth. If only it could last for a little longer.

He released her.

She forced herself to let go of him.

Adam's gaze locked on hers. She wasn't experienced when it came to men, but she recognized the desire shining in his eyes. Her blood pressure spiraled into the red zone.

He looked like he wanted to kiss her.

Megan wanted him to kiss her.

His mouth was so close to hers, mere inches away. His warm breath, sweet with a hint of chocolate from the cupcakes, caressed her face.

She parted her lips in invitation.

Kiss me.

A wish. A plea.

He drew back slightly. "Drive safe on the way home."

Her heart dropped to her feet. He was saying good-night, not trying to kiss her. She cleared her dry throat. "You, too."

The two words were all she could manage.

"See you on Tuesday," he said.

Not if Megan could help it. She'd never had this kind of reaction to a friend before, not even Rob. The less she saw of Adam, the better. He made her feel entirely out of control.

She wasn't a swooning, obsessed fan, wanting a one-night stand with her idol. She was a professional. Okay, an intern, but if she wanted a permanent job she had to stay focused and not think about Adam Noble.

Not now, not ever.

CHAPTER SIX

ADAM loved shooting. Stepping into a role and losing himself in a character were second only to the adrenaline rush of succeeding at something difficult and dangerous. But life on the set was like moving from an aquarium to a fishbowl. His world became smaller and more visible. At least to the cast and crew.

That was a small price to pay to do what he loved.

Adam parked near the set. One of the perks of being a movie star was a reserved parking spot. His car was one of three vehicles in the VIP lot. Not surprising given the sun was just now clearing the horizon. He liked arriving early to give himself time to relax and prepare.

He always started his day with a cup of coffee from the refreshment table. Craft Services put out a spread of snacks and drinks to tide them over between the catered meals they were fed.

One of the electricians shouted a greeting.

Adam waved.

Spending twelve to fourteen hours with the same group of people gave him a chance to get to know the cast and crew well. But only a week in, he knew this production would be different because of two women—Megan Calhoun and Lane Gregory.

One was as sweet as a cupcake. He'd had barely caught sight of Megan since shooting began. But she'd been on his mind and in his dreams since last Sunday night. Two places no woman belonged. Thinking about sex was one thing. With

Megan, it was different. Okay, he might have thought about what she looked like naked and sleeping with her, but he'd also been imagining her pretty smile and her captivating eyes. Adam didn't have time to dwell on those things, however appealing. He needed to focus on his feelings, rather Maxwell's feelings, for his wife, Calliope. She was the only woman who could take up residence in his thoughts.

The other was his costar, Lane Gregory. She was the best of old Hollywood and new, but the woman was relentless in her pursuit of, well, him. Attention, gifts, innuendos. Adam had taken to hiding in his trailer whenever he could, something he rarely did while shooting. He preferred being where the action was. A good thing Lane wasn't an early riser.

"You're late," Lou, who worked for Craft Services, said. "I thought you might have slept in this morning."

"And miss the first pot of coffee? No way." Adam greeted the man with a handshake. "How did your daughter's softball game turn out?"

Lou grinned. "She hit the cycle. They won six-two."

"Excellent," Adam said. "There could be a scholarship in her future."

"Hope so." Lou handed him a steaming cup and a blueberry muffin, nicely warmed with a pat of butter softening on top of it. "Your standing order, sir."

"Thanks."

As Adam turned, he caught the scent of perfume wafting in the air. Not any perfume. Lane's.

Damn. She must have figured out his morning routine.

Maybe he could ditch her before she saw him. The costume department was nearby. He could sneak in and see if Megan was there. Interns always got the crappy call times. He wouldn't mind saying hi to her.

An oh-so-appealing image of her filled his mind. He'd missed seeing her.

On second thought, as tempting as paying her a visit might sound, he'd better not. On his mind was one thing. Under his skin was another. That was the one place he didn't allow a woman. It was safer that way.

"So it's true about you being an early bird." Some men might consider Lane Gregory's breathy voice sexy. Adam had at one time. But now the sound grated on his nerves. "I thought if I got here early enough we might be able to...rehearse in my trailer."

He should have gone to see Megan.

No way did he want to be alone with Lane. Not without a bodyguard. Maybe two. He might be strong, but the woman was dangerous. And not in a good way. "I have a few things I need to do."

Lane was beautiful. He'd give her that. Her long blond hair, porcelain skin and blue eyes were the envy of many women. Her curvy figure enticed men. She smiled coyly. "I can think of a few things we could do together."

Not in this lifetime. Adam pointed to her left hand where a huge diamond, iceberg-size, shimmered beneath the morning sun. "I doubt your fiancé would appreciate that."

Adam sipped his coffee. He needed to be alert to handle Lane's flirting.

She moved closer. "I doubt he'd mind if our rehearsing made the chemistry onscreen stronger."

Bull. He stepped back to put some distance between them. Just look at Rhys Rogers. The young actor's career was DOA thanks to "rehearsing" with Lane, and Hugh Wilstead's not-in-the-least-bit-understanding response. The studio head had the Midas touch and the respect of the industry. When Hugh spoke, everyone listened. No way would Adam cross him, not for a roll in the sack with Lane, not for anyone.

Lane, however, lived in a different reality. She'd grown up in the movie industry. She was spoiled and pampered and expected the world to fall at her feet. Pretty much the exact opposite of someone like Megan. He would have to try another tact. "Lane, beautiful, talented, Lane. Look at you. Look at me. All we have to do is stare at each other and the screen will sizzle with chemistry."

She gave him a sultry look. "Why not rehearse until passion explodes?"

"We'd end up with an R-rating or NC-17."

"I wouldn't mind."

Adam would. He wanted this film to be the best it could be, but there were limits to what he would do to achieve that goal. Lane was one of them. "Nothing personal, but I don't mess around with married or engaged women."

"Honorable. Dare I say noble?" She smirked. "But rules are meant to be broken."

"Some rules, yes," he admitted. "Not this one."

She winked. "We'll see about that."

She pranced away, her hips swaying seductively.

Adam was usually up for a fling with his costars, but Lane's engagement was only one reason he didn't want to sleep with her. She was all about artifice and deception. The total opposite of someone fresh and honest like…

Megan.

She stood outside the costume department. She wore a green jacket, jeans and canvas shoes. The shoes sparkled. Those were different than the sneakers she'd been wearing before. A black trendy-looking messenger bag hung on her shoulder. He hadn't seen that before, either. But her wild curls were still piled on top of her head. He wondered if she ever wore her hair down.

She had her cell phone pressed against her ear and a big smile on her face. Adam remembered the way she'd looked at him at the observatory. He'd thought she might want him to kiss her. But while waiting for another sign, he'd remembered his decision not to kiss her.

He wondered who was making her smile. Maybe that idiot best friend of hers.

Adam bit into his blueberry muffin to mask the bitterness souring his tongue.

Time to head back to his trailer. He needed to review his lines, not think about some woman who wanted another guy.

Walking away, Adam glanced over his shoulder. Megan was

still on the phone, but she was no longer smiling. She looked…
concerned. Maybe even upset.

Unease balled in his stomach.

Man, he was being stupid. No reason to overreact. Megan
was simply talking on the phone. So what if her smile had fal-
tered for a moment? It could be her boss or her landlord. Her
business wasn't his business. He should get out of here. Now.

Except his feet wouldn't budge. A protective instinct, the
same he'd felt whenever his mom used to introduce him to a
new "uncle," sprang to life.

The look on Megan's face, the way she ducked her head,
bothered Adam. It didn't matter who was on the other end of
the call. He didn't like the idea of anyone upsetting her.

She was too sweet, too nice.

This might not be his business, but Adam didn't want to
leave her on her own if she was upset. And he wouldn't. He
didn't have to be anywhere for another hour and a half.

He positioned himself at a table where he could see Megan
more clearly. This was as good as any other place to enjoy his
muffin. He took a bite and watched her.

Megan stood outside the costume department so happy to hear
from Rob. Not a text, but an actual phone call. She hadn't spoken to him in over a week. His texting had been erratic, too.

"It's good to talk to you, Meg," he said.

Her heart swelled with affection. With Rob in her life, she
would never be one of these people who died and her body
wasn't found for months because no one noticed she was missing. "I know. It's been insane here. Crazy busy. I've never
worked so hard in my life."

"Have you met anybody?"

"Oh, I've met lots of people." Megan listed the various crew
members she'd befriended. She thought about Adam, too, even
though she'd wanted to avoid him. Thankfully, he hadn't been
around much except during shoots. She'd seen him only in

passing. He would wave or nod in her general direction. The way he'd done to others when they'd had lunch at the cafeteria.

Megan should be happy he treated her like everyone else and wasn't going out of his way for her. That was what she wanted. Distance. Except staying away from him and being treated the same as others didn't feel as good as she thought it would. She no longer felt…special. Silly, but true.

"That's great you're making friends," Rob said. "But I wanted to know if you met a guy yet."

She let the words sink in, unsure what to say or think. This was the first time Rob had ever mentioned her and another guy. She didn't like it. "You mean someone to, um, date?"

"Yes."

Adam popped into her head. Too bad the only thing "date" and "Adam" had in common were the number of letters in the words. She pressed her lips together. "No, but I've been, um, busy."

Though others, including Kenna and Rosie, had been flirting with guys since the shoot started. Megan couldn't help but compare each man she met to Adam. So far none came close to the friendly, handsome actor.

"Too bad," Rob said.

Weird. He sounded…disappointed. "What about you? Have you met anyone?"

"Actually, I have."

The air rushed from her lungs. She nearly dropped the phone. "Really? I mean… That's great." She tried to sound interested, happy. "Who is she?"

"Someone you know. Knew. Pru Bradford."

Megan recognized the name. She tried to place it. "Prissy Prudence from fifth grade? The girl who never wore anything but frilly dresses and fancy shoes?"

"Yeah," Rob said. "She still wears dresses, but she's a lot prettier now. She works at an art gallery. She loves to cook and you should see the things she knits. So talented."

Megan's heart plummeted to the pavement. Splat.

"She doesn't sound like your type at all." Meow. Megan's claws were showing. "You've never shown any interest in art." Not that Larkville had any "arts" to speak of. That was one thing that made her feel as if she were suffocating there. "Or knitting."

Or sewing. Her sewing.

"A couple of shirts Pru's made are hot."

"I've designed some hot dresses," Megan countered.

Ouch. That sounded kind of desperate.

"For who?" he asked.

She grimaced. "Me."

"I had no idea," Rob said.

That was because she'd kept the dresses a secret. She figured no one would like them so why open herself up to more criticism. "The local cattleman's dinner or the library dessert benefit don't exactly call for haute couture."

But it was more than that. People hadn't tried to understand her. The high school drama teacher had been a despot who wanted no input on costumes. The Larkville quilting bee didn't appreciate the ideas and creativity Megan brought to their gatherings. The entire town, especially her mother, had wanted to break Megan as if she were a wild mustang needing to be tamed.

"That's true," he agreed. "But I've got to admit, it's hard to picture you all dressed up with makeup and your hair done."

Rob saw her as Cinderella before her fairy godmother arrived, not a beautiful princess the prince wanted to marry. That stung. "We might have grown up together, but there are a few things you don't know about me."

"Yeah, it's been fun learning about Pru."

Ouch. Rob hadn't a clue. Megan blew out an exasperated puff of air. "I bet."

"I know what you should do," he said. "Find yourself a boyfriend so you can doll yourself up and wear one of your dresses."

Megan grimaced. First a date, now he wanted her to find a

boyfriend? Rob had parked her in friend zone and let the meter expire. She dug her toe into the asphalt. "I can't conjure up a date out of thin air."

"Have you thought about online dating?"

Yeah, right. She would be the one woman to end up catching the eye of an ax murderer or psychopath. "Not my style."

"There's a guy out there for you, Meg, I just know it."

Yeah, you.

But that wasn't looking likely now. Not as long as Prudence was in the picture. Megan thought about what Adam had said.

Find another guy. Someone who will appreciate you. Spoil you. Kiss you until you can't see straight.

She sighed. "For all I know he could be right under my nose."

Or on the opposite end of this telephone call.

"That's the spirit. I want you to be as happy as I am," he continued. "There's nothing better than starting fresh in a new town with a new job, new apartment, new girlfriend."

Her stomach roiled. Thank goodness she hadn't eaten breakfast yet or she might be sick. "Things are moving fast."

"Sometimes you just know."

His words speared her heart. She forced herself to breathe. "Sounds...serious."

"I really think Pru could be a keeper," he confessed.

Rob had never talked this way about a woman. Megan couldn't believe he was talking about Prissy Prudence. Okay, they'd been ten years old when she moved, but how much could a person change in twelve years?

Megan didn't want to know the answer. "Keep me posted."

"I will," he said. "I plan on bringing Pru to the Fall Festival in October. She hasn't been back to Larkville since her family moved away."

It was May and Rob was talking about October? Megan cleared her dry-as-sandpaper throat. "The more, the merrier."

Forget caffeine drinks. Megan needed to mainline chocolate to survive today.

"Pru loves going to the movies," Rob said. "Maybe we could visit you in L.A."

The thought of watching Rob and Pru hold hands and kiss made Megan nauseous. "I have a small studio apartment. It might be a little cramped."

"We don't mind."

Could things get any worse? She didn't want to know the answer to that, either.

"Pru would love to see some movie stars in person," Rob continued. "Adam Noble is her favorite."

At least Megan had something to contribute to the conversation. "Adam is the lead actor in the film I'm working on. He's a nice guy. Very friendly."

An excellent pillow and backrest, too.

"You know Adam Noble?" Rob sounded impressed.

That surprised her. He wasn't into movie stars. "We've met."

"Wow. That's so cool."

The excitement in his voice had Megan staring at the phone in disbelief. Who was this person on the phone and what had he done to her best friend?

"I have a brilliant idea," Rob said. "Pru's birthday is coming up. Could you get an autographed picture of Adam Noble for her?"

Seriously? Megan's shoulders couldn't sag any more or they'd be hitting the ground. She needed a T-shirt with the words *Sucks to Be Me!* imprinted on the front and *Doormat* on the back. "I don't know. When's her birthday?"

"July. It would mean a lot to me."

They could be broken up by then. Or engaged, an evil little voice whispered. "I'll, um, see what I can do."

"I can always count on you. Best buds forever."

Until some other woman clawed her talons into his heart and carried him away from her. Anxiety grabbed hold of her. "I should get going."

She would rather face an angry Firebreather than stay on the phone with Rob any longer.

"Good talking to you," he said. "I'm almost glad Pru was busy so I had time to call you on my break."

Almost? That wasn't a nice thing for Rob to say. Megan gritted her teeth. He'd always treated her like an all-star. Now she was second string. Telling him to dump the girl probably wouldn't be a smart move. She'd better think of something else to say. "You know me. Always there for my best bud."

"Don't forget about Adam Noble's autograph," Rob said. "If he could personalize it to Pru that would be awesome."

"Awesome," Megan repeated. What had Adam said when she used that word when they had lunch?

That's a strong adjective.

She supposed it would be awesome for Rob and Prudence.

Megan couldn't imagine a guy like Adam asking her to get his girlfriend something for her birthday. He probably wouldn't get a woman a toolbox, either. That had been Rob's birthday present for her. Okay, she'd used a screwdriver to put together a table she bought. Still…

So. Not. Romantic.

But when you were a "best bud," romance didn't factor into gift selection. Anger surged. All her plans for a future with Rob were vaporizing. Plans or fantasies? The latter looked more likely at the moment.

"Text me and let me know when you have the autograph," Rob said.

Megan disconnected the call. Talking to Rob had drained what energy she had left.

"Good morning."

She jumped, startled to see Adam. What was he doing here so early?

"Here you go." He handed her a steaming cup of coffee. "What's going on? You look like you lost your best friend."

"I think I might have."

"Rob?"

"He thinks he found a keeper."

"That has to hurt."

She thought for a moment. "I'm more angry."

He smiled at her. "That's better than sad."

Nodding, she took a sip. The coffee was black. Strong. She choked. "I didn't realize you drank sludge."

"The stronger, the better. Especially on Fridays."

"I've been dragging since Wednesday."

"You'll get used to it."

"I have a feeling I'm going to have to get used to a lot of things."

"This must be messing up your plans."

"Wreaking havoc."

"Anything I can do to help," Adam offered.

She'd spilled most of the details about Rob. Might as well tell him everything so she would look like a loser only once. "Actually, there is. I don't know if it's against the rules or anything, but would you mind signing an autographed picture for Rob's girlfriend, Prudence? I mean, Pru. It's going to be a birthday gift from him. You're her favorite actor."

Adam's gaze narrowed. "He asked you to do this for him?"

Megan nodded, realizing how silly she must look.

His brow slanted. "Does Rob know how you feel about him?"

"Sort of."

"Say again?"

"Well, I once told him how I felt." The mortification of that still made her cringe even after all these years. "That didn't go over well. But I've dropped hints."

"Hints?"

She nodded. "He'll figure them out."

"And you still think the guy's smart?"

"Unless he's pretending to be oblivious."

Adam frowned. "You need to get away from Rob."

"He's in Texas."

"Doesn't matter where he is," Adam said. "You can do much better than someone like him."

"Maybe." But as she spoke the words her heart screamed, *Definitely!*

"How did he figure out we know each other?" Adam asked.

"I told Rob about you."

Adam's smile crinkled the corners of his eyes, sending her pulse rate into overdrive. "So what did you tell him? How much taller I am in real life? Or hotter? Or that I'm a very comfortable pillow?"

His lighthearted tone told Megan he was joking, but her cheeks warmed. Friend or not, Adam probably wasn't interested in hearing her whine about some other guy she was into. "I, um, told him you were starring in the film I was working on."

"The hotter and pillow comments might have made him jealous."

"Rob isn't the jealous type. He wants me to meet someone out here."

Adam raised his hand. "You met me."

"I mean a guy."

He flexed his arms, striking a he-man macho pose. "Do I look like a girl?"

She grinned. "No, but Rob was talking about a guy I could date."

Adam's mouth quirked. "So now I'm undateable."

Megan gave him a look. "You know what I mean."

"What?" He sounded surprised. "We went out. We could do it again."

"No, we can't."

"Because I'm the lead actor."

She nodded. "I keep waiting for Eva to give me the talk she gives everyone who works for her. But so far I've been spared."

No doubt Eva didn't think any movie star would be interested in a lowly intern from a nothing town in Texas.

"If I wasn't off-limits, would you go out with me?" he asked. "Say a real dinner at a restaurant, not a friendly picnic."

She remembered how romantic Adam had made everything

at the observatory and how close their lips had been when he hugged her. He'd seemed to want to kiss her, but backed away. She thought he wanted to be friends. Now she reveled in how he looked at her. He made her feel like Cinderella being asked to dance by the prince.

Her heart pounded. Heaven help her, she would say yes to him. No doubt about it. Megan swallowed around the lump in her throat. "You are off-limits so it's a moot question."

His frank appraisal made Megan want to cover her face with her hands and hide. But she kept her chin up and her posture straight, even if she was quivering inside.

"Fair enough," he said.

There was nothing fair about the way he made her forget everything, including Rob. Adam Noble was dangerous. Every instinct told her to get away from him. Now. "Thanks for the coffee. I have to go."

As Megan hustled into the costume department, she ignored the urge to glance over her shoulder and see if Adam was staring at her. She had to be realistic, not set herself up for more disappointment. Her hopes were already being dashed. She didn't need to let Adam in on the action, too. She didn't have a fairy godmother waiting to appear and wave a magic wand to make everything better. Fairy-tale endings didn't happen for girls like her. Even if, in her heart of hearts, she wished they did.

CHAPTER SEVEN

FRIDAY night, Megan turned down an invite to go out with the crew to a bar. She didn't want to be antisocial, but tiredness had finally gotten the best of her. Home in bed was the only place she belonged.

Saturday flew by. Sleeping in late. Laundry, napping. Her phone didn't ring or beep. She wanted to make the most of her free time. Rosie had told her once they were on location they might only get a day off a week.

By Sunday, Megan got antsy. She kept thinking about the lot, wondering how other people were spending today. Well, not all the crew. Adam.

She needed to have her head examined. Or better yet, find something to do so she would stop thinking about him.

Plopping onto a chair, she hit the power button on the television remote. Maybe she could find a movie to watch. A comedy would be good.

Megan surfed through the various channels. Adam appeared as the Roman god Neptune, standing on top of a wave. She let go of the remote.

Talk about gorgeous. She sighed.

What in the world was she doing? Megan was practically swooning over the guy. She turned off the TV.

No reason to go gaga over Adam Noble. Crushing on him was a total waste of time. He was the last person she should ever date, her internship aside.

She'd spent her entire life in the shadows. No one except her father and Rob had ever paid any real attention to her and made her feel important. She wanted to matter to someone, be an equal, not be overshadowed by his larger than life personality and in-the-spotlight career. Any woman who dated Adam, even his flings, ended up in the public eye, on view and scrutinized. No thanks. She'd had enough of that in Larkville.

Megan knew what would take her mind off Adam. She reached for her sketchpad and pencils.

Time to design a sundress worthy of the vintage fabric she'd purchased at a thrift store. The bodice seemed like a good place to start. Something fitted, a little retro looking to match the fabric. Slowly, the dress took shape both in her mind and on paper.

A knock sounded at the door.

Megan jumped. She glanced at the clock. Two hours had passed by. She'd been concentrating so hard she'd lost track of time. She rose. Probably Mrs. Hamilton from downstairs. Yesterday the elderly woman had needed help to locate her cat, Jack, who kept running away. Megan had found the orange tabby rummaging in the recyclable bin and returned him.

She opened the door. Shock rocketed through her.

Not Mrs. Hamilton. Adam.

He stood on her porch wearing a pair of board shorts, a plain white T-shirt and flip-flops. Somehow he made the casual clothing look like haute couture. His hair was mussed. Razor stubble covered his chin. He held a pair of sunglasses in one hand and a manila envelope in the other.

Megan clutched the doorknob. She tried to speak, but her tongue felt two sizes too big for her mouth. A million questions ran through her mind.

He greeted her with a charming smile that reached all the way to his clear green eyes. "Hello."

"Hi." She forced the word from her Sahara-dry mouth. "What are you doing here?"

He held up the envelope. "I have your autographed photo."

One question answered. Might as well ask the next one
"How did you find out where I live?"

"My assistant, Veronica."

That didn't explain how his assistant had gotten the address
Connections, perhaps?

Adam glanced over his shoulder. "Mind if I come in?]
didn't see any paparazzi following me, but you never know."

She had more than enough reasons to not want him in he
apartment, but she also didn't need a picture of her and Adam
together finding its way to Eva.

Megan loosened her grip on the knob and stepped back
"Come on in."

As soon as Adam entered, his wide shoulders and six-foo
height made the apartment feel ten times smaller. His male
scent enveloped her. He smelled spicier today. Maybe he'c
used a different soap or aftershave.

He looked around. "Nice place."

Thank goodness she'd cleaned up yesterday and made he:
bed this morning. The apartment wasn't big, a large roon
with an efficiency kitchen and eating area off to one corner
two closets and a bathroom. But the small space had a lot o
character with high ceilings, crown molding, picture rails, tal
wood pane windows and hardwood floors.

"It works well for what I need," she said. "It's in a safe are
and reasonably priced."

He handed her the envelope. "Here you go."

"Thanks." She still couldn't believe Adam was here. "Bu
you shouldn't have gone to so much trouble delivering it in
person. I'll be at the lot tomorrow."

"I don't have a lot going on today."

A guy like him? She found that hard to believe. "I appre
ciate it."

"You weren't at the bar Friday night."

Megan hadn't thought a big-name star like him would han§
out with the crew. "I was tired."

He slanted a brow. "Nothing else going on?"

"What do you mean?"

"Rob."

Oh, man. She wanted to die of embarrassment. "I haven't been throwing myself a pity party if that's what you're asking."

A sheepish grin formed on Adam's lips. "It was."

She grimaced. "I'm not a total loser. I was worn-out Friday night. The only thing I wanted to do was go home and crawl between the sheets."

Adam glanced at her queen-size bed with a brown-and-pink-striped comforter, light blue bed skirt and coordinating pillows on top. "Sounds like the perfect place to spend a Friday night."

His flirtatious, almost suggestive tone sounded warning bells in her head. She frowned. "It was. I slept. Alone."

Amusement danced in his eyes. "You look rested."

What was he doing here? She squared her shoulders. "I am."

"You were missed at the bar."

Yeah, right. No one ever missed her. Not when they hardly noticed when she was around. "That's nice of you to say, but I'm sure Kenna and Rosie were too busy flirting to notice I wasn't there."

"I wasn't talking about them," he clarified. "I missed you."

She hadn't been expecting that. "Oh."

"I sent you a text that night, but never heard back."

"I silenced my phone when I went to bed. I didn't want to be woken up. I never turned the sound back on."

"It's good to see you're okay."

Realization dawned. "The autographed photo was your excuse to come over."

"I wanted to make sure you were okay."

She didn't know if she should be annoyed or pleased. "I'm not some mentally unstable, psycho chick who would hurt myself."

"I know that."

"Then why are you here?"

He shifted his weight between his feet. "I remember how

upset my mom got when things didn't work out with a guy she liked."

"Pity party?"

"To the nth degree," he admitted. "She would stay in bed for days and cry her eyes out. If I hadn't brought her food, she wouldn't have eaten."

Sympathy replaced Megan's irritation. "Who took care of you while this was going on?"

He raised his chin. "I took care of myself."

Megan couldn't imagine. The only person she'd ever taken care of was her nephew, Brady, when she babysat. "How old were you?"

Adam walked farther into her studio. "It started when I was four. She can still be like that, but now she has a household staff to take care of her when it happens."

She knew the hardships Jess and Brady had been through. Adam might look like the golden boy, but his childhood sounded like it had been rough.

Megan touched his arm. His muscles tensed beneath her palm. "Adam…"

He shrugged off her hand. "It's nothing. Really."

His words didn't match the emotion darkening the color of his eyes. But he'd come over here out of concern for her. No way would she push or pry into something he didn't want to talk about.

"Well, you'll be relieved to know that not only have I not had a pity party, I also haven't shed one tear all weekend."

Which, come to think of it, was really weird. She had cried over Rob for much less over the years. Those sobfests used up boxes of tissue.

Why hadn't she cried this time?

Adam stared into her eyes. "Your eyes are clear and bright, not red and swollen."

She smiled smugly.

His gaze raked over her. "But you're still wearing pajamas."

Heat stole up Megan's neck until her cheeks burned. She's

een so busy working on the sundress design she hadn't show-
red and changed. She glanced down. Bare feet. Purple zebra-
triped fuzzy pants. A black camisole. No bra.

Oops. She crossed her arms over her chest, holding the en-
elope in front of her like a shield. As if that would make a
ifference now…

His eyes, no longer dark, twinkled with mischief. "Don't
e embarrassed. You look cute in your jammies."

Cute. The word sent a shiver down her spine.

Guys called their female friends cute. Women, at least those
hat men wanted to date, were labeled sexy. Not that she wanted
o date Adam. She didn't. But she was wearing a cami with-
ut a bra.

And then she realized what was going on. Adam wasn't
mpressed with her average body. Why would he be when he
vas surrounded by knockouts like Lane Gregory's on a daily
asis? Megan bit the inside of her cheek.

"No worries," he added. "Women go out in public wear
ng a lot less."

She remembered the women at the beach when she'd first
et Adam. Those tiny bikinis barely covered anything. If he
idn't think her body wasn't a big deal, she wasn't going to act
mbarrassed wearing her jammies and being braless in front
f him. She uncrossed and lowered her arms.

"Check the picture," he said. "Make sure it's what you
anted."

"You mean what Rob wanted," she corrected.

Megan opened the envelope flap and removed an eight-by-
en glossy photograph. A gorgeous shot of him from an up-
oming release, a movie, based on the watermark in the corner,
tled *Navy SEALs*. She read his inscription.

Pru,
Happy Birthday! Thanks for being such a great fan.
Appreciate all your support.
Love,
Adam

"Thank you." His thoughtfulness warmed Megan's insides "This will make Rob happy."

Adam's gaze met hers. "I want you to be happy."

Her heart skipped a beat. Maybe two. Okay, seven.

Looking down, she slid the photo back into the envelope She placed the envelope on top of the table. "I am happy. have my internship, this charming apartment and am makin; new friends on the set."

"So you've put Rob behind you?"

"He's with Prudence," Megan said. "Not much I can d about that."

"You could tell him how you feel."

Megan had lost her dad. She couldn't face the thought o losing Rob, too. That was a distinct possibility, more like hundred percent probability, if she told him her true feelings It was safer to plan and dream. "I can't."

Adam raised a brow. "Even if it means losing him t Prudence?"

The question swirled through Megan's mind. "I don't know.

"You might want to think about it." Adam strode to he chair where she'd been working on the sundress design. H set his sunglasses on an end table and picked up her sketch book. "What's this?"

Megan inhaled sharply. "Nothing."

"It looks like something." He studied the page. "You dre this?"

Her muscles bunched. She'd never forgotten the way he mom laughed at Megan's first and only attempt to put on fashion show. She should have known better, but she'd wante her mother to be proud of her and tell people about both he daughters, not only Jess. "I was playing around this morning.

"You're talented."

What else was he going to say? *You suck?* "Thanks."

"Don't duck your head. I've been dragged to enough fash ion weeks and costume meetings to know talent when I see it.

She straightened. "Design classes were my favorite in co

lege. Nothing like putting on a piece of clothing that started
with nothing more than a few lines on a sketchpad."

"This is for you?"

Maybe she'd been trying too hard to fit in. She raised her
chin. "I might wear jeans at work, but that doesn't mean I
wear them 24/7."

"You also wear pajamas."

"I should change."

"Not on my account."

Disappointment shot through her. "You're leaving."

"Not unless you want me to go."

"I don't." The words rushed out before she had time to think.
"Unless you have somewhere else to go."

"I'd rather stay here," he said to her unexpected relief. "But
I'm a casual type of guy so there's no need for you to put on
something else. Pajamas are the perfect attire for a Sunday
afternoon. I take it you were planning to take it easy today."

Megan fought the urge to cringe. She had asked Adam to
stay. Here. With her. Maybe she needed her head examined,
after all. "Um, yes. A little design work. Order a pizza. Watch
a movie or two."

"Pizza and movies are two of my favorite things."

"O-kay." Her insides twisted with unease. "But you'd have
more fun riding some wave or jumping off a building."

"This will be fun enough." He sat in her chair, crossing his
feet at the ankles. "I'm not allowed to do any of my normal
activities while we're shooting. Don't want to put the production in jeopardy."

"Thank you from someone grateful to have an internship
during the shoot."

"You're welcome."

A beat passed. And another.

Megan didn't know what to say or do. Lying on a bed of
knives might be more comfortable than this.

She didn't know if Adam was bored or lonely or simply a
big flirt, but nothing like this had ever happened to her before

with a guy other than Rob dropping by, much less a movie star. She wasn't sure how to handle it. Or him.

"So what kind of movie do you want to watch?" Adam asked. "A romantic comedy?"

"Straight comedy." Something romantic wouldn't be a smart idea with him here. Who was she kidding? Nothing about spending time with Adam was smart. In fact, she could be in real trouble if anyone in the costume department found out he was here. But she couldn't deny a part of her enjoyed the attention. She would have to be careful not to let that enjoyment go too far. "The cable has streaming videos on demand. You pick a movie. I'll order the pizza."

The thought of spending a Sunday afternoon relaxing had appealed to Adam on a gut level. He never hung out and did nothing. He was looking forward to it. Except being around Megan was far from relaxing.

Forget about watching the movie on the television, he wanted to look at her.

As if on cue Megan shifted positions on the bed, rolling onto her stomach. The scoop neck of her camisole gave him a better view of soft, ivory skin. His temperature shot up.

"This is a funny movie," she said.

Adam looked at the television screen. "Yeah."

His gaze wanted to stray back to her. It wasn't just her nice breasts or her expressive eyes, but the way her curly hair fell halfway down her back.

He was attracted. Very attracted.

That was bad. Very bad.

A perfectly good bed was going to waste at the moment but he didn't care. Not when he felt as if he was struggling to remain in control around her. Not physically, though there was an element of that, but emotionally. Considering Adam didn't do emotion, he wasn't sure what to think.

She laughed at something from the movie.

He hadn't a clue what, but the sound curled around him like a lover's embrace.

What the hell was going on?

Okay, she was smart, funny, unpredictable, pretty, though she would disagree about that.

But none of those things explained why he lowered his guard around Megan. Something he never did. Worse, it didn't seem to be a conscious decision.

Maybe it was her honesty or her straightforwardness.

Maybe parts of Maxwell were seeping into Adam's real life.

But he couldn't believe he'd told her about his mom. No one, not even his agent, knew any of that. Adam hadn't even needed a lot of prompting.

Bad, bad, bad.

He didn't want anyone to know about his childhood and family. It was nobody's business and better left in the past.

Or forgotten altogether.

There was a reason he had flings not relationships. He'd learned the hard way that love only ended up hurting. It didn't last.

Which was why Megan should stay in the friend zone. Sure, he wanted to sleep with her. A friend with benefits. That might get her mind off Rob, but would that be the best thing for her? Adam's consideration of Megan's feelings was enough to tell him to stay far away from her. At least when it came to a physical relationship. He liked taking risks, but he wasn't stupid.

What if he really liked Megan? She was different enough she could turn his world inside out.

Not worth the risk.

Monday, Megan couldn't believe how the atmosphere on the set crackled with tension, a one-hundred-eighty-degree shift from Friday. Unforeseen delays had put a wrench into the schedule. Tempers flared. Voices rose. The background artists sat around with nothing to do except take up space.

An unexpected break gave Megan time to return Adam's

sunglasses. He'd forgotten them at her apartment yesterday. Passing them off in public rather than private would have been better. His friendliness and confidence appealed to her and sent her hormones into overdrive whenever he was near. But she hadn't seen him on the set.

At his trailer, Megan removed his sunglasses from her pocket. She'd cleaned the lenses last night and placed them in a padded holder so they wouldn't get damaged.

She had it all planned out—return the sunglasses, thank him for keeping her company yesterday and then say goodbye. No matter how much fun she had with him or how attractive he might be, keeping her distance was the smart thing to do.

This morning Eva had mentioned staying away from the lead actors. It was a generic warning, but a warning nonetheless. One that set warning bells ringing in Megan's head. A good thing Adam seemed satisfied with being friends. What guy spent an afternoon sitting on a bed and watching movies without making a move? Not one who was attracted to her. She must have her own spot reserved in the friend zone.

His trailer door was ajar.

Megan heard a voice, Adam's voice. He was rehearsing lines.

She waited at the door. He stopped talking. Something thudded. A book?

Megan knocked.

The door opened more from the weight of her hand against it.

"Not now," his harsh voice barked.

Megan felt like she'd been slapped, but she didn't think he knew it was her. She couldn't see him through the crack in the door. He doubted she could see him. "I have your sunglasses."

"Keep them."

She tried not to take his impatient tone personally. His moodiness was a total shift from how lighthearted he'd been yesterday. But she wasn't keeping his sunglasses. She wanted nothing to tie her to Adam, not even a little bit. For the sake of her internship, she rationalized. "I'll set them inside the door."

"Whatever."

As Megan opened the door farther, she saw Adam. He faced to the right side of the trailer, giving her a view of his profile.

Deep lines on his forehead and around his frowning mouth matched the tension in the air. He stared at the script in his hands. His grip tightened until an edge crinkled. With a shake of his head, he smoothed the wrinkles on the page with his thumb.

She hated how pained he seemed. But he'd made it clear he didn't want company. Time to get out of here. She set the sunglasses on a table.

As she backed out of the trailer, the door creaked.

He cursed. "Just go."

She hesitated. Adam looked like he needed a friend or a hug, but she doubted he'd admit it. "I'm going."

He glanced up from the script. "Megan?"

The emotion in his eyes filled her with compassion. His gaze, usually full of confidence and strength, contained a look she knew well—one of nerves and self-doubt.

Megan's heart melted at his unexpected vulnerability. "Sorry, I didn't mean to bother you. I wanted to return your sunglasses."

He dragged his hand through his hair, looking tortured. "Ignore me. I'm in a bad mood. The scene I'm shooting soon is killing me. I can't get the lines right."

She had no idea he took his acting so seriously. "I wish there was something I could do to help."

"There is." He handed her the script. "Read Calliope's part."

Maxwell's wife. Lane Gregory's role. Megan's stomach knotted. "O-kay, but I'm better dressing and undressing actors than being one."

Adam didn't crack a smile. He pointed to a line. "I'm going to start here. Ready?"

She nodded, even though she felt completely out of her element.

"Tell me the truth." He gazed deeply into Megan's eyes, making her insides quiver. "Are you involved in this?"

Megan glanced at the script. "Unbelievable. After everything we've been through…"

"Calliope."

His anguish, both visible and verbal, gave Megan goose bumps. "Max."

"Answer my question."

"You know my father. He thinks women are incapable of anything other than shopping and sex. He has never involved me in his business dealings. Legal or otherwise."

A beat passed. And another.

His nostrils flared. "Do you love me?"

His words sounded…mean. Spiteful. Wrong.

"Of course, I, um…" Her tongue stumbled over the next word. She lost her place in the script. "Sorry."

"It's not you," Adam said. "Those four words get me every time."

Do you love me?

A warm and fuzzy feeling flowed through her. She could fall in love with him.

Correction. Not Adam, Rob. She could fall in love with Rob.

Wait. She was already in love with Rob. At least she thought she was. She clutched the script.

"The emotion is off," Adam continued.

"You sounded mean, angry."

He blew out a puff of air. "I'm hitting the wrong notes. Maxwell wouldn't feel that way here. He's confused, trying to figure out what's going on and who set him up."

The frustration in Adam's voice tugged at Megan's heart. She wanted to help him. She'd never acted, but she'd spent plenty of time at the theater in college. She'd taken film courses because character and story could be enhanced by costumes. Surely all those hours hadn't been a waste of time and tuition.

She thought for a moment. "What do you want Calliope's answer to be? Not you, I mean, Maxwell."

Adam's brow furrowed. "I know what she says."

"So do I." Megan waved the script. "But is that the answer Maxwell wants to hear? Is he expecting her to say she doesn't or is he hoping she does? That might help you figure out the right emotion to use."

Adam closed his eyes. His lips moved, but no sound came out.

She stayed quiet so she wouldn't disturb him.

A minute, maybe two, passed. His eyes opened. The creases on his forehead remained, but they weren't as deep. The lines bracketing his mouth relaxed. "Let's try it again."

The dialogue flowed smoother this time. Megan still wasn't sure what she was doing, but knowing she was helping made her relax a little.

"You know my father. He thinks women are incapable of anything other than shopping and sex. He has never involved me in his business dealings. Legal or otherwise."

A beat passed. And another.

"Do you love me?" Anxiety gave an edge to the anticipation in his voice.

"Of course I love you." She sounded husky, unnatural.

"Prove it."

The potent mix of hope and fear in Adam's gaze mesmerized her. The line she was supposed to say flew from her mind. She glanced down at the script but the words had blurred.

Megan parted her lips, as if that would be enough of a prompt to make her remember what she was supposed to say.

"If you won't," he said. "I will."

Adam lowered his mouth to hers. His kiss jolted her. She gasped, but didn't back away.

Heat. Sparks. Proverbial fireworks.

His lips moved over hers with an expertise that left her breathless and wanting more. He touched her with only his mouth, but sensation pulsated through her until she curled her toes.

She arched against him, wanting to be closer to him. Her arms circled him. Her hands splayed his back.

The fireworks continued. The kissing, too.

She'd never been kissed like this, never felt this way before. She wanted it to keep going.

Slowly Adam ended the kiss and stepped back.

Her lips tingled. Her heart pounded.

Adam looked at her with a strange expression in his eyes as if he were waiting for something.

Another kiss? Anticipation soared. "What?" she asked.

He blinked twice, then turned the script toward him. He ran his finger along the page, as if he'd lost his place, too, and pointed. "It's your line."

He sounded a little breathy. From the kiss? She hoped so because that was exactly how she sounded, too.

Megan focused on the words and reread. The script called for a passionate kiss between Calliope and Maxwell. Her heart dropped to her feet. The kiss hadn't been an impromptu one. It had followed one of the lines of dialogue.

Adam must have gotten caught up in the scene and kissed her, assuming she was going along with it, too.

Except she'd thought the kiss was for real. But while kissing him might have felt like the Fourth of July, the fireworks hadn't been real. This was a rehearsal for when he kissed another woman, a beautiful, sexy woman. Nothing more.

Instead of fueled by a mutual attraction and heat, the kiss had no real emotion to it. At least not from Adam. He flirted and was used to kissing women while acting. This wasn't about her or him but his career. That was where his vulnerability lay. If he truly had any interest in something deeper than friendship, he couldn't have kissed her so passionately, then stand there like it meant nothing.

But he *was* standing there as if nothing had happened between them.

Megan struggled to breathe. She needed to get away from him. Now.

"I need to get back to work." She handed him the script. "You don't need me anymore. You nailed the line."

His gaze remained on her. "Thanks for the help."

Megan didn't know how to reply because right now she was wishing she'd never stepped foot in his trailer. That kiss would stay with her a long time. Maybe forever.

"You're welcome," she said.

With that, Megan exited the trailer. She hurried back to the costume area. She touched her lips, still tingling and swollen. Losing herself in Adam's kiss had been a severe lapse of judgment, one she couldn't repeat. And wouldn't.

No matter how much she might want to kiss him again.

CHAPTER EIGHT

A THIRTYSOMETHING makeup artist named Basil patted Adam'
forehead with a towel after the shoot had finally ended. Th
man beamed as bright as the silver earrings dangling from hi
earlobes. "You were simply amazing, Adam. If that kiss wit
Lane isn't nominated for an award, if it doesn't win, I'll eat
big fat beef burger."

He looked at Basil. "But you're a vegan."

Basil winked. "Exactly."

A satisfied feeling settled in the center of Adam's chest. Th
big emotional scene with Lane had gone off without a hitch
He wished he could take credit for his performance during a
the takes this afternoon, but that belonged to one person—
Megan. He'd gotten himself so worked up about flubbing hi
lines and making a fool of himself that he hadn't been able t
think straight. She'd been a voice of reason, an angel savin
him from embarrassment, a devil kissing him until the onl
thing he could think about was her. And more of her kisses.

Aware of Basil's gaze, Adam smiled. "Thanks. Appreciat
your support."

Basil pulled the towel away with a flourish. Not surprisin
given the makeup artist's passion for flamenco dancing. "Th
pleasure is all mine."

Adam glanced around to see if Megan was on the se
Producers and invited guests sat in an area to the right of th
set with cushy leather couches to lounge on and monitors t

watch. The rest of the crew was either scattered among the cameras, lighting or other equipment.

No Megan.

He'd wanted her to see how well he did. He wanted to thank her. The way she'd kissed him this morning had rendered him speechless. He'd been turned on and uncertain at the same time. Not a good combination.

"You naughty boy," Lane whispered from behind him. "Not letting me know you kissed like that. I was hoping Damon needed another close-up."

Adam hadn't been thinking about Lane while kissing her. Calliope hadn't entered his head, either. Only Megan. She might seem like a forever type of girl, but she had kissed him back eagerly, almost recklessly. Maybe acting the part of Calliope had given her the chance to break free of whatever was holding her back and making her cling to her so-called plans. He had to wonder how reckless she might be willing to be with him.

"Just playing my part," he said.

"We should practice for our upcoming love scene." Lane blew softly in his ear, making him want to scratch the affected skin. "Your trailer or mine?"

The woman was relentless, even though her fiancé was somewhere on the set. "I told you my rules."

Lane frowned. "I thought you were a player."

Adam wasn't about to play with her. "You're in a league by yourself. I wouldn't want to try to compete there."

Confusion clouded her gaze.

This was his opportunity to go. "I need to change. So do you."

As Adam walked toward the dressing rooms, crew members gave him kudos and atta-boys for his work. Everyone said they couldn't wait to see the dailies. Neither could he. That acting nomination was getting so much closer Adam could taste it.

It took him over a half hour to reach the dressing room due

to receiving so many accolades. Rosie was waiting for him
Megan, too.

Today kept getting better and better. Adam smiled at the
two women, but his gaze lingered on the intern.

Megan's cheeks were no longer flushed. Her lips didn't look
as swollen from kissing him this morning. A lanyard with
laminated pictures of actors in their costumes hung around
her neck. Comparing a character to the picture gave the costume dressers a fast and easy way to determine continuity
between takes. He kicked off his shoes. "Sorry it took me so
long, ladies."

"No worries." Rosie placed his shoes into a labeled bag
"You earned every single one of those compliments. Great job.

"You were watching?"

Rosie nodded. "We all were."

Megan must have watched, too. That pleased him. But she
wouldn't meet his eyes. Adam didn't know if that was because
of their earlier kiss or the scenes he'd shot. He liked the idea
she might be jealous of him kissing Lane all afternoon, but that
was probably stretching things given her feelings for Rob, the
engineering bozo with the supposedly high IQ.

"Thanks," Adam said.

"Texas has been enlisted to help today," Rosie explained
"Kenna was called in to assist with Lane, who's acting more
like a spoiled brat than America's sweetheart."

His fault. Now the crew would have to put up with Lane
being in a bad mood. He'd be buying the rounds on Friday night
after Damon showed this week's dailies. Spending money on
the crew was better than fooling around with Lane. "I'm sure
you'll show Megan the ropes."

"Speaking of ropes." Rosie winked. "After seeing the way
you kissed Lane, Texas might have to tie me up to keep me in
line with you."

Adam's gaze met Megan's. "Promises, promises."

She blushed, turning her cheeks a pretty pink.

"Let's get you out of this costume," Rosie said.

A wicked idea formed in his head. Remembering the feel of Megan's lips on his, her sweet, warm taste, he wondered what it would be like to have her undress him. Adam flexed his fingers. "I have stuff on my hands. Would you mind?"

"I'll get a wet cloth," Megan offered.

"No, we've taken long enough. We still have to get ready for the close-up shot." Rosie removed his accessories, checking them off on her inventory list and placing them in Ziploc bags. She pinned that to the accessory holder, a muslin sleeve that was a foot to a foot and a half long. "Unbutton Adam's shirt for him."

Megan inhaled sharply.

He almost felt bad for her deer-in-the-headlights expression. Emphasis on *almost*. He planned to make the most of this unexpected opportunity.

Megan's fingers trembled as she reached for his shirt button. Her nervousness tugged at his heart. "I don't bite."

"He doesn't." Rosie removed his watch and placed it in a Ziploc plastic bag. "Adam's more a nibbler."

"You know this how?" he asked jokingly.

Rosie grinned. "I have my sources."

"Sources that are wrong," he countered.

Megan's fingers fumbled. She finally unfastened one, but she wasn't smiling.

Maybe this hadn't been such a good idea.

"So you're a biter, then?" Rosie teased.

Megan's fingers slipped off the next button. Her fingertips brushed his chest. Heat pooled where she touched him.

Some strong physical attraction…chemistry there. But he'd known that from their kiss.

Her flushed cheeks deepened from pink to red. "Sorry."

"I'm sorry. I should have had Basil deal with my hands before coming here." Adam wanted her to laugh, not be nervous and tense. "You're doing great."

Rosie's phone beeped. She checked the touch screen, then grimaced. "I'll be right back."

With that, she dashed out of the dressing room.

Megan's hands froze. "Your hands are fine. Basil took care of them, didn't he?"

Adam smiled sheepishly. "I knew you were a sharp one."

She placed her arms at her sides. "Hurry up and unbutton your shirt before Rosie gets back. Pants, too. I'm not unzipping your zipper."

Adam would have loved her to unzip him, but he'd given Megan enough grief. He did as she'd asked.

She readied a hanger for his shirt. "You and Lane were great today. You, especially. I didn't think you could be any better than you were this morning. I was wrong."

Others' compliments paled in comparison to hers. "I was hoping you were there."

"I wanted to be there," Megan admitted. "But I didn't realize there would be so many takes for one kiss."

He handed her his shirt. "They have to get all the angles."

"Well, it gave me plenty of opportunity to see how you acted out the scene with Lane compared to the one with me."

"It was the same."

"During the main takes, you kissed Lane longer."

Interesting, Megan had noticed that. Maybe he shouldn't have downplayed the kiss in the trailer. But her rock-his-world kiss had caught him off guard. Self-preservation had made him act as if the kiss had been nothing when it had been something. Something big. "Not intentional."

She stared down her nose at him. "None of my concern if it was."

The lines around her mouth and tight voice begged to differ. He wondered if that meant she wasn't so dead set on the guy back in Texas in spite of what she'd said. "I was taking Damon's request to make the moment more emotional, but wasn't timing any of the kisses."

She lifted her chin. "I didn't time the kisses, either. But the ones with Lane were definitely longer."

Satisfaction flowed through him. Megan was jealous.

"That's only because every time I kissed Lane I imagined I was kissing you."

Excitement flashed in Megan's eyes, but quickly disappeared. "Yeah, right."

"I'm not joking." He glanced at the closed door to the dressing room and lowered his voice. "Just so you know, you're a much better kisser than Lane Gregory."

Gratitude shone in Megan's stunning brown eyes. "If I wasn't afraid of someone walking in or the fact I decided not to kiss you again, I'd plant a big fat one right on your lips for saying that. Whether it's true or not."

"Trust me, it's true." He liked her sassy response, but he hated how she didn't see herself as desirable. He wanted to kiss all the uncertainty out of her. "But why don't you want to kiss me?"

"Other than the fact that you're the star and could have me fired quicker than snapping your fingers?"

Her words stung. "I would never do anything to hurt you or get you fired."

She buttoned his shirt. "You say that now, but you could change your mind."

"I'm not like that."

She placed the hanger on a clothing rack. "No, I don't think you are."

Her words didn't make him feel much better. He unbuckled his belt. "What else?"

As she faced him, he unzipped his pants.

She gasped, covered her eyes with her hands and turned away from him. "What are you doing?"

"Taking off my pants."

Megan kept her back to him. "I thought you'd go into the bathroom or something."

"Why would I do that?" He didn't understand why she was so upset. "This is a dressing room."

"But I'm here."

"Come on. It's not like we're twelve."

She didn't say anything.

Adam supposed she might not be used to the lack of modesty. "I'm sorry if I surprised you, but actors dress and undress in front of people all the time. I don't think twice before stripping down to my underwear."

She lowered her hands from her eyes, but didn't turn around. "Are you wearing underwear?"

A little prudish, but still cute. "Do I look like the commando type?"

"Must I answer?"

He smiled. "I'm wearing boxer briefs. Fully covered. Satisfied?"

"Take off your pants and hand them to me." Megan didn't look at him, but reached behind her. "I'll hang them up."

"Turn around. If you're going to be in costume design, you can't get all wigged out by a guy undressing in front of you." He slipped out of his pants, but didn't hand them to her. "It's not like you haven't seen a naked man before."

Glancing over her shoulder, she met his gaze. "I haven't. At least not in person. Unless you count sculptures in museums."

He stared at her in disbelief. No way could she be...

"Please don't look at me like that," she pleaded. "I might not have slept with anyone, but that doesn't mean I have some sort of incurable disease or a giant *V* on my chest."

V for virgin. His throat tightened. "Most women your age have had sex."

Her eyes darkened. "I'm not like most women."

No, she wasn't.

Squaring her shoulders as if she were facing a troop of armed soldiers rather than a guy in his underwear, Megan faced him. She kept her gaze focused on his face. "Give me your pants."

He handed them to her. "Does Rob know?"

"I have no idea." She zipped the pants. "He knows I haven't dated much."

"You've been saving yourself for him."

She cringed. "That sounds so…pathetic."

"It's sweet and romantic."

Like her.

She buckled his belt. "If the crew finds out, they'll think I'm a freak or frigid or something."

"Having sex while working on a shoot happens, but not everyone is doing it."

He wasn't. That would surprise the crew more than Megan being a virgin. But he wasn't going to tell her that.

"Maybe Rob knows and that's why he doesn't want me." The hurt and embarrassment in her voice made Adam's stomach hurt. "Because I'm inexperienced."

"If that's the case, Rob is not only an idiot, but also a total moron."

"I suppose giving it up to the first guy I see would be pretty stupid."

Not if she were giving it up to him. He was the guy she was looking at. Introducing Megan to sex would be fun. He would be better doing that for her than someone as clueless as Rob.

"I mean I know what my sister has gone through being a single mom." Megan hung up the pants. "That's a road I don't want to follow."

"Having sex doesn't mean you'll automatically get pregnant."

She removed his wedding band and placed it in the plastic bag with his watch. "Not having sex guarantees I won't."

"I'll concede that point." Adam might want her, but he wanted it to be the right choice for her. "You shouldn't just give it up. The first time is a big deal. Or it should be."

There. He'd said what needed to be said, told her good advice and provided the necessary support. If this were a romantic comedy, he would have given the perfect best friend performance. Now he wouldn't have to feel guilty when he took her to bed.

Oh, the things he could teach her. Playful images filled his mind.

"That's the real reason I've waited," she said. "I want my first time to be with someone I love and trust and who feels the same way about me."

Damn. That didn't describe Adam at all.

Talk about a bummer. But maybe this was for the best.

Someone with a big heart like Megan would never treat sex as simply a physical act of gratification. She would become attached and want a relationship and other things Adam wasn't willing to give. She deserved all those things. He wanted her to have them. Best to curtail his flirting with her.

"Wait for that right guy." Adam couldn't believe the words had come out of his mouth, but he kept going as if some alien being had taken residency in his body, especially his heart, and pushed out any thought of selfishness. "Having sex isn't something you do to fit in. Don't let anyone push you into doing something until it's the way you want it to be."

Her smile brightened her entire face. It was as if the sun had appeared after being covered by clouds. Simply beautiful. Breathtaking.

"Thank you. I don't feel like such a freak now," she said. "You're really something, Adam Noble. Just when I think you can't get any nicer, you do."

His heart slammed against his chest. He struggled to fill his lungs with air. What was happening?

Megan wasn't the anomaly. He was.

If any of his friends had heard him, they'd confiscate his player status, delete all the hot chicks' phone numbers from his contact list and laugh him right out of town. Adam swallowed. "Just don't let anybody know."

The V above her nose deepened again. "About being a virgin?"

"That I can be such a nice guy." His jaw tensed. "I'm a leading man, not a best friend. You'd be wise to remember that."

He'd spoken the words for his sake as much as hers. Unfortunately, Adam had a feeling he might be the one struggling not to forget them.

* * *

Hurry up and wait. That seemed to be how things worked on the set. The days ran into one another, one week into the next. Megan had finally gotten into the swing of things, but she never knew exactly what she would be doing each day when she arrived at the lot.

The only problem, if she could call it a problem, was Adam. Megan thought they were friends, but she no longer saw him except at meal times or if she went onto the set to watch a scene being shot. If she didn't know better she would think he was avoiding her.

Maybe he was.

I'm a leading man, not a best friend. You'd be wise to remember that.

Did he mean he wasn't a friend type or her friend? Not knowing frustrated her. But what could she do about it? She wasn't supposed to be hanging around him. She couldn't force him to be her friend or spend time with her or make him kiss her again.

Strike the kisses. More of those were bad ideas.

But she missed her conversations with him, his smile, his sense of humor.

Tuesday evening, Megan followed Kenna and Rosie out of the wardrobe department. The two women had taken Megan under their wing, both professionally and personally. Even though they were older than her, they didn't seem to mind her being younger and new to the set. She enjoyed working with them and hanging out during meal times and breaks, talking about work, fashion, men. It was the kind of relationship she had always wanted with her sister. The kind of relationship Jess had had with their mother. But Megan hadn't told them, or anyone, about kissing Adam while they rehearsed lines. She wanted to keep that secret. Her secret.

An outdoor scene was being shot tonight so call times had been shifted later. Everyone would eat dinner, then prepare for the shoot.

Kenna rubbed her hands together. "I hope there's salmon."

"Beef brisket and corn bread would be nice," Megan said.

"Homesick, Tex?" Rosie asked.

"No." Megan hadn't heard from her family. Not that she'd thought about them much the past few days. Rob, either. That was odd. Guess she was busier than she realized. "But I'm hungry."

Whatever they were serving for dinner smelled delicious.

Craft Services provided all the snacks and drinks the crew could want, but a caterer, in this case a Cordon Bleu–trained chef, prepared meals. The food was to die for. Tasty, healthy and priced right—free. Megan was on her feet so much, working crazy hours, she was losing weight in spite of food being available all the time.

"You know what they say." Rosie picked up a plate. "A well fed crew helps a production run smoother."

"Let's hope that's true tonight," Kenna said in a low voice. "Rumor has it there are lighting 'issues.'"

Rosie sighed. "I hope not. I don't want to be here all night."

"Tony had an early call time," Kenna said of her gaffer boyfriend who she met on the set. "He hinted things weren't going well."

Delays happened for a variety of reasons—equipment breaking, weather for outdoor shoots, props and lighting. Some setups, especially exterior scenes, could be complicated and take hours.

Megan stood behind her two friends in the line for dinner. "A good thing we could sleep in this morning."

"I needed the rest," Rosie said.

Megan picked up a plate. "Me, too."

Waking without an alarm had been so great. Dreaming about Adam Noble, not so much. She needed to get him out of her thoughts once and for all. He hadn't even placed her in friend zone. He didn't want to be her friend.

Better that way, she kept telling herself. Maybe one of these times the words would sink in and not bother her so much.

Megan went through the buffet. The delicious aromas made

er mouth water. No brisket, but she helped herself to a gen-
rous helping of pulled pork, steamed green beans, a baked
weet potato with butter and brown sugar and a glass of iced
ea. She joined Rosie and Kenna at a table.

"Where's your dessert?" Rosie asked.

Megan placed a napkin on her lap. "I'll get a brownie later."

As they ate, they discussed fashion trends for the fall. The
opic turned to an upcoming awards show.

Kenna scooped up another forkful of salmon. "I can't wait
o see what people will be wearing at the Viewers' Choice
Awards."

Rosie nodded. "I love seeing all those gowns on the red car-
et no matter what the awards show."

"There are so many of them. They all start sounding the
ame," Megan admitted.

Kenna nodded, and started ticking award ceremonies off
n her fingers with exaggerated yawns. Midlaughter, Megan
ealized Adam stood next to their table with a plate of food in
ne hand and a glass of water in the other.

"Mind if I join you?" Adam asked,

Megan's heart bumped. She opened her mouth to speak, but
othing came out. He gave new meaning to the term "smart
asual" in his cerulean polo shirt and khaki pants. The shirt
ntensified the green in his eyes. Her pulse accelerated.

Stop staring.

She glanced at the other two women, who motioned for
Adam to sit.

Adam took a step toward the empty chair next to her, much
o Megan's delight. Maybe he wasn't ignoring her, after all.
But then he changed direction to her dismay. He pulled out
ae chair next to Kenna on the opposite side of the table from
Megan and sat. "Thanks."

Disappointment tugged at her. Too bad she hadn't picked up
brownie. Chocolate sounded good right now. Megan stabbed
er fork into her sweet potato and took a bite. Brown sugar

and butter didn't have the same emotional benefits as a chunk of chocolate.

Adam stared across the table at her. "Do you like award shows?"

"I've watched them on TV," Megan said.

"What you see on TV is staged," Kenna said. "The real fun is when the red light on the camera goes off. The emcee tells funnier jokes."

Rosie nodded. "And the seat fillers run around in their gowns and tuxes while someone races to the bathroom."

Adam placed his cup on the table. "I did that."

"Race to the bathroom?" Megan asked.

"Sit in empty seats during breaks," he said.

Kenna's mouth formed a perfect O. "I had no idea."

Adam shrugged. "It was a paying gig. One where I didn't have to fall out of a building or roll across the top of a car."

Rosie smiled. "Lucky you. I don't have that kind of claim to fame, but I have been enlisted to make impromptu fashion repairs in the ladies' powder room as well as tape breasts to ensure no nip slips."

Adam winked. "That sounds like a better gig than mine."

The man was incorrigible. A total flirt. And absolutely gorgeous. Megan stared at the food on her plate, but nothing looked appetizing any longer.

"I've only attended some after-parties," Kenna said.

Rosie stared over her cola can. "Those are much better than the awards show."

"Why is that?" Megan asked.

Rosie grinned. "Drinking, dancing, more drinking."

Kenna looked at Megan. "We should try to get invites for a party after the Viewers' Choice Awards so Tex can see what it's like."

Megan's first instinct was to decline. She'd never been into parties, but then again, she'd never been invited to many. "That would be fun."

Adam's mouth quirked. "You'd want to go?"

She thought for a moment. Dancing sounded fun. "Yes, I would."

Rosie batted her eyelashes at Adam. "Maybe some hot actor nominated for favorite onscreen couple could get our names on some after-party lists."

He squinted. "What's wrong with your eyes?"

Rosie punched his shoulder. "You're worse than my brother."

Adam laughed. "I take that as a compliment. I'll see what I can do about getting you ladies on a couple of lists."

"Thanks." Kenna rubbed her hands together. "That gives us two weeks to plan our outfits. Think you can do it?"

Megan nodded. She wondered if Adam would be at the same party. Not that it mattered.

"We'll need at least a week to figure out what shoes to wear," Rosie said. "Though I'm sure we'll be barefoot by night's end from all the dancing."

"You mean when the sun comes up," Kenna said.

Adam grinned at the redhead. "I like how you think."

Picking up her iced tea, Megan wondered if he knew Kenna was dating Tony. Not that who Adam flirted with or liked was any of Megan's business. For all she knew, he'd hooked up with someone on the set and that was why he hadn't been around. She wasn't thirsty, but she sipped her tea to give herself something to do other than think about him.

"You're the planner," Adam said to her. "Anything your partners in crime are forgetting for your big night?"

Megan set her glass on the table. Invite, dress, shoes… Hair and makeup."

"Basil!" Kenna and Rosie said at the same time.

Adam grinned. "Looks like you're all set."

"All set for what?" Eva asked, standing next to the table.

CHAPTER NINE

THE appearance of Firebreather cast a pall over the table. Conversation screeched to a halt. Excitement died.

Kenna and Rosie stared at their plates. Megan, too. She wanted to avoid making eye contact with their boss, if only to keep from being sent on an errand.

"All set for their night on the town," Adam said, rather bravely, Megan thought.

Eva arched a brow. "With you?"

Kenna looked up. "We know better than that."

Rosie nodded. Megan, too.

"So you've explained my rule to the intern," Eva said.

It wasn't a question.

"I heard about it, too." Adam's jaw tensed. "Not that they have anything to worry about from me."

Eva's hard gaze didn't waver from Adam's. "Did you know Lane had Annie Rockwell fired because her fiancé made a passing comment about how attractive the woman was?"

Megan hadn't heard that. But she knew who Annie was. The pretty assistant camerawoman had a Zumba-instructor worthy body.

"I'm not like that," Adam said through clenched teeth.

"Maybe not," Eva agreed. "But better safe than sorry. These three women are important, talented members of my team."

Important? Talented? That was the first compliment Eva had ever given Megan. Pride flowed through her.

"I'd hate to lose any of them due to an…indiscretion," Eva continued. "And finding a replacement in the middle of a production would be a real pain."

"No worries." Adam cracked a smile. "We're all friends here. Just friends."

He hadn't been treating Megan like a friend lately. More like an acquaintance, a not so fond one, or a stranger.

"You can't have too many friends." Eva looked around the table until her gaze came to rest on Megan, who shifted in her chair under the watchful stare. "The shoot has been delayed two hours. Be back before nine."

With that, Eva walked away, but kept glancing back.

"Firebreather is on the warpath," Rosie mumbled.

Nodding, Kenna stood. "I want to go find Tony."

"Have fun," Megan said. "This is my chance to check out some of the other sets on the lot."

"I'll see you ladies, later." Adam stood. "I'm off to soundstage three to say hi to my agent."

Rosie stood. "Maybe you could get Texas headed in the right direction so she doesn't get lost?"

Spending time with Adam appealed to Megan, but not this way. She didn't want him to feel obligated to be with her. "Thanks, Rosie, but I drove all the way from Texas on my own. I'm sure I can figure out which way to go."

"We don't want Rosie to worry," Adam said. "I'm happy to show you the way."

Megan leaned back in her chair. This wasn't what she wanted. Adam, either. He wouldn't have offered to escort her without the prompting from Rosie. Hurt pricked at Megan. She would prefer him to *want* to be with her. Not be so much like…

Rob.

The realization took Megan's breath away. Her insides twisted. No way did she want another situation like that in her life. Once was bad enough.

Time to grab a brownie or two and find something else to do.

No, Megan realized. That would be stupid. She wanted to

see the lot, and she would. But she didn't need Adam pointing her in the right direction. She could find her own way.

Adam was alone at the table with Megan, but didn't dare sit again. Not when he felt like a moth to her flame. He'd been trying to stay away from her. Not flirt. He should have eaten dinner in his trailer.

Except, he'd missed her. Like Rosie, he didn't want her wandering off and getting lost. "Ready?"

Megan rose and walked to the garbage can with her plate and cup.

What the… He did a double take.

She wasn't wearing jeans. He'd noticed she was wearing a button-up shirt with a lace-trimmed camisole underneath when she was sitting, but now that she stood he could see her complete outfit…

He blew out a puff of air.

The stylish tunic and leggings showed off her long legs and accentuated the curve of her hips and narrow waist. She'd exchanged her sneakers for a pair of leather flats. Pretty. Fashionable. Hot.

He followed after her. "New clothes."

She nodded. "I went shopping."

"You look great." He'd wondered what she had done on her time off. Not that he'd been thinking about her 24/7. Okay, maybe he had. "You must have had fun shopping with Kenna and Rosie."

Megan raised her chin. "I didn't go with them."

Her reply surprised Adam. Unless Kenna was with Tony the gaffer, the three women hung out during breaks. "Did you go shopping on your own?"

Her nose scrunched. "Huh?"

"Never mind," he said. "Let's go."

"Thanks for telling Rosie you'd get me going in the right direction," Megan said. "But I have a map. I'll be fine on my own."

No way. For some unexplained reason, Megan brought out his protective instinct. Must be some leftover character stuff from that SEAL commando he'd played. But Adam couldn't deny he liked being with her, too. Even if it went against his better judgment. "I'm going that way. It's no problem."

She stared at him.

He stared back.

Stalemate.

"Okay," she said finally, sounding annoyed. That bothered Adam. He'd hardly seen her. He would have thought she would want to spend time with him.

Megan walked alongside him in silence.

"How are things going?" he asked.

"Well." She looked at each of the buildings they passed, as if they were more interesting than him. "How about you?"

"No complaints." At least he'd had none until now. They'd never lacked for subjects to discuss. "Is something wrong?"

"No."

"You're quiet."

She shot him a sideways glance. "I didn't think you wanted to talk to me."

"Why would you think that?" he asked.

"You've been avoiding me since that night in your dressing room."

Damn. She'd nailed it. He hedged. "We've both been busy with the shoot."

Her gaze met his. "I made you uncomfortable."

Hell, yes. She made him uncomfortable. Not only then, but now. The scent of her shampoo filled his nostrils. He remembered the taste of her lips.

What was going on? Adam brushed his hand through his hair.

"You don't have to answer. It's pretty clear I do." She stopped at an intersection. "This is where we part ways."

He wasn't ready to say goodbye. "I'll go with you."

"Soundstage three is the other way."

The hurt arcing through him caught Adam by surprise. "You don't want me to go with you."

She set her jaw. "No."

Her firm tone dug into him, as did her answer. "Why not?"

"The truth?"

He nodded once, bracing himself for what she might say.

Hurt clouded her eyes. "I thought we were friends."

He tried to understand where she was going with this. Tried and failed. "We are."

"Your actions imply otherwise."

Once again she'd called him on his bad behavior. Okay, he had been acting like a jerk. But being with her confused him. He wasn't sure what to do or say. Avoiding her meant he didn't have to deal with the uncertainty, something that reminded him too much of his childhood. "I'm a guy. I don't put a lot of thought into what I'm doing or saying."

"Sounds like most men."

Rob? No, Adam didn't want to go there. He wanted Megan thinking about him. "Would it help if I apologized?"

"Only if you mean it."

"I do," he admitted. "I'm sorry for acting like a jerk. Again I'd promise not to do again, but I'm a guy so who knows what will happen?"

A smile tugged on her lips. "At least you're honest."

"I am." He grinned. "And so are you. You don't hold back what you are thinking or feeling."

That familiar V above her nose returned. "With you, no."

He wanted to see a big smile back on her face. "Hey. Before you head off on your own, let me show you one thing."

"Your agent…"

"Sam can wait," Adam said. "Please."

She looked off into the distance, not really focusing on anything. But she wasn't zoning out. She was…thinking, no doubt performing a pro/con analysis to his offer.

"One thing," she said finally.

Relief washed over him. He took her hand.

She stiffened, but didn't pull her arm away. "What are you doing?"

"Showing you something."

Holding her hand, he led her across the street and through the alley of two buildings. This part of the lot was empty except for a helicopter flying overhead.

A few minutes later, anticipation revved through him. Adam hoped she liked this. He released her hand and covered her eyes.

She tensed. "What is going on?"

"Hold on." He coaxed her forward around the corner. "I want this to be a surprise."

"I'm not big on surprises," she said, sounding irritated.

"Trust me. You'll like this one. Keep your eyes closed." He positioned her in the middle of the street and removed his hand. "You can look now."

Megan opened her eyes and gasped. "It's New York."

They stood in a replica of Times Square, complete with large video screens and neon lights. He motioned to the street with both hands. "Welcome to the Big Apple."

Excitement filled her eyes. She spun around. "The set looks so real."

The same awe filled her voice as the first time they'd walked through the lot together. He was happy she hadn't lost that sense of wonder after being on the set. "Movie magic."

Her mouth slanted. "Or a talented group of set designers and carpenters."

Adam grinned. Practical. That was his Megan.

Not his, he corrected. Well, his friend.

"It's amazing," she said. "I've never been to New York, but I feel like I've been there now."

"Never been to New York with your interest in costume design and fashion?"

"Nope. I've always wanted to go. Experience the city that never sleeps. Get a taste of some glitz and glamour." She touched the brick facade of one of the buildings. "But I..."

As her voice faded, sadness filled her eyes.

He touched her shoulder. "What?"

"It's nothing."

"It's something." Adam gave her a reassuring squeeze. " understand if you're still angry at me for the way I've been act ing, but I am your friend and I'd like to know what's going on.'

Megan took a breath. And another. "My mom never wanted any of us to go to New York. I finally realized why after m sister found an unopened letter hidden beneath my mother' jewelry box. It was written by my dad's first wife, Fenella. The return address on the envelope was New York City."

"The rancher and a city girl."

"Yep. I'm assuming my mom didn't want my dad anywher near his first wife. Nor any of us." Megan peered in the window of a storefront. "Fenella was pregnant with twins when they di vorced. I have a half brother and sister that I never knew about.

"That had to be a shock."

Megan nodded with a pained expression. "It's been a littl weird."

Adam guessed more than a little. Losing her dad, findin out about new siblings. Megan had been through a lot in th past year. "Have you met them?"

"No, but one, Ellie, is now living in Larkville," Megan saic "I didn't have time to go home before leaving college for L.A so I haven't met her. I'm glad to be here and not have to dea with it. Is that bad?"

Adam gave her a half hug. "Sounds smart to me."

She glanced up at him. "Thanks."

"Anytime." Something seemed to draw them closer. A par of Adam liked the feeling, but another part of him wanted t get the hell out of Dodge. "I have no idea what my father's lif was like before or after us. I've always wondered if I had an secret half siblings."

"Is there any way to find out?" she asked.

"I hired a private detective, but he couldn't find any trac

of my father. He told me Noble most likely wasn't my father's real name."

Megan gave Adam a squeeze.

The gesture, her warmth, comforted him. This time he wasn't about to shrug it off. Or her.

"My father was a con man. A charming liar. If he kept the same M.O. and moved on to another town and woman, I could have half siblings all over the place." Adam gazed down at her. So pretty. Compassion gleamed in her eyes. "We're a pair, aren't we?"

She nodded once. The light from the streetlamp made her lips glimmer. "But we're very different, too. Small-town girl and a famous movie star."

Adam didn't care about their differences. He wanted to kiss her. Badly. He could if he wanted to. The set was deserted except for the two of them. Silent except for their breaths. No one would have to know.

Megan parted her lips, a sign she wanted a kiss.

All he had to do was lower his head a couple of inches, to capture her lips with his. He knew how she would taste and feel.

His pulse quickened.

But something held him back.

I want my first time to be with someone I love and trust and who feels the same way about me.

A kiss was a long way from having sex, but he couldn't forget what she'd told him. He liked Megan, more than he'd liked anybody in a long time. Maybe ever. But he knew better than to love and trust anybody. Going down that path only led to heartache and disappointment. Places he had no intention of going. Watching his mother experience it over and over again was enough.

Gold flecks flamed in Megan's eyes.

He wanted to kiss her, but he wouldn't. Not until he explained what he was willing to give and what he couldn't. As soon as he figured out what that would be. Until then, he'd better stop thinking about her that way. "You'll get a taste of the movie star life at the after-parties."

"I can't wait to see all the dresses in person."

Her excitement pleased him. He wasn't that surprised she was more interested in the fashion than the stars wearing them. "You should be at the red carpet."

"That would be so cool," she admitted. "But attending an after-party is more than I imagined I'd do out here. I'm happy with that."

The hint of wistfulness in her voice stirred something within him. She might be content going to the after-party, but he felt the urge to do something more for her, to make her forget all she'd been through these past months with her family.

Megan had never been to New York. Larkville didn't sound like the most happening place. But he could give her a taste of the glitz and glamour she wanted to experience. More than she'd get attending an after-party. "Go with me to the Viewers' Choice Awards."

She let go of his arm. "What?"

"I want to take you to the awards show. You can experience one of Hollywood's big nights from start to finish," he said. "Rosie and Kenna can meet us at one of the after-parties."

"I...I don't know."

"What's not to know? Awards show, after-parties, a handsome escort."

"I appreciate the offer, but—"

"No buts," he interrupted. "All you have to do is say yes and you'll get to walk down the red carpet with me at your side."

That got her attention. Anticipation sparkled her eyes.

"Imagine seeing all those gowns up close and personal."

She moistened her lips. "That would be...nice."

"Not nice. Awesome," he countered. "I promise you'll have a great time."

"I'd really love to go." Concern clouded her gaze. "Except I...can't."

He hoped this had nothing to do with Rob. "Why not?"

"Eva. If she found out…"

Not Rob. Adam smiled. "Don't worry. I'll take care of Eva and any concerns she might have about you and me being… friends."

Megan threw her arms around him and hugged him tightly. "Thanks."

He hugged her back, inhaling her sweet scent. She felt so good in his arms. Sweet torture. "Thank you."

Megan felt as if she floated through the rest of the evening. Not even the lighting delays could bring her down. She couldn't believe Adam had invited her to the awards show, especially when he was up for an award. She wanted to tell Kenna and Rosie, but not until he'd had a chance to talk to Eva about it.

The only thing that would have made things better was if Adam had kissed her. She thought he might until she realized he saw her as only a friend. The way she wanted him to see her, Megan reminded herself. She shouldn't complain about that.

Except his invitation made her wonder if more than friendship was…possible.

The next day, she double-checked the racks of clothing for the background artists. Excitement had kept her awake most of the night. She still felt as if she were floating.

"So Adam Noble invited you to the Viewers' Choice Awards."

The sound of Eva's voice made Megan spin around. She held clipboard in front of her chest and took a steadying breath. "I hope that's okay."

Eva pursed her red-glossed lips. "Are you sleeping with him?"

"No." Megan's voice came out sharper than she intended, but she hadn't held on to her virginity this long to give it up to the first gorgeous guy who'd paid attention to her. No matter how tempting. "We're…friends."

Friends who had shared kisses in his trailer hot enough to melt the rubber soles of Megan's tennis shoes and had her

dreaming of more kisses, but Eva didn't need to know that
Especially since no more kisses had followed. And wouldn't

Friends, Megan reminded herself. She wasn't ready to take
that plunge into something more.

Eva studied Megan's face. "He said the same thing. Tha
you were just friends."

Disappointment bounced down to Megan's feet and back
up again. Maybe she was more ready than she realized. No
she needed to be smart about this. Her internship came first
Not romance with a guy who'd told her and her boss they were
just friends. She tilted her chin. "It's true."

"I didn't believe him, but I believe you."

Megan blushed. "May I go with Adam?"

"If I say no?"

"I won't go. This internship is more important than attend
ing an awards show."

"Good answer."

Eva wasn't going to allow it. Megan's shoulders sagged.

"Stand up straight," Eva snapped. "You can't have bad pos
ture when you're on the red carpet."

Megan straightened. Excitement stirred beneath her ches
"I can go?"

Eva narrowed her blue eyes. "Yes, but you'd better not d
anything to make me regret this."

"I won't. I promise. On my father's grave." Megan wante
to hug Eva, but thought better of it. "Thank you."

Eva's assessing gaze traveled the length of Megan. No doul
assembling an inventory of all the things wrong with her. I
would be a long list.

She fought the urge to squirm. She wouldn't give Firebreathe
the satisfaction.

"The Viewers' Choice Awards is a formal event," Eva sai
finally. "Do you have anything appropriate to wear? Shoes
Accessories?"

Her boss's critical tone bristled. "I have a dress."

"Off the rack?"

Megan raised her chin. "I made it."

"For a class?"

"For me."

Surprise flashed in Eva's eyes, but vanished as quickly as it had appeared.

The dress was one she'd mentioned to Rob. Stunning, if Megan said so herself. Glamorous, sexy even. Not the typical style she would ever considering wearing, but that had been part of the challenge. The fun. The dress wasn't doing much good hanging in her closet.

"Bring the dress in tomorrow," Eva ordered.

The thought of showing a talented costume designer like Eva Redding her dress knotted Megan's stomach. "I… I…"

"You're my intern," Eva said. "I'm not going to allow you to embarrass me and Adam by showing up at a huge media event in the wrong dress."

Good point. "I'll show you the dress tomorrow."

In his trailer, Adam played a game on one of his consoles. His cell phone beeped. A text message had arrived. He glanced at the touch screen. The text was from Megan.

Thanks for talking to Eva!!!! I can go to the awards show with you!!!!!

All the exclamation points made him smile. He typed a reply back.

Great!

Adam had looked for her this morning, but hadn't seen her. He missed her smile. He typed another text.

See you at lunch?

As soon as he pressed Send, he winced. Why was he tortur ing himself like this? Hanging out with a woman he couldn' have was stupid.

Her response arrived quickly.

Yes!!!!

A thrill flashed through him at the thought of being with he What was a little bit more torture, especially when she had suc gorgeous eyes and a very pretty smile and made him feel lik the king of the world? Even though he knew better, he typec

See you then!

The next day, Megan carried a garment bag containing he dress into the costume department. She was awash with nerve but a hint of excitement that Eva might like the dress ker Megan from wigging out completely. She found most of th wardrobe crew waiting for her.

"Show us this dress of yours," Eva ordered.

With a trembling hand, Megan unzipped the bag and re moved the dress. The purple fabric shimmered and sparkle She showed the front of the dress to them.

Kenna gasped. Rosie grinned. Two others stared in disbelie

Eva studied the gown. Her blank expression gave nothin away as to her opinion of the dress. "Show me the back."

Megan turned the dress around.

"Interesting," Eva said.

Megan had no idea if interesting was good or bad. She wa afraid to ask so she kept her lips pressed together in a ha smile.

"With a couple fixes, it'll work for the Viewers' Choic Awards," Eva said. "The bow has to go. The slit needs to k higher."

Megan tightened her grip on the hanger. It was already sl to her midthigh. Any higher…

"What shoes?" Eva asked.

Megan pulled out a pair of sandals. They were the dressiest shoes she owned.

Every person in the room shook their head. A few looked horrified by her choice of footwear.

"No," Eva said. "You need a higher heel. Slingbacks or a T-strap. Silver."

The others nodded their approval.

"I'll buy a pair," Megan said.

Eva shook her head. "I'll take care of it."

As Megan stood there holding her dress, her coworkers debated what accessories she needed as well as what to do with her hair and makeup. More people joined in on the discussion until a plan had been made, one without any input from her. She felt like a mannequin in a store window. Was this how Adam felt during a fitting and when he was being dressed for a shoot?

"You'll get ready here." A rare smile brightened Eva's face. "You'll be feeling like Cinderella by the time we're finished with you."

Megan wiggled her toes. She would have never believed Firebreather had it in her to be a fairy godmother. Or Adam her prince. "Thanks."

She would happily enjoy the fairy tale for the night. Even if a part of her wished it could last a little longer.

CHAPTER TEN

PRODUCTION was halfway over. Shooting continued amid delays, including an unexpected rain shower on a day scheduled for an outdoor scene. Script changes slowed. The shoot would be moving on location shortly. That would mix things up a bit and make this bubble world of the set even smaller.

Adam was looking forward to getting away from the lot. Being on location meant fewer distractions. More time to spend with Megan.

He exited the set following a close-up shot, his eyelids heavy and his feet dragging. He had an hour and a half break. He wanted to make the most of it. No video games, no phone calls, no texts. His assistant, Veronica, was making sure his bed was turned down and a white-noise machine running.

Napping wasn't his usual way to relax on the set, but a fling wasn't happening. At least not with the one woman he wanted. No one else interested him as much. At least he had a new friend.

"Adam." One of the grips ran up to him. "Chas is looking for you."

Damn. Adam didn't want to waste his break talking to the producer. Now if it were Megan… He would see her at lunch. Mealtimes were their main time together. It reminded Adam a little of high school, except students got some action. He wasn't getting any—no kisses or hand-holding even. But celibacy was turning out to be good for his acting. He could almost taste a nomination. "Tell Chas I'm getting a cup of coffee."

Adam trudged his way to the food and drinks table. He yawned, fighting a bone-weary tiredness that had set in over the past week and a half. A busy schedule and sleepless nights didn't go well together.

He downed half a cup of coffee. Maybe that would wake him up. Though it might wreak havoc with his nap.

"Looks like you could use a jolt of caffeine." Chas joined him at the coffee station. "Or a nap."

"Between the shoot and PR for the SEALs film, I don't have time to breathe." Adam had been running from one thing to the next, wherever he was told to go. The one constant amid all the chaos was Megan. She was always on his mind, day or night, awake or asleep. A little weird considering he'd kissed her only once. An air of mystery hovered around her. Maybe it was because they hadn't slept together. But with only a few weeks left of the shoot he wasn't going to analyze it too much. "I've lost track of the number of radio phone-in interviews I've done."

"Keep up whatever you're doing. The dailies look great," Chas said. "Everyone thinks I'm a genius for wanting you to play Maxwell."

Adam drank more coffee. The strong, hot drink tasted good going down his throat. "I never did ask why you were so set on me for the part."

"My wife," Chas admitted. "She's been a big fan ever since Neptune."

That one role had changed everything for him. He hoped bigger things happened with this film. "So she's the true genius."

Chas nodded. "And she knows it, too."

The sound of wheels rolling on the asphalt made Adam glance to his left. Megan pushed a clothing rack to the costume department. A camera bag hung off her shoulder. Worn jeans hugged her thighs like a second skin. A scooped-neck burgundy shirt with a sleeveless sweater over it complimented her ivory skin. More stylish than a plain T-shirt. If only she'd wear her hair down instead of clipped on the top of her head...

Megan's gaze met his.

Her beaming smile took his breath away. He waved, then watched the gentle sway of her hips as she passed by.

Chas tsked. "Texas, huh? I had no idea."

Adam's gaze jerked from Megan's retreating backside to the producer. "What was that about Texas?"

"I didn't realize the two of you were an item."

Unease slithered down his spine. "We're not."

"Could have fooled me the way her eyes lit up when she saw you."

Yeah, they had lit up. He'd noticed that a couple of times. Her smile seemed wider and brighter. It didn't mean anything. She must be getting excited about the Viewers' Choice Awards on Saturday night. Adam was looking forward to it. He'd been nominated, but he wanted to see Megan all dressed up and walking down the red carpet. "We're friends."

They were friends. Except when was the last time Adam had wanted to see a friend so much or thought about a friend all the time or dreamed about them? Hot dreams. Naked dreams. He gulped.

Chas winked. "I know what kind of friend you are, one who funds shopping sprees after a night of hot monkey sex. No wonder you're so tired lately."

The producer's wink-wink, nudge-nudge tone bothered Adam. He didn't like the insinuation that Megan might be trading sex for clothes. "We're friends, period. No sex or shopping sprees."

Chas shrugged. "Well, given the way she looks at you, if you want her, she won't put up much of an argument."

A weight pressed down on the center of Adam's chest. "Megan might surprise you."

She had surprised him. He knew the kind of romantic relationship Megan wanted. It was one hundred and eighty degrees different from what he wanted.

Maybe there was some middle ground where they both could be satisfied with more than their friendship right now. Or maybe things would continue as they were until production shut down and that would be it. They would say goodbye and move on to their next projects without looking back on what might have been. The thought of not talking to or seeing her again bummed him out. He drank the rest of his coffee.

"Hugh wants to see you," Chas said.

An image of Rhys Rogers dressed as a clown, complete with red nose and frizzy orange wig, performing at a kid's birthday party appeared in Adam's mind. Dread coupled with a sense of foreboding knotted his gut. "Hugh's never wanted to see me before."

Chas nodded. "Don't worry."

"Easy for you to say. You aren't the one rolling around in bed with Hugh's fiancée."

During yesterday's love scene shoot, Lane had her hands all over Adam. If she'd become Calliope and gotten wrapped up in the moment, he wouldn't have minded so much. But what she did had nothing to do with acting like a husband and wife making love and everything to do with Lane being a sexual predator and him her prey. Damon had been pleased with the shot, but no one, not even the watchful director, knew what Lane had been trying to do to Adam under the sheets.

Talk about awkward. He was relieved that Megan hadn't been allowed on the closed set. Nonessential crew members were kept out during sex scene shoots. A good thing because Adam hadn't wanted Megan to feel uncomfortable about his acting with Lane.

"I'm serious. No worries," Chas said. "Hugh has a favor to ask. That's all."

The studio head was rich and powerful. Adam had nothing Hugh would want or need. "When and where does he want to see me?"

"Now. In his office."

So much for a nap. Adam tossed his cup into the trash can.

"Leave it to Hugh to know this is my biggest chunk of free time until lunch."

"He knows everything that happens around here."

Adam wondered if Hugh knew what his fiancée was up to, even when the cameras were rolling. Somehow Adam doubted it.

"Hugh always reciprocates favors," Chas said in a low voice. "He's a good person to have in your debt."

"I'll keep that in mind."

Five minutes later, Adam entered Hugh Wilstead's office. Floor-to-ceiling windows along the back wall overlooked the entire lot. Movie posters covered the other walls along with a USC pennant and a Stanford flag. Framed photographs and awards filled bookshelves. Impressive.

"Hello, Adam." Hugh rose from behind a giant mahogany desk with a telephone and a laptop on top. The studio head wore a gray suit, yellow tie and white button-down shirt. Except for the patch of gray hair at his temple, he looked to be in his mid-thirties. He shook Adam's hand firmly. "Thanks for stopping by. The shoot is going well."

Adam nodded. "Solid script. Talented cast. Great crew. You're going to have a winner on your hands."

"I like your confidence." Hugh motioned to a black leather chair. "Sit."

Adam did.

Hugh sat and leaned back in his chair. "I find myself in a bit of a dilemma. I have to be in Europe this weekend. A meeting I can't get out of."

Adam had no idea what this had to do with him, but Hugh didn't sound pleased. "That's too bad."

"Lane is not happy about it," Hugh said. "When she's not happy, everyone around her will be unhappy."

So that explained Lane's tantrum this morning. At least it hadn't been because Adam had turned her down. Again. "We don't want Lane unhappy."

"That's why I need a favor."

Adam should have known this "favor" might have something to do with Lane. He doubted Hugh would want him to sleep with his fiancée. The guy didn't look like the type who shared his toys. But Hugh Wilstead was someone you wanted in your corner. Especially if they owed you a favor, as Chas had mentioned. "I'm happy to help out, what do you need?"

"The Viewers' Choice Awards are Saturday night. Lane's nominated," Hugh said. "I'd like you to escort her to the event, as a personal favor to me."

No freaking way. Adam's stomach roiled at the thought of spending the evening with Lane instead of Megan. "I have a date."

Hugh straightened. "That does complicate matters."

Adam nodded. He remembered the excitement dancing in Megan's pretty brown eyes when he'd invited her. He couldn't wait to show her the glamorous side of the movie industry. "She's excited to go. I would hate to let her down."

"No doubt," Hugh agreed. "But this is just one awards show. There will be others."

Not for months. Who knew where either of them would be by then? He couldn't imagine them together, but the thought of not being with Megan made Adam shift in his seat. He liked having her around.

Hugh's gaze hardened. "You're a smart man. You'll think of a way to make it up to her. The way I'll make it up to you."

The carrot dangled. The consequences of saying no to Hugh weighed on Adam's mind as much as the benefit of saying yes. He'd worked hard to get where he was. He didn't want to derail the momentum of his career over something like this.

But he couldn't stop thinking about Megan. She would be disappointed and rightly so. He took a deep breath, feeling trapped. No matter what he decided someone wouldn't be happy. Someone would be hurt. He didn't want that person to be Megan.

A few weeks ago, he would have said yes to Hugh without any hesitation. But the thought of hurting her tightened a vice grip around Adam's heart. She'd come to mean a lot to him. The depth of his feelings for her took him by surprise.

"This is a difficult spot to be in," Hugh continued. "We never want to let down the women we love."

Whoa. Adam clutched the chair arms. Hugh might love Lane, but Adam didn't love Megan. Okay, he liked her. Megan was nice. Pretty. Hot. He enjoyed kissing her and being with her. He cared what happened to her. But nothing would ever come of it. She wouldn't be around for long. No one ever was.

Friendship was one thing. But love…

No way. He didn't love anybody. Except his mom. And that hadn't always turned out so well with men flitting in and out of their lives. Love was uncertain, out of control and left you hurting when it went south. Which it always did.

Why would anyone want to fall in love?

He didn't plan on it, but Megan…

I want my first time to be with someone I love and trust and who feels the same way about me.

She wanted to be in love, but that didn't mean she'd fallen for him?

Could have fooled me the way her eyes lit up when she saw you.

Well, if you want her, it doesn't look like she'll put up much of an argument.

Chas noticing those things about Megan bothered Adam. He didn't want a relationship or a girlfriend. He didn't want any sort of attachments to slow down his career or put his heart at risk.

Or hers.

Megan had her whole life ahead of her and big plans, ones that would take her away from him. If she'd developed romantic feelings for him, then his not taking her to the awards ceremony would be a good thing for both their sakes. Neither of them could afford to get in too deep.

"You and Lane attending the awards will drum up early pubicity for the movie," Hugh added. "It will help your SEALs film, too."

Adam found himself nodding, ignoring the voice inside his head reminding him about Megan. He'd promised her a good time. He hated breaking his promises. He remembered how badly it stung when his mother broke hers.

Hugh steepled his hands. "So I can count on you for Saturday."

It wasn't a question. Adam thought about Megan. Her expressive eyes told him what she was feeling. Her smile warmed his heart. The sound of her laughter brightened his day. The intoxicating scent of her made him dizzy with desire. With all those things in mind, Adam knew exactly what he needed to do about the awards ceremony.

"Yes, you can count on me," he said. "I'll take Lane to the Viewers' Choice Awards."

That would slow down whatever this thing was he had for Megan and keep it from going any further than friendship. He didn't like the way he kept reacting to whatever she said or did. Or the way she could always sense how he was feeling. He didn't like the way he felt off-balance when he was with her and unsettled when he wasn't.

This was for the best. Even if Adam wasn't looking forward to having to tell Megan.

In Lane Gregory's dressing room, Megan secured a diamond-encrusted watch on the actress's slim wrist. She double-checked to make sure it was fastened correctly. Dressing actresses sure beat being stuck fixing broken zippers or doing laundry after everyone went home. "Is that too tight?"

Lane moved her wrist back and forth. Her lips were set in a frown, and she'd been snapping since they arrived. "No."

While Kenna kneeled on the ground fixing the hem of Lane's skirt, Megan checked the photograph showing what the actress had worn when the previous scene had been shot.

Hair, earrings, scarf, blouse, jacket, watch, wedding ring, skirt belt, shoes.

Scenes weren't shot in chronological order. Lane had worn this costume last week. Everything had to be the same as then

Megan checked the photograph again. "The scarf knot is on the wrong side."

Kenna stood. "I'll fix it. Get me some double-stick tape."

Megan rummaged through their supplies of safety pins needles, glue and anything else that might come in handy to find. A cell phone buzzed.

"Someone get that for me," Lane said.

Megan grabbed the phone off a table, then handed it to her

As the actress read the text, her features relaxed. The frown disappeared. "Thank heavens, he came through for me."

Megan glanced at Kenna, who shrugged.

Lane handed the phone back to Megan. "Thanks, sweetie."

Definitely in a better mood after that text message. Megan placed the phone back on the table. "Good news?"

"Yes." Lane checked her reflection in the mirror. "I've been so upset since I found out my fiancé couldn't take me to the Viewers' Choice Awards."

Hearing the words *Viewers' Choice Awards* sent a thrill shooting through Megan. She couldn't wait to go. Not only to see what an awards show was like, but to spend quality time with Adam. She saw him only if their breaks and mealtimes coincided. His days off were full of personal appearances for his upcoming movie release. They might be just friends, but she missed him when they were apart.

Adam starred in her dreams. He'd pushed Rob out of her mind and made her wonder if her heart had truly ever belonged to her best friend. Or if her dreams about Rob had been one big schoolgirl fantasy she'd clung to into adulthood.

Not that she was ready to give her heart to Adam. But the thought of kissing him again had been on her mind.

"You're nominated for an award," Kenna said.

"Best actress." Lane shimmied her shoulders, sending the

scarf every which way. A good thing they had tape to secure it in place. "But my dearest, devoted Hugh came through for me."

Megan handed Kenna the tape. "He isn't going away?"

"He's still going, but he's found the perfect man to escort me to the awards ceremony." A canary-eating grin settled on Lane's face. "Adam."

Megan's heart slammed against her chest. She clutched the back of a chair to keep her knees from buckling. Not her Adam. She wanted to tell Lane she was wrong. Lane had to be wrong. "Adam?"

Lane laughed. "Adam Noble. You know, my costar and leading man."

I'm a leading man, not a best friend. You'd be wise to remember that.

His words echoed through Megan's head. But that didn't mean... It couldn't...

Adam had invited her. He'd asked Eva's permission. The entire costume department knew. There had to be some sort of mistake. "I—"

Kenna touched Megan's shoulder and sent her a compassionate yet pointed look.

"I'm sure you'll have a great time," Kenna said.

"With Adam as my date, I know I will." Lane looked at Megan. "Did you have something to say, Texas?"

"I, um, hope you win."

Lane pushed her blond hair behind her shoulders. "Me, too."

Hurt swirled through Megan, making her throat burn and her eyes sting. Adam had promised her a good time. He'd promised.

He probably figured since they were just friends, she would understand why he couldn't take her. That he had to put his career first over a friend, a woman he wasn't sleeping with. A woman who was nothing compared to a glamorous actress like Lane Gregory.

Anger burned. Megan couldn't believe Adam hadn't called her first and at least asked if she minded or cared. But he hadn't. Of course not. He was the star. Adam Noble could do whatever he wanted. And had.

Worse, this hurt more than anything with Rob ever had. Pathetic. She should have stuck to crushing on him. It might not have gone anywhere, Rob might not have made her heart go pitter-pat like Adam, but at least she wouldn't have felt like someone had done jumping jacks on her chest.

Megan wondered what excuse Adam would give her for taking Lane to the awards. She couldn't wait to find out, but one thing was certain. She doubted whatever he told her would be the truth.

A knock sounded at Adam's trailer door. He grimaced. The last thing he wanted was any company. He needed to figure out what to say to Megan. If only Veronica hadn't stepped out…

Another knock.

Adam opened the door. "Megan?"

Her mouth was set in a firm line. "May I come in?"

He motioned her inside. "What's going on?"

She took a breath, then exhaled slowly. "Lane told me you're taking her to the Viewers' Choice Awards."

Damn. He hadn't expected that to happen. "I was going to tell you."

"Then it's true?"

The disappointment in her voice hit Adam harder than a left hook to his jaw. He felt like a jerk, a selfish jerk who had made a decision solely on what he wanted and felt.

But it was for the best. He would only end up hurting Megan more in the long run. Better now while her heart wasn't tied too tightly to him. Or his…

No, that wouldn't happen. His heart was safe. He made sure it was always safe.

He moistened his dry lips. "Yes, it's true."

The color drained from her face. "I…"

Adam hated seeing her like this. The last time she'd stood in his trailer they'd kissed. He wished they could go back to

hat time. "I'm sorry you had to find out this way. I was going
:o tell you at lunch."

Flames flickered in her eyes. "That's supposed to make
ne feel better?"

He met her gaze. He knew she'd be upset. Now he had to
)wn up to it. "No."

"I don't understand."

"It's not you…" As soon as he said the words he knew he
houldn't have said them. Not only because they were cliché,
)ut also because they were a lie. His going with Lane had as
nuch to do with Megan as it did Hugh Wilstead. Adam's mouth
asted like sand. "Lane's fiancé is a powerful man."

"I might be only an intern, but I know all about Hugh
Wilstead."

"Then you know when he asks you to do something, you
lo it or pay the consequences," Adam explained. "I've worked
oo hard to get where I am to screw up everything now by re-
using."

She raised her chin. "So you did this for your career?"

Not completely. A Golden Globe–size lump of guilt lodged
n his throat. No way could he tell her the entire reason, of how
ier feelings and his had played into his decision-making. He'd
)een more open with Megan than any other woman—person—
n his life. But he wasn't going to share that. He…couldn't.

"This is how Hollywood works," he explained instead.
'Costars go to awards shows and premieres together. Some
;o as far as pretending to date. It's part of show business."

She didn't say anything, but blinked. Her eyes glistened.

Damn, he didn't want her to cry. "I know how much you
vanted to go to the awards. You can still go. I'll get you a
icket."

She shook her head. "I want to go to the awards, but I
vanted to go with you."

Her disillusionment in him was clear. He'd let her down.
3ig-time. But it couldn't be helped.

"I'm sorry," he said. "I'll make it up to you. I promise."

A shopping spree on Rodeo Drive would be good. She liked clothes. He would love to see her try on some sexy cocktail dresses and a bikini or two.

Love?

No, he wouldn't like that. Veronica could take her shopping instead.

Megan arched a brow. "Like you promised me I'd have a good time at the awards ceremony? No thanks."

His gut clenched. "Megan…"

"Eva was right about actors playing by different rules."

"I said I was sorry, what else do you want from me?"

"Nothing," she said firmly. "I get being friends with the costume intern is awkward. But I thought that was okay because you seemed more grounded than some of the other talent on the set. But I realize you live in one world. I live in another. Maybe we would have been better off keeping it that way."

"That might have been the smart thing to do, but we didn't."

"We still could."

"No." The word rushed from his mouth before he knew what he was saying.

"Why not?" She eyed him curiously. "It's not like we're BFFs."

They weren't, but Adam didn't want to say goodbye to her. "We're still friends."

"Are we?" Confusion filled her voice. Her lower lip trembled. "The truth is, I've been wondering whether we could be more than friends. But now I realize how foolish that line of thinking was."

Damn. Letting her go was the best thing Adam could do for both of them, but that didn't stop him from reaching for her. "Megan."

She backed away. "There's nothing left for us to say."

With that, she exited his trailer.

He plopped into a chair, feeling more alone than he'd ever felt in his life.

CHAPTER ELEVEN

Two days later, Megan stood in the workroom sorting through the dry cleaning she'd picked up earlier. Wardrobe pieces needed to be labeled and organized. Tedious work, but detail oriented. It kept her distracted, something she needed right now.

She yawned, stretching her arms over her head. She needed more coffee or an energy drink to get her through the day after not sleeping well last night.

Megan ripped off the plastic covering a crisp, white button-down oxford shirt that had been laundered and lightly starched. She removed the cleaner's inventory number stapled to the tag, relabeled the shirt with the character name, Maxwell, and scene number seventeen so she could stick the clothes in the proper garment bag and hung it on the rack. Adam's rack. She grimaced.

She didn't want to think about him, but traces of him were everywhere. Here and at home.

A bouquet of wildflowers had been sitting by her front door when she arrived home the day she found out about his taking Lane instead. A note card had been attached.

"Let me make this up to you."

Nothing more than Adam feeling obligated to make amends like he had with lunch after they'd met. Well, that was his problem, not hers. She had given the flowers to her neighbor, Mrs. Hamilton. The tears glistening in the elderly woman's blue eyes let Megan know she'd made the right choice giving the flowers away.

But she had been serious about not wanting anything from Adam. She wanted to put this behind her, move on and…grow up.

Being disappointed was one thing. But that had been part of her daily life for as long as she'd been alive. When her older sister, Jess, the Golden Girl of Larkville, had gotten herself knocked up by a man who wanted nothing to do with her or their baby, Megan had thought her mother would see her differently, perhaps more positively. Instead, her mother had said she always thought Megan would be the one coming home pregnant, not Jess. Even when Megan did everything right she was still wrong.

What bothered her most about what happened with Adam was how she'd ended up feeling so hurt over this. Going to the Viewers' Choice Awards would have been fun and an interesting experience. But the excitement she felt, the anticipation of Saturday night, revolved around Adam, not the awards show.

Yes, Adam had been a jerk the way he handled this. He couldn't help that she'd heard from Lane, but he still hadn't been planning to tell Megan about it until lunchtime, a few hours late. That was inconsiderate. But knowing her father, her brothers and Rob, she got that men didn't always think like women. Their sense of timing seemed off. Case in point, Rob.

She also understood that Adam had a choice to make. He chose his career. Yes, it sucked to be her in this instance. She didn't like what he'd done. But if push came to shove wouldn't she have made the same choice? She'd told Eva as much.

What was she to Adam, anyway? Not his girlfriend. Not his best friend. Not a close friend if you went by how long they'd known each other and the amount of time they'd spent together. She would have been his date for one night. Nothing more.

The bitter truth stung because Megan had wanted to believe it could be more. Different. Better. But it was just like…

Rob.

Realization washed over her with hurricane force winds. Her legs wobbled. She leaned back against a table.

What a fool she'd been.

Megan had taken all her wishful thinking about Rob and transferred it onto Adam. Another crush on a friend. Dreaming about what could be rather than the reality of the situation. Pretending things would change when they never would.

She was still the same little girl who loved to escape into animated princess movies where the evil mother—make that stepmother—would be defeated, the princess would be rescued by a handsome prince and all would live happily ever after.

None of what she'd been feeling and thinking had been any more real than the fairy-tale cartoons. Not with Rob. Definitely not with Adam.

In some ways, Megan was still trying to do what her mother wanted. Fit in and gain respectability so she wouldn't be seen as odd or different. With Rob, the grandson of the mayor. And with Adam, the handsome movie star and lead actor on the set.

She straightened and squared her shoulders.

No more.

No more crushes.

No more wanting what she couldn't make happen.

She didn't need anyone to define her or give her respectability or help her fit in. She could do all those things herself. She should have a long time ago.

But it was never too late to start.

She tore the plastic wrap off a purple silk blouse. One of Jane's wardrobe pieces.

Megan swallowed a sigh. Moving forward, she reminded herself.

Kenna and Rosie burst into the workroom with laughter and glowing faces. The two looked like they had won the lottery.

Rosie waved a white envelope in the air. "You're not going to believe this!"

Megan hung the purple shirt on a rack so it wouldn't wrinkle. "What is it?"

Kenna rubbed her hands together. "Three tickets to the Viewers' Choice Awards. One for each of us. They're up in the balcony, but who cares? We get to go!"

Rosie bounced from foot to foot. "Plus we're on the lists for the after-parties and have a limo at our disposal for the entire night. We'll be living the high life."

The sinking feeling in her stomach told Megan where this high life had probably come from. "Adam."

Rosie touched Megan's arm. "Please don't let what happened with Adam stop you from going out. Our having a blast doesn't have anything to do with him."

Megan stared at the tickets. "I told Adam I wanted nothing from him."

"So? He's given all three of us something." Kenna grinned. "He's obviously trying to get back on your good side."

Megan wasn't going there. "More likely trying to assuage a guilty conscience."

"Who cares what his reasons are?" Rosie did a little dance. "We're going to the awards show. We have our own seats. We can get into the after-parties. Nothing else matters."

Uncertainty rushed through Megan like water released from one of the dams on the Rio Grande. "I don't know."

"Well, I do," Kenna said firmly. "You're disappointed. I would be, too. But you've put on a brave face and haven't been all mopey or let it interfere with your work."

Megan knew throwing herself a pity party wouldn't solve anything so she'd thrown herself into work.

"That's how it's done in Texas." She had no idea what was happening back home on the ranch. Or Austin. She hadn't heard from Rob since he let her know he'd received Adam's autographed picture. Truth was, she didn't miss hearing from him. Her feelings for Rob weren't as deep as she originally thought. Rob was safe, stable and familiar, not the love of her life.

As much as she longed to escape Larkville, she now realized she'd wanted something to keep her connected. Otherwise, she eared she would be all on her own. Her parents were dead. Her siblings were too busy with their own lives. That was where Rob had come in. He'd shown interest. Made her feel wanted. So had Adam. But she wasn't wanted. Not by her family or Rob or…Adam.

"My dad used to say everything happens for a reason. This no different." Maybe what happened with Adam was so she'd figure out what had been going on all these years with Rob. And with her. "I think the two of you should go and have a great time. Tony can use my ticket. I'm going to sit this one out."

"You are not sitting this one out," Eva announced from the doorway of the workroom.

When had she showed up? Megan hadn't noticed her standing there.

Eva strode into the room as if she owned the place. Given she was the costumer designer on the shoot she sort of did. "You're going to the awards show, but not with Kenna or osie."

Megan stared in confusion. "Adam—"

"You're not going with him, either," Eva interrupted. "My godson, Zachary Carleton, will be your escort. He's been nominated for Best Action Hero and his date had to have her appendix removed. Her loss is your gain."

Kenna shook her head. "Nothing like this ever happened to me when I was interning."

Rosie nodded.

Zach Carleton was an up-and-coming handsome actor who was around Megan's age. Hot didn't begin to describe him. She wanted to pinch herself to see if she were dreaming. "I appreciate all that you've done for me, Eva, but I have to be honest. I don't understand why."

Eva's eyes softened. "Once upon a time, a young costume designer fell in love with an older handsome actor. She thought he'd fallen for her, too, but instead he got bored and the costume designer was fired."

Megan's mouth gaped. "You?"

Eva nodded once. "But I didn't handle myself as profes
sionally as you have. These past few days you've shown wha
you're made of. And after seeing your gown, it's obvious yo
have talent. You deserve to go to the awards and sit up front

A chill shivered down Megan's spine. "I don't want to em
barrass your godson. I'm going to be so nervous."

"It's okay to be nervous," Eva counseled. "Just don't let
show. Whatever you do, don't drink too much during the da
and especially before the show starts. You don't want to hav
to spend all your time in the ladies' room and miss the fur
Because I can guarantee you're going to have the most won
derful time. Zachary will see to it."

Firebreather *was* a fairy godmother. "Thanks, Eva."

"Be here at eleven o'clock on Saturday morning," Eva sai
"By the time we're finished with you, Mr. Adam Noble is goir
to be kicking himself for taking the wrong princess to the ball

Outside the Shrine Auditorium, Adam held Lane's hand a
she exited the limousine. Her fingers were thin and bony. H
wished he were holding Megan's hand.

Don't go there. Stay in the moment. The cameras are rollin

The sound of applause and camera shutters going off fille
the afternoon air. Things started early on the west coast so th
show could be shown in prime time on the east coast.

A female shrieked.

A chorus of women yelled, "Neptune!"

Lane raised a brow. "Such devoted fans."

With a smile in place, he waved at the ladies. "The be
fans in the world."

The hem of Lane's gold-colored gown swished around h
feet. Her gold, jewel-encrusted designer shoes—she'd told hi
in the limousine how much Hugh had paid for them—add
four inches to her height, but she was still half a foot short
than Adam. Diamonds dripped from her ears, wrist and nec
More presents from Hugh, Adam assumed, but Lane had

aid. The magic of double-stick tape kept the extremely low-
ut bodice from allowing a wardrobe malfunction, much to the
ismay of males in attendance. All except Adam. He wasn't
nterested. Now if it were Megan...

He forced his attention back to the red carpet.

When he released her hand, Lane didn't let go. "Smile at
ne cameras, darling."

He pasted on his most charming smile, one he'd practiced
nd perfected over the past two years. A photo-shoot smile
hat had graced many a magazine cover. If Megan had been
is date, his smile would have been real.

Don't think about it. Her.

Two steps down the red carpet reporters tossed questions
t them like Frisbees on the beach.

"Where's Hugh?"

"Who designed your dress?"

"Is it true your onscreen romance has become an offscreen
ne?"

"Are you wearing an Armani tux?"

"How's the shoot going?"

"Are you excited about the premiere of *Navy SEALs?*"

Adam's smile didn't falter as he answered questions. His
ns watched the red carpet shows on television so he didn't
ush through the gauntlet, but strolled at a snail's pace from
porter to reporter.

Lane rose up on her tiptoes to whisper in his ear. "Isn't
is fun?"

Every minute with Lane sucked five minutes of life out of
m. But this was part of the job. Movie magic carried over
life in Hollywood. Much of it wasn't real. Pretend couples,
ublic relation lies, phony smiles, sucking up. Whatever he
id would be repeated back to Hugh Wilstead so Adam had
be careful and keep his guard up. That took all the fun out
ght there. "Superfun."

"Make the most of it." A twinge of desperation sounded in
ane's voice. "If they don't all want you, you're done."

No wonder she went after her male costars. She needed t
be the queen of the set to prove she was still desirable. Tha
she wouldn't be tossed aside by someone newer and prettie
That was why she'd had Annie fired. Jealousy.

Adam never would have thought he'd feel sorry for Lan
but he did.

Behind them at the beginning of the red carpet, a flurr
of activity announced a new arrival. The high-pitched femal
screams were deafening.

"One of those teen idols must have arrived. The girls a
ways go crazy for them." Lane waved to a girl in the crow
who stared at the actress with total adoration. "Is it anyone w
should bother saying hello to?"

Adam glanced back to see Zach Carleton signing autc
graphs. Security was holding back crying girls. There'd bee
ongoing discussions about Zach and Adam playing brothe
in an action movie that had been green-lighted, but the tw
had never met. "It's that new kid. Zach C. He's up for Be
Action Actor."

Adam knew this because he'd never been nominated for a
individual acting award before. Best Kiss—he'd won twic
Best Ensemble—Neptune. Best Onscreen Couple—he'd kno
if he won that later tonight.

"Oh, he's cute. Young, but lots of staying power." Lar
smirked as she waved to more fans. "Or so I've been tol
Who's he with?"

Adam glanced back. Zach held on to the hand of a woma
with long, dark curly hair as she pirouetted, showing off
sexy shimmering purple gown with an even sexier slit up t
side. The woman was jaw-droppingly gorgeous and your
like the actor.

Adam took a closer look. She almost looked like… His hea
stalled. It was. Megan. He exhaled a sharp breath.

"What?" Lane asked.

Zach rested his hand at the small of Megan's back.

Adam's jaw tightened.

Zach whispered something into her ear. She smiled shyly. Zach laughed.

A wave of jealousy crashed through Adam like a sneaker wave.

The two looked cozy, comfortable with each other like a... couple.

Adam's blood pressure spiked.

"Oh, my..." Lane sounded like she had seen a badly decomposed body. "Look at the way his ascot matches her dress. Purple shimmers, really? It's all so senior prom-ish."

Maybe, but in a refreshing, wholesome, appealing way. Megan captivated him. It looked like Zach felt the same way.

Adam could hardly swallow. Sweat dripped down his back. They're young. Attractive. It works. The press seems to agree even the attention they're getting."

"Well, I'm not impressed." Lane blew a kiss to the fans in the grandstand. "Zach's date looks familiar. She must be one of those television actresses."

Adam waved to the crowd, but his gaze kept straying to Megan. He couldn't help himself. "She's not an actress."

Lane struck a pose for a photographer. "I recognize her from somewhere."

"She's Eva's intern." The words barely made it past the lump in his throat.

Lane froze. "Texas?"

Adam nodded, afraid if he said anything he'd reveal how upset he felt.

She glanced back at the couple that had barely moved two feet due to all the attention they were receiving. "How did she end up with him? Looking like *that?* Here?"

Adam knew Megan had been hiding something, but he hadn't realized it was this. "I have no idea."

But he intended to find out.

Megan felt like Cinderella at the ball. She'd been feted on the red carpet, allowed to talk about the gown she'd designed for

herself with a fashion reporter, made to feel like a fairy prin
cess by her charming escort, Zach. He even kissed her on th
cheek when he won the award for Best Action Actor.

Now she was at an after-party with Zach thrown by a to
studio. No expense had been spared with the elaborate deco
rations. An award-winning DJ mixed the music. Stars from
television, music and film filled the dance floor. Rosie, Kenr
and Tony were here, but Megan had lost track of them for th
umpteenth time that night.

She held on to Zach's hand, mindful of the other dance
around them. "Tonight has been magical. I feel like Cinderella

He grinned. "Except there's no reason to be home by mid
night. I can assure you the limo won't turn into a pumpkin."

As he twirled her around, one of her shoes flew off. Sh
would find it after the song ended.

"I owe my godmother for finding me such a beautiful date
Zach said.

She stared up at him. "Thank you."

She did like Zach, but unfortunately she just didn't feel ar
sparks. Only friendship.

"I wish I didn't have to fly back to the shoot and be the
for the next three months," he said. "It would probably soun
stupid to ask you to wait for me."

Affection for Zach grew. The kind she had for her brother
"Not stupid. Extremely sweet."

Hope filled his eyes.

"Who knows where I'll be or what I'll be doing in thre
months. Same with you. But you've got my cell number," sh
said honestly. "Give me a ring when you're back in town."

By then he'd surely have found someone else to pin h
hopes on.

He nodded enthusiastically. "I will."

The music came to an end. A man waved at Zach. "Wou
you mind if I said hello to someone?"

He really was a nice guy. Younger than her, but very cu
"Go ahead."

As Zach pushed his way through the crowd to reach his friend, Megan searched for her missing shoe, hobbling with ne shoe on, being careful so she wouldn't twist an ankle. She earched the dance floor, but didn't see it.

Where could her shoe be?

Adam appeared at her side.

Her heart danced a jig. He looked so handsome in his tux. om Ford, if she wasn't mistaken.

"Lose your date?" he asked.

"He's saying hello to a friend. But I did lose a shoe."

Adam pulled something from behind his back. He held up er silver slingback heel, the match to the one on her foot. va and the wardrobe department had purchased the shoes for Megan. A gift for their favorite intern, they'd claimed. She reninded them she was their only intern.

Megan reached for the shoe. "Thank you so much."

He pulled it out of her reach. "I've got it."

As Adam kneeled, she stuck out her leg, toes pointed. Her urple nail polish glimmered in the light from the ballroom handeliers. He gently placed the shoe on her foot. As he pulled n the strap, his thumb brushed her ankle, sending a rush of ensation up her leg.

Her temperature surged.

"How's that?" he asked.

She cleared her dry throat. "Fine."

Adam stood. He held out his hand, palm up. "Dance with ne."

Temptation flared. She shouldn't. "Our dates—"

"Are off with others," he interrupted. "What's one dance etween friends? I do consider myself your friend even if you on't think so."

Megan wasn't ready to have this conversation. If she danced vith him, she wouldn't have to talk to him. "One dance."

She placed her hand on top of his. Adam led her onto the lance floor.

"You're the most beautiful woman here tonight." He took

her into his arms. His hand rested possessively at the small
of her back, pressing her close while he held her other hand.
His thumb stroked her palm, sending little pleasurable thrills
sliding over her.

"Thank you," she said, awash in sensation. She hated the
way her body reacted to him. "I had lots of help."

His gaze raked over her. "The dress?"

"I made it, but others refined my design."

Appreciation warmed his green eyes. "Stunning."

"I'm happy how it came out."

"I'm jealous."

She drew back. "Excuse me?"

"No favor is worth seeing you with another man." Contrition
echoed in his voice. "I should have never agreed to bring Lane."

A mix of emotion swirled through Megan. She wished his
words didn't bring her so much pleasure. She needed to be cautious around him. But she also knew she would remember this
moment, this dance, forever. "Some lessons are hard to learn."

Desire shone in his gaze. "I won't make the same mistake
twice. Come on."

Holding on to her hand, he led her off the dance floor and
into an alcove outside the grand ballroom. Megan didn't want
to cause a scene so went with him.

As soon as she knew they couldn't be seen, she pulled her
hand out of his. "What do you think you're doing?"

"It's time I admit defeat," he said. "I want you."

She half laughed, half choked, a reaction based on a combination of nerves and self-preservation. "This isn't the real me."

"I know who you are." Adam's appreciative gaze traveled
the length of her. "The way you look now. That part has always
been inside or you would have never made the dress. You've
been too nervous, too scared, to show anybody who you really
are. In Larkville, in college and here."

Adam knew who she was. He understood her. The realization pleased her as much as it scared her. Crushing on Rob

ad been safe. Adam was proving to be as dangerous as she'd
riginally thought.

"I've seen the real you," he continued. "I like what I see.
And I'm finally ready to admit that."

Her heart pounded double-time to the music in the ballroom.
f the rapid tattoo of her heartbeat continued too long she might
yperventilate. A part of her wanted to flee, to pretend none
f this had ever happened. It was too risky, too dangerous to
er peace of mind, to her heart.

But the look in Adam's eyes held her captive. She couldn't
ave moved if she wanted to. But she also couldn't forget the
ay he'd acted and treated her.

Megan stared down her nose at him. "So you're going to
pologize and call it good? And when it happens again? And
gain—"

"I've been a lousy friend." He sounded sincere. "I'm sorry
bout that, but when I'm around you I don't always think
traight."

That she understood. Being near him seemed to short-circuit
er brain. "I know the feeling."

"I want us to try again."

All the reasons this was a bad idea shouted inside her head
t once, the noise deafening. But she couldn't deny the excite-
ent pulsing through her at the same time. "At being friends?"

He nodded. "We have to start somewhere if we're ever going
o be more than friends."

Her lips parted in surprise.

More than friends.

The words echoed through her trembling heart. Dare she
ope?

Adam lowered his mouth. He kissed her with a hunger that
ook her breath away and left her wanting more. This wasn't a
ractice kiss. There was no script he was following this time.
he kiss was…real.

She clung to him for support and strength and more kisses.
e left no doubt in her mind that he wanted her.

Megan couldn't deny she wanted him.

He wrapped his arms around her and pulled her close. Megan went willingly. Her hands splayed his back. She relished in the moment, in the sensations pulsating through her. Kissing Adam was all that mattered. Being with him made her happy.

She pressed harder against his lips, exploring his mouth with her tongue. With each passing second, the heat intensified. An ache built deep within her. She wanted more, so much more.

A moan escaped her lips. At least she thought it came from her mouth, but she wasn't certain.

Adam dragged his lips from hers. The desire in his eyes matched her own. He seemed as shaken as her.

Her lips burned from his kiss. She fought the urge to touch them. "Why did you kiss me like that?"

"Why did you kiss me back?"

Her cheeks burned. A part of her wished she were still kissing him. "I asked my question first."

He traced her lips with his fingertips, sending goose bumps down her arms. "You mentioned you'd thought about us being more than friends. I wanted to show you what that might be like. Pretty good, huh?"

Awesome was the only word to describe it, but Megan couldn't let Adam know that. She didn't want to lose herself in another fantasy world. She needed to stick to reality and real relationships.

But Adam's kisses had felt real. Tingles were still shooting through her. Maybe her feelings for him weren't a crush as they'd been with Rob. Heaven knew, they felt more real and grounded in something true between them. "Mission accomplished."

Mischief shone in his eyes. "I was hoping it might take a little more convincing."

Megan was so tempted. "We're here with other dates."

Adam grinned. "I take full responsibility for that. But another kiss—"

"Zach and Lane might be wondering where we are." The

ords spewed from Megan's mouth faster than a bucking bronc to the rodeo arena. She was truly flattered, but nervous. They might be looking for us."

"I'm not going to let this drop."

She didn't want him to let it drop, but she needed time to nink about things. About him. And what she wanted or didn't ant. She had to be careful. "I know."

"I want a second chance."

"I know that, too." She moistened her swollen lips. "I'm ot sure us being more than friends makes sense right now."

"Think about more kisses and other stuff we could be doing ogether."

Disappointment shot a hole through the haze of desire still ulsating through her. "I'm not up for a fling."

"I don't do long-term."

She sighed. "I'm not sure where that leaves us."

"We can agree to make the most of the time we have to-ether during the shoot," he suggested. "You should learn how o have fun and date. That doesn't have to mean sex, but it can nean more kissing. I can show you what romance is all about."

Megan knew there was more to being with a movie star nan red carpets and dancing. Keeping sex out of the equa-on would allow them to get to know each other while they ere busy working on the shoot. But she couldn't forget one ning. "Eva—"

"Or not so much kissing and romance." He didn't hesitate t all. "I'm okay with that, as long as we're spending time to-ether. But it's totally up to you."

No one had ever given Megan a decision like this to make. he liked the way it made her feel. Empowered. Reckless. Let's make the most of the time we have left. I'm willing to ave fun and see where this goes."

Adam grinned. "Sounds good to me."

Megan, too. She just hoped she wasn't making a big mis-ake....

CHAPTER TWELVE

BY THE time production moved out of Los Angeles and on lo cation outside of Albuquerque, New Mexico, Adam couldn have been happier with Megan giving him a second chance Her sweet personality and sense of humor kept a big smile o his face. He wanted to keep things uncomplicated, but occa sionally and only in the privacy of his trailer where they ha no chance of being seen, they shared sizzling hot kisses.

Once the shoot finished, they would move on to other pro ects in different locales. But Adam wondered if they migh keep seeing each other still. Perhaps spend a few days togethe back in L.A. or have Megan visit him on the set of his next film

He walked to his trailer parked outside an old school bein used as a prison. Each step brought a puff of dirt flying int the air. No wonder Megan had been up half the night doin laundry; keeping costumes clean was a full-time job.

"Adam," Lane called after him.

He groaned inwardly, but stopped and waited for her t catch up to him. "Hey."

She smiled up at him. "You killed it today."

He ignored the flirtation in her voice. The woman neve gave up. "Thanks."

"I was wondering if you wanted to have dinner tonight? Lane asked. "I heard there's a steak house about twenty min utes from here."

Funny, but he thought he'd heard her say she didn't eat re

neat. Guess she hated being stuck out in the middle of nowhere so maybe she was willing to expand what she ate. But
no matter what the reason for her invitation, he wasn't going
anywhere with her. "Thanks, but I can't."

Adam was having dinner with Megan. He couldn't wait to
see her when she returned to the set from the motel. No doubt
tired from having to wash so many clothes. Maybe she'd want
a back rub. He bit back a grin. He didn't want Lane thinking
his smile was meant for her.

She scrunched her nose unattractively. "What's your excuse
this time? You have a date?"

Adam was tired of dealing with her. He rocked back on his
heels. "Yeah, I do."

Her mouth gaped. "With who?"

When he didn't answer, Lane named several costars and
female crew members.

"Nope," he said.

"That only leaves…Texas." Lane made a face. "Please tell
me you aren't dating that lowly intern."

Intern, yes. Lowly, no way. Megan had more class in her
little finger than Lane had in her entire body. "Okay, I won't
tell you."

With that, Adam walked away. Lane yelled his name, but he
didn't turn around. The shoot had only a couple more weeks
to go. But he'd put up with enough from Lane Gregory. Maybe
this would get her off his back once and for all. He hoped so
because the only woman he wanted to think and worry about
was…Megan.

Megan tested the iron on a white motel pillowcase. She'd spent
the morning washing clothes. Scorching a piece of wardrobe
would not be good and being forced to make a mad dash to replace something didn't appeal to her in the slightest, not when
he could be spending time with Adam.

Ever since the party after the Viewers' Choice Awards
things had been going well. She was getting to know him and

understand him. She felt comfortable with him. She'd been thinking this could turn into something...more.

The iron seemed fine. No marks were on the pillowcase. She grabbed one of the prison jumpsuits. She'd iron out the wrinkles. Then put the ones from the last scene back in.

The joys of continuity and out of sequence shots.

Four hours later, she turned off and unplugged the iron. Mission accomplished. The prison garb was finished. She could return to the set. And Adam.

Anticipation shot through her. She'd missed him today.

As she cleaned up and put things away, she heard footsteps outside the motel. A knock sounded.

That was odd. Everyone from the shoot should be on the set. Must be the motel manager.

Megan opened the door. "Eva."

The designer's face looked pale and drawn. She wouldn't meet Megan's eyes.

"Is everything okay?" Megan asked.

Eva entered the room and closed the door behind her. "No, it's not."

Megan's first thought was something bad happened on the set. To Adam. She dug her fingernails into her palms. "What's wrong?"

"You've been fired."

Fired? Megan stared at Eva in disbelief. No one had voiced any complaints or suggested Megan wasn't doing a good job. She hadn't been late to one of her calls or taken any sick days. "Why?"

Compassion filled Eva's eyes. "One of the lead actors demanded it."

The air rushed from Megan's lungs. Her stomach knotted. Her knees threatened to give out. She plopped onto one of the double-size beds in the motel room. "Not..."

She couldn't say his name. A weight pressed down on the center of her chest, making it hard to breathe.

"Not Adam," Eva said.

Relief nearly knocked her to her knees. Megan shouldn't ave doubted him for a minute. But if not him... "Lane iregory."

Eva nodded once.

Megan's shoulders sagged. "I don't understand. I haven't vorked with her much, but when I did she was always nice to 1e. Why would she have me fired?"

"Jealousy."

She drew back. "Lane has no reason to be jealous of me."

"You're young, talented, thin and pretty. Sometimes that's ll it takes. But in this case, you've also caught Adam's eye. .ane doesn't like that because she wants him all to herself."

"She's engaged."

"Hollywood is a world unto itself. Things happen here that 'ouldn't happen anywhere else," Eva explained. "If it's any onsolation, Adam went to bat for you. I was impressed with ow he took on Hugh Wilstead. But Hugh sided with Lane."

Numbness set in. At least Adam had tried. Fought for her. hat counted for something. Okay, a lot. "So what happens ow?"

"You need to gather your things, pack and fly back to L.A."

"My internship?"

Eva shook her head. "I'm sorry. The work I need done is ere."

Emotion clogged Megan's throat. She'd worked so hard only have the internship end because of a jealous actress. Her iroat burned, but she wasn't going to cry. She needed to be rofessional about this. She raised her chin. "I understand."

And she did.

Megan had been warned about getting involved with the lent. She'd been told a lead actor could have anyone fired at 1y time for any reason. But she hadn't realized it could turn it *this* way. That a woman engaged to another man would e jealous of Megan's relationship with Adam. She'd naively ought things would work out okay.

What was she going to do?

The thought of leaving Adam and returning to Larkvill made her nauseous. She wrapped her arms around her stom ach. "I was hoping my internship could lead to something mor permanent. I don't want to go back to Texas."

"Then don't."

Her gaze met Eva's. The fierceness in the designer's blu eyes made Megan's heart pound.

"Don't let a jealous harpy like Lane Gregory stop you fron going after what you want," Eva said. "You have the talen You have a little experience now. You also have connection: Make the most of them."

Megan did have those things. Most important she had Adan Not that she'd ask him to find her a job, but maybe he coul introduce her to some costume designers. "Thanks, Eva. I'v learned a lot."

"You've done a lot." Eva's eyes gleamed. "Leave the cos tumes in here. I'll have Kenna take care of them. As soon a you finish packing, a car will take you to the airport."

"Seriously?"

"Lane demands it. She claims you are too big a distractio on the set."

This was unbelievable. "Can I say goodbye to everyone?"

"You're not allowed back on the set."

Everybody was there. Including Adam. Her hands trembled "Will you tell people goodbye for me?"

"Yes."

That was something. "What happens when I get back t L.A.?"

"Relax for a couple of days. Rewrite your résumé. Conta everyone you've met in the business and let them know you' looking for any kind of costume or wardrobe position. Feel fre to use me as a reference."

"Thanks." Megan appreciated the advice, but she realize she was as much on her own here as she had been in Larkvill Forcing herself to breathe, she went to the closet and pulle out her suitcase.

Ever since arriving in Los Angeles her life had revolve
around the shoot. She knew no one who wasn't working on
the film except her neighbor, Mrs. Hamilton. Megan never had
looked for a job. She didn't know how to begin.

But she would have to figure it out. Maybe Adam would
know what she should do. Megan hoped so because she hadn't
a clue. Worse, she wouldn't be able to see him for a couple of
weeks. Those were going to be the longest weeks of her life.

Damn. Lane hadn't wasted any time. Adam charged through
the entrance of the small airport in this middle-of-nowhere
town.

He'd fought for Megan, even stood up to Hugh Wilstead during a heated conference call with Lane, Eva and Chas. Damon
was too busy with the shoot to deal with something like this.

So much for being owed a favor. Hugh hadn't listened to a
word Adam said. The cuckolded producer had bent over backward to appease his jealous fiancée. Adam's efforts had only
meant he hadn't been able to comfort Megan and drive her to
the airport. But he was here now to see her off and say…

Goodbye.

He had to say it. Do it.

Twice now, Megan had gotten hurt being with him. First
the awards show and now being fired. He kept putting his own
selfish desires ahead of what Megan needed. He needed to protect her. That meant letting her go.

His shoes echoed on the tile floor. The place was nearly
empty except for uniformed workers and a lone, dejected-
looking woman sitting in a chair with luggage at her feet.

"Megan."

She jumped out of the chair and into his open arms. "I'm
so happy you're here."

He hugged her, wanting to hold her one last time. "I'm so
sorry."

Megan wrapped her arms around him. "Eva told me you
fought for me to stay. Thank you."

"Lane is psychotic. It'll be better if you're away from her."

Megan looked up at him with red-rimmed eyes. "But tha means I'll be away from you."

Her vulnerability sliced into him like a knife's blade. H wanted to pick her up and cradle her on his lap so he coul kiss her until the hurt disappeared from her face and a smil returned. But if he did that, she'd experience more hurt. H couldn't allow that to happen. "The shoot's almost finished."

Megan rose on her tiptoes and brushed her lips across his

So tender. So sweet. Nothing would keep them apart back i L.A. Not Eva and her rule. Not Lane. They could be togethe finally and take things to the next level.

No, they couldn't. He couldn't.

Adam stepped back. "Megan…"

She stared up at him. "I'll be counting the days until you'r back in L.A."

Adam took another step back. "I'm only going to be ther for a day or two, then I'm going on location for a new project.

"Oh."

The one word spoke volumes. He hated letting her dow the way other men had let down his mother. "The shoot wi last three, maybe four months."

Confusion added to the hurt in her eyes. "But…"

Adam wanted to look away, but he couldn't. She was alway so honest and open. He wanted to be, too. "This has been fur but we said we'd make the most of our time together."

"And now that's over."

Over. That sounded so final. Better this way, he reminde himself. Better for Megan. "We agreed."

"I know, but I thought…"

The slight quaver in her voice knotted his gut. He wante to know what she'd been thinking. "What?"

"Nothing," she said. "I was wrong to expect more. I see no you never intended this to be more than one of your flings."

"It wasn't a fling. We didn't have sex." But they had hun out and kissed. Really hot kisses. And grown closer, closer tha

e'd been to any other woman. He swallowed. "I like you
ot. I was thinking we could keep hanging out whenever I'm i.
..A. We're young, there's nothing wrong with just having fun."

"But there could be so much more than that between us."

However tempting that sounded, he wouldn't allow himself
o be swayed. "My life is… I'm no good for you."

Her eyes darkened. "What you really mean is continuing
vhat we have would be too complicated."

"I'm not looking to settle down."

"The easier, the better."

"Nothing wrong with easy," he agreed.

"Except the best things in life aren't easy. They take effort
nd a lot of work." Her jaw tensed. "It's interesting how you
vork so hard to perfect your roles, but you couldn't care less
bout putting that same kind of effort into your relationships."

He had to be strong for both their sakes. He put his hands
p, as if to hold her at bay. "We're friends. We aren't having
relationship."

She pursed her lips. "That's only because you're too afraid.
ou like to end things before they go bad."

He hated how her words hit the bull's-eye. "I end them
hen it's time."

"The shorter the relationship, I mean, fling, the better." Her
harp tone surprised him. "That's why you're backing off, be-
ause you can finally see something that could be long-term."

"I don't do long-term." He saw she expected a lot from him,
ore than he was willing or capable of giving. She deserved to
ave what she wanted. "You're better off without me."

"So who would I be better with? Zach?"

Thinking of Megan with another man ripped out Adam's
uts. "No way."

"Rob?"

"He's the wrong guy for you."

"Who's the right one, then?" she pressed. "I thought it was
ou."

Her words stabbed his heart, but Adam couldn't let her see

w much she'd come to mean to him, as a friend and more
e'd allowed Megan to see more of him than he had with any
other person. What if he pursued something with her? Then she
decided to leave him rather than him being the one to leave
It wasn't a risk worth taking because people always left. No
one had ever stuck around him and his mom. Not his dad. No
any of the other men who claimed they wanted to be his father
but really didn't.

"Look at me," Adam said for his benefit as much as hers
"My life is crazy. Being followed by the paparazzi, traveling
all over the world for months at a time, doing whatever extreme
sports I can. You have an amazing talent. You don't want to
tangle up your life with someone like me. Face it. I'm not
picket-fence kind of guy. You'd only end up unhappy with me.

"Wow, all this so I'll be happier."

"I want what's best for you."

She narrowed her gaze. "What if I don't want a picket-fence
life? What if I want a costume design career that takes me on
location for months at a time while shooting a film and gives
me the opportunity to do exciting things, also?"

He couldn't afford to believe what she said. "If that kind
of life is what you really want, then you need someone more
solid to be your anchor when it's time for you to come home.

"Is that what you need?"

He needed her. If only… "I'm doing fine on my own."

"You'd do better with me." Her gaze didn't waver from his
"I want you to be my anchor. I can be yours."

"I've hurt you twice," Adam said. "You even lost your in
ternship because of me. It's best if you move on from all the
trouble I've brought you."

"Have you forgotten you're the one who said he wanted
second chance with me?"

"I haven't forgotten. I had my second chance, now it's time
to move on." He tried to sound flippant. He wasn't sure if he
succeeded. "You need to learn that not every fun time with
guy leads to more than friendship."

"Unbelievable." She laughed. "So far, you've been the best friend, the bad boy and now the protector. Which character are you going to play next?"

His muscles tightened. "What are you talking about?"

"You're searching for excuses," she said. "You act all brave when it comes to your extreme sports. Riding the gnarliest wave or whatever else you're risking your neck doing. But you're a coward when it comes to life. To love. You're using these characters, these roles you've played, to hide behind and keep people from getting close to you."

The temptation to flee was strong, but he stood his ground and squared his shoulders instead. "That's not true."

"It's very true," she countered.

"You don't know what you're talking about." His voice sounded harsh. He didn't care. "I'm not a coward."

"Just calling it like I see it."

"So am I." Adam liked Megan. She knew him well, too well. He wasn't willing to take a leap of faith and trust things with her would work out because he knew they wouldn't. He would not put himself through that kind of hurt. "I like challenges, but not ones where I have no chance of succeeding."

"That's too bad. Sad, really." She blinked. Her eyes gleamed, but no tears fell. "If you aren't willing to risk yourself, your heart, you'll never succeed at what matters most in life. And you'll wind up...alone."

CHAPTER THIRTEEN

THREE days remained on the shoot. Adam had never been s[o]
damn miserable in his life. The only thing that kept him fro[m]
sitting himself down at the local tavern night after night wa[s]
the need to give this shoot his best effort. He needed to sa[l]
vage something from this project. He doubted he'd be seein[g]
an acting nomination now due to the tension on the set be[-]
tween him and Lane.

The actress used people and spat them out, but that didn[']
make her happy or feel less alone. Adam didn't want to end u[p]
like her, yet he felt so lonely, even surrounded by crew men[]
bers. He'd wanted to avoid getting hurt, but he'd been hurtin[g]
ever since Megan left.

His cell phone rang. The ring tone told him it was h[is]
mother. She was on an extended tour of Europe after her cruis[e]
He hoped nothing was wrong. He hit Answer on his touc[h]
screen. "Mom?"

"Hi, Adam. I hope your shoot is going well."

Her cheerful tone lessened his concern. "I'll be back in L.[A]
in a couple of days. How's the vacation?"

"Wonderful." His mom sounded like she was smiling. "[I]
met the most perfect man."

Adam grimaced. Not again. He prepared himself for wh[at]
was no doubt the beginning of yet another end full of hear[t]
break and tears. "Who is he?"

Probably another in a long line of jerks.

"His name is Joseph Weber. We were seated at the same
ble for dinner. It wasn't love at first sight, but it didn't take
e long to know I'd finally found my Mr. Right."

Yeah, Adam had heard that before. "I'm going to have the
ıy checked out."

"No need, dear, unless it'll make you feel better," his mother
id. "Joseph owns his own security company in San Diego.
e's an upright and law-abiding man."

Adam would still have him checked out. "At least you don't
ve too far away from him if you keep seeing him when you
t home."

"Oh, we will." His mother sounded confident, but she usu-
ly did at the beginning of a new relationship. "I know I
ven't been the best mother. I put my needs ahead of yours.
ıt I always knew I'd find what we both needed. It took me
ıger to find than I thought it would, but I think you'll like
seph as much as I do."

Adam's heart squeezed tight. His mom sounded like she
as floating on air. He wasn't looking forward to her crash-
g and burning. "You'll have to introduce us."

He wanted to believe this time it would work out for her,
en if the odds were slim to none.

"I'll call when I'm home," she said.

As soon as his mom said goodbye, he disconnected from
e call. He tightened his grip on the phone. He didn't want
s mom hurt again. It took everything in him not to reach out
the one person who he felt most comfortable with. The one
rson he wanted to see, to hear, more than anything.

Megan. He missed her.

Being with her lifted him up and made him stronger. When
was with her, he wanted to be a better man. She'd cared
out him in a way no one had before, and he'd let her go.

Megan had been right.

He'd been a coward. Even his mother had been braver than
n. She'd never given up trying to find Mr. Right. Even if
'd ended up with a lot of duds along the way. Whatever his

mom kept searching for had to be pretty special if she ke
risking her heart to find it.

Adam hadn't even tried. He'd been too scared of being hu
to risk it. He couldn't help himself. He'd held off everyone, eve
his own mom at times, because of what his dad had done a
those years ago. Adam had even copied him by being an act
and a ladies' man. Someone who might disappoint, but cou
never be disappointed.

But Adam wasn't his father. He cared about people, abo
his mom, about Megan.

People changed. Megan had grown and changed before h
eyes. She'd helped him do the same, too.

What was he doing?

He couldn't let his chance with Megan slip away because I
was afraid. The risk of having her bail on him at some poi
was worth it to have her in his life now. The excitement of bei
together and trusting they could make it work would be lil
riding a wave or jumping out of an airplane. There weren't a
guarantees, but that didn't mean it wouldn't work out.

Maybe it could. If it weren't too late.

Fatigue wore Megan down. She placed a pair of faded jear
the only remaining item in her dresser, into the suitcase lyir
on her bed. She'd packed everything and wished she cou
pack away her broken heart, as well.

She could hardly sleep. Food didn't appeal to her. Nothi
did.

Darn Adam Noble.

Megan was angry with him for not being willing to take
chance and at herself for falling for another man who could
love her back. Sadness gripped her heart like a fist and would
let go. Emptiness, too, as if her insides had been hollowed c
and left bare. Nothing, not even Rob offering to visit witho
Pru, had made Megan feel better.

But she wouldn't always feel this way. At least she hoped n

She rolled her suitcase to the front door. Everything s

owned. Three boxes and two suitcases worth of stuff were ready to be loaded into her car. The furniture had come with the apartment, except for her little table. That would go in the car, too.

She glanced around the apartment. Even though she'd spent more time at the lot, and on location, this had become home, the one place—the first place—where she fit in and could be herself. No hiding. No pretending.

Not that she would ever go back to doing that again.

Lesson learned. Even if her family might not agree.

When she returned to Larkville in October for her father's celebration and a family reunion with her new half siblings, they would all have to accept it. Accept her. And even if they didn't... Well, she was a stronger, more confident woman now than when she left.

She double-checked the locks on the windows. She'd given her perishable food to Mrs. Hamilton downstairs, who still had out the vase from the flowers Adam had sent.

Thinking about him made her chest ache.

Best to forget everything to do with him. That was the only way to heal. She wasn't the first woman who'd had her heart broken. Unfortunately, she wouldn't be the last.

She'd cried enough. No more pity parties.

Someday she could look back on this and laugh at the time she went out with a famous movie star. Someday. Too bad that couldn't be today.

With a sigh, Megan loaded the table, suitcases and boxes into the back of her car. She decided to take one last look around the apartment to make sure she hadn't forgotten anything.

Inside, her footsteps echoed on the hardwood floor. It sounded as if she were in a cave. She recalled talking to a screenwriter while working on a one-day shoot as a stylist two weeks ago. He had told her about the Writer's Journey, a method used to plot scripts. Megan had accepted the call to adventure when she took the internship. Now she wanted

out of the innermost cave. The rest of her life was waiting fo
her. And maybe, just maybe, she would find the elixir—the
treasure—to have made this journey worthwhile.

Best get finished with this portion so she could move on t
what came next. Her plans hadn't turned out like she expected
but she was coming to realize that was okay.

She double-checked the closet, the bathroom and the smal
kitchen. All the drawers and cupboards were empty. Time t
go.

"You're leaving."

The sound of Adam's voice sent a chill down her spine
Every nerve ending stood to attention. Once again, a millio
and one thoughts ran through her head. She focused on one—
don't lose it.

Slowly, she faced him. "Yes, I am."

Adam stood four feet away from her. His hair was damp, a
if he'd gone for a swim or showered recently. He wore a pa
of board shirts and a faded T-shirt.

So handsome. Gorgeous. But looks didn't make a man.

Whether on the set or off it, Adam played roles. She wasn
sure who the real man was now. Too bad because she'd liked th
Adam she'd gotten to know on set, but for all she knew he wa
as make-believe as the character he was playing in the movi

She raised her chin. "What do you want?"

His gaze met hers. "You."

The air rushed from her lungs. She didn't know what to sa
He took a step toward her.

Self-preservation made her back away from him. He wa
too handsome, too charming. She couldn't allow herself to b
swayed by him. That had happened twice already. "I have
go."

"Where?"

"Portland, Oregon."

"The beautiful Pacific Northwest."

"I hear it's very green and rains a lot," she said. "I was c
fered a job on a shoot there. Someone heard about me fro

Iugh Wilstead. Imagine that. The man whose fiancée had
ie fired."

"It's funny how things work in this town."

"No kidding," she agreed. "I tried to find a position on my
wn, but kept coming up empty even with Eva as a reference.
ot enough experience was the standard line I kept hearing,
I heard anything at all."

Adam took a step closer. "Someone must have called in a
ivor."

"I'm just happy for the chance." Megan didn't know why
ie was telling him all this. She needed to shut up. He'd made
is choice. She'd made hers. She stared down her nose at him.
Not that it matters to you."

"But it does."

Huh? Megan started to speak, then stopped herself. She
asn't sure how to respond. Or if she should.

Adam crossed the distance between them in two long
rides. "I'm sorry, Megan. I was an idiot for the way I acted
the airport."

Emotion swirled through her. Part of Megan wanted to
row herself into Adam's arms and kiss him. The other part
anted to see him on his knees groveling at her feet.

He touched the side of her face. "I want to make it up to
u. I want us to be together."

Warmth flowed through her. His words filled her heart with
pe. She cared about him. She wanted to be with him.

But no matter how she might want to believe what he said
as true, Megan didn't dare. He'd said it himself. He wasn't
e right man for her. They'd already played this scene and it
dn't ended well. She looked away. "I have to go."

"I'm not talking about a fling," Adam said. "I'm talking
ig-term."

Her gaze jerked up to his. "You don't do long-term."

"I haven't," he admitted. "That doesn't mean I can't. Forever
th you sounds awesome to me."

Her mouth gaped. She closed it. His words wouldn't let th
hope in her heart die.

"I miss you, Megan. I don't want to lose you."

She was tempted. Oh, how she was tempted. But that roa
would only lead her to where she was now...brokenhearted.

Megan moved past him. Getting far away from him was he
smartest move at the moment. "I'm sure you'll find someon
else on the set to keep you company. If you haven't already.'

"I love you."

She froze. Her shoes felt as if they'd been glued to the floo

"I love you, Megan Calhoun," Adam said. "I understan
why you're upset. If you want to leave, go. I don't blame yo
But if there's a part of you who wants to take a chance on
risky guy like me, here I am. I'm yours."

Her pulse rocketed out of control.

His gaze implored her. "You were dead-on about me pla
ing roles. But not with you. It was only when I got scared, r
alizing how close we'd gotten, that I wasn't myself. It's wha
did when I was a kid to survive. But you showed me it cou
be different. I could be myself. I want to be with you, Mega
I'm willing to do whatever it takes to keep you in my life."

Her heart pounded so loudly she was sure people in tl
next apartment could hear it. She stared at Adam with a m
of surprise, affection and respect. The sincerity in his ey
and the way he stumbled over his words made her believe l
was telling the truth.

He loved her.

Fireworks exploded inside her. "I love you, too."

Adam pulled her toward him. He lowered his mouth to he
and kissed her firmly on the lips. His arms wrapped arou
her. She went willingly, eagerly. She melted against him, a
lowing his kiss to consume her. This was where she belonge

"I want to spend the rest of my life with you." He ran t
side of his finger along her jaw. "But first I want you to
after your dreams."

The love in his eyes matched the way she felt. "They're al-
ady coming true."

He removed something from his pocket—a ring box.

The air rushed from her lungs.

"This is a promise ring. I don't want you to feel rushed or
y pressure. But I promise—" he slid it on the ring finger of
r left hand "—when you're ready, I'll replace this with an
gagement ring."

She stared at the silver ring. The diamond sparkled. She
uldn't imagine any engagement ring being more beautiful.

"It's…" Megan struggled to find the perfect word. "Stun-
ng."

He kissed her hand. "Not as stunning as you."

She studied him. "Are you sure about this?"

"I'm not sure what the future will hold," he admitted. "But
n sure I want you in it. I'm committed to making this work."

That was good enough for her. "A part of me wishes I didn't
ve to go to Portland now."

"Why? There's so much to do there—climbing, skydiving,
terskiing, year-round skiing on Mount Hood."

His daredevil ways hadn't changed. She smiled. "Let me
ess, you want to BASE jump off Mount Hood?"

"No," he admitted. "But I have in mind a few adventures
us. Ones we can do and experience together to create mem-
es."

"Too bad we'll have to wait to do those things until we're
ether."

Mischief gleamed in his eyes. "My shoot is in Portland, too."

Megan didn't know how he'd managed that, and she didn't
e. They were going to be together. That was what mattered.
e rose on her tiptoes and kissed Adam on the lips, hard.

"And I have an adventure for us…in Larkville." She had
idea what it would be like to bring him home, but she had
eling it wouldn't be bad. "We're celebrating my dad's life
he annual Fall Festival in October. My entire family will

be there, including my half siblings. I'd love it if you wou
go with me."

"I'm in." Adam didn't hesitate. "I can't wait to meet yo
brothers and sister."

"*Sisters,* remember—I have a brand-new one!" Mega
smiled a bit nervously. Adam looked at her and grinned.

"It doesn't matter how many sisters you have, you'll a
ways stand out."

Megan blushed. "Well, you're the one who's helped me
stop hiding and start having adventures!"

"And the lessons have only just begun."

He kissed her again, a kiss worthy of a Viewers' Choi
Award for Best Kiss. Or maybe the MTV Movie Awards ga
out that one. Either way, Megan knew she and Adam were t
real winners no matter what happened after the screen fad
to black.

Happily ever after. Sounded like a perfect ending to he
She had a feeling Adam would agree.

* * * * *

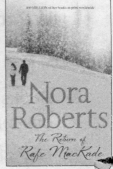

2 Free Books!

Join the Mills & Boon Book Club

Want to read more **Cherish**™ books? We're offering you **2 more** absolutely **FREE!**

We'll also treat you to these fabulous extras:

- Books up to 2 months ahead of shops

- FREE home delivery

- Bonus books with our special rewards scheme

- Exclusive offers and much more!

Get your free books now!

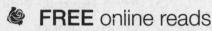

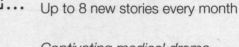